BORN OF BLOOD & SHADOWS

JAMYE SMITH

JAMYE SMITH

BORN OF BLOOD AND SHADOWS

To the readers who were told they didn't have a choice.

Farrah, who waited four years for this book.

Paperback ISBN: 978-1-964350-00-4

Ebook ASIN: B0D1Q4LPKM

Editing:

- Developmental Edits: Kate Studer
- Line editing: Kate Studer
- Proofreading: Megan Heenan

Design and Art:

- Cover Design: © 2024 by Giulia F. Wille Art www.giuliafwillearts.com IG: giulia_fw.arts
- Character Art: Copyright © 2024 Damián IG: damian.in.the.den

AUTHOR'S NOTE

A full list of CW can be found on my website.

Want to listen to the playlist while you read? Here's the Spotify link:

PROLOGUE

Her last day had come, marked by the arrival of a great storm. Thunder rumbled in the distance, a warning to the clergyman, who rushed toward the witch's cottage with half the town's garrison, that he best hurry before the rain ruined his kill.

She watched the torchlight in the distance as it made its way toward her home. The chant—*kill the witch*—repeated over and over, growing louder the closer they came. There was a soft knock on the back door. Cecilia pulled herself away from the window and opened it to find an old woman standing in a dark green cloak. She lunged at the woman, hugged her, and whispered, "Oh Marguerite."

The old woman was as close as a sister and the only remaining witch in their coven who hadn't been discovered. Marguerite broke from her embrace and rushed inside. "Cici, they're coming. We must hurry."

She nodded curtly. Cecilia's husband came up behind her and rested his hands on her shoulders. She turned around and fell into his embrace. A shudder ran through her before she pushed away and called out to their daughter. "Ameris, come here, darling."

A young girl the age of ten appeared from a side room, holding a satchel. She knew there was nothing good coming from this exchange. "Mommy, I don't want to go."

"My darling girl, Marguerite is going to take care of you."

"Will you come back?"

It was as if her daughter had delivered her death, for she knew this was the last goodbye and the last time she would see her. The town knew nothing of the girl. A choice Ameris's parents made for this very reason. The risks were too great for anyone to know of her existence.

"No." Cecilia turned her head as tears threatened to fall. Taking a breath, she looked at her husband before meeting her daughter's eyes once more and continued, "But my love for you will never fade, even if your memories of me do. Never let them find out what you are." She had to be strong in these final moments, even if her trembling hands betrayed her.

"What about Daddy?" Ameris looked to her father with a sadness not meant for one so young. He bent down and hugged her fiercely.

"I love you, but I must stay with your mother. One day you will understand. Go now and remember the story I just told you. Tell it to Marguerite."

"I will keep her safe." The old lady draped another green cloak over the girl's shoulders, put up her hood, and picked her up.

The girl cried out and tried to fight, but the old woman held her tightly. Lightning flashed as she left through the back door and made her way into the forest. The storm was driving its way toward them and would soon arrive to envelop the village.

Minutes later, the guards rammed through the door, tearing the couple apart. As the guards dragged them to the open field, Cecilia watched the guards set her home's roof on fire, quickly engulfing it in flames. Terror coursed through her, knowing her fate would be the same.

Cecilia and her husband were tied against roughly constructed pyres. The town's favorite method to kill a witch was to burn them.

The crowd swarmed upon the couple like vultures waiting for their victim to fall. Their jeers and words of hate pierced her soul. Cecilia's tears fell freely as she held onto the hand of the man at her side and looked at him. Her words caught within the mounting storm, but he saw them—*I love you*—and returned his own.

"Forever and always."

"Today we rid our village of a witch and her consenting husband. A man who allows witchcraft is as guilty as the witch herself." The clergyman's dark gray cloak swirled around as he set the torch to the wood. The hungry flames rose up the pyre, catching fast in the wind.

"They will burn in the depths of hell!" The clergyman's promise rang out, and the crowd burst into rancorous excitement.

Cecilia had saved her magic for this moment and cast a spell that blocked her and her husband's physical pain, even as their bodies withered among the flames. Her magic would still triumph over their hate and cruelty.

Acrid smoke filled the air, mingling with the scent of burning flesh and hair. Cecilia knew their time was fast approaching as her breathing became shallow and each beat of her heart was slower than the last. Their bodies were failing, skin and muscle contracting and ripping apart.

Marguerite struggled to keep Ameris back as she clawed at the old woman. But at something Marguerite said, Ameris dropped to her knees and clutched her heart.

Before the fierce cry of her daughter was released, Cecilia looked at John, and he nodded. She chanted, and as she did, unbearable pain ignited. John screamed, and the crowd cheered.

Her magic understood the sacrifice she was making. It protected her until she drew upon their remaining life force, channeling it into protection for Ameris.

You will not be found and meet the same fate.

With her last ounce of magic, Cecilia cast a spell into the storm. The clergyman's eyes went wide, and the villagers screamed, scattering as a jagged and blinding light barreled toward them.

Cecilia looked at her daughter once more, her heart cleaving in two at the pain on that small face. She closed her eyes for the last time, knowing Ameris had been drowned out by the resounding boom from the lightning that struck the pyre and shattered it, killing anyone too close.

CHAPTER 1
AMERIS

I should be scared, but there is beauty in the chaos.

A violent storm is churning in the distance. Despite the agonizing pain that ripples through my body, I find myself drawn to the cliff's edge, observing the stormy sea. The maelstrom of elements that converge during this weather makes my magic want to rip itself out of me.

It's like thousands of sharp pins are trying to force their way out from beneath my skin. My magic hates being bound within me—a sentiment I share.

Even though the storm is miles from making landfall, rumbling thunder reaches me. Grey and black clouds fill the predawn sky as wind whips my hair around my face. Lightning flashes, and I marvel at its jagged brilliance. It illuminates a ship that's trying to outrace the waves that claw at it. Waves that want to pull the ship into the watery depths of the ocean.

Despite the pain coursing through my body, goosebumps still rise along my arms—a warning I ignore. I'm unwilling to tear my gaze away from the way the elements feed off each other to make something that's as terrifying as it is beautiful.

I want that much power.

But it's out of my reach. My own magic is locked away within me, bound by my late mother. Yet, it's never stopped me from trying to use it, even when pain wracks my body from the inside out. After the first excruciating moments, I can settle into the pain and push it to the back of my mind. Function through it.

Reaching out, my hand flexes, fingers quivering as the cold air swirls about. I channel every ounce of my will toward the tempest within the storm, imagining invisible tendrils wrapping around its wild heart. My desire for control and dominance over my magic causes it to pulsate within me as I attempt to pull the churning clouds to shore. My magic wants to be released—to be used.

But nothing happens; the storm indifferent to my presence. A raw, violent scream tears from my throat in frustration. I lash out and kick at the rocks beneath my feet. They spiral off the edge and disappear into the frothy waves, which swallow them greedily before crashing against the cliff.

Cold droplets of seawater break into mist, spraying me as if the ocean is releasing a cruel laugh against my futile attempt. For thinking I could control the elements. The salty spray stings my eyes, momentarily blurring my vision, a bitter reminder of the power I don't have. Witches have limited access to the elements; we can only harness their energy for our craft.

I want control over them—wind, fire, water, and earth—like the fae did. It's something I've dreamed of since I was young. My mother used to spin elaborate tales of the fae we inherited our magic from.

Beside me, Honey shifts uneasily, letting out a nervous neigh, hooves pawing at the rocky edge. With each wave that crashes, she takes a small, hesitant step back. She knows we should go. "Shh. I've got you. We're okay."

My godmother, Marguerite, will figuratively kill me if she discovers I'm here, but the villagers will actually kill me if I'm caught. My mother was burned at the stake for being a witch, along with my father, who was complicit in her existence. My magic withered with their last breaths; it was their attempt at keeping me from meeting their same fate, but it also made me weak. A part of my soul fractured that day. Lightning illuminates the sky, and I flinch at its abrupt flash.

Anyone the villagers suspect of being a witch is killed. I'm not sure if it's fear or jealousy of our abilities that drives such violence. They make up silly beliefs, like only witches would brave this weather.

Maybe they're right. I am the only one who comes out during a storm, and I am a witch.

Marguerite has not missed the obvious longing in my heart when we go to the beach to collect seaweed, and my gaze falls to the ocean. The only reason I still live in this village is because she needs me.

We're the only witches left, and when I needed her, she never left my side. I wouldn't leave her to these wretched people. Besides, *she* is my village, and its elder, always telling me what I need to hear, even if I don't like it.

The only problem is I don't want to hide who I am like Marguerite does.

I want to revel in the power.

To be a witch.

And if I don't find a way to unbind my magic, I'm afraid my path will end in an early death. Each year that passes, the magic festers, the pain worsening when it storms.

I can't help the part of me that hates my parents for leaving me vulnerable. I have no magic to protect myself from the villagers that watch my every move.

The wind surges, pulling me from my thoughts. I raise my arms, extending them wide, letting the frenzied air flow about. It whips around, tugging at my clothes and swirling strands of my hair. Raindrops begin to fall, kissing my skin, a herald to the downpour that is sure to come.

Eyes to the sky, I let the elements wash over me as I reach down and pull vigorously at my magic once more. I try again, exerting all my energy to conjure a bolt of lightning. To watch a jagged slice cascade through the clouds. But my magic cannot break through; it's just out of reach and pummels me in the gut at my attempt.

Nerves now alight, my hands curl into fists, the tips of my fingernails digging into the soft skin of my palm. The magic within is coiled tightly, and I crave its release.

Pivoting, I mount Honey. She immediately moves back from the edge and tries to head home. Except, I'm not ready to leave, and we enter a dance, pulling and pushing against each other until I get her back in place. I rub her neck, her chestnut hair slick under my touch. "We're leaving soon."

Rolling grey clouds swallow the ship, solidifying the sailors' doom. Rain falls harder, tiny daggers assaulting us from the sky, soaking my skin as I watch—waiting.

Sure enough, it comes barreling out of the heavy darkness, too fast to stop, and crashes against the rocky coast. The resounding boom from the ship splintering sounds like thunder.

Good. Their destruction means our survival.

No one will come to their aid; and I won't waste this opportunity to scavenge the ship. Marguerite and I need whatever I can find to sell for food, necessities, and ingredients for our tinctures and balms.

The villagers are wary of me and Marguerite, even though they purchase our wares. They tolerate us, but if suspicions are raised, we'll burn, just like my parents.

Sometimes I wonder if death would be easier than the pain and the villagers' constant glances and whispers. But I push through because I'm not willing to give up on finding a way to unbind my magic. To get retribution against those who have wronged me and my family.

Not only that, but to obtain the power I so desperately want in order to protect Marguerite and myself.

To control my own fate and live free from other's decisions on how my life should be lived.

I release tension on the reins, and Honey gladly pulls away from the cliff's edge as I guide us toward the wreckage. We've taken this route many times, but never in this weather. Solid ground turns to mud, and Honey's hooves skitter and slide against it.

"Woah. Woah," I call out as a sudden lurch sends me sideways. My heart skips a beat as my thigh muscles tense. Quickly righting myself, I lean back into the saddle and exhale. I urge her on, but she only whips her head to and fro, straining against the reins and refusing to go any further.

"You're doing good. We're almost there." I stroke Honey's neck repeatedly, reassuring her as I nudge her forward. She relents, not wanting to be in this rain longer than necessary. *Get what you need and get out.* Thank the stars, we make it down the path to the beach with no more incidents.

A jagged shoreline, brutal and deadly, meets the ocean that spreads beyond it. The ship leans against the rocks, hull shredded —no match for the ocean's ravenous teeth.

Large holes remain where cannons should be, exposing the hold. The mast is cracked in half, and the ripped sails that remain snaps back and forth in the wild wind.

I was certain this wasn't a survivable wreck as I watched the ship crash into the rocks. Confirmation comes in form of the sailors who didn't drown at sea, who lie among the scattered crates that line the beach, unmoving until the frothy water thrashes at the sand beneath them, like greedy hands wanting to claim what got away.

Unfortunate for them, but a blessing for me. It's all part of the balance of nature, and I will not waste my chance at surviving.

My hair whips around, its wild strands tangling in the wind as

Honey's hooves pound against the sand. In the distance, the ship's timbers groan and splinter. It's dangerous, a death wish even, but everything in my life is that way. My own breath, my magic, how I steal what we require—all I've known is danger, so I face it with the same resilience as everything else.

I will survive.

As we approach the wreck, my mind traces the path I'll take. The quarterdeck remains intact, the captain's quarters just below; the windows, now glassless, will ease my entry. Plus, that's where the jewels and gold will be, or my best bet to grab anything valuable.

I pull back on the reins and steer Honey into one of the cliff's alcoves, giving her reprieve from the elements, and tie her to a rod I hammered into the rock ages ago. There's always a shipwreck or goods that wash up along this stretch of beach.

Though heavy clouds still fill the sky, the worst part of the storm has moved inward, slowing the rain. Trudging across the beach, my feet sink into the wet sand. Generous in size, the ship rises before me as I approach. Not wanting my satchel to get in the way as I ascend, I swing it around my shoulder, where it lies against my back.

I climb slowly, making sure my footing is sound before moving up. The swollen wood is slick under my touch. This is going to take longer than I want, but dying won't get me anywhere. So, slow and steady it is.

Water slides down my face, blurring my vision as I grab the next spot, but my hand slips, and I falter. Careening sideways, a scream tears through my throat when my body slams into the wood from the force of the wind.

Pain lances through my twisting shoulder as I hold on with every ounce of strength I have. My heart pounds under my ribcage, filling my ears, and drowns out any other sound. When I've steadied myself, I lean my head back, assessing my options.

The windowsill is only three feet above me, and there are no more footholds.

I force myself to calm down, focus, and breathe.

In... Out...

In... Out...

One foot at a time, I find stable footing. I'll only have one shot to make it up there. If I fall, it's going to be in an attempt to reach the window. Not flailing like a fish out of water.

Why do I get myself into these situations? I hope the sand is soft.

Before I can muster the courage to jump the distance to the window's ledge, I take a deep breath, ribs expanding until I can hold no more, and expel the air.

Relax.

Repeat.

A few more breaths conquer the nerves that plague me. I can do this. On my last exhale, I push through the muscles that burn and catapult myself up, using what strength I have left.

A hand grabs mine.

I scream, my heart beating faster than I thought possible as I'm pulled through the window. Landing hard, I roll onto my back before jolting up.

A gruff male voice fills the cabin. "Where am I?"

CHAPTER 2
AMERIS

Crimson liquid trickles down my forearm. I flick my gaze to it, adrenaline and shock blocking the new source of pain. I'm momentarily stunned by the man who stands hunched against the other side of the cabin, with one of his well-defined arms leaning on the wall to support himself.

No one should have survived.

His long, auburn hair, disheveled and bloody from a gash on his temple, falls into his face. Cuts litter his skin, visible through his torn and ragged clothing.

Other than his injuries, his light complexion is smooth, and bronzed by the sun. He doesn't have the leathery, deeply suntanned skin that often marks a seasoned sailor. And he's not wearing normal sailing garb. It's a style I've never seen before, with remnants of elaborate stitching on his white shirt and pants made from velour.

"Where am I? And don't make me ask again." The words come out through heavy breaths, his head tilting in my direction.

Only the angry slant of his eyebrow is visible through the hair that masks his features. I assess him before answering. There are wounds and bruises that circle his wrists. Tendrils of fear coil in my stomach, for only prisoners, traitors, and deserters end up with those—or worse. *Shit. Shit.*

"You're on the coast of Baylon," I stutter as I come to my senses.

We're only about a foot apart, and I crave the safety of distance. I slide my foot toward the cabin door, which is barely clinging to its hinges, ready to bolt if he tries anything. The ship groans as the wind continues to lash outside, threatening to make my movements unsteady.

"I've never heard of it." His features relax as he pivots and leans against the wall. Sky blue eyes briefly lock onto me. His brows pull together like he's confused before his head lolls to the side and he slides down, collapsing into a hunched sit.

Halting my movement toward the door, I wait a few heart-beats before I nudge him with my boot. No response. His effort to pull me up must have taken the last of his strength. I exhale, relief washing over me. Now, I have the chance to find what I came for—something of value.

Pain radiates up my arm, taking over my senses now that the more immediate danger has subsided. The gash is bleeding more freely, dripping off my arm onto the wooden floor. I need to wrap it, and soon.

This cabin is a wreck. Books are strewn about. Papers line just about every surface. Lanterns and trinkets cover the floor. Lovely. I'll be wasting time trying to find what I came for. The desk bolted down in the center is the only thing unmoved by the wrath of the storm. I kick over a lantern and shove debris out of my way. It's a miracle I didn't crash into anything when he pulled me up.

Picking up a soaked and shredded velvet curtain, I take the knife from my boot, cut a long strip off, and wrap my arm. I heave the rest of it to the side, and a wide smile forms when a small wooden chest, tipped over on its side, reveals itself at my feet.

But, of course, this day wants to curse me. It's locked.

Quickly looking around for something to use, I notice an iron candlestick stands upright on the desk, melted wax around the base holding it in place. I jerk it back and forth, and when it breaks away, I waste no time slamming it against the rusted metal lock over and over. It does nothing. I stifle a frustrated scream and resort to kicking the chest.

"Come on! You stupid thing. Break already!" I realize I'm not being quiet in my annoyance. I glance back at the man—still out. Thank the stars.

Using what remains of my wanning strength, I slam the heel of my boot once more against the lock. It finally gives, and exactly what I was hoping for greets me when the lid pops back.

A bag full of coins.

When I place them in my satchel, the weight of the coin pulls the strap of my satchel further into my skin. An icy chill distracts me from my bounty, winding its way down my spine, when I notice something else within the chest. Small bumps rise along my skin. Sketches of humans with pointed ears and maps with scribbled notes about where to search for fae.

The more I rifle through the pages, the more documents there are detailing records of fae captives. These shouldn't even exist, let alone be left for anyone to find. I gather the papers and stuff them in my satchel.

Get off this ship now, I tell myself. I got what I came for. But my curiosity about the man gets the better of me. Each step I take toward him is slow; the creaking wood under my feet feels too loud; and my breath too erratic.

It's impossible.

I prod his thigh with the tip of my boot. He still doesn't move, doesn't even flinch. My hand trembles slightly as I reach out and lift his hair. I suck in air and release a breathy laugh. His ears are longer and slightly pointed at the tip—the mark of a fae.

Memories of fae bargains run through my mind as I move towards the window. He may not be fully conscious, but if we enter a bargain—I help him in exchange for him teaching me magic—then he'll be honor-bound, forced to follow through.

Suddenly, his hand juts up, grabbing my wrist tightly. I yelp in surprise and shoot backward, but his grip is strong, and he yanks me forward.

"Get me off this ship. Now." His eyes are unfocused, gaze drifting, but his voice is forceful. Each word pronounced with authority. A command.

I reel against the way he demands I help him. "Or what?" I'm not here for the goodwill of survivors, even if he's a fae, and he has something to offer. Helping people is what got my mother killed. What can get me killed.

"I saved you from falling. You owe me." He responds without looking at me.

"I owe you nothing." I yank out of his grip, and he collapses once more. I step away from him, ready to leave him and this ship behind.

"What are you willing to give me in return?" I turn toward him again.

He tries to lift his head, but it sways, too heavy in his current state. "Anything."

Well, I wasn't expecting it to be that easy. He's desperate, and this is my chance. "I want you to teach me about your magic and how to use it."

"But you can't…" He shakes his head. The struggle to remain conscious is clear. He tries to look up at me but fails. "Fine. I agree." The words tumble out, slow and slurred, right before he falls unconscious again.

A wide smile paints my face.

Finally, I have a way to learn more about my magic. But it doesn't last. It dawns on me that if the sailors were hunting fae and he was a captive, someone will come looking for him. I run to the window and look outside. Dawn should have breached the horizon by now, but the clouds still dampen the light. I need to get out of here before whoever was expecting this ship shows up.

I shove the cabin door aside, snapping it the rest of the way off the hinges, and step out onto the upper deck. Heavy rain once again slams into my face. I throw my arm up to shield it as a second bout of angry wind whips my hair around.

The storm did the damage I knew it would, but I'm still in awe of nature's power. The snapped mast lays across the deck, blocking the path to the other end.

Any step in the wrong direction will send me falling below. I gently make my way to the damaged rigging, avoiding the splintered wood and gaping holes. Pulling the knife from my boot, I cut what I need of the ropes.

Drenched, I return to the captain's quarters and make a knot, carefully looping it under his muscular arms. Needing an anchor point, I scan the room. The desk bolted to the floor will have to do. I don't have time to find something better.

Hooking my arms under his armpits, I drag him away from the wall. He's heavier than he looks. Each step I take strains the muscles in my legs as I drag him in front of the broken window. I clench my teeth through the burning, a combination of the exhaustion from climbing, his weight, and the pain caused by the storm.

When I lay him down, his shirt shifts, loosened from where it's torn, revealing the smooth skin beneath. Contoured lines of his pronounced muscles rise and fall with each shuddering breath he takes.

Focus, Ameris.

I clear out all the remaining glass before I sit behind him. Propping one foot on the wood frame while resting the other on his back, I pull the rope around my back, creating a pulley. The rough strands of it scrape my palms when I twist it around my hands.

Without a second thought, I shove him out the window. I

quickly place my other leg on the opposite side of the wooden frame and lean back, bracing for the weight that will come. The muscles in my thighs tighten, straining, and my back arches at how the rope cuts into my skin. Slowly, I lower him. Another few releases, and he'll be safely down.

Crack.

I whip my head around. *Oh no.* My anchor point is about to break; the leg of the desk is at an angle. It snaps off before I can do anything, and I'm thrown through the window from the sudden release of tension.

Sky and sand swirl in a blur as my body free falls, the rope wrapping around me like a coiling snake. It pulls taught and jerks me to a stop before I hit the ground. The rope tightens around my stomach and pain explodes, white filling my vision. I hang in the air and dry-heave, swaying back and forth.

The sand is only a few feet away. I need to cut myself from the rope, but any movement I make burns as it cinches tighter. Groaning, I struggle to bring my leg up. The knife in my boot feels miles away. My fingertips graze the smooth wooden handle, but black pushes in at the corners of my vision as the sound of the crashing waves begins to fade, replaced by ringing.

When I finally have the knife in hand, I turn as best as I can and work the blade against the rope, each cut searing my body. I pause, the burn along my abdomen too much, and look up. The leg of the desk is stuck behind the window frame. I blow out a strangled breath.

This was a bad idea.

I should have left him and never looked back. I push past the pain and continue sawing the last tendrils of rope connecting us to the ship. Each frayed strand that comes loose promises relief. At the last cut, it comes, momentarily flooding my body. Until I land on top of him, face down in the sand.

I'm not so good at this savior thing.

My muscles protest, screaming at me to stop moving when I

roll over and lay beside him. I give into them and take a moment, breathing in the salty air. The dark grey clouds have lightened, and the sun is rising—a sign I've been here for far too long.

"Ugh. This is not my day." Wet sand filters through my fingers when I push myself up. My eyes narrow, my facial muscles tighten into a wince as searing pain wraps around my belly, and I lean back on my shins.

One more deep breath, and I focus on standing up even though my body revolts against the agony caused by every movement. I hobble over to Honey and guide her over to where the fae lies on the beach. Honey kneels on command, and I maneuver him onto her back.

Kicking at the sand, I cover our tracks and thank whatever gods—human or fae—for the timely convenience of finding him during a storm, so it will wash away our time here. At least, that's what I tell myself. When we reach the rocky path, I mount Honey, doing my best to push through the pain, because if any villagers or sailors were to find us here, it would mean our deaths.

Except, arriving at our cottage with a male fae might be even worse—because I don't know what to expect from Marguerite.

CHAPTER 3
XANDER

A scream wakes me. Ocean waves crash. Groaning wood.

Too much energy spent on the storm. I spend what's left on helping a human.

Strawberry blonde hair. My vision is too unfocused to see her features.

The human wants to know magic, but they cannot do magic.

I agree anyway. I need to get off this ship.

Darkness takes over again.

CHAPTER 4
AMERIS

The sun finally breaks through the clouds, which dissipate under its heat as the garden comes into view. Every color is vibrant in the golden columns of light that split the sky to touch the ground.

Droplets of water sparkle on the leaves of various plants. The world is alive and buzzes around me. I take a deep breath, letting the wet earth fill my senses. Elements swirl around us. The sun's fire, the earth's power, the wind's whisper, and the water's ease.

They caress my skin in a gentle touch, and I blow out a breath. The mental anguish never ceases, even when the physical pain does, especially during the aftermath of a storm when the heightened elements linger.

We approach the cottage, and Marguerite's slender form glides under the vine-covered trellis that arches over the bridge to the flower and herb garden. I can't help but marvel at how, despite her seventy years, her movements are fluid, like a never-aging goddess.

This morning is no exception, with the morning light enveloping her, casting a warm, golden hue over her delicate, tawny skin. Her crown of white and grey hair is artfully gathered into a bun. She leans down to gather fennel but looks up as I dismount Honey.

The deep lines in her face crease. "Dear girl, what is this? And your arm, what did you do this time?"

Marguerite doesn't comment on my absence or return. But her expression tells me all I need to know. She's angry. "It's a long story. My arm isn't important. I couldn't leave him where he was. Especially after I saw these." I lift the fae's hair away from his ears to show Marguerite the pointed tips.

Her face pales, the anger dripping away, replaced by worry. Dropping the basket of fennel, she asks, "Did anyone see you on the shore or spot you bringing him back here?"

"No."

"You fool. You've done a lot of stupid things in your twenty-four years, but this tops it." Marguerite says as she shakes her head. She pinches the bridge of her nose, lost in thought.

"Not this again." A dramatic sigh escapes. I can't help it; she's always doing this. I fold my arms over my chest instead of quipping back as I wait for her response. I wasn't sure what to expect, but I can tell her disappointment is laced with fear, and that wasn't on my list.

"Someone will come looking for him, Ameris. They will kill us when they come." She removes her fingers and slowly looks up at me, sadness etched into the lines on her forehead. Her voice rises, anger lacing her words, as she gives me a hard look. "Do you want to burn like your parents did? They died for you!"

I shrink back, the sting of her words a dagger to my heart. She sighs and shakes her head. Marguerite has taken care of me since my parents were killed and raised me as her own. She protected me and kept us as safe as she could from the villagers. They never realized I was a child of my mother's. But I don't want to talk about my parents; they're dead, and this is the present.

I hand her the documents I found on the ship. "I took these. And there were no other survivors. He's probably alive because he's a fae. I need him. He can help me with my magic. Then I can protect us. You know I have it in me. I just need to break through the chains my parents put on my magic. I'll kill anyone who tries to harm us."

"Come. You've already brought him here, and you clearly have much to learn. What fate wills is now decided." She walks toward our cottage and, with a raised hand, waves for me to follow.

Marguerite is concerned about us being seen but doesn't offer to help me get him inside, leaving me to handle my own perceived bad decision.

Yet, the only bad decision would have been to leave him on that ship, losing an opportunity to have a fae teach me magic. He's the answer to my problems. He has to be.

Honey's steps against the pebble walkway and the birds' chatter fills the late afternoon air. At the front door, I pull a piece of carrot out of my satchel and bait Honey to kneel. I drag him off, stumbling backwards under his weight, and heave him against the door frame.

Marguerite steps outside and watches me, doubled over, breathing hard before she cracks a smile and helps me carry him inside the cottage. When we're past the doorway, she sets his legs down. "I'll take Honey to the stables. Place him on the pallet in front of the fire."

Sweat drips down my back as I drag him across the floor. The fire in the hearth isn't ablaze, but it's putting off enough heat to make the room uncomfortable. I'm about to lay him on the blanket in front of the hearth when Marguerite walks in.

The rich, woodsy-sweet smell of helichrysum follows her as she walks to the kitchen. Pulling a mortar from a shelf, she grinds the yellow flower down. I watch as she adds fresh yarrow, pine needles, beeswax, and a small amount of water.

A salve for his wounds. It is a common mixture we make for the townsfolk. They let their judgment towards us slip just enough since we've healed about everyone in town. But if they heard of any other magic being done, they wouldn't hesitate to bind us to stakes and burn us for having magic.

She looks over at me. "You need to undress him. It won't do any good if you leave him damp. Especially damp and covered up." She turns back to the mixture and continues using the pestle to grind it together.

"But I... That's..." My cheeks flare. "I can't do that. Isn't that inappropriate since he's unconscious?"

"Well, dear girl, your actions have consequences, and you need to take care of him. You didn't drag him all this way to let him die." She pauses and looks at me. "Did you?"

I stare at her for what feels like a millennium. When I blink, she laughs. Her eyes lighting up. She is doing one of those lesson moments again. Never ending lessons are her way—always looking for a way to teach me about life through practicality.

"I'll do it," she says. "Make the tea. Finish mixing this, clean yourself up, and get two blankets." She chuckles as she walks over to us.

This woman is going to be the end of me.

Dried lavender hangs from the ceiling amid other herbs and flowers. I crush them and let the broken pieces fall among the lemongrass leaves on the thin cloth I've laid out on the worn oak counter. Bringing the edges of the cloth together, I tie the ends to create a bulb, then place it in a cup and gently pour boiling water over it.

As the hot liquid cascades over the cloth, the energy in the water shifts, drawing out the essence from each plant to strengthen it.

Feeling the magic emanating from the tea—almost palpable in the air—I tear my gaze away and divert my attention to cleaning myself up as it steeps. This is my torture. Magic taunts me. It wants me as much as I want it.

After dressing in dry clothes, I grab two blankets from a storage cabinet, the tea and salve, and return to Marguerite. She's undressed our unexpected guest, leaving a folded cloth over his groin, yet every crease and line of chiseled muscle is exposed. I take a moment to appreciate him, and my word, he is gorgeous—the picture of a warrior god in restful slumber. My parents told me about the unnatural and alluring beauty of the fae, but nothing about them looking like *this*.

Marguerite has tended to the wound on his temple, and now she gently wipes the sand off his body with a rag, willing it to fall away. I love the beach and ocean, but hate the sand. It's a beast of its own, clinging to the life of its carrier.

Still fatigued, my muscles protest when I sit cross-legged at his head and pass Marguerite the salve. I slowly part his perfectly formed lips, bringing the cup to them. Ever so gently, I tip it, allowing a small amount of liquid to trickle down his throat.

Marguerite works on his other wounds, chanting an incantation as she applies the salve and wraps them with cloth. I've never seen her use magic while healing, and I am mesmerized by the steady pace she works at, which matches the rhythm of the chant. She repeats the spell for each wrist and ankle.

He was bound. Dread pools in my stomach. The kind of humans that can capture a fae are not the kind I want to cross paths with. I hope Marguerite is wrong and no one comes looking for him. Taking those documents might not be enough to protect us.

No. It was enough. No one survived, and no one saw us.

Movement interrupts my thoughts. His fingers twitch and legs slightly jerk. He murmurs as his head moves back and forth. Marguerite and I share a glance, and she quickens her pace. Just as she finishes tying the last bandage, his eyes snap open.

Fiery sky-blue eyes bore into mine as if they know me. "Rhiannon."

The word comes out harsh—deadly. His arm shoots up in a sudden, sharp motion, and he grips a handful of hair with predatory precision, forcing my head to jerk to the side. A jolt of pain erupts from my scalp as my nerves scream in protest. Beautiful and dangerous. Got it.

Marguerite holds out her hand, and his arm instantly drops as he slips back into sleep. I look at Marguerite, hoping for an explanation.

But her eyes are wide with alarm.

"Marguerite, what's going on?"

CHAPTER 5
AMERIS

arguerite distances herself from him, sitting at the round wooden table on the opposite end of the room. Her hands rest on her knees, but her gaze remains on us, contemplating something. She looks like death has knocked on her door. It's not a look I'm used to, nor like seeing.

A shiver snakes its way up my spine, uneasiness spreads from each vertebra as I unfold my legs and place his head down. I unfurl the blankets and place them over him.

"Please tell me why he said that and why it's distressing you." I take the seat opposite her and fold my hands on the table before leaning forward. She knows something.

Sitting back in her chair, she releases a deep sigh. "You are more powerful than you know. With that power will come responsibility and hard choices."

That's not an answer, so I try again. Plus, she's not making sense. She knows my struggle with magic. "Who is Rhiannon?"

"It's a long story." Marguerite rises, the legs of her chair scraping against the floor. She leaves and heads down the hall to her room.

Leaning back, I drag my hands down my face. I guess that's all I get for the evening. She has that tendency, only saying what she needs to, and then walks away.

But this time, Marguerite returns, placing a weathered leather-bound journal between us. "We've guarded a secret for a long time. Rhiannon was one of the original fae, but they haven't been around for centuries. So, if he's here, saying that name aloud, that's a problem, especially if he was on a human ship. And you brought him to our home."

She opens the journal and pulls out a folded piece of paper, handing it to me. The yellow edges give away the paper's fragility. Gently unfolding the paper, a painting of a woman with golden brown hair, a sharp jaw, and green eyes that closely resemble my own is revealed.

Our features are so similar, except for the hair. I assume this is Rhiannon. My eyes flit up to Marguerite before looking down again at the portrait. I hardly know what to think right now. "Am I a reincarnation?"

"No, you are not her, but you are her descendent. She starts, letting out a breath before she continues. "Your mother and I never understood it, but swapped theories that you would have the same magical abilities she did." She looks over at the unconscious fae. "We must be careful with him. We don't know how old he is or what side he was on when Rhiannon ruled."

"When she *ruled?*" I ask, emphasizing the word.

"She was their queen before she was banished."

"I'm sorry, what? Why was I never told any of this? And why do you think I inherited her power? I'm not even half-fae."

"We never knew the answer to that. Only figured there was a chance you could once we saw how much you resembled her." She grabs my hand and squeezes it. "It's why your parents bound your magic when they were caught. They wanted to protect you from the same fate. And I never told you about Rhiannon because there was no reason to."

"What they did made me weak. I want my magic, to be able to access it—you know that. It's why I saved him. I want to be able to protect you, as you have done for me all these years."

Marguerite nods, a sad smile on her lips, like there is more that she won't say. "It is time for this to be passed on. This grimoire has been passed down through the generations of our coven. Contained within are all the spells we know and the few I created."

"Would you have ever given this to me if it wasn't for him?" As much as I love her, a spark of anger flares when she hands me the grimoire and then walks away without answering my question.

My parents never told me any of this, and then they left me unprotected, thinking it was better not to have access to magic. And Marguerite, keeping it from me for all these years, knowing what potential I had. It fuels my desire to learn from him even more.

Not only to release myself from the physical pain but because we are the only two witches left. It's our heritage, and I will not forsake it. I will figure out a way to unbind my magic, and then this town will pay for what it did to my parents and to me.

The grimoire smells like moss, forests, and old books. The faded leather cover houses a combination of well-worn pages and ones that look untouched. I open it, and the paper that greets me is decorated with elaborate designs and beautiful writing. The writing changes as I flip through the pages—a mix of elegant and plain script, penned by different people.

Moving my hands over the words, I feel as though I am connected to my ancestors. Flipping back to the beginning, I study the beautiful words inked in kohl, surrounded by colorful vines and thorns. I trace the vines with my finger, moving around the border, surprised to find the drawings are raised. My gaze wanders to the opposite page, a blank space waiting to be filled.

A sharp prick to my finger interrupts my reverie. I wince and jerk it away from the vines. A drop of blood splashes on the blank page, and I stick my finger in my mouth to stanch the bleeding. It must have been a trick of the light—I *am* tired, but I could've sworn I saw words forming before the blood soaked into the page.

Movement in my peripheral diverts my attention from the grimoire. The fae is lying on his side, propped up by his elbow, staring at me. Heat from the fire so near to him causes his bare skin to glisten from sweat. I force my gaze away, again, from the way it highlights every curve of his muscles. His eyes are piercing daggers, and before I can register another thought, he jumps up and rushes toward me, faster than any man I've met.

"Margur—" The rest of her name gets cut off as his hand wraps around my throat. The chair under me crashes against the floor from the force of his movement as I'm lifted from it. Oh stars. He's naked, and if he wasn't trying to strangle me, I might be turned on right now.

"You," he says with a deadly tone and strength to match as he pushes me up against the wall. "How are you alive, and why didn't you you come back?" Towering over me, his auburn hair falls into his face as he leans down, eyes narrowed.

Terror courses through me as I claw at my throat, trying to pry his hands off my airway so I can answer his question.

My eyes widen as I struggle to breathe. I grab onto his wrist where it's wrapped in bandages and twist. He winces from the friction against his wound, and the pressure on my throat lessens. I suck in a greedy breath, and tears spring to my eyes, but it's only seconds before the force is there again.

Squirming under his grasp, legs flailing, I do the only thing I can think of to stop him. I bring my leg up as best I can, kneeing him in the groin. He bellows and doubles over, dropping to the ground. My body crashes to the floor in a heap, choking and coughing as I gasp for air.

Craning my neck, I see he's standing again, staring down at me with a fire in his eyes. "Have you lost your strength after hiding among humans, Queen?"

When he takes a step towards me, I scramble away from him and push off the floor. Oh stars, did he expect an even fight, thinking I was her? I bolt for the kitchen, to the knife on the counter. It's my only hope since there is no way I can overpower him, but he might think twice about approaching me.

"Marguerite!" I rasp, my voice too cracked to make a noise worth hearing. Heavy footsteps sound behind me. My heart pounds just as hard in my chest. Inches away from the counter, my hand falls short of reaching the knife as his fist finds purchase in my hair. My head snaps back, and I'm pulled against his hard chest. Neck exposed, his hand wraps around it once more.

My breath is stolen again, and blackness swirls among my view of the kitchen. Relief comes just before I black out, hot air rushing back into my lungs as his hands slip from my hair and neck. I hear a thud, and I blink back my vision. He's dropped to his knees, elbows resting on the stone floor. His fingers are pressed into his temple, his face pinched in pain as he violently rocks back and forth.

Marguerite stands in the doorway to the hall, palm exposed in his direction. "You will not harm her. I will release you, but you will not try that again." The words are stern, like a mother scolding a child.

His only response is a grunt. The moment Marguerite releases him, the tension in the room shifts. It doesn't lift, but lessens. His face relaxes, and he takes a deep breath.

"Ameris, get a pair of your father's pants and a shirt for him."

At her command, I gladly step away and go to my room. We never got rid of their clothes. I couldn't part with them. Letting go was too hard. When my hand hovers over a tan shirt, memories flood. I bring it to my face, pulling in the scent of my father—sea spray and musk. He worked as a trader, his husky form coming up the garden trail, skin red and peeling from the harsh waters of the sea.

I grab a white shirt and brown pants and return to the main

room before I get lost in the past. Marguerite stands on the opposite side of the table, eyes on him. He sits with perfect posture, a blanket on his lap, staring back at her. Like two wolves ready to fight for dominance. "I wasn't going to kill her."

"That's not what it looked like. Give him the clothes." Marguerite instructs, though her eyes never leave him. "You have no power here and are at my mercy. Should you try that again, you will regret it."

I throw the clothes at him, hitting him in the chest. Each step I take resonates with a thud, echoing my growing frustration as I stalk away from them. I reach for the herbs and gather what's needed to make a salve for my aching neck, hoping to ease the pain and stifle the bruises I know will surface.

I look over my shoulder and catch him glaring at me. I send a glare of my own back at him. He attacked me, thinking I was someone I have no knowledge of.

Plus, seeing someone wearing my father's clothes with so much anger emanating from him hurts. So much that it causes my own anger to flare—my father was so gentle-hearted, it's almost blasphemy.

To make matters worse, my father's clothes fit him well—too well—with his form filling them out where they should be baggy. The collared shirt falls into a deep v-neck that shows off his collarbone and the lines of his chest muscles. The pants are just tight enough to show off the sculpted legs beneath before tapering off below the knee.

Marguerite continues talking to him as I finish making the salve and apply it to my neck. "Rhiannon is gone from this world. It has been three hundred years since she passed into the stars."

Even with my back to them, I can feel his gaze still on me. So much hatred. Rhiannon must have really pissed him off. I turn to watch as Marguerite commands him. I enjoy seeing her like this; she's normally reserved and kind.

"Lies! Why are you hiding Rhiannon?" he yells, rising to his feet. The clatter of the chair hitting the floor reverberates through the cottage.

Marguerite raises her hand again, and his hands go to his head once more. "I know your kind. But you do not know mine. Do not test me again. Your unnerving strength will not work against me. I can take you down with a wave of my hand. Is twice enough?"

"What do you mean?" he grits out.

"You are no longer in Elysium. I don't know what you did to find your way to the human world, but there is no going back," Marguerite says stoically. "And if you are not careful, you won't live long in this place. It has been many years since a fae has been here, and stories have turned into legend and myth. But humans hunt your kind, nevertheless. We are your best chance at survival."

He gives a single, decisive nod. In response, Marguerite lowers her hand, releasing her hold over him.

The rigid set of his shoulders softens, his brows unfurl, and he picks up the chair. Sitting down, he crosses his arms over his chest. "I know I'm not in Elysium—or even the capital city, Solarium, where I'm from. The ship I was a captive on sailed far and wide."

His eyes dart between me and Marguerite, a perplexed look etched into his features. "Who are you? How can she look so much like Rhiannon if you are to be believed?" he demands, his voice laced with contempt and disbelief.

"This is Ameris—Rhiannon is a blood relation from many moons ago." I smile curtly and lift my hair to show my rounded ears when he looks in my direction. He narrows his gaze, considering me as Marguerite continues. "I descend from Carthis. We are not fae, but carry the blood of them within us. And you are?"

"Xander," is all he says, distrust written all over his expression.

He stands, but Marguerite stops him with her sharp words. "Boy. Sit Down."

I chuckle at his look. He is so arrogant. It seeps off him like steam after a summer rainstorm.

"I am no boy. I have passed two centuries—a blink compared to your brief life." His defiance and disregard sing of status and wealth. It's so similar to the way the upper class behaves here in Navarine. Those in power are all the same. They feel entitled, as if things are meant to be given to them, demanding respect but not giving any in return.

"Yes, but that only makes you about thirty years old in our world. So, boy, if you keep it up, you will not live to see a hundred more." Her stare is hard and unwavering.

It's the same look that always scares me. You don't mess with Marguerite when she gives you one of those.

"Let him go, Marguerite. He thinks he's better than this place. It's not worth our time. He may have magic, but humans have weapons." The distaste is heavy on my lips.

"You did not waste your breath saving him to let him go so easily," she chides.

"Humph. I think I'm the one who saved her," Xander retorts, assessing me.

"I would have made it." I bristle. "And you'd still be in chains if I didn't help you. What were you doing on that ship? There are wounds around your wrists. You were not their guest."

"Those humans used me for my magic and thought they had bested me. So long I waited, for the right moment, and then I brought the storm raining down on them."

"So, you can harness the energy of water?" Marguerite interrupts.

"You know the way of our magic?" Xander turns to Marguerite and studies her.

Marguerite responds without hesitation. "As I said, we are descendants of the three fae from the Elysium Court who were banished to this world. Our ancestors have passed down stories of your world, and the magic we have comes from them, even if it has manifested differently."

"Impossible," he mutters.

She continues, ignoring his interruption. "Witches cannot manipulate the elements like the fae can, but we are born with the innate ability to use magic. We can craft spells, create tonics and salves from nature, and possess other gifts. Ameris might be the only exception." Marguerite nods her head in my direction.

A devious smile comes before I remind him what he agreed to. "That's why you will honor your bargain."

CHAPTER 6
XANDER

"I would never make a bargain with a human to my disadvantage." My words are laced with venom, fingers curling into fists at Ameris's words. Bargains are a fae's worst nightmare, like a curse that works its way through our body. Controlling us.

Now that my rage has subsided from waking to someone I thought was Rhiannon, I notice the differences, even if her beauty matches the late queen's. Ameris's skin has a light golden glow, much warmer than Rhiannon's porcelain.

The fire catches on the pink tones in her long blonde hair, flowing unbound and wild around her shoulders. They look so alike, even in their differences, that I am still hesitant to believe these two. Yet, I also know that Rhiannon would never have been subdued like Ameris was, and they have no reason to lie.

"Try to deny it. Say you won't teach me magic," Ameris taunts.

"I—" A deep rumble comes out instead of words, which stick in my throat. No matter how hard I try to force them up, I cannot say that I refuse to teach her magic. I want to rip the smug smile off her face.

"And you owe me a life debt," she presses.

"I saved you from falling."

"Doesn't mean I would have died. You, on the other hand—I saved you from your fate."

"Enough," the old woman interjects. "A bargain was made, and you are bound to follow through."

"The thing about bargains, human, is that unless you specify the conditions, every other option is on my side. We like to extend, find workarounds, whatever it is we can to get out of it. Remember that, for you might find yourself regretting a bargain in which you think you've gained the upper hand." I lean back in my seat, enjoying my turn to give a smug smile. I receive great satisfaction in the way Ameris's body tenses and her eyes narrow. Marguerite sighs and shakes her head.

She huffs indignantly. "Help me, please. Starting now, until I can do magic. Then you are free to do whatever you please."

"Hmm. Perhaps." I draw out the moment, reveling in Ameris's anguish that is bubbling to the surface. She knows I have a loophole, a way out of our bargain. I could teach her magic forty years from now, or when she's near her death bed. So long as I fulfill the bargain. But I can use this to my advantage.

"Help me get back to my world, and I will help you starting now."

"That's not possible," Marguerite offers. "Otherwise, we would not exist as we do. I imagine Rhiannon would have returned to your world if she could."

"All I want is your help in finding a way back. I am putting no time limit on it. I will live beyond your life span and exhaust all means possible to find a way."

"I will help you, but can't guarantee I will find the answer," Ameris responds.

"Very well." I turn my attention to Marguerite. "Now, tell me more about this magic—spells you called them—and what makes her so different."

"There isn't much more to the magic than what I already told you. For Ameris, as you can see, she looks like your queen. That was our first inclination when she was young—that she would be able to do magic that none of us could. Manipulate the elements. But being able to wield magic in this world will get you killed. We are hunted and burned for our gift."

"You know, like the chosen ones in stories, with exceptional abilities? Except I'm not here to save the world." Ameris smiles, but there is something more beneath, something dark.

"We have no such stories." I respond with pinched brows.

"If you two plan to practice magic, you must be very careful, or both of you will meet your end," Marguerite cuts us off with a warning.

"Show me one of your...spells," I request, wanting to understand how they use our magic.

"Was giving you a terrible headache to the point of breaking you not enough?" Marguerite chides.

"I want to see it, not feel your wrath," I respond.

Marguerite sighs. "Ameris, get me some dirty water."

"Why are you indulging him?" Ameris asks.

Marguerite places a hand on her hip, her impatience showing. "Do you want his help?"

Ameris stalks off and out the cottage door.

"Can I trust you not to try anything else?" Marguerite inquires when Ameris is out of earshot, giving me a pointed look.

"I give you my word." After all, I am nothing if not a man of my word.

Not a moment later, Ameris returns from outside, holding a tin cup of muddy water, tiny leaves and debris swirling within it. She hands it to Marguerite, who places it on the table in front of me. Ameris stands back, an untrusting look crossing her features when the old lady steps away and gathers more items.

I chuckle. "I won't harm you intentionally again." She gives me a pointed look, and I shrug. "You can't blame me for mistaking you for Rhiannon. The war between her and Oberon got my father killed and is the reason I lost my throne."

She lets out a scoff, rolling her eyes. "I should have figured you're a scorned prince."

Her insinuation ignites a flicker of irritation. My brows furrow as I lean forward, pressing my hands firmly on the table. "Not a prince. An appointed heir."

"Well, isn't that better? The chosen one." An insulting laugh escapes before she continues. "Let me guess: you want to get home so you can claim what's yours?"

"Not claim. Reclaim," I say through gritted teeth. "From the bastard who stole it and banished me." My hands clench into fists at the memory of Oberon overthrowing Rhiannon and stealing what is mine. When I make it back to Elysium, I will make him pay for what he did.

"Well, I guess we'd better get to work on helping me with magic then. Since I'm the one with the spells and all." She raises an eyebrow and waves the brown leather grimoire back and forth.

I give a half-hearted smile as Marguerite returns to the table. She pours salt around the cup, completing a circle, and lights a candle. "Feel the water the way that it is now. For us, this water is dirty, could have contaminates that would make us sick. I am going to do a purification spell."

Deepening my connection to the element, I find it's muddled, other elements blocking the purity of the water. Wrinkled hands hover over the bowl, moving in circles, and words unknown to me spill from her mouth.

The water swirls as she chants, pushing everything other than the element at its core to the sides of the bowl. It slowly changes, the water becoming purer with each minute that passes. When she's done, all the things that were in the water have poured over the sides and now lay on the table.

"Drink." She hands me the cup. "Ameris, get three bowls of

stew from the pot over the fire. I need sustenance, and I'm sure you two are hungry."

"The winter solstice has passed, and the sun has set early. We do not go out after dark. Take the last room on the left and rest."

CHAPTER 7
XANDER

The next morning, I step out into the sun. Beaming down in full force, it heats my skin while the wind whispers a promise of relief. Crisp air fills my lungs, a tell of the coming winter. To be on solid ground for the first time in months is a pleasure I almost forgot the feeling of.

My body doesn't sway with the creaking wood in the wind. No water swishes around my feet. There are no chains around my wrists. I'm not being forced to use my magic by the sailors who captured me.

I soak in the energy of this world, but the stillness here is different than on the open sea. It's heavy and reserved, like the magic knows it's forbidden and only allows itself to be used at its willingness. And it sets me on edge—this whole place does. But at least I'm free of my captors, even if I'm stuck in this bargain with the human girl.

Ameris looks up, her smile disappearing as I approach. "What do you want?"

Placing a hand on her hip, she leans into the curve of it. I trace the lines of her body that narrow at the waist, following them up to her neck, where the skin has turned color from the bruises made by my hands. The imprint of them still lingers.

Redness blooms along her cheeks in opposition to her narrowed glare. Her attraction is clear, and I will use it to my advantage. Find a way to get home and take back my throne.

"If you aren't here to help, the least you can do is stop staring."

"You're one to talk about staring." I raise an eyebrow.

Ameris scoffs and slams the tool she's using into the ground, splitting the dirt before pulling it back to pry potatoes from where they cling to the earth. I can only imagine what she's thinking as a satisfied smile cracks across her face.

She has that spark that can easily be ignited, filling the space she occupies if she wishes—just like Rhiannon did.

"Look, I just want to get this bargain over with, as I'm sure you are. Teach me magic, and you can be on your way." She drops the potatoes into the woven basket at her feet.

"I do apologize for my part in that." I nod toward her neck. She didn't deserve what I did, but the blinding rage at seeing someone I thought was Rhiannon overtook me. It's not in my nature to harm innocent people. I can't bear to see the discolored skin—or her resemblance to Rhiannon. But she doesn't need to know that. I walk past her toward the woods.

She grabs my arm before I can get out of reach and shoves the basket of potatoes into my arms. "Be useful and take these inside."

"I have other things I want to do." I try to rebound the basket toward her, but she steps back, hands raised.

"I don't think so. You owe me a life debt, and we made a bargain. You will help me every day until I can do magic." Ameris shrugs and smirks, pushing me to the water pump. Water flows over the potatoes, rinsing the dirt off.

I give her a deadly look, but have no retort. She knows I can't get out of helping her. Being indebted to someone is a fae's worst nightmare. I push past her and head back inside the cottage.

"Put the basket by the hearth," Ameris says as she gathers

balms, medicine, and small bags of dried leaves, putting them all in her satchel.

"Do not take him to the village." Marguerite coughs. She sits in front of the fire, a shawl tightly wrapped around her shoulders. Her hands move fast for her age, twisting needles between different ends of thread. It's the same commanding voice she used with me last night. I learned my lesson not to test her.

After dropping the basket next to the empty chair across from Marguerite, I cross the room and lean against the kitchen island. I observe them, soaking in how Ameris disregards—almost ignores—Marguerite. Humans must not care for the wisdom of their elders.

"I told you no one saw us. You're not feeling well this morning after exerting so much magic. You were supposed to deliver the medicine today, and we need more food." She continues packing her satchel, adding a handful of potatoes to it. Looking up, she shrugs at the old woman. "Plus, he can carry the sack of grain."

Marguerite stops working the material and turns to us, a warning in her look. "That is what your horse is for."

"You worry too much. Honey needs the rest after yesterday too." Ameris nods, letting me know she's ready to leave before walking out the door.

I don't move, unsure of whom to listen to. I've always been the one to give orders, to decide for others. But I have to adjust to this new world. I am no longer the appointed heir, and I have no one to command. And even though I don't have elders here, Marguerite is still one in this world.

"Ameris!" Marguerite calls after her. When there is no response, she huffs out, "Stubborn girl, doesn't listen."

Marguerite's gaze locks on mine, and her eyes gloss over like an oracle's for the briefest moment before she blinks and they return to their usual deep brown. My jaw tenses, and I fidget uncomfortably under it before she addresses me. "The winds have shifted, and the birds flock from left to right. Go with her to the village. But before you go, promise me you will take care of her. She will need you."

"Why should I make such a promise?" I cock my head at the old woman and cross my arms over my chest as tension creeps between my shoulders. Asking a promise of a fae is not something to take lightly. Life debts and promises are not things we like to dabble in. Too many unknowns.

"Because I'm telling you to. The moment she saved you from that wrecked ship, the tendrils of fate shifted and began weaving ours together. You must bear the burden of what may come." Her tone is flat; no feelings behind the words. She speaks of what signs she sees.

"I will agree...if you tell me the location of where the first fae entered this world." My father's warning echoes in my mind. Never enter a bargain. Never make a promise. If you must, then enter that bargain with one of your own. I will protect her—until I can find a way out of this world and back to my own. After all, I didn't agree on how long I had to protect her.

"It's not far from here, a few miles at most." Marguerite waves me off and returns to her needlework. "Go then, but be careful. This world is not a friendly place."

"That's not a good enough answer." I push off the table and am about to leave the cottage when she responds.

"Promise me before you leave, and I will show you tomorrow. I'll take you there myself." Just below her soft tone sits an urgency.

I take the chance, knowing I'll likely regret it. "I promise."

A promise left open to interpretation. Taking care of someone can mean more than one thing. Stupid humans forgetting to require specifics. By the time I leave the cottage, Ameris is several paces down the dirt path. A quick jog is all it takes to reach her.

"You don't listen to your elders?" I want to better understand why Marguerite would think she needs protecting.

Ameris shrugs, her gaze never leaving the path. "She's overprotective, has been since my parents were killed. That was a long time ago now, and I've learned to navigate life among the villagers who are already suspicious of us and dislike us."

"What happened?" I kick a stone down the path, and watch it skip along until it careens sideways, out of reach.

"The villagers burned my mom for doing magic and my father for allowing it." She curls her fingers into her dress and doesn't elaborate any further. The wind picks up and teases a loose strand of hair that she tucks behind her ear. Rolling her shoulder, she adjusts the satchel to her other one.

I extend a hand, offering to carry her satchel, but she refuses. "My parents are gone as well."

Neither one of us says another word. The sun sits high in its midday position, taking the chill of the morning and replacing it with cool day. Farmed fields along the path host a variety of plants. Some I've seen in my world; others are new to me.

More homes appear closer together as the town comes into view. We pass stone houses, varying in shades of grey and brown. Roofs are laid with cascading rows of small wooden pieces, cracked and weathered.

These dwellings are dismal compared to the beauty of the fae buildings. There is no beauty to be found here. Yet, magic whispers on the wind—tentative and reaching, as if aware that someone among these humans possesses the ability to wield it.

We take the winding roads through the town until we enter its square. Buildings pressed together flank the space; some connect, and others are so close not even a cart could fit in the alley between them. Devoid of greenery, no flowers, or plants, this place is bleak. The only color in this town comes from the stalls in the center of the square, which are covered with colorful fabric and filled with various wares.

Before we enter the village Ameris holds out her arm and turns to me. "Listen, Marguerite and I already live in a precarious state, waiting for one of the villagers to accuse us of being witches. Most of the villagers want so badly to burn a magic wielder at the stake. Please... don't cause a scene."

I nod as I take in the villagers milling among the vendors. Some are yelling at each other, arguing over the price of goods for sale, while others have calm exchanges. Animals roam about, eating rotten vegetables that lay in piles in the corners of connected buildings. At one end sits a grand stone building with vaulted roofs, and a bell tower that rises from its center, reaching into the sky.

The wind shifts, and a presence similar to the ones on the ship stirs, pulling my attention to a dark alley. But as we pass by and it comes fully into view, there is no one there—just the lingering sense of being observed.

Strange. No one survived. I made sure of that. Perhaps it's the lingering souls who were lost to the sea. I return my attention to Ameris, wanting to tell her we should head back and come another day, but she must not have noticed I stopped and continued walking to a stall without me.

The old woman behind the counter, with russet skin and wispy hair pulled into a bun, looks up at me as I come up and stand behind Ameris. Judgment passes before her gaze returns to Ameris, who nods in response to her question about me being with her.

Her smock is of good make; blue lace overlays the brown fabric at the top in an intricate pattern, stopping at her waist, where it flares out into pleats. I wonder what this merchant is doing selling wares when her clothing suggests she does not need to engage in such business ventures.

Ameris pulls out a few of her tinctures, exchanging salts and cloth with the woman. She gives the old woman's hand a squeeze once they've finished.

She grabs onto my forearm, and her nails dig into my skin as she drags me away. "Could you be any more obnoxious? You shouldn't stare. People take offense to it. Especially since you're not known here. Stay with me this time."

"I will do that which I choose. But proceed, and I will follow." I tip my head toward the remainder of the stalls.

Ameris scoffs, letting go of my arm before turning her back to me. I stay close as requested, soaking in all the details I can about this girl and who she is.

When she mingles with the other merchants, her smile is a practiced ease. But I see through it—she hates them. It appears pleasant, but there's a subtle tension around her eyes, a thinly veiled display of cordiality.

A short, bald man at the next stall stands behind the counter and watches us approach. His nostrils flare, lips curling back into a sneer, barely able to contain his disgust. Leaning forward, his gaze hardens.

"What do you want, witch?" His contempt is clear as a spring creek.

Ameris stiffens, releasing a breath; the smile now brittle as she speaks. "Gene. So nice to see you as well. We are healers; let us not forget we saved your wife."

"And by our savior, if she wasn't alive, you'd be dead," he snarls, venom lacing every word.

Ameris extends a handful of coins, ignoring his threat. "I'll take the dried grapes, apples, and a sack of grain."

He reluctantly bags the dried fruits in a cloth, unwilling to refuse her money, and sets it before Ameris. She drops the coins into his open palm, and he weighs them in his hand, running them between his fingers before pocketing them. "It'll be ten more."

"What? That's ridiculous. I'm not paying you more." She grabs the paper bag, but he snatches her wrist back and stops her from leaving.

"Do you want to end up dead like the last one?" Teeth barred, he tightens his grips on her wrist, fingers pressing into her skin until she drops the bag. Ameris winces as she twists out of his hold. She looks around, checking to see if anyone is watching, rubbing her wrist before quickly pulling her sleeve down to cover the beginning of a bruise left behind.

Unable to hold myself back, I yank the merchant up by his collar, so our faces are inches apart. I lower my voice, coating it with a dangerous edge. "You pocketed her money without first stating a price. To me, that is an agreement. We will take the products and leave your stall. Do you have a problem with that?"

I release my grip, shoving him back. He falters, scrambling to regain his balance. "Uh, uh. No."

His eyes widen in alarm, fear mixed with surprise, as his gaze flicks from me to her. "Yes, I'm with her," I confirm. "You'd do well to remember that, as I won't be so nice next time."

Ameris stands rooted to the spot, eyes wide, shock written starkly across her face. Her expression quickly changes, dancing between anger and concern, a storm of emotions playing out in the span of a heartbeat. I pick up the bag of goods and extend it towards Ameris. She hesitates, her hand hovering in mid-air, before taking it. I lug the sack of grain up and sling it over my shoulder. "Let's go."

"You'll regret that!" Gene yells as we turn to leave.

His yell draws the attention of those around us in the market. But his continued disdain kindles the flame of my contempt for disrespect, and I act on impulse. The bag of grain slams on the top of his stall table, my fist flies after it, landing a hit on his jaw.

"No," I assure him. "You will."

CHAPTER 8
AMERIS

uck. I should have listened to Marguerite.

My feet move back of their own accord as I watch Gene's body fall. Dust rises from the impact of him hitting the ground. He doesn't stir, momentarily stunned, just as I am. This is not good. Xander was already getting too much attention, and now a crowd has gathered.

Why does Marguerite have to be right when it matters? A string of curses escapes with my next breath. I slink into the crowd that has surrounded us to watch the spectacle as a few men flock to Gene's side, helping him up. His gaze locks onto Xander's, eyes blazing as he spits blood to the side.

I don't wait for Xander as bystanders start to murmur, wanting to put distance between myself and the crowd.

My heart pounds with each step I take. Looking over my shoulder, I take in the people in the market, but they're not looking at me—only at the tall, handsome man that no one knows, who is now following me.

I duck into a narrow alley, and my breaths come in a detached cadence, each one faster or slower than the other. Rough brick presses into my back as I lean into the wall of the alley.

When his form comes into view, towering over me, I rush up to him with fire in my veins, burning through me. The words come out full of fury, and I can't stop my hand as it slaps him across the face. "What is wrong with you?"

He doesn't say anything; just watches as I run trembling hands through my hair, thoughts spiraling. Heavy breaths escape me as I pace back and forth.

Each step is like a drumbeat to my mounting rage. Emotions and thoughts swirl in a chaotic whirlwind. I warned him. Asked him nicely not to cause a scene.

The villagers will never forgive what he did, and I'll be lucky if anyone does business with me again. But... Xander is imposing, standing tall and proud, and they may think twice before coming after us.

I storm back up to him and poke him in the chest. "What were you thinking?"

Xander stiffens, jaw clenching, when he grabs my hand and removes it. He drops it against my side, like I'm not worth his time. "He was disrespectful. Putrid human trash."

I lose it, a frustrated scream escaping through gritted teeth. My hands clench, and when I uncurl my fingers, sparks of electricity shoot from them, hitting him in the chest. I inhale sharply as pressure leaves my body along with the magic, but it quickly returns, cutting off my breath.

He startles, stepping back before raising a brow. "Interesting. Is that normal?"

Movement from my peripheral steals my attention from what I just did. Two men stand at the entrance of the alley, watching us. Both men are stocky; thick muscles cord their arms, showing through the sailors garb they wear, though it's tattered and dirty.

"Well, well. So, it was a witch who stole our fae captive." The man with black hair and a pinched nose grins, like he's just earned a grand catch.

They saunter towards us, and I steal a glance down the alley, but it's a dead end.

And here's Xander, leaning into the shadows of the alley, watching them with an unreadable expression, arms folded across his chest. One foot is nonchalantly crossed over the other, the toe of his boot gently resting on the ground.

My god, he looks like he could care less, I balk at him. This is not the time. This is bad. Worse than the encounter with Gene. Oh gods, I wasn't careful enough on the ship. They're a few feet from us when Xander's words interrupt my thoughts.

"I would stop where you are." Xander pushes off the wall and stands partially in front of me. The men laugh, swinging iron chains from their hands.

"You forgot something on the ship, witch." The other man, with white hair and a tanned face ruined by sun damage, says. He holds up a set of manacles, opening and closing them, the rusted iron echoing between the narrow walls. "We'll be taking what's ours now, and we won't say a word about you to your lovely town council."

Fear pounds its way through my heart, coiling its tendrils tightly around my body. I think about Marguerite and what they'd do to us, because I don't believe them. I would be a witness not only to a fae but to their dealings. I grip Xander's arm, a plead to do something, and he tenses under my touch.

Before I can process another thought, Xander moves so quickly that if I hadn't been just holding his arm, I would've missed his movement. He snaps the neck of the man with the manacles, whose body drops gracelessly to the ground.

Xander's yanked back when the other man wraps an iron chain around his neck, trying to choke him. Unsure of what to do, I watch in horror, even though I kind of enjoy seeing him suffer in a similar way he treated me the first time.

"Ameris—magic—" Xander struggles to speak as he pulls the chain away from his windpipe, which is now bright red and blistering. His plea wipes the dark thought from my mind.

"I told you I can't do magic at will!" Frustrated and wanting to help, I grab the manacles from the ground.

Xander shakes his head as I'm about to throw them to him. He's struggling against the iron chain. He headbutts the man, who howls in pain as blood leaks from his nose.

I swing the manacles around the back of the man's knees instead, hitting him in the thigh. He loosens his grip just enough, and Xander slips from beneath his grip, bending and grasping for breath.

The man vaults towards me and tackles me to the ground. My right cheek slams into the cobblestones, and pain shoots up into my skull and through my hips. The pressure of his body is gone as quickly as it came. I'm still on the ground when I turn to see him jump back up and go after Xander.

But Xander has already recovered. He closes the distance between himself and the man in a blur. His arm wraps around the man's neck in an iron grip.

Despite the man's bulk, his eyes widen, bulging. He's no match for Xander, who looks like he's handling a rag doll, snuffing the life out of him with ease. With a cold, dismissive motion, he hurls him to the side, like he's nothing more than the sack of grain he was carrying earlier. The body lands with a dull thud, a lifeless heap, discarded next to his dead companion.

"Are you hurt?" Xander squats before me, taking my chin in his hand, and tilts my head to the side, inspecting the scratches on my face. I look into his eyes as they search mine. A flicker of concern lies within those sky-blue irises, gentle, like there is a soft side to him behind his annoyingly prickly exterior.

"I'm fine." I jerk out of his grip. Stars, my right side is throbbing from the fall. I groan as getting up proves difficult, but I wave off his help. When I step forward, I stumble, my knees roaring in pain. His hand grabs my elbow, steadying me. "What are we going to do about them?"

"Leave them here." Xander drags the two bodies behind some nearby crates so they won't be visible to anyone looking down the alley.

I balk. "We can't leave them there. If someone finds them, there will be an investigation. We have to do something."

"What do you suggest? There is nowhere to go but back into the market. Shall we wait for someone to arrive and explain they attacked us?"

"Can't you use magic to cover them up? Anything?"

"It doesn't work like that. There is nothing water can do to help. What about you? Burn them with that little electric shock you gave me."

"I can't do magic when I want to. Sometimes it just happens when I'm overly emotional, but it's rare and I can't control it."

"It appears we have a dilemma."

"I should never have brought you," I mutter. All I wanted was for him to help me learn magic and be done with it. Why couldn't he have minded himself until our path's separated?

He ignores my comment and walks ahead of me, peering out of the alley and into the square. "Let's go."

The pain in my knee and hip makes it difficult, I hobble forward, barely making it a few paces before gripping the wall for support. Great. I'm coming to regret my decision to help this fae. He has been nothing but trouble.

CHAPTER 9
AMERIS

Xander waits outside, keeping watch. We agreed it was best for me to do this alone. I join Marguerite, who sits in front of the hearth, sipping tea. The blackened stones are the holders of tales long past. Sitting in the chair across from her, I stretch my legs out and lean back, releasing a long sigh.

My nerves are firing on high. As the pressure beneath my skin mounts again, I need to occupy my body with something. I grab a potato, put a knife to its tough skin, and begin peeling while I explain that we will need to leave. "I messed up."

With each stroke of the blade, I recount what happened at the market to Marguerite. She listens quietly, no reaction or expression; only stares into the fire, deep in thought. The low burn of coal cracks and pops every so often—the only sounds that reach me—along with the grate of the knife and the thunk of a potato. Marguerite's voice is soft against the silence. "He has a darkness in him. Be careful."

"Don't we all?" It comes out a little too loud and forceful as I recount my anger at him in the market and how it sparked my magic. How I so badly want that which escapes me. Marguerite doesn't acknowledge that I think we should leave. She just keeps on about this darkness; but it's too late for that, I've already seen it.

"You are right... But the difference is whether you let it manifest and burn your soul so deeply that it shines black as night, or just let it be another part of your life that sits until it's needed."

Silence takes over because there is no answer I can provide that is not debatable. I bury that dark part of me to be the polite and amiable girl who lives outside the market when I interact with the villagers. When all I really want to do is rage against the village that makes my life hell.

Marguerite balances me, pulling me back from the edge. Reminding me that these people only know what they've been taught to hate.

"You will either burn or shine, my dear. There is only one way this ends. I must pass on to you all my knowledge. It is time. Give me your hands." Marguerite's soft voice fills the emptiness, with no judgment in her tone.

Putting the knife down, I wipe my hands against the smooth fabric of my dress and hold them out. Her weathered, wrinkled skin is soft as she takes my hands into her own. The moment our skin touches, she begins an incantation, her voice low and rhythmic. "*Transfere omnes memorias nostras in hanc unam.*"

A sudden heat flares, searing into my skin like a brand, building with each word she utters. My muscles stiffen, and I pull back in a reflexive urge to escape the burning. But Marguerite's hold is surprisingly firm, her eyes pinched in concentration. "Close your eyes and repeat after me."

I do as instructed and repeat the incantation over and over. "*Ego libenter omnes memorias accipio.*"

Each time the phrase passes my lips, my throat burns, and white light blazes behind my eyelids. Words come out hoarse and painful until I can no longer stand it. "Marguerite..."

"Hush girl. Push through the pain, and do not interrupt again. Now, continue." She squeezes my hands tighter.

I lean into her grip, putting my forehead to the back of her hands. My body and mind blur and bend as images and voices swirl, intensifying the more we chant. Nothing makes sense. My throat is raw, the words barely come out. Just as I cannot bear it anymore, Marguerite's rhythmic chanting stops.

"Open your eyes and look at me."

It's not our cottage I open my eyes to. Vivid visions, or perhaps memories, overwhelm me as if I am physically reliving them—filled with loss, love, pain, and pleasure.

Pain racks my body; every muscle tenses and flares in revolt, like liquid fire is flowing through my veins, burning me from the inside. I double over, my brain on the brink of bursting through my skull. In an instant, it switches to an intense, brittle cold that threatens to crack my bones.

My breath catches in my throat as I'm pummeled over and over with visions of someone else's life.

Conversations of magic, nature, and balance. Rhiannon stands at the edge of a body of water, staring at a half-moon bridge. The water is so still; the bridge reflects perfectly, creating a precise circle. It's beautiful and eerie. All these memories and emotions happen so quickly, I can't process them all. As the pain subsides, my breath comes easier, and I take each one greedily, gulping in the warm cottage air.

Exhaustion moves through me like a summer storm. Abrupt and violent. I drop from the chair onto my knees, collapsing onto my back. My body lies parallel to the floor as I stare at the wooden rafters.

An angry rasp is all that I can manage. "What was that?"

"The fastest way to teach you what I know." Marguerite looks down at me, unaffected.

Heavy footsteps draw my attention to Xander, who stands in the doorway, looking from Marguerite to me. His expression is unreadable. He turns and leaves, saying nothing. Ugh, figures. He's a brute with no tact. I roll over and push up onto my hands and knees. A deep ache sits within my muscles, as if they want to tear from the inside out. Marguerite helps me up and walks me to the table. As I slide into a chair, she walks away and returns with a cup of water.

"Drink." She pushes the glass toward me. "You should talk to him."

My response is coated with irritability. "There is nothing to talk about. He's ruined our lives. We need to leave."

"We all must face our demons one day. When that day comes, whether tomorrow or next year, it will either be by choice or by force." Marguerite says, a knowing look crossing her features, like she's been living with this expectation her whole life.

"Why do you always have to make statements like that?" I groan.

She smiles. "Probably because I'm old."

My mood slips through the cracks of this taxing day as I laugh. A deep, belly-shattering laugh—the kind that comforts you and lets you know everything will be okay.

Even though, deep down, I know it won't be. As I look at her and she looks at me, I can't help the feelings that wash over me. She is my impossible Marguerite. The wise old woman with the wisdom of a hundred women.

Even though time is of the essence, I want to know what kind of magic that was. "Marguerite, what just happened? What did we do?"

"It is an ancient spell that allows one person to transfer knowledge to another if they can withstand the pressure and pain of it. It's not meant to be used frequently and only reserved for special times. Since Xander's arrival, our fate has shifted. I don't have time to teach you everything." The last words are emphasized as she gestures toward the glass of water. "Now drink."

"Fine. But..." She cuts me off and tells me to drink again, stubbornly nodding her head in the water's direction. She waits, unrelenting, until I finish the glass. Once I'm done, she grabs the glass and walks away before I can say anything else.

Bending to rest, my forehead touches the table as I process the experience I just had. I only have a moment though, before we need to pack and leave. I want to tell Marguerite what I saw, where I saw Rhiannon. Ask her if she knows the place.

When I look up, it's not Marguerite. I drop my head back down, not wanting to think about him, let alone see him.

"You're hurt—again." The words are as conflicting as his stare this afternoon.

"No shit. I was tackled, and I just had an awful experience with Marguerite." I roll my eyes, even though he can't see me. "So yeah, I'm hurting. Again." I let loose an exaggerated sigh. "Do you need something?"

"No. But we need to go," he responds, "sooner rather than later."

"Where are we even supposed to go?" The tenor of my voice rises, each syllable like a dagger thrown to inflict the pain from that question that cuts through me.

"This isn't my world. I cannot offer you suggestions," Xander says, matter of fact, no ill intention apparent behind his statement.

We sit there in dreary silence for a few more minutes before I get up and head to my room. The edges of sleep creep in, a promise to ease some of the pain and fatigue. But I can't rest; we have to prepare to leave the only home I've ever known. I change into a shirt and pants, my preferred clothing when I'm not visiting town. Plus, they'll be easier to travel and ride in.

When I sit on the edge of the bed to pull my boots on, my eyelids droop. They're so heavy from the day that I can barely keep them open. I blink slowly, battling the urge to let them close. I can't stop myself as the weight of my body sinks into the mattress.

CHAPTER 10
AMERIS

"Ameris! Wake up!" Marguerite bursts into my room, jolting me from the edge of sleep.

The rhythm of my heartbeat accelerates, spurring me into motion. I must have fallen asleep. Dammit. Jumping out of bed, I rapidly blink the haze away, but it isn't from sleep. Smoke hangs in the air, swirling about. The acrid and charred scent of wood burning reaches my nostrils as my brain registers something is very wrong. Panic rises as I ask, "What's going on?"

"They're here." Marguerite scuttles around the room, tossing items into my satchel. She pushes the satchel into my arms and turns me about, pushing me out the door. "He knows what to do."

We rush through the thick smoke in the hallway, the heat intensifying as we near the kitchen. The wooden rafters are ablaze, like an angry fire god has reached down a hand and has our roof in its grasp.

The elements are raging around me, fire consuming the oxygen in the air to fuel its hunger. I rear back, bringing an arm up to shield my eyes. My lungs constrict, forcing a slew of coughs to escape as I try to breathe in the stifling air. Heat presses in on me, searing my skin as we make for the front door.

Cold air sinks its talons into my skin when we stumble outside. Eyes wide, I gasp, my hand coming up to my mouth. It's not from the winter chill, but from the five bodies scattered across the ground. Gene is among them, along with a few of the villagers who helped him. One of the other men is dressed similar to the sailors who assaulted us in the alley.

Waves of emotions crash through me. My fingers run through my hair as I hold onto my temples and pace back and forth. This is really happening. I knew we needed to leave, but my home is burning.

Fire.

Like my parents.

Everything I've ever known. *Gone.*

The world blurs as tears gather in the corner of my eyes. I try to blink them away, but it's no use. A shaky breath tears through my chest, along with the wetness that slides down my cheeks, its slow descent in opposition to the raging fire.

Xander waits with Honey, already mounted. I quicken my pace towards them, relief washing over me even though Honey's on edge. Her muscles are taut, soaked in unease, with another rider atop her and the flames crackling nearby.

She's more than just my horse; she's a constant companion. The last gift my parents gave me, and in their absence, she became my solace. Helped mend the fractures their deaths left behind. Reaching her side, I gently run my hand down the length of her neck. "It's okay, girl. You're okay."

I lift my gaze to meet Xander's. Crimson liquid speckled across his skin glistens in the firelight, highlighting the angles of his face. Blood is splattered on his white shirt, which is split from a long gash running across his chest. He killed them all. Protected us instead of leaving.

He offers a solemn nod and extends his hand to me. But this

isn't right. I refuse and turn to Marguerite. "Why aren't you on this horse?" The words escape in a rush, confusion mixed with worry. Marguerite should be the one riding with me. "He's capable of running."

Ignoring me, she looks to the cottage, deep lines crossing her forehead as a thought seemingly occurs to her. "I forgot the grimoire."

Marguerite runs back into the inferno, jumping through the flames that now flank the front door.

"Marguerite!" No, no, no. She's trying to save us and the grimoire that contains all our knowledge. I throw the satchel to the ground and run after her.

Xander's yell for me to stop is like a whisper lost in the woods. I should have listened to her when she told me not to take him to the village.

Heat sears my skin, a punishing reminder that everything is soon to be ruined, a pile of ash that will be swept away with the breeze. A high-pitched whistle fills the space, one of the wooden beams splits away from the ceiling and crashes in the middle of the cottage.

Flinching, I jump back, narrowly avoiding the flames that roar up. Marguerite is stuck on the other side with the grimoire in hand.

I take in the partially destroyed room, looking around for anything to put over the flames long enough for her to jump over. I grab the edges of the rug; the rough fabric cuts into my palms as I tug, but it's stuck.

Throwing things aside, panic strikes, holding my chest in a vice-like grip.

There's nothing that will work.

She has no way to escape.

"Ameris. Stop. It's no use. I am an old woman; you must go and save yourself." Marguerite's voice pulls me back to her. She tosses me the grimoire. "You will find all you need to know within its pages."

"No!" The sound tears through my throat at an octave I didn't know I was capable of.

She blows a kiss and raises a hand in goodbye. "Leave me. Take him home and go with him."

Not again. No…no…no…

Not someone else I love, stolen by the angry flames in their passion for destruction.

The fire taunts me, forming my parents' silhouettes among the red and orange. I will not let Marguerite suffer for my actions. A tingle of magic pulses, and I pull at it with everything I have. It builds along with my desperation, my need—I couldn't save my parents, and now I face losing another person I love.

That cannot happen again. The need to quell the fire takes over, and I attempt to force my magic to comply, even though it never has. I don't care; I have to do something, anything.

Marguerite watches me, speaking, but the words don't reach me, even though I know she's telling me to stop. The last words to form on her lips are 'I love you,' before she nods her head and steps back, away from me. I can no longer see her.

She's gone.

"Marguerite! No—" Guttural, raw screams repeat the words over and over until there is no air left in my lungs.

The magic churning within me spins out of control, and instead of taming the fire, the room erupts. I'm thrown backward, wood and debris spreading out around me.

Ringing sounds in my ears as Xander pulls me up and tries to drag me out of the now ruined cottage. I claw against his arms, my fingernails ripping into his skin, until I slip through. He pulls me back, wrapping my body in a vice grip, his strength overpowering me.

"We have to go! More will come when they don't return."

Xander's voice registers slowly in my muddled brain, but the word *go* is loud and clear. He picks me up, throwing me over his shoulder, and runs out of the cottage. My fists pound against his back as I watch the cottage's roof finally cave in and a firework's display of sparks shoot into the night sky.

Sobs rack my body as I go limp against him. Everything numbs. All emotion drained; I've become an empty well. There is nothing I can do. Again.

I hate being helpless. If only I had access to my magic.

Hardly aware of my own presence, like the world has turned into a veiled dream, I don't fight anymore when Xander puts me down. He grips my shoulders, his gaze searching mine, but there is nothing to find.

Xander slides the satchel around my shoulder, then lifts me onto Honey. Only the galloping of hooves beneath me and the woods coming in and out of focus as I hold onto the man who left Marguerite behind break through the numbness.

Just as it did the day I found him, the world laughs at me, its spite falling down in the form of rain.

A new sort of pain blossoms along my back as my body lurches against Xander's. I look back to see an arrow lodged in my shoulder and other riders following us.

Maybe I deserve to have my muscles torn apart; I only wish it would've hit my heart. To stop it. I would gladly welcome a fall, for the earth to bury me into its depths.

But I know better than to hope for that. It would be too easy. I release my grip, holding my arms out to the night, a plea for it to take me. An arm reaches back to steady me, keeping me in place. I never win. Everything blurs together as I slump forward.

Shouting comes from behind me.

A racing heart in front of me.

Green is the only thing I see before darkness takes over.

CHAPTER II

XANDER

The bastards came sooner than I expected. This is on me. A miscalculation on my part. The thud of an arrow sounds, followed by the impact of her body against my back. Dammit. "Ameris!"

A soft groan is her only response. She doesn't move or make another sound, but her grip is still present, which eases my concern. We could have been better prepared for this. When I returned early and saw her so distraught and weary, I wanted to talk to her. To make sure she was okay, but I couldn't find the words, and it was clear she wasn't interested. I didn't want to add fuel to her already brewing hatred of me.

That was the wrong choice. Marguerite told me they would come, and I, being overconfident, failed her too. And now I have a promise I cannot break—to protect Ameris. I won't break faith, even if Marguerite is no longer here to bind it.

Plus, I have my own reason for protecting her. She is the only connection I've found to Elysium in all my time in the human world, and I won't waste this opportunity.

The wind shifts, a whistle slicing through the air as an arrow flies past my ear. Determined to catch us, the men are relentless in their pursuit. A smirk curls at the edge of my lips—they have no idea who they're up against, but they will soon find out. They know what I am, but these men couldn't have been on the ship.

Even if there were another survivor, I never allowed the sailors to know my full strength. It was the one thing I could control when I was a captive.

The rain will become my weapon. If only it had started before we left, I could have saved the cottage. I did what I could, but it was too late. The cottage was turning to ashes, and I had to get Ameris out of there. Otherwise, she'd be gone too.

Water's vibration, a melodic and benign force, can become fierce and deadly once manipulated. Its vibration is all around— the low rumble of movement. I let it flow through me, using it to pull the dark clouds together, forcing raindrops to lash into the faces of our pursuers and inhibit their ability to see us.

Heavy sheets of vicious rain fall behind and beside us, but never in front. I control the pattern so that the path ahead is dry and urge Honey to go faster.

When the pounding of our pursuers hoofbeats ceases, falling rain and the noisy chatter of the woods is all that remains. Pulling the reins, I slow Honey to a trot. I have no sense of place in this shadowed forest, in the inky blackness from the heavy clouds that cover the sky, so I let go of the storm.

As it clears, the moon and stars shine through, their brilliance just as beautiful as in Solarium. They echo my world's night sky, allowing me to at least know what direction we are heading in.

Taking us off the path, I guide Honey through dense shrubs. We travel for a while longer, until a clearing opens up far enough from the path to give us coverage. I ease off Honey, one arm on Ameris to keep her stable, and notice she's clutching tightly onto her satchel. The last thing Marguerite gave her.

The long arrow juts out of Ameris's shoulder, blood staining her shirt around the wound and trailing low down her back. This is not good. I ease her off the saddle and into my arms. Gently setting her body on the ground, I remove the satchel and roll her onto her side, so the arrow doesn't cause more damage.

Barely opening her eyes, they narrow into slits, face donning a scowl laced with pain and confusion. Her eyes turn glassy as she stares into the dark of night. "Did that all happen?"

"Yes." It's all I can manage as I kneel next to her.

She closes her eyes again and winces.

"I need to remove the arrow from your shoulder. I will likely need to stitch the wound as well."

Ameris leans into me, her shoulder sitting in the crook of my neck when I guide her into a sitting position. I steady her, taking in the eyes that are swollen from tears long since dried. The wind from our ride has tousled her hair. She looks like a beautiful disaster. A storm at the tipping point of catastrophe. I take the grimoire from her satchel and hold it out. "Here, look through this while I work on your shoulder."

Her hand reaches out, a moment of hesitation passing before her fingers brush against mine, slowly taking it from my grasp. She looks up at the sky, then back to me. "Why did you leave her?"

"I had no choice." Moving beside her, my fingers graze her hair, and a few strands flow through them before she pulls it around to the front. Blood slowly finds an escape from the wound. Removing the arrow will let it gush forth like a dam breaking. "This is going to hurt," I warn.

"We always have a choice." She drops her head, rolling her shoulders forward. The words hold no conviction; no emotion. They are just that—words spoken by someone who wants to believe there was a choice to be made.

Gripping both ends of the arrow, I snap the shaft and pull the tip from the front of her shoulder. Ameris takes a heaping gulp of air before a scream rips from her lungs. She jerks forward, but I hold her firmly.

"I can't do this, Xander." Ameris breathes out as she looks over her shoulder at me.

The way her eyes have lost focus and no longer have that spark of life shatters my soul. It brings me back to when I lost everything. While I am partly to blame for this, I will do whatever it takes to get home, even if it means using her for magic.

Even if it means tending to her every need so she follows through with helping me get back to Elysium, and then to the capital, Solarium.

It won't help if I leave her to bleed out. I need to repair her wound. I rip a piece of fabric from the bottom of my shirt and hand it to her. "Wrap this around your fist. Bite it when I'm stitching. It will help."

She cocks an eyebrow. "You could act like you care more."

"If I didn't care, I wouldn't have offered or be attending to your wound at all," I throw back. "Can I finish?"

Ameris looks up at the night sky, then nods, a hiss escaping when she hunches forward. I delicately lift the hair that fell onto her back and place it over her shoulder.

A shiver runs through her body. I can't be certain if it's from the cold that has crept into the night or from my touch. I rip more cloth from my shirt and wipe away the blood from around the hole in her shoulder.

Along with dressings, Marguerite had the foresight to include aid items in her satchel. I thread a needle and pinch her skin together. "Are you ready?"

"Do it." Ameris nods and places her wrapped fist into her mouth.

The needle pierces her flesh, and I quickly and precisely work it through the torn skin, slowly closing the wound. A stifled scream escapes, and her jaw flexes as she bites down on her hand. She's outwardly handling the pain well, but her body betrays her. A tremble starts in her shoulders that soon gets her whole body shaking.

"I need to cut some of your shirt off to tie it around your shoulder," I say as I finish. "So it will hold the dressing in place."

"I'll do it," she says, spitting her fist out.

"No, you shouldn't exert yourself. You..."

"I said I'll do it," Ameris responds curtly, cutting me off.

I hand her the knife, intrigued by her resolve, her spitfire spirit that doesn't give up. Ameris holds her shirt out and works the blade against the fabric. She's struggling; her muscles still weak from the magic she did earlier and the energy she used in the cottage. Frustrated, she tosses the blade to the side and rips at her shirt with too much force—too much effort. A small cry escapes, but she grits her teeth, cutting it short. I watch every pained movement as she struggles to separate the strip from the rest of her shirt.

"Here. Let me." I place my hand on hers. She'll injure herself if I let her continue.

She jerks her hand back as if my touch would pain her and continues to try, letting loose a frustrated grunt. My hand wraps around hers, halting her, and she looks up at me. I offer a small smile. She doesn't return it, just blows out a breath and releases her grip on the fabric.

I pick up the blade from the grass and make the last jagged slices, cutting away the strip I need before I wrap her shoulder.

"You need to rest and get some sleep. You lost a lot of blood. I'll keep watch."

She turns onto her side, away from me, and says nothing else. I would start a fire, but it's too risky with our pursuers. Likely, it wouldn't bring her any comfort after losing her home and Marguerite. To ward off the chill of the night, I drape both our blankets over her, then find a spot nearby, pressing my back against the rough bark of a tree.

Fixating on the steady rise and fall of her back, I hear the soft, rhythmic breaths of deep sleep. She's lost everything. I should care, and I do to a degree. But she's more than just a pretty girl who reminds me of the queen I served. This human, seemingly no one, and her inherited magic are the key to my return and to getting my throne back. If Marguerite is right, and she can control all the elements like Rhiannon, then not only will her resemblance be of use to me, but so will her magic.

There are humans in the fae lands of Elysium, especially in Solarium, who show up without any memory of where they came from or how they got there. They started showing up shortly after Oberon's rule. He preached they are offered a better life in exchange for a service contract. I'm not sure how many fae believe this, but no one questions Oberon.

I wonder if this will happen to her. If she will forget who she is and where she came from, although I doubt it. She has fae blood, so whatever magic affects the other humans likely won't work on her.

I'll keep my promise to protect her from others who would harm her in Elysium. But I will also use her to get what I want. She's important—at least for now.

CHAPTER 12
AMERIS

The pain from my wound is nothing compared to the turmoil in my soul. The ache in my chest, where my heart should be, is crippling.

Cold air flows into my lungs as I take in a breath and stare up at the morning twilight.

Stars pulse against the deep blue before it cascades into a lighter shade; the sunrise will soon make its appearance.

Tears come that won't stop, slowly filling my eyes. My vision fractures, like my soul; everything now swirling between cold, pain, and darkness. Two kinds of pain fight for control, physical and emotional, thrusting me back and forth between them.

Marguerite.

Marguerite.

Rising, I reach out to pick up the grimoire, but instead hover over the knife that lays beside it. Temptation spawns deep within to wield it, wanting to inflict a wound upon Xander, just as he's caused one within me.

I glance over at him, and sure enough, he's still awake, watching me. "I can keep watch."

He nods and closes his eyes. It would be so easy, but I ignore my urge for vengeance—for now.

I pull the grimoire into my lap, stopping on the same page as I did the other night, and lose myself in the delicate drawings on the border. Trailing the edges of the page along the thorns, I'm not disappointed when my finger is pricked again.

A single drop of blood hits the page. Crimson liquid morphs into black ink. The page requires a blood offering, and with a fresh wound, I have plenty to offer.

The pads of my fingers slide under the dressing, and I suck in a breath, biting my lip as I dig into the stitches on my shoulder. When I pull it away, warm blood coats my hand.

Dragging my hand down the paper, blood smears across it before soaking in. Black tendrils appear, inching their way across the cream-colored page. Elegant script snakes across its surface, swirling to form words.

I found it. I could feel it pulling at my soul. A nagging feeling that if I followed my instincts, the place would be revealed to me. Each step and every day, the feeling got stronger, knowing I was on the right path as I kept going. It took days to journey to the lake. But the day finally came. It was a warm day with no breeze, but when I stepped out of the woods and onto the bank, the water shimmered and danced in excitement. I swam to the center and floated there, feeling the power of the place enveloping me. Whispering to the world, I asked for the answer to my most desired question: How could I return home?

But the answer eluded me. It was difficult to find. It took years of trial and error. The answer came as I felt the sun's burn on my face playing with the wind's kiss on my cheek. Humans. This is their world, and their blood would be required to open the rift. Our blood. Together.

Oberon used blood magic to send us to this place, and blood magic must be the way to return. He will pay for what he did. I took a human man who stumbled into the woods. He was to be my sacrifice. My savior. But it failed. It wasn't until a hundred years later that I saw the man who would become my love—and he saw me. I knew, in that moment, the spell would only work if the human's blood is given freely. I cannot force this magic to work because our worlds were never meant to meet.

"Blood Bond."

The whisper escapes with my breath. The blood of both human and fae has to be given willingly for the spell to work. Rhiannon found where our worlds meet and created a spell that bridged the gap between them. It's all here on this page, as if I was meant to find it.

The bridge constructed by my design is to be a conduit for the magic. By the light of the full moon and the force of a jump into the water, the spell will not fail. Cut each other's palms and join hands. With your hands held together, you must speak these words to bind yourselves together.

Blood of my blood.

Let the worlds we belong to open to us.

The force of our bond will not break us.

By the stars decree, two souls become one.

But be warned—if this spell is ever done, there is no going back. Two who perform the spell cannot break their bond. You will forever feel the presence of whomever you bind yourself to. And I cannot know the implications of returning. I do not know if you will be able to return to the human world. Blood magic is not to be trifled with.

Slamming the book shut, I shove it into my satchel. Marguerite passed on the memories of my ancestors, including

Rhiannon's time in the human world.

I don't fully understand them, and I can't recall the memories at will, but embedded in my subconscious is the location of the lake. My instincts should guide me there, just like Rhiannon, serving as the light of a candle in the darkness. I didn't know Rhiannon—or even Marguerite—was capable of magic like that.

Spinning and morphing, my thoughts get the best of me. I lay back on the ground and stare at the moon, still shining brightly in the morning light. There is only one day until it's full.

One day until I bind myself to this male, whose arrival, though unwittingly, brought about so much loss.

All I wanted was to free my magic and myself from the pain it causes, learn to control the elements, and then Xander would have had his freedom. Damn him.

My whole world literally went up in flames due to his outburst in the market. Everything I have no longer exists; there is nothing left in this world for me. I finally get to start over in a new place, but without anything. No Marguerite.

What else did she keep from me, waiting for the right time? A time that's now too late. And what's to become of Honey? I don't —no, I—I just can't think about that right now.

Tension coils itself around my body, tightening like a snake. I take a deep breath and release it. When it doesn't let go, I turn my focus to the forest that is alive around me. The sound of chirping and a soft breeze brush across my skin, while leaves dance across the forest floor in the light wind.

Sunlight filters through the trees, casting columns of light that pierce the shadowed underbrush. I inhale deeply and slowly release my breath, trying to ease the tightness in my chest and the overwhelming emotions of losing everything I've ever known.

My shoulder throbs as I stretch, pulling at the wound I re-injured. Pain stops me from leaning as far forward as I'd like. This injury is going to get annoying.

"It will take a while to heal."

Xander's voice is like sandpaper against wood, an irritating sound I don't want to hear right now—even if he did patch me up, which I'm grateful for—because the loss of everything I've known outweighs his one good deed thus far.

I don't respond. Instead, I throw a scathing look that tells him I know—that I'm not new to wound recovery.

Xander's expression remains unchanged, offering only a nod of acknowledgment. He then rises onto his knees and reaches for the pile of wood I hadn't noticed before. He starts building a fire below a roughly constructed platform.

"I found some mushrooms and tubers. I'm surprised your world is so similar to mine. These grow in Elysium too." Xander puts them on the platform and watches as they brown. When satisfied, he removes the platform from over the fire, letting the food cool.

"Looks like you were busy all night," I push out. I should be grateful, but he's also the reason I'm here.

"I was concerned the men who chased us would find our trail. Which is why I didn't light a fire until now."

With a grimace I slide the satchel over my good shoulder and get up. Xander picks up the saddle to ready Honey to leave. I stand a few paces away, observing as he clumsily drops the saddle onto her back and fumbles with the straps. He wrestles with the buckles, his lack of experience evident in every awkward movement. The moment he feels my gaze, his body tenses, and he turns to look in my direction.

I walk up to them and grab the edge of the saddle. "Move. I'll do it. Put out the fire and get your stuff," I command, my words clipped and sharp as I adjust the saddle's position.

Xander snatches my wrist and, gripping it tightly, pulls me into his chest. The saddle drops to the ground, sending a cloud of dirt swirling around us.

He stares down at me, his brows pinching together as he

speaks, his words laced with a snarl. "Don't think you can push me around. My kindness should not be mistaken for weakness."

My breath hitches, and I lose my composure as the nearness of him startles me.

Under his ripped shirt, the bare skin of his smooth, muscular chest is on display, and I notice the wound has healed to a thin red line. I flit my gaze to his rolled-up sleeves; faded pink lines etched around his wrists are the only signs of the wounds he had when I first found him.

Looking up, I notice his expression has shifted. He's smirking, like he knows he's gotten under my skin. Damn him. I don't like being caught off guard.

"We heal quickly." He lets go and stalks toward the fire, kicking dirt onto the flames, smothering it, and roughly picks up his pack. "And yes, we have horses, but I never readied them."

I glare daggers at his back, irritation licking against my skin. Turning my attention to Honey, I blow out a breath. She has been with me since she was a filly, and if anyone is going to care for her, it'll be me. I run my hand down each leg, feeling her muscles, searching for any tender spots. I move to her back, careful not to be in her blind spot, where she might kick even me.

"Do you even know where you're going?" Xander asks. There's an edge to his voice, laced with stunted excitement.

"Yes, I'm following Rhiannon's lead. Her memories are driving me toward it. It's what Marguerite passed onto me the other night." I don't expand.

I kick a fallen branch, irritation flaring that I now have to bond myself to him so that he can return home. I suppose I don't *have* to, but I have nothing else keeping me here. At least through our bargain he still has to teach me elemental magic and I can practice freely in his world—a liberty I could never have enjoyed here.

Xander's stops abruptly, tilts his head to the side, and turns it in the direction we just came from. His voice goes cold and hard like ice, sending a chill through me. "Time to go."

He picks up the saddle and throws it onto Honey's back, haphazardly buckling it before rushing to me and sliding his hands around my waist with a firm grip. I try to jerk back, but he lifts me onto Honey's bare back.

"What—" I adjust my seat and give him a questioning look, but his demeanor has shifted—all hard edges and seriousness.

"We're not alone. Give me your hand."

Steadying myself, I extend a hand and look around for the source of his panic. Xander exhales a deep breath and hoists himself up behind me.

His arms slide along mine; the heat of our skin making contact cuts the cold air. My body reacts to his closeness, betraying me and our situation, sending a flutter of butterflies into my stomach. His chest presses into my back as he leans forward, and I feel all of him against me.

His body silently betrays him as well; I feel the way his breath hitches and its slow exhale. My cheeks flare, and I suck in a breath, muscles tensing when his thighs lock against mine. He envelops me like a lover would.

We may not like each other, but that doesn't mean we don't find one another attractive.

A soft, barely audible chuckle escapes from him, probably finding amusement in the ill and inappropriate timing of how our bodies clearly lust for one another.

He rests his hand over mine for control of the reins, but I don't let go, so he moves our arms together. Using the loose end of the reins, he smacks Honey's hide, spurring her into a gallop.

CHAPTER 13
XANDER

The pounding of hooves fades as we put distance between our pursuers. Removing my hand from hers, I relinquish full control of Honey to Ameris. I hover my mouth against her ear. "Guide us to where we need to go."

We've been riding in silence for an hours before a rustle catches my attention—the unnatural crack of a branch, a misplaced crunch—unmistakably out of place in the once quiet forest. Heavy breaths, along with the snorts and hoofbeats of their mounts, sound like the grinding of stones to my heightened hearing. They've been tracking us.

This is not good.

A cold realization washes over me. We are far from safe, our trail too easy to follow. Ameris's need for food and rest delaying us the night before. Dammit. I should have tended to her wound and kept us moving through the night. But I let my own thoughts and desires become a distraction, thinking we'd made it far enough. Panic prickles against my nerves.

The surrounding forest blurs as we race ahead. My heartbeat pounds, body flooded with adrenaline, in tune with each step

Honey takes. Turning my head to check, I let out a curse. Four men are on our heels, two with their bows readied. An arrow whizzes by my head, a lethal whisper in my ear. We're not going fast enough to outpace the danger.

A hail of arrows follows, each one a deadly shadow encasing us. One grazes Honey's leg, and she reacts instinctively and suddenly.

Bucking wildly, we have no hope of holding on without the saddle. I wrap my arms around Ameris as our bodies are tossed off, determined to shield her. My back slams into the ground, taking the brunt of the fall; the air knocked from my lungs.

Honey kicks and runs off. Ameris's wail of agony pierces the air with as much force as the arrows still flying toward us. She tries to scramble after Honey, clawing out of my grip, sinking her hands into the earth. I yank her back, pulling her down as a sword arcs in her direction.

There isn't enough water around; its vibrations weak, but I pull it all to me. Barely enough comes together to make a funnel around us, forcing the man back and blocking any further arrows from hitting their mark. At least they won't be able to see us. For now.

"Ameris! Use your magic!" I yell at her over the roar of the funnel. "You used it before in the market. Heightened emotions can make fae magic flare. I know you're angry."

"Stop it Xander. I don't know how to access it. It never comes when I try! I told you that!" Ameris grapples with the satchel that is tangled around her neck, her frantic fingers slipping against the fabric. In a flit of frustration, she pulls it loose and tosses it to the side. She rocks back and both, gulping down heaving breaths.

"You hate me; you hate these men. They cost you Marguerite, and now Honey. Get vengeance." I need her help, so I deliberately provoke her, feeding the emotions that I know are likely overwhelming her right now.

There isn't enough water for my magic to pull from other than our shield. Making it impossible for me to take all these men while the archer still lives. It's too risky when I also need to defend Ameris. "There are four men. Use your magic to feel where they are and strike!"

Her hands run through her wind-swept hair, pushing it off her face. Tears spill from her eyes, rolling down her cheeks, before they too are pulled into the funnel. My heart shatters, like a knife stabbing through a mirror, but now is not the time for sympathy.

"Ameris." I say her name with more force and urgency. "Feel for the vibrations around you that your magic reacts to. It will lead you to it. I imagine after all these years of hiding your magic, you'd do anything for a chance to use it against the people who cause your suffering."

She looks at me this time with hatred in her eyes. Good. She slowly looks at the water funnel that is protecting us. Her once-bright eyes turn dark with ire.

The setting sun bathes her in a golden light as it cascades through the trees, transforming her. She looks like fury encapsulated into a being. She commands me, her voice laced with an angry venom, ready to spread through with no antidote.

"Drop it."

The moment I release control, knocked arrows point at us. Slowly, like a nightshade, the legendary beast of Elysium stalking its prey, Ameris turns in a circle. She takes in each man as they keep their weapons ready. They have no idea what they've done. What was culled from the stars when Honey was harmed.

"He comes with us. Fight it, and you'll find an arrow through your hearts," the bald man commands.

Ameris falls to her knees and forcefully digs her fingers into the soft earth, covering her hands up to the wrists. A guttural scream rips from her throat, raw and full of agony. Her arms shake violently as she heaves, her body rocking back and forth. The men are momentarily stunned at her display.

The ground trembles in response to her intense emotions, as if it too feels the weight of her suffering. It surprises me. I thought she could control the air, electricity, but if she's doing this, then she's more valuable to me than before. In awe of her raw power, I give her this moment, let her soak in the magic she can command. Brown and green roots move like snakes in tall grass, slithering over the ground, creeping upon their prey.

"Your turn," the bald man says to me. "On your knees."

I tilt my head and smirk as roots wrap around each of their bodies, constricting their limbs. One of the men tries to leap to the side, but the knotted wood takes him down, pinning him to the earth. Motioning with her free hand, Ameris drags them to us and forces them to their knees. I saunter over to the bald man, a wide smile plastered on my face, and grab an arrow from his quiver, trailing the sharp tip along his clavicle.

"You'll pay for this," he says with a sneer.

"No. You are going to pay for what you've done." I pick up a quiver of arrows, pull one out, and thrust it into his chest, pushing it through to his lungs. The light fades from his eyes, and blood pools at his lips, spilling from the corners as he gasps for air. "That was for the horse."

"Wish I would've killed it." His last words are barely audible through the gurgles of blood filling his airway. He dies, a crooked smile lingering before his head slumps to his chest.

Sweat glistens on their brows, and a heavy scent carries on the wind. Though they try to hide it, the other men's eyes are wide with fear, as clear as this evening's sky.

As they should be. I move to the next man, and before I can pass the same judgment, Ameris's hand clasps around the new arrow I've pulled from the quiver.

"My turn." Ameris's words are vicious and deadly. A warrior ready to cut down their enemy.

The arrow balances on my open palm, an offering. I take a step back, giving her the spotlight. She looks at me after removing it, and hate fills the green of her irises. When she pivots to face the men, her strawberry hair whips around, flowing out behind her.

She has become death incarnate, ready to deliver judgment.

Twirling the arrow between her fingers, she glares at the men and leans into her hip. "Did you kill the old lady?"

"Since you are going to kill us either way, you'll never know."

The one that spoke looks up to the sky and back at Ameris. He's made peace with his death. No more words will fall from his lips.

"Well, then, this is for her," Ameris says as she stabs him in the neck. His eyes widen as she pulls the arrow out. Blood flows freely. His body jerks, and his arms strain against the bindings. As he chokes on his own blood, she delivers the last words he will ever hear: "Your soul will never find peace so long as I live."

Ameris doesn't give the other two a chance to speak before slicing their throats; the arrow tumbles from her hand as she makes the last jagged cut.

She walks away, her legs giving way beneath her as she crumples onto her shins; the vines binding the men fall with her. The magic takes its toll, even more so since she's never done something like this before.

"This is your fault. You have cost me everything. I hope whatever this is," she motions her hands around us, "is worth it."

As I approach, the resentment radiates off her like steam rising after a summer rainstorm. "Ameris—" I start but am interrupted by the coldness in her eyes that threaten to bite if I continue.

"Don't." She picks up her satchel, returning it to her shoulder.

I don't press her, busying myself instead with unsaddling the men's horses. Dropping the saddles and packs to the ground, I tie the horses to a tree and walk off in the direction Honey ran. We should release the horses, and Honey might as well have four other horses for company.

Ameris won't like it, but I doubt Honey will be able to make the trip with us. It'll be yet another thing for her to hate me over —to blame me for. The icy walls around her will now be near impenetrable, and I will have to do everything I can to break them down. I have a promise and a bargain to fulfill, and a throne to win back.

If I have to use lust and attraction to my advantage, I have no qualms about forfeiting my morals to free Solarium, and all of Elysium from Oberon's iron grip.

Honey isn't far off, and I guide her back to where Ameris is riffling through the men's belongings, shoving a knife into her boot. She refuses to look at me, taking bread and dried fruit and putting them into her satchel.

"Ameris."

"What?" She snaps before looking up, then her face lights up, and she rushes over, hugging the horse around the neck.

"We have to let her go."

"I know." Ameris sighs deeply, running her hand down Honey's mane. She nods, takes the bridle out of Honey's mouth, and steps back.

"She'll have the other horses."

Honey stands there, tail flicking, waiting for a command. Ameris hesitates, a solemn expression shadowing her features, before she pats Honey on the neck and pushes her away. The horse kicks and runs off to join the others. Tears well in Ameris's eyes, but she turns before I see them fall and walks away.

CHAPTER 14
AMERIS

Something in me snapped. I've never taken a life before, but they deserved it. And it cost me. Fracturing who I am with each blow dealt. Seeing Honey injured and running scared released a rage I have never known, and it took over. Heat rushed through my body, and fire burned through my veins. I acted without thinking. The memory of their unkind eyes, laced with the realization that death had come, still lingers, along with the red stains on my hand.

Digging my fingers into the dirt, I reach back to that feeling—to when I connected with the earth and anchored myself in its strength, bending it to my will—but it's gone. I vow I will master my magic and never be vulnerable again.

My breath hitches, and tears come again.

Losing Marguerite.

Letting Honey go.

The pain of loss is too much. Sorrow coats my soul, thinking about having nothing to return to. I don't want these emotions. They shred my soul, taking pieces of me that will never return.

Not only do I have to contend with them, but I'm heading into the unknown. A new world, and I have nothing.

Alone.

That is what I am now.

Xander hooks his arms under one of the men, about to move him, but they deserve less than that. "Leave them where they lie on the ground. They can stay there and rot. Let animals ravage their bodies and tear them apart."

I adjust my satchel, grab a bow and quiver, and walk through the trees, putting distance between myself and the scene of destruction. When death's lingering presence is no longer heavy in the air, I stop to check the position of the sun. Aligning my body with the time of day, I turn to each cardinal point of a compass.

"What are you doing?" Xander asks, his presence suddenly filling the space.

"Finding which direction to go. Due east, then straight until we reach a lake with a bridge. The full moon is tomorrow night. We'll have to walk through the night if we want to reach the bridge in time."

"I will lead us there." Xander walks away, and I suddenly feel very alone in these woods as the distance between us grows.

I rush to catch up, following a few paces behind. We travel in silence for what feels like hours, staring straight ahead with no conviction. I'm exhausted from all that's happened. But boredom sets in, so I pin my eyes to the back of Xander's tunic and use it as imaginary target practice for the blade I want to sink into it.

"Full moons are symbolic in Elysium. Are they in your world as well?" Xander's question feels harsh after the long silence.

"Yes. I have to cast a spell under the full moon."

I still haven't told him about the bond, but I don't want to. Maybe it's irrational, or petty, but part of me wants to make him pay for what's happened.

Plus, I don't even fully understand what the bond will do or how it will affect us. But I hope it brings him torment as payment for the cards that were dealt when our worlds collided. That he will feel the crushing weight of my grief, the pain of my loss. When he bonds his life to mine, I'll serve as a constant reminder of what I gave to him after he took everything from me.

He doesn't ask anything else, and we fall back into silence as the day passes. The sounds of the forest blur together, a constant buzz. At this point, my feet are following what my incoherent brain is telling them to do. One foot in front of the other.

Light from the setting sun filtering through the trees has lost its luster. The only sound that is clear is the cawing of a raven, its cry as bleak and black as my heart feels. I shouldn't question why this is happening to me. Life is unfair—it always has been.

Memories of Marguerite and Honey swirl through my mind; there are moments when I chuckle, then burst into tears. This will pass. I know it will. I went through this when my parents died. The pain is so visceral in those first moments—first days—but it eventually fades like a well-worn saddle.

As if he senses my thoughts, Xander looks at me over his shoulder. His face is blank, giving away no emotion. Even though it's my fault that I brought him into my life, what he did in the market brought on the chaos that is ripping through everything I've known.

The worst part is that I will have to bind myself to him—willingly. Though the need, the burning desire, to learn how to use and control my magic is stronger, and if binding myself to him is what it takes, then I'm willing to pay the price.

Since I look like and have the power of their most revered ruler, maybe I can take it all for myself in his world. Make the most of the new life that awaits me. I will haunt Xander's every move, make it my vengeance to thwart his every attempt at getting the throne back.

The light of the setting sun has faded, and darkness bathes the forest in shadows and silence. Moonlight, even this close to a full moon, has difficulty lighting the forest floor, making it hard to see Xander and what I am walking through. I am about to call to him when I stop short; his outline inches from my own.

"You could've said you stopped. I almost ran into you." The words come out harsher than intended.

He turns to face me as he shifts one of the saddlebags we took to his other shoulder. "Fae vision is better than humans. I can see in the darkness where you cannot. We can stop until the moon reaches its zenith and more light can make its way through."

"Just tie a rope around your waist, and I will hold on to it."

"I am not a mule," he quips.

"I can barely see what is in front of me." Rolling my eyes, I continue, "I'm just a human, remember?"

"I will not tie a rope around my waist. Take my hand, and I will lead you. Or we stop for a few hours." His voice carries an unwavering finality, each word stern and inflexible. There are no other choices.

"We don't have time to stop." Reluctantly, I take his outstretched hand, and even in the settling cold of the night, his warm palm grips mine tightly.

"We will stop, even if it's brief. We need at least one hour of rest. Once there is enough light coming through, you can let go." A softer tone coats his words this time, almost like there is concern mixed with his command.

Knowing he can see me, I nod in response. We continue forward, this time with my hand in his.

My eyes adjust to the darkness shortly after we resume walking. I can't see anything in detail, only the outlines of trees and shrubbery. Snapping branches and the crunch of fallen leaves greet me as they pass underfoot. As the night progresses, a mist presses in on us, the cool droplets brushing against my face with the softness of velvet.

The warmth of the sun is gone, and the mist coupled with the brisk air sends a shiver through every part of my body, gooseflesh prickling along my arms and legs. I will my hand not to shake in his, not wanting him to offer any help or cause us to stop.

He doesn't say anything; simply rubs his thumb across the top of my hand, not enough to warm me, yet it sends another kind of warmth through. Stars, how can my body enjoy his touch when my brain finds his presence vile?

Forcing myself to ignore his gestures, I turn my thoughts to how nice it would be to have the ability to see in the dark. Then I wouldn't have to rely on him or hold his hand. But we must keep moving if we want to make it, and I have no other path but forward to walk. So my hand stays within his. I sigh, annoyed at myself.

Time warps in the darkness. There is no way to tell how long we've been walking under the cover of the trees. Every step sends a throb through my aching feet, hunger gnaws at my stomach, and my bones feel brittle from the damp cold that has permeated my clothing.

To top off my endless misery, sharp pain radiates through my shoulder, refusing to be ignored amid every other awful thing to happen over the last two days.

Sweet relief comes when Xander lets go of my hand, and we finally stop. I stand there, letting the cold wash over me, the warmth of his touch gone. I surrender to my body's desires, allowing my legs to buckle and bring me to the ground.

"I will gather wood in the immediate area and start a fire."

Wincing, I reach into my satchel and feel for the grimoire. Pulling it out, I run my hands over the binding, thinking of the women who owned it before me and the power it contains. Wondering why, only now, it was time for me to find my power. To know its capabilities. Why couldn't I have used it before—when it mattered.

Sounds of the night break up its dreary silence; crickets play their chirping melody among the screeching of an owl. I'm grateful for the noise, an antidote to the poison of my thoughts. I stare at the moon until the snapping of twigs and the crunch of leaves alert me to Xander's return.

Curiosity gets the better of me. I might as well learn some things before I make Elysium my new home.

"What was Rhiannon like when she ruled?" I ask, then pause, finally adding, "And tell me about Oberon."

CHAPTER 15

XANDER

"Let me get the fire going, and I will oblige your request." I set the pieces of wood down, running my hands over them, pulling any moisture out so they burn. This would be easier if I had fire magic. Instead, I rub my hands together, drilling one piece of wood into another. When the ember dust accumulates, I transfer it to the tinder bundle and lightly blow on it to fuel the fire.

"I felt that. The embers sparking to life," she says as she stares into the building fire. "I've never been able to feel that before."

Ameris has the grimoire in her lap, sitting cross-legged with her shoulders hunched, hair falling forward. She trails the binding, as if she longs for the people to whom those words belong to reveal their secrets. Darkness lingers within her green eyes. I'm rarely uncomfortable, but it is unsettling. Haunting even.

"Deep emotions heighten our magic. It flows differently, stronger, and more electric," I answer, working the fire until it burns well enough to light the immediate area and give off some warmth.

The silence is palpable until I ask, "How much do you want to know?"

"We have nothing better to do, so tell me a bedtime story." Sarcasm drips between her words.

I chuckle before beginning. "Rhiannon was fierce. A force to be reckoned with, whom no one dared to cross her. She was a fair ruler and took care of her citizens, but she did not have patience for those who liked to play games. She was, unlike other fae, direct and straightforward. Our kind likes to play word games."

My eyebrows pinch and my fingers press into the palms of my hand when I speak again. "Oberon is selfish and ruthless, but a coward. He was part of the court, always on the heels of those who were important, and always lurking in the shadows. Oberon knew he could never challenge Rhiannon in her abilities, so he sought other magic."

"Hmm," she hums thoughtfully, the only response she offers while thumbing through the pages.

"Rhiannon's patience grew short with Oberon," I continue, "and one day at court Rhiannon embarrassed him after he tried to trick her with words and gifts. He wasn't seen again until he showed up with a following and a type of magic no one had seen before."

"Oberon changed her in ways we don't understand as he started to reintegrate himself into our court. He was after all the son of the previous king, so he had standing, even if he wasn't ruling. Rhiannon became worrisome, always muttering about Oberon and treachery. Her actions grew erratic."

"She morphed into a different being, no longer the queen we had loved for centuries. In the end, she was right; Oberon declared her unfit to rule and that he would take the throne. There was a battle, and Oberon won, banishing Rhiannon."

"I see. Tell me about your rebellion." She looks up, and the fire illuminates her silhouette against the dark woods. She's a blank slate; no reaction or emotion paints her features regarding what I've told her.

Flames lick in front of her, pulsing in rhythm with her breathing. She has no idea the effect she has on the elements. Learning what she is capable of could make her more powerful than Rhiannon.

"When Rhiannon and her court fell, many of the fae were in shock. It can happen in our world. One leader challenges another, and the winner takes all, but it is not common. The throne was supposed to pass to me because she had no children. I am the son of her general, and she decided I was best suited to rule next. Many in her court did not like the idea of Oberon ruling, so a few approached me, wanting to fight against him."

My gaze flits from the fire to Ameris. She's looking down at her grimoire, like I'm not here, not speaking.

"Are you even listening?" Annoyance laces my words as I grab a few more logs and toss them onto the pile of burning wood. Sparks shoot into the night sky, breaking her attention.

"Yes. Xander. I am." Her head snaps in my direction, and her gaze is one that could kill. "Just because I'm not looking at you doesn't mean I didn't hear what you said."

A sharp, exasperated breath escapes my lips. I want to snap back, but I still need her to get home, so I hold my tongue. My attempt at niceness has been futile, and it sends ire through my veins. Instead, I shake my head and push up from the ground, done with her, before I say anything I'll regret.

The only thing that really matters is getting back to my world.

Leaving the warmth of the fire, I step into the coldness of the surrounding forest. The stillness of the night, paired with the subtle sounds of the creatures that own it, help relieve the boiling anger that was rising moments ago. I allow it to redirect from Ameris to thoughts of what I lost.

Loss is a tough battle to fight. Something ripped from your grasp, leaving a gaping hole where the thing was before. The throne. My throne. The title was mine to inherit. Oberon wrenched that away from me. Drove a sword through my father's heart, ripping my heart out along with it.

He will pay for what he has done. He must fall, no matter the cost. We were so close to launching the attack on the palace. Everything was in order. The plans secured.

Or so we thought. Until he was waiting. I seethe thinking about the black tendrils of his magic, latching onto me, binding me before I could even break in. He knew. Someone betrayed our plans. When I return, I'll find out how, because no one should have been able to with the binding magic of our hideaway. The magic would have killed anyone who spoke ill of our efforts. Anyone who betrayed us.

What will I find when I return to Solarium? Has the rebellion fallen or continued the work we started? Shrouded in the darkness of the night, I lean against a tree and wonder what my future holds.

How this seemingly normal human will change my fate. Will she bring the destruction of Oberon or the reverence of Rhiannon? The possibilities run through my head until a shuffle of movement pulls me from my thoughts.

Ameris lays on her side, her hand propping her head up. Using the light of the fire to trace the pages of her grimoire, her eyes move across the pages.

Witches, she called the humans born from fae. Their magic was born from Rhiannon's. Of course, she would find a way to live on. She never did anything that didn't benefit her in the end. Across the distance, my fae hearing picks up murmurs, but Ameris is speaking in a language unknown to me.

My gaze traces the outline of her figure. How the curve of her hip dips into her waist, rising to meet the delicate shape of her breasts. Through the scooped neckline of her shirt, the elegant shape of her collarbone shows.

Her face is bathed in a warm, golden glow that highlights her features. Too bad we didn't start out on better terms. I've noticed the way she mirrors my appreciation and attraction.

We could have offered each other a distraction, our bodies colliding in a purely sexual desire that leaves no room for other emotions. It's more than that, though; she could easily rule alongside me, her power and presence a compliment mine. But we are too far gone for that to ever happen.

CHAPTER 16
AMERIS

"It is over the next ridge. We made it on time. The full moon is due to rise in a few hours."

"I never doubted us," Xander says. His eyes relax, but his face is stoic as ever.

"Neither did I." *Ass.* I give him a sharp side-eyed look, eyes narrowing, then continue up the hill until I reach the top.

The hill slopes down into a clearing with a small lake. Two small opposing tributaries flow into it, the water darkening in the middle, a sign of its depth. The setting sun bathes everything in hues of gold, mingled with rich greens, yellows, and browns.

Autumn-colored leaves, still vibrant in their orange and red hues, linger among the almost barren branches of the trees in the clearing. Their fallen comrades rest along the bank, flanking the edges of the water.

A perfect half-moon bridge arches across the water, its reflection in the still water below creating a symmetrical circle. I'm captivated by nature's own majestic painting; it's more beautiful and serene than anything I have ever seen.

This is the location where my life ends and begins again. Even though my magic is blocked, all the vibrations stir potently within the air, the magic swirling, almost as if I can see it. Maybe—just maybe—the new world will be better than mine. I'll still be alone, but at least I'll have someone to tutor me on how to access and use my magic to its full extent.

"Can you feel it?" I ask as Xander walks up beside me.

"Yes. There is power in this place." He looks out, his gaze sweeping over the clearing, but then it lingers on the bridge before he continues ahead of me. I follow him as he makes his way down to the water's edge. "I'd say there is about an hour remaining before sunset. Based on the previous nights, it'll be another few hours until the moon is in position."

I approach the bridge, appreciating the intricate craftsmanship. Yet, it's as if whoever built it did so with magic, not manual human labor. It's too perfect. The two sides are formed from pillars of rocks, interlocking and fitted seamlessly together, like they were forced up from the earth, cascading in an upside-down waterfall before meeting, forming the bridge. When the moon fills the circle, I will cast the spell, our blood opening the way to Elysium.

I move away from the water's edge. "Let's go through my satchel before it gets dark and choose what to take with us. We won't need everything. I don't even know if we can take anything."

A fallen tree lays on the ground, covered with moss and mushrooms. I find an open spot and sit, emptying the contents of the satchel onto the ground in front of me and sort through what's left of our meager supplies. I hand him a rope. That is always useful and has saved me too many times to count. I add some nuts and dried berries to an empty vial and stick it back in my satchel.

"Do you want any of this?"

"No. I need nothing from this world." Xander barely looks at the herbs and vials on the ground before turning back to the water.

Ugh. I only keep the salves, leaving everything else on the

forest floor while Xander lights a small fire. Fading light from the sun falls beyond the trees, darkness setting in as the moon's glow takes over the night sky. I suck in a breath when I move my injured shoulder around to loosen the joint and warm my muscles. Stretching is something Marguerite taught me the importance of. Anything I do will have the lingering touch of her. Scooting to the ground, I rest my back against the stump and gaze into the sky as thoughts of tomorrow bombard me. I soak in the constellations that have been my guide and the idols of prayer.

Stories of the gods and goddesses, of love and war, hope and honor, and death and destruction wash over me, comforting me in these final hours. For after tonight, the sky will no longer be my own, as foreign to me as the fae standing nearby. Xander breathes deeply before sighing, and I can tell he's about to say something.

"I don't want to talk to you right now." I cut him off harshly before he can begin, not in the mood. I want as much of this night to myself as I can get.

Suddenly, Xander is before me, materializing like a summer storm. A dark fury fills his gaze as he grabs me by the shoulders and yanks me up, the abrupt movement jarring my injured shoulders. Tears of pain well in my eyes as my yelp of agony pierces the quiet clearing, echoing around us. Seething, I try to jerk away, but he's too strong.

"Look. At. Me." Each word is slow and dangerous.

I try to avoid his gaze, but he holds me firmly until I look at him.

His tone shifts, and a genuine sadness replaces the anger. "I'm sorry. I understand loss. I know it."

"You know nothing!" I jerk again, and this time, he releases his hold.

"I watched my father die in front of me, protecting Rhiannon. I got banished to this world!" he yells, his returning anger boiling to the surface. His shoulders tense, and he balls his fists. "Everything that was mine was ripped from me. I was supposed to be the next ruler of Elysium!"

"Yes, Xander, but you are not still standing beside the person who caused all your loss."

He turns away from me and paces, each pound of his foot like he's sending pent up energy into the ground.

Xander's fingers rake through his auburn shoulder length hair, pulling it away from his face in an agitated manner. His lips narrow in barely contained frustration. He grabs a small log from the ground, his knuckles turning white as his grip tightens around the rough grey bark.

With a deep rumble, he hurls it into the woods. I flinch when the log collides with a tree and splinters on impact; its echo like a boom of thunder.

His gaze returns to mine. His irises are ice cold as he stalks toward me, stopping inches from me. "I didn't ask for this to happen! You are the one who dragged me from that ship and into your home. Take responsibility where it's warranted, Ameris. Your actions also carry burdens."

Glowering, his heavy breaths invade my space, and it drives me forward. I shove him, but he stands, unmoving, as solid as a carved stone monument. My fist swings before my brain registers it, slamming into his chest.

My voice rises along with my punches. "You are the reason I have lost everything! The men who came, destroying my house, killing Marguerite, and now Honey? They were looking for you!"

The pounding of my fists is something I cannot control as a scream rips from my throat and a well of hot tears fall. It feels good. Releasing the pent-up anger. Time slows as I punch and punch until my hands hurt. Xander hasn't moved an inch.

He's just standing there, tall and stiff, letting my emotions bang against his chest. Finally, he takes hold of my wrists and gently lowers my hands.

"I know, and that is my burden to bear." His voice is soft

before turning harsh. "But that doesn't mean my pain is any less real."

How can he be those two things at once—kind and harsh, angry then calm—all while I'm heated and unwavering in my conviction that he is the reason for everything I've lost?

But he's right. I did save him. Instead of bringing me comfort, it just fuels my need to hurt him back. It might be petty or juvenile, but it's the only emotion I can latch onto that won't send me spiraling into oblivion. That will keep me strong.

Xander leaves me there, arms hanging limp as I compose myself. I wipe my tears away and push my hair out of my face, pulling it up into a topknot.

Is this what falling apart feels like?

Never knowing, from moment to moment, which emotion will rip out of you? My head feels heavy, and my eyes burn. I want to fall asleep and never wake.

Instead, I close my eyes and pull in a breath, expanding my lungs to fill every part of them with air, and then I slowly release it along with what just happened, leaving it all behind in this place.

Hours pass in the night's stillness, accompanied by sounds I may never hear again. I close my eyes, appreciating the beauty that lays hidden in the quiet places of this world.

Sitting up, I move closer to the fire and pull the grimoire from my satchel. I open the first page and see the signatures of Rhiannon and all those that followed, including none other than my mother's and Marguerite's. A pang hits my heart, and I turn the page before tears can fall.

The spell is complex; I repeat the strange words over and over, tracing their curves on the page.

Ut ligatis meum sanguinem tuum. Tua fata mea usque nunc tenetur. Semper coniuncti sumus.

Bind my blood to yours. Your fate now bound to mine. Forever more, we are connected. The spell symbolizes our connection to life, death, and soul—that we will be bound by blood.

Xander returns and lies on his back, one arm under his head, in front of the fire opposite me. He stares up at the canopy of trees that spare us only a few stars.

"I'll keep watch tonight." His gaze never leaves the sky above.

I put the grimoire away and bundle my jacket, placing it on top of my satchel. Turning my back to Xander, I rest my head on my makeshift pillow. There is a chill in the night air. I pull my knees to my chest, hoping the fire will keep me warm as I repeat the spell over and over before sleep takes me.

CHAPTER 17

XANDER

"It is time." I reach out my hand to Ameris, and hers hovers over mine for a brief moment before accepting it.

The unusual construction of the bridge towers above us. At twelve feet high, it was not meant for the average passenger to cross. This bridge holds intention. You don't come unless you mean to jump from it. I realize this must be where the humans that have found their way into our world have come from. No wonder they don't care to fall into bargains with us.

"I'll lead the way up." I begin the ascent, finding placeholders for my hands and feet. Jagged and uneven stone presses into my hands as I climb, the way steeper than it looked from below. "The rocks are rough. Watch your hands."

Checking on Ameris, I see she's right behind me, following my path. The top is just as treacherous as the way up; the narrow walkway only wide enough for one person to cross at a time.

Moisture glistens in the moonlight, pooling in some areas. I step tentatively, but my foot slides out from under me, and I pitch backwards. One of Ameris's hands grips my bicep, the other anchoring itself on my shoulder, helping to steady me.

"Thank you." Gaining stable footing, I inch closer to the center of the bridge, gazing upon the water beneath it.

The moon's brilliance is reflected below, almost reaching the top of the completed circle. There are only a few minutes before it fills the remaining space. We reach the middle and face each other, our gazes locking for a moment before she kneels.

"I have to cast a spell." Ameris sets down a curled leaf with a stone in the middle, a weight to hold the fragile thing in place.

The mixture of light and dark orange is bright against the grey stone of the bridge. When Ameris rises, she slides a blade from her boot and motions for my hand. I extend it to her, and she presses the tip of the blade against my palm.

"I must cut your palm, and you have to cut mine," Ameris says, seeking my approval.

I nod, giving her permission to proceed. I don't care what I have to do; getting home is my top priority. Ameris slides the blade across my palm. The sharp sting is immediate, but I make no sound, pushing down the pain, and offer no reaction as she tilts my hand to the side.

Blood runs down my palms, dripping from the lines in my skin. It collects in the leaf below, a few drops splattering off the rock.

She pulls a cloth from her pocket and cleans the blade before handing it to me and exposing her palm. Ameris closes her eyes and nods. I cup her hand in mine and slide the cold metal across her skin.

Her involuntarily jerk is accompanied by a sharp intake of breath. The pain always comes, but it's expected when you've been in fights, had cuts, and have been stabbed before. "It'll pass. Try not to think on it."

I mirror her process, tilting her hand, letting the blood drip down to meet mine. Ameris slides her hand out of mine, and she throws the rock into the water below before picking up the leaf. Swirling the contents, the crimson liquid mixes together before she pours it into the water as well, a small crimson waterfall that spreads into the dark water below.

Ameris faces me again, holding out her wounded palm. "That was our sacrifice to the earth, but we must also link our blood, solidifying that both parties agree to enter into this of our own free will. Hold my hand, and when I squeeze, jump. Whatever happens, do not let go until we surface."

I quickly push down the flare of hesitation, too brief for her to notice, because I'm willing to risk the consequences of doing blood magic. This is the only option.

Even if my subconscious knows this is a bad idea, I intertwine my fingers into hers and press our palms together, gripping her hand tightly.

She raises our joined hands; our blood intertwines and runs down each of our forearms. Her voice is rhythmic with repetition as she chants the incantation, repeating it three times.

A heavy weight presses on my skull before moving through my shoulders and over my body, lingering for a moment before disappearing. A vice grip takes my heart. Sucking in a breath, I gasp for air through the constriction before it passes.

Ut ligatis meum sanguinem tuum. Tua fata mea usque nunc tenetur. Semper coniuncti sumus.

The last word barely escapes Ameris's lips when her grip on my hand tightens with fierce pressure.

Something's wrong. Her body convulses in a sudden and violent shudder. A heart-wrenching scream claws from her throat, her knees buckle, and she falls, pulling me with her. I kneel beside her, putting my free hand on her trembling body. "Ameris!"

"Jump... Us... Now... Don't let go," she pants, her eyes losing focus.

There is no time for questioning. The moon has been at its peak in the circle for long enough. I could lose this chance to get home if I tarry any longer. Swinging my legs over the edge, I scoop her in my arms the best I can while still keeping our hands together. It's not the best position, but it'll have to do.

I unceremoniously scoot over the edge, barely holding on as we fall into the icy water below. It hits like a punch to the face, the shock of it quickening my pulse. Flowing fast and fierce, the water tosses us about, nothing like the calm surface I split just moments ago.

Realization dawns. We're in a damn river—a freezing one at that—but the water is mine to control. I push out my magic, warming the surrounding water and slowing our movement. My lungs burn. Each second that goes by is one closer to not only my end but Ameris's as well. Keeping hold of her hand, I release her legs and swim towards the sun that shines through the surface, using my magic to ease the burden.

It's daylight. We're probably somewhere north since the water is so cold. I break the surface of the water not a moment too soon. My lungs relax as air flows into them.

Pulling Ameris above the water, I bring her body close to mine. Even with my magic, I struggle against the force of the raging river, trying to keep us above the surface.

As we're pushed downstream, I take a breath and re-focus on my magic, creating a jet stream to propel us to the bank. When my feet hit the rocky bottom, I walk backwards, pulling her out of the water. Holding onto her hands makes this tricky, but I make it far enough back and lay her down.

Nothing ever good comes from using blood magic. Especially since she is untrained in her own magic, and she performed a powerful spell. I should have known it wouldn't be as easy as she made it sound. I know better.

But I let it happen because I wanted it to.

Leaning my head down, I listen to her lungs expand and collapse with effort.

Dammit.

Placing my free hand on her chest, I search her lungs, tuning into the vibrations of the water trapped within them, and I pull it out. She jerks up, coughing and spitting, expelling the clear liquid. Gasping for breath, it takes a few minutes until she settles, and her breathing normalizes.

Ameris looks at our hands, still held, and shakes her head like I did something wrong. "You held on."

"You told me not to let go." I scowl, my deep breath coming out in puffs of white.

She swivels her head, taking in our surroundings. Barren trees are decorated in ice spikes. Sunlight brightens the world, reflecting on the frost that covers the ground. There's not much to see in this winter wasteland. The freezing air quickly takes hold; her limbs shake, and her lips are starting to turn from pink to blue.

"What happened? Do you know where we are?"

"What happened?! You used blood magic and passed out. I picked you up and jumped into the water. We ended up in a river, and I got us to the shore."

Ameris removes her hand from mine. The wounds have sealed, but faint white lines linger, like the blood transformed into etched ink that trails down both of our arms. Her eyes widen, and she juts out her chin. "I had to use blood magic! Or we wouldn't have gotten here."

I balk and let out a breath, jaw tightening, before asking her, "I don't get a thank you for saving your ass?"

Through chatting teeth, Ameris fires back, but her words are slow. "Why would I thank you? I'm the reason we're here. You should thank me."

She has some nerve, but I don't push it. On the verge of freezing, with the bite of winter surrounding, is not the time for this conversation. "I think we are in the high north, which is not a place we want to be. There are dangerous beasts, nightshades, and other life forms we don't want to encounter. We need to move south, and fas—"

My warning is cut off by the sound of snapping branches and a snarl. I whip my head around as my stomach sinks, terror coating my insides. Fuck.

White coats of fur flash between the trees. The nightshades slow, pacing, waiting for their prey to react. Menacing horns rub against bark, their hardened spines protrude from their backs, and frosted breath flows between rows of jagged teeth that are perfect for shredding.

Though nightshades may be rare, these are the beasts our children are warned of in bedtime stories. They seek destruction in the world, born from the use of blood magic. A fusion of beast and demon.

Before I can decide what to do, the nightshades run forward. Reacting, I grab Ameris's hand and jump up, yanking her upright, pulling her behind me as I run.

"Xander! I can't run like you!" Ameris yells, but I barely hear her over the yaps and snarls from the beasts following their prey.

We only make it a few paces before her hand slips from mine. I skid to a stop on the frosted ground and slip as I pivot, landing on my knees.

Ameris scrambles back on her ass, her eyes wide. She tries to rise but slips on the frosty ground. When she realizes there is nowhere to go, she stops moving, rising to her knees. Three of them circle her, while the fourth stands with its hackles raised, snarling at Ameris.

The nightshade slowly approaches, its sharp teeth inches from her face, holding its ground, but it does not attack. Ameris looks into its eyes, staring it down, looking as fierce as the beast she faces.

Panic spikes through my veins, and my heart pounds against my chest. All rational thought melts away, replaced by a burning desire to eradicate any threat against her.

A fierce protectiveness that I don't understand flows through me, as if her life is more important than my own. It must be the blood magic; this encounter being so soon after she cast the spell.

I rise and creep closer to her, pulling moisture from the air and frost from the ground, creating two daggers. I throw the first, launching it at the one poised to attack Ameris. It whips its tail at the oncoming dagger, catapulting it to the side without glancing in my direction.

Ameris breaks her eye contact to look at me and shakes her head. I halt at her command but stay on edge, ready to attack.

CHAPTER 18
AMERIS

The beast's gaze hits me with an intensity I've never experienced. Like it's searching my soul, assessing me. Taking two steps back, it sits on its haunches, still imposing and terrifying. Its snarl relaxes, snout twitching as it sniffs the air between us.

I have the urge to reach out and touch it. But that would be stupid. It would shred me to pieces. Except, somehow, I know it won't.

I hope.

Tentatively, I reach out my arm. Inwardly, I wince, waiting for my end in this wretched cold. Of all the places the bridge could lead to, it just had to be this frozen wasteland. Nothing but dead trees around. What a miserable place. Even more so because I hate the cold.

When nothing happens, I slowly rise to my feet and take a step. The beast does nothing but stare at me. Another step closer, and I've placed myself at death's door should the nightshade so choose.

It looks at the other three, and they stop circling. Instead, they move behind me. The hair on the back of my neck rises; I'm uncertain of what they are doing. I turn and watch them sit at attention, as if waiting for a command.

I bow to the nightshade that appears to be in charge, instinct driving my actions. Perhaps it's from the knowledge that Marguerite passed to me—something from Rhiannon's time. It returns the gesture, lowering its head and stretching out a paw in front of it. The next thing it does surprises me.

I thought it might simply let us pass, but no, it sits next to me and nudges my hand like a dog. I rub its head and run my hand along its white-ridged spine, feeling each vertebra that protrudes.

I sense all the elements within you, but there is also a darkness that lies within your soul. You will come into great power, the kind that gives us pause. Very powerful indeed, but you lack control. She is you, but not. Your smell is unique. What is your name child?

Did it just speak to me? Even though I know there is no one else here, I can't help but look around. Returning my attention to the nightshade, I take a moment to process.

The beast slowly blinks.

Okay, yes, that just happened. This can't be normal. Xander is terrified of these beasts. The *she* that's being referred to must be Rhiannon. "Ameris. Rhiannon is my ancestor, but I'm human."

Pleased to meet your acquaintance. I am Lorcan. The beast bows its head. *Should you ever need us, we will answer your call.*

Xander moves towards us.

The beast snaps to attention, teeth barred, and ready to attack again. I run my hand along its back again, reveling in the protection the beast offers.

I whisper, "He's not a threat, but rather my guide to safety. As if it understands, the nightshade falls back and walks away with its pack in tow.

"We won't be bothered as we travel south." I stride toward Xander. When I reach him, I turn and watch the nightshades walk into the woods.

Xander raises an eyebrow, disbelief written all over his face. "What just happened?"

"I'm not entirely sure." I can't stop myself from shivering now that my adrenaline has settled, and my body's responses have returned to normal. "Let's go. I'm freezing, and my bones are turning brittle."

Xander grabs my arm, stopping me. "Are you okay?"

"I've had better days." Is he seriously asking me if I'm okay after that experience? Of course I'm not okay. The last week has been one shitty event after another. "Let's go. Walking will help me warm up. But we'll need to stop when we get a chance to dry our clothes."

"We may not last that long. It's perpetually cold here. If we are safe in the woods, as you say, then we should stop now. Build a fire and warm up while our clothes dry."

"Fine."

I pivot, moving deeper into the woods, grabbing limbs and leaves, and return as Xander hunches over a pile of kindling he's collected. He's determined to get a fire started. It shows in the scowl that falls over his features.

The same determination as when he never let go of my hand, even after we surfaced in this world. I attribute it to the bond he knows nothing about. I should tell him that now that we're here, there is no taking back what happened. His life is forever bound to mine. I sensed his panic as he watched me face off with the nightshade. The beating of his rapid heartbeat, in tune with my own. I wonder if he even noticed.

"What happened to you? On the bridge?" Xander asks, concern lacing his words.

"After I cast the spell, your essence—and magic—started flowing through my veins. It was burning me from the inside out. The icy water was a relief to the blaze running through my body. That's the last thing I remember before I woke up on the riverbank."

But that's not all that happened—it was like his essence also flowed through me along with flashes of my mother: the day she died and cast the spell to bind my magic. The last words she spoke—*you will not be found and meet the same fate*—her last moments shattered into a million pieces. The shroud over my magic fell away, breaking whatever spell she used to protect me all those years ago.

And when it all came crashing in, my body couldn't take the pressure; the explosive well of power that was locked away for so long wanted out. I've never felt so light, so free.

The edge of pain, like a blossoming headache, that was always there is gone. I can also now feel the way the world responds differently to me; everything is heightened, all the elements' vibrations flow about. Power—magic—it's there, unrestrained.

"I felt an immense pressure, like my heart wanted to stop beating, something latching onto it, squeezing tightly. Then it passed." Xander pauses, considering me for a moment, as if he is going to say something else. A question lingers in his gaze; instead, he shakes his head and returns his attention to the fire he's trying to start.

I think about what the nightshade told me and pull the grimoire out of my satchel, expecting it to be a soggy mess, but it's a perfectly preserved book. Rhiannon protected it using magic to preserve it through the ages.

My stiff clothes crack with frost as I crouch next to Xander and reach out my hand toward the kindling. I close my eyes and focus on heating it, putting pressure against it. A dull heat fills my belly, and I mentally grab onto it, building the heat with intention. Weaving it faster as it pulses, I open my eyes at the pop of a spark catching.

I flinch, a memory surfacing of my parents and Marguerite trapped within flames, but I shove it down before it can suffocate me. Logic prevails, knowing we need fire to stay warm and to help dry everything out.

"Keep going." Xander blows on the sparks.

I pull harder, going deeper, pushing magic into the kindling. Forcing the fire, I want to see. It grows in front of my eyes. The flames lick at each other and the wood it wants to devour. I channel that, the way the fire gets satisfaction from burning and destroying.

But my thoughts go to my home, to Marguerite, and I lose control. The flames shoot up into the air, singing my hands. I stumble back, falling to the icy ground, which becomes a relief for my palms and eases the burn.

Xander jumps back and drops the wood he was adding to the fire.

"You need to learn control." His gaze flits from me to the fire, watching as the flames reach a height they shouldn't be capable of. "We can dry our coats, but then we need to undress." I snap my head in his direction, and he coughs. "Not fully. We should sit close together for warmth while our clothes dry. I dug some dirt out of the ground, so we don't have to sit in the frost."

"Yeah. That makes sense." I nod at his words and move closer to the fire.

The flames slowly recede as my breath evens out. They pull me into a trance as they dance, burning happily amongst the wood it devours. Standing close, I hold out my hands for warmth and to feel the way it vibrates—erratic and angry. I want to hate my mother for blocking my magic, but she thought she was protecting me.

Still, if I had access to magic when my home was burning— controlling the power in the fire—I could have stopped it. Failure blossoms in my chest; I should've been able to save Marguerite. Trying to ignore the tears that threaten to fall, I switch my thoughts back to what Xander said. I consider his affinity for water.

"Can't you pull the moisture from our clothes? Like you did with the wood?" I ask, impatient with the cold.

"I hadn't thought of that." He rises and hangs his coat from a branch near the fire. Gathering the fabric in his hands, he slowly slides his fingers against the brown material.

I watch and wonder what it would feel like if his fingers were on my skin.

What. I mean, he is attractive, but I do not like him.

I subtly shake my head and watch as water drips from the bottom of the coat, turning to ice before it hits the ground. He faces the fire, holding the coat so the heat warms it. "Take your clothes off. When you are done, tell me, and I will pass you the coat."

"How about you run your hands down my clothes while they're still on me?" *Oh stars.* I slap my hand over my mouth, shocked at my own audacity. I really just said that. *Ameris, get it together. You're supposed to not like him.*

Xander whips his head in my direction. A surprised but intense look greets me, and before my next blink, he stands in front of me. My traitorous heart beats faster at how near he is. Why does he have to be so attractive? The one benefit of being bonded to him—he's nice to look at, even if my resolve is being tested.

"I would be happy to oblige." He quirks an eyebrow.

"I bet you would." I tilt my head up to look into his blue eyes, which hold a spark of mischief and curiosity mixed with desire.

"I've seen the way you look at me. You find me attractive." He trails his fingers up my arm, over my shoulders, moving delicately along the artery in my neck. Then he cups my cheek and runs his thumb along my bottom lip.

"I could say the same for you." I can't help the arousal that sparks, like tiny lightning bolts coursing through me at the contact of his skin against mine. I don't back away from him, even though part of me is unsure this is what I want.

"We don't have to be in love to enjoy the pleasure of sex." The corner of his lip quirks up in a devilish smile.

"Enemies do make the best lovers." I offer back, moving my own hands along his chest.

My breath hitches when his fingers roam again, tracing the outline of my body, slowly trailing down my arms to my waist and over my hips.

He leans down and brings his lips within inches of mine. "I don't want to be enemies or lovers. Just two beings taking advantage of an opportunity."

I respond without a second thought and close the distance. My stupid, traitorous body and mind. If I didn't hate him so much, I'd have wanted this sooner. I'm far from innocent, enjoying the sexual encounters I've had for the fun of it.

But it's easier to be angry and to push him away.

I want someone to be angry at.

But by the stars, this is divine. And just like that, our tongues are exploring each other.

"Ameris." My name leaves his lips in a deep rumble as he pulls away, far enough for his mouth to worship my body, moving to my jaw and neck.

I arch it back, a moan escaping my lips, butterflies ricocheting through my insides, but I need his mouth on mine. My fingers move to his hair, bringing him back to deepen our initial kiss. Xander's hands explore my curves, sliding over my waist and hips before cupping my ass. He picks me up, and the next thing I know, my back is against a tree and my legs are around his waist.

The hardness of his arousal presses against my center the deeper our kiss goes. A moan escapes my lips. He might have been taking the water out of my clothes, but I'm wet again, a heat settling in my lower abdomen.

This is torture, but in the best possible way. I've never had such an intense moment with a man. It's as if this is more than just two people wanting to use the other for pleasure, but a deep-rooted need for him to touch me everywhere. A primal need for him flares within me.

And then it clicks.

Panting, I pull my head back from his mouth, breaking the moment as I push out of his hold. He sets me down, and I step around him, heading to the fire.

The blood bond.

Dammit. I should have known it would be more than just a bond to connect our lives to one another. The bond wants to connect us in desire—a primal need for the other person—to love and need them deeply.

I'm not interested in falling for the man who ruined my life.

"That was—something." Xander leans against the tree, a crooked smile lighting one side of his mouth.

"It won't happen again." I retort, trying to act unfazed, but my lips still tingle from the kiss, and I curse myself.

"But it should," he quips.

"Don't look." I say, shooting him a glare. He raises his hands and turns his back to me. I undress quickly, throwing my clothes at his feet before grabbing the coat he dropped on the ground. I stand before the fire with the coat open. No point in wearing dry clothes if my undergarments are damp. The warmth is immediate and soothes the cold that tried to return.

I swap the coat around and stand with my back against the fire. I watch him work at the rest of his clothing, and the thought of his hands running over my body creeps in again. *Stop it, Ameris.*

Xander holds out my clothes without making eye contact or saying anything. When I grab them, he wastes no time. He removes his shirt, the muscles in his back flexing with each movement. But instead of smooth skin, I notice scars all over. They cross in places and vary in size. Some look like they could be from stab wounds; another looks like a brand. I hadn't noticed them when I brought him back from the ship. Did he get those in his world or mine?

My world. No, I have no world—no home.

When he moves to undo his pants, I focus on dressing instead of how he is undressing. I shake the thought again. This is going to get annoying. When Xander is done, he comes to stand on the opposite side of the fire.

Both of us are looking into the flames' mesmerizing dance, swaying this way and that, always together and separate. That is how we will be. A flame that cannot be divided but will reach out only to be pulled back together. Burning brighter and hotter together.

But I don't want another flame in my life, and I will do everything I can to snuff it out.

Grabbing dirt from the ground, I smother the flames. "Let's go."

CHAPTER 19
XANDER

I haven't been able to stop thinking about the way her body felt against mine. Her need was apparent, just as she clearly relished in mine.

She seems to have erased it from her mind. I thought she would have opened up, but no, it's as if we never had that moment by the fire, as if nothing changed when we finally gave into desire.

Ameris rarely responds when I talk to her. It always seems to put her on edge. I knew this was going to be hard for her—to not only lose everything but also leave everything she ever knew behind. I still have a responsibility to protect her, to fulfill the promise

I made, a bargain to honor, and I intend to see them through, even if she pushes me away.

The farther south we travel, the greener the landscape becomes, but it lacks the usual emerald-colored grass. A hilltop peaks in the distance, one I know by heart, signaling we are close to Solarium.

As we crest the hill, I wait for her reaction, and it does not disappoint. Ameris's features relax, and awe takes form as she looks upon the capital. Her green eyes are lit up, a vibrant and ethereal glow radiating from the reflection of the setting sun.

"Oh my." The words escape under her breath. "I've never seen anything so beautiful."

"That is Solarium, the capital of Elysium and my home." The palace stands upon a hill, shining like a beam of light, drawing all who see it forward.

Crafted of white marble washed with pearls from the hands of the first fae. They spared no detail in its construction. The rest of the city fans out around it, forming rings of homes and businesses, larger to smaller, then out into farmland and into the woods that circle it.

"This view never gets old." I revel in the view before making my way down the hill toward the forest that surrounds the city.

"Are we going through the main gates? Where are we even going? We never actually talked about that," Ameris notes.

"Well, you never asked." I expect a snappy response, but Ameris is too busy staring at the capital and the radiance it emits with the sun setting behind it. "I promise to bring you here again. When the sun rises, it's even more beautiful."

Her eyes bore into me. "You promise?"

I offer my hand in confirmation, in truce, as we descend the hill, but she refuses. I veer left into the woods east of the city instead of towards the main road leading into the city. "Yes. I wouldn't make a promise I don't intend to keep. We are taking a hidden route. I don't need anyone knowing I'm back. Not yet."

That would ruin my plans. And I won't be stopped a second time. I will take back what is mine and ruin Oberon for what he has done.

The decay along our route is Oberon's doing. Plants that should be in bloom lay shriveled and brown. Grass, once a deep emerald color, is now yellow and dying.

The shadow magic he uses is seeping into this world, and he will ruin it before the era is over. Oberon is corrupting our source of magic, so we can never challenge him. Either he doesn't care, or he doesn't understand what is at risk. In his quest for vengeance against those who wronged him, he will rip everything apart so that even he cannot survive in his world without magic.

"You still haven't said where we are going." The tail end of her words taper off as she takes one last look at the city before entering the forest. "Tell me now."

My gaze lingers on her silhouette, highlighted amidst the rays of the setting sun. Every contour of her form is bathed in the amber light filtering through the forest; her beauty, though different, radiates like Rhiannon's once did.

"We are going to the underground," I explain. "To the hiding place of those in the rebellion. The ones fighting against Oberon."

"The one you told me about before we entered Elysium?"

I nod. "It's not much further, and it's best to enter before darkness falls. There are beasts in this forest as well."

I turn and walk away—something I seem to do a lot when all I really want to do is grab her hand and walk together. I let my thoughts stir to when I started having feelings for her. What is it about her? Her fighting spirit? All I know is that when I nearly lost her in the water, I panicked, and I never want to feel that again—never want her to be in danger again.

Thick undergrowth eases my pace as we traverse through the forest. There are no paths this far; the ground is uneven, and bushes threaten to maim our legs or tangle between them.

Decay hasn't taken hold in the forest close to the capital. Oberon must not want the citizens to know what sins against our world he is committing. Darkness spreads as the golden ray filtering through the trees slips away.

The grand oak comes into view just as the sun sets; it's light enough to showcase the beauty of this tree. Its base is six feet wide, and it stands a hundred feet tall.

"Place your hand on the tree." I instruct, lifting my own and placing it against the dark brown bark. I flex my fingers into its rough texture, a reminder that this is not a fever dream. It's real, and I'm home. The sacred phrase of our rebellion comes easily, eternally etched into my memory: "I pledge my life to this land and offer my magic for passage."

Ameris sucks in a breath and looks at me; her expression shifts from surprised to understanding. "The tree is thrumming under my palm. Its power radiating through me and pulling at my magic."

"To enter, you must be pure in your intentions and offer what is most precious to us—our magic. We offer the tree continued strength and life in exchange for protection. Step back." We remove our hands as the tree's roots shift, revealing an opening in the ground. "Please, let me guide you until we get far enough in, where you can see."

This time, she doesn't refuse. Her hand slips into mine, and it sends a chill down my spine, sparking a desire to pull her into me, but darkness takes over as we're closed in. I blink and pull in a deep breath.

Exhaling, I open my eyes to the darkness transformed. The curtain of blackness lifts to grey and white. Smooth, carved earth interwoven with thick and delicate roots line the tunnel ceiling. The familiar scent of damp earth lingers as we move down the path to the main chamber.

It's strangely quiet as we approach, but the faelights are active, and they are only on when someone is present. Vaulted ceilings and a large chamber open before us, transforming the earthen tunnel into grey marble streaked with white and brown, like the inside of a grand palace. I lead Ameris from the overlook and down the curved stairs to our right.

Faelights sparkle, held in lanterns hung along the walls. Some float freely along the ceiling, giving the appearance of daylight even in this massive cavern. It should be full of hundreds of people milling about, vendors selling their goods, laughter echoing through the stalls. Even guards that are normally posted at the exit are nowhere to be found.

"It's magnificent. Was this created by magic?" Ameris lets go of my hand and grabs the intricate wooden railing, leaning into it as her gaze sweeps over the space.

"This was here long before any of us remember, but likely. There are many cavities that spread out from the main room. There is also a passageway that goes directly into the capital."

"How were you able to keep it a secret from Oberon if it has been here for so long?" Ameris descends the rest of the stairs, taking in the breath of the space.

"We did not discover it until the fall of Rhiannon. Many of the fae fled the capital during the war and into the surrounding woods. A group of them stopped to rest under the great oak, and it opened for them. The magic that flows through this place is older than anyone alive, and no one alive understands it. We cannot speak of this place with an intention to do harm to it or its inhabitants. The words will not come to those who try."

"Where does it exit into the capital?" she asks, walking through the now empty space.

"It exits in a grove in the center of the city, but we won't be going there. You won't be going to the capital." The words come out harshly. I don't correct myself because the last thing I want is for her to go into the city. "They will know you are a human. I don't need you getting mixed up in a bargain you didn't intend to make or getting taken by Oberon's guards."

Ameris scowls but doesn't respond. When we reach the bottom of the cavern, voices drift from a passage to the right. I follow them, and as we approach, the deep baritones emanating from a familiar voice carry as we get closer to the war room that was built at the end of the passageway.

"Xander," Ameris grabs my arm, halting me, "I don't want you to tell them about my magic just yet. I want to get a handle on it first."

"I'm going to have to tell someone so they can teach you." I pull my arm out of her grip and start walking again. I'm antsy, ready to reach the voices I haven't heard in so long. To see my friend's faces again.

"We made a bargain. You are supposed to teach me magic." She hisses and forcefully grabs me again, turning me to face her.

"You can access more magic than I can teach." This is a conversation for another time, one we could have had the entire journey here.

Her fingers dig into the flesh of my forearm, eyes narrowing. With a tongue as sharp as a blade, she says, "Don't tell them that."

"As you wish." I bow, then pivot, taking long strides, not wanting to be stopped again. until we're just outside the door that was left slightly ajar. Strained, argumentative voices reach us through the door that was left slightly ajar. I know who is speaking, but the words create a pit in my stomach.

"We have no way of getting to him. He's already decimated our stronghold. Those who fled are too terrified to come back. We lost a lot of our numbers."

"But we have to continue to fight back, or the decay will spread until all of Elsyium is gone—every forest, river, and city. Hunger and desperation will turn to chaos as resources dwindle, forcing the fae to fend for themselves in the face of starvation."

"Jesper, tell us then, what do you have planned?"

I rap my knuckles against the door: once, two fast raps, and a final one, the announcement of someone familiar so the room knows part of the crew is entering. I'm not sure what to expect as I pull the door open and step inside the war room.

No one from our world has ever returned after being banished.

CHAPTER 20
AMERIS

Disbelief and shock paint the faces of the four fae sitting around a long, rectangular table made of golden oak, similar to the trees of the forest we traveled through. I sink further into Xander's shadow, not ready to be seen.

"What in the maker's name?" The fae looks nothing like the ones described in the bedtime stories my parents told.

He's handsome, even though age lines have worn his otherwise flawless olive skin. His white hair is parted, the right styled in a braid adjacent to a shorn strip above his ear. The rest of his straight strands are pulled into a messy bun that rests on the crown of his head. He has the air of an elder and is dressed as finely as any noble would be, but looks no older than a man in his forties. A white shirt sits under his regal royal blue tunic, paired with black pants that are stitched with golden thread.

It's the same type of clothing Xander had on when I found him. Refusing to remind myself of the events that led us here, I divert my attention to everyone else in the room.

Three other fae sit at the table, wearing a similar style of clothing in various colors and patterns. They look younger than the one who spoke, but I know looks are deceiving considering the fae have long lives.

Unease burrows itself into the pit of my stomach, drawing me to the gaze of the female sitting across from the older fae. She's fixed on me like a predator that's found its next victim. Like I was the first thing she saw when we walked in. If stares could kill, I wouldn't be standing.

The fire blazing in the hearth at the back of the room accentuates her dark brown skin and slender features, and gives the gold flecks in her brown eyes their chilling glow. Two rows of braided black hair stop at the nape of her neck, and the rest of her tight curls flow freely over her shoulders, stopping at her ribs.

Not even a second after the older fae speaks, the force of her forearm slams against my shoulder, dagger drawn against my throat.

The dagger's sharp edge presses into my skin. I suck in air through clenched teeth, a sting flaring from the spot where the dagger ever so slightly cut into me. Her other arm pins mine to my side, a quick reminder that even if they don't look deadly, they are.

I look down my nose at her. It's the only thing I can do. With my neck exposed, any movement will be my last. Even still, my body floods with magic that begs to be unleashed to protect myself.

I don't know what would happen or even what element would come forth if I let it have free rein, so I hold it all back. The thrum of magic pulsing in my veins comforts me, knowing I could rip her apart if I willed it.

"Give me one reason I shouldn't slit her throat." She slides her gaze to Xander. "And how the hell did you get here?" Disgust rolls off her tongue in waves. That my ancestor elicits such a reaction hits me harder than the blade to my throat.

"Lay off, Zorria. This is not Rhiannon," Xander commands, putting his hand on her shoulder to pull her back.

She shrugs him off. Without pushing the blade any deeper into my skin, she leans into my neck and inhales. Stories flood back to me about the fae who can smell emotion, sense it from the way our human bodies react to situations and use it to their advantage to trap humans in bargains they cannot escape.

"You're afraid." The words are a whisper against my ear. Slowly removing her dagger, she sheathes it against her thigh and steps back. She returns to the table and leans against it, folding her arms against her chest, but her deadly glare doesn't vanish.

She has mistaken my disappointment and irritation at allowing myself to be cornered for fear. I'll let her think that; better for them to think me weak. That way, they'll feel they have nothing to fear from me. But one day, they will fear me, a promise that crosses itself in my heart.

"Ameris, meet Zorria, Jesper, Zeke, and Lyle." Xander nods in her direction, then to the older Fae, and the other two sitting at the table, who are clearly amused by Zorria's reaction.

"She gets like that," the one named Zeke says. "I've had to deal with it all my life—my sister." He nods toward Zorria.

I flit my gaze between the two of them—the same dark brown skin, same round face with defined cheekbones, and gold-flecked eyes—features so similar they could pass for twins. Except his tight black curls float about his head, whimsical and free. And from his demeanor, it's clear they are nothing alike.

The older fae, Jesper, rises from his seat and comes to me. He holds out his hand, an offer he must assume I'll return. I hesitate, considering what it would mean if I didn't return the gesture. Silence stretches in my decision, but I oblige. I don't need to start making enemies. Even though I'm sure I've already made one of Zorria without trying.

He takes my hand and places a kiss on the back of it. "Welcome. I apologize for Zorria. She and Rhiannon didn't end their relationship on good terms. It's remarkable. You look so much like her. Tell me, how did you come to meet Xander and end up within these walls?"

"I found Xander unconscious on a wrecked ship." In my peripheral, Zorria shifts, and I glance at her. She has an eyebrow raised, disbelief now mixed with her disgust. No apology will come from her. Definitely starting out as enemies. Great. Returning my attention to Jesper, I continue. "I realized he was fae, so I pulled him from the wreckage and brought him to my home. Rhiannon is my ancestor. I inherited her magic. I cast a spell, and here we are." Speaking the words aloud threatens to break the dam I've constructed, which holds back all the pain of losing Marguerite and Honey. Xander can explain it to them. I refuse to give my energy to these fae. I owe them nothing.

"I see." Jesper gently drops my hand and turns to Xander. They clasp arms and bow to each other, touching their foreheads for a moment before he continues. "It's so good to see you. It's been two years since he banished you. Lyle, do you mind getting them something to eat and drink? Please sit."

"Ameris." Lyle stands and bows their head before leaving the room. The dark green robe they wear flows about them, covering their pale skin. Lyle's presence is calm and serene, like an evergreen tree surrounded by freshly fallen snow.

I nod in response. I hate this—feeling as if everyone here thinks they know me, a mere human, because fae have heightened senses. For Zorria to react so quickly, her hatred of Rhiannon was more powerful than her ability to sense my humanity.

Xander places a hand low on my back, guiding me to the chair Jesper pulls out from the table. I fight the comfort of his touch caused by the bond, wanting to shove him off. Instead, I focus on the seat that promises the rest my exhausted body desires.

My chest tightens as Jesper's words repeat in my head, and I consider that time might run differently in this world. It's only been a week since I found him in the shipwreck, and he's been gone for two years. Or was he a captive for that long?

It doesn't matter. We're here now. I exhale a small breath, forcing the tension in my body out with it. If I ever get home, I might be years older than when I left. But I have no home to return to, and no one waiting for me. Anxiety spreads; a hollowness begins to carve itself out in my chest, eating away at my heart.

Xander slides into the seat next to me, telling Jesper about all that's occurred since he woke up in the human world. But distraction from his tale and the answer to my questions comes in the form of Zorria, who chooses to sit directly across from me.

Unrelenting in her inspection, she watches my every movement. Either she's trying to intimidate me or plotting the next best spot to place her dagger. I match her stare until Lyle places a plate of food and a mug in front of me.

"I hope this food satisfies you. The drink is our wine. Go easy with it until you know how it will affect you." Lyle gives me a small smile, then places the other plate and cup down for Xander. They clasp Xander's shoulder and squeeze. "It's good to see you again."

Variations of fruit and vegetables fill my plate, different colors and textures, some similar to the human world and some different, accompanied by buttered bread.

It all looks delicious. I glance up to thank Lyle, but they've left the room. Trying a bite of everything, it's all so good and full of flavor. Taking the mug, I drink deeply, not caring about Lyle's warning. The wine is sweet, tasting of elderberries and honeysuckle with an undernote of spice. It goes down easily. I'm about to take another drink when laughter fills the space.

"Whoa there, little lady." Zeke's eyes crinkle at the corners.

"I'm not a little lady," I retort.

"It is just a saying." Holding up his hands in surrender, he adds,

"That wine is not kind to mortals." He finishes his statement with a wink.

Right now, I don't care what is kind to mortals. I finally have something to drown out my sorrows. Even if it's momentary. Brining the cup to my lips, I drink the rest of it in one go. I've had wine before, but the warmth of it hits me immediately, flowing through my body.

"Just like all the other humans, thinking she can be one of us," Zorria spits out.

That's all it takes to bring the buried rage to the surface, forcing my body up as the chair I was occupying scrapes against the stone floor behind me.

Zorria rises with me, ready to fight. "What are you going to do, mortal? You may look like our lost queen, but you will never be her."

She's right. I will never be Rhiannon, but I'm not trying to be. I have the same magical abilities and my own witch ones as well. So, I vow to be better than her—stronger and more powerful. Even if I need to learn how to control my magic, I'm not afraid to use it. I never want to be weak and vulnerable again.

I slam my hands on the table, and flames spring to life, engulfing the surface of the table. Everyone jumps back in surprise. "I'd appreciate if you stopped disrespecting me. I may be a mortal, but I can use magic just like you."

Zorria's eyes widen in shock. I'm also in shock, even though I keep it from showing, because I'm not sure how it happened. It must be my magic reaction to my emotions like Xander mention. Just as quickly as the flames appeared, they subside.

The table isn't ruined, but black, charred steaks cover the surface. Kicking my chair back, I stalk out of the room. I don't know where I'm going, and I don't care.

What I need right now is to be alone. To process everything and have a moment for myself. I follow the passageway until it opens into the main cavity where we entered.

As the wine makes its way to my brain, I stumble a few times. My vision blurs, and I'm so hot now that I just need to get out to breathe fresh air. I call to the air surrounding me. The vibrations are soft and smooth, and I let them guide me through the passages until another entrance opens to the night air.

Raising my arms to the side, the wind moves through my fingers and tousles my hair as I walk out onto the ledge. It pulls the emotions from me, releasing pent up tension in my body. Standing at the edge, the smell of cold air and pine trees washes over me.

Drunkenness finally masters me, and the inhibitions I didn't know I was holding slip away. I stand there until the sway of my body is too much, and I sit, letting my legs dangle over the ledge. I dare not look down for fear I will topple over in my drunken state.

The woods in the distance sway in the wind. At least that's what it looks like. My head bobs with the freeness of the drink. Laying back, I stare at the night sky. The stars shine brightly; I recognize some of the constellations while others blur together.

I am not the same as I was two days ago. The thought filters through my mind without my consent. My eyes close as a tear slides down my temple. The wind whistles a melody, and I let my body relax into the drunkenness the wine provides. Another presence shifts the air, becoming heavier as footsteps approach.

"Hey there, little lady."

Zeke.

"You should keep your sister in check." My stomach churns with the strength of the wine, and I keep my eyes closed so as not to make it worse.

"There is a lot of history there that you know nothing of." His tone is soft but stern.

"I don't care. I'm not Rhiannon and don't want to be treated like I am."

"So, you have the ability of fire. Impressive."

"What are you doing here?" Impatience oozes from my words. I wanted to be alone. To relax.

"I'm here to make sure you get safely back to where you will be staying. Xander is still speaking with Jesper. Zorria would've pushed you off the ledge. Lyle has already retired for the night. And, since you don't know where you are or where you're going, you need me."

I pry one eye open and immediately regret it. There are three Zeke's with their arms crossed in front of them, leaning with their backs against the stone wall. So, too much wine then. Good to know if I plan to drink less next time. Silence stretches for a few moments before he speaks again.

"I tried to warn you about the wine." Zeke chuckles. The sternness is gone, replaced by lighthearted joking.

Opening my other eye, colors swirl and pulse. Bad idea. I definitely should've listened when they warned me about the wine. Turning my head to the stars, they dance in the darkness. Sitting up takes more effort than I care to admit. My limbs are heavy, and my head is swimming. Bile comes up without warning, and I lean over the edge, letting the contents of my stomach empty into the void below.

My body pitches forward from the motion, but Zeke grabs my shoulder and pulls me back, saving me from certain death. He hauls me up from my armpits and wraps one of my arms around his waist for support. Walking proves difficult as my feet do not want to follow the instructions my brain gives. I only make it ten feet before my legs give out and I land on my hands and knees. Pain jolts through me, the rough stone biting into my kneecaps and palms.

A laugh escapes as I roll onto my back. "You can leave me here."

"What kind of hosts would we be if I allowed that?" With one arm under my knees and the other across my back, Zeke effortlessly lifts me up. I wrap my arms around his neck as he carries me through the winding corridors that I have no memory of walking through.

"Where are we going?" I slur out. Oh gosh. How embarrassing.

"I'm taking you to your room." He looks down at me with a smile on his face.

Focusing on the next words I want to say, I try my best not to slur. "I want some water."

~

There's no way to tell how long I have been laying in this bed. Only faelights and the fire in the hearth lights the room. The only good thing is that I don't feel hungover.

No head pounding or dry mouth. In fact, I feel rather rested—the best sleep I've had in a long time. Except, I'm sleeping in the same clothes I've worn since we left my home. The only time they, and I, could be considered even close to clean was when we entered this world in the river.

Looking around the room, I can tell a lot of care went into furnishing and designing the space; it doesn't look like it's underground. White, wood paneled walls make it feel like a suite at a lavish inn.

The four-poster bed I'm lying in is behind the couches that sit in front of the fire. I get out of bed and go to the bathing chamber to my left. It opens up to a polished stone room with its own fireplace. No smoke emanates from either fireplace, and, thankfully, there is indoor plumbing. If they can use magic to do these two things, then I'm going to enjoy what my magic can do.

Two buckets of water sit by the fire. I dip my finger in. It's lukewarm, though; if I'm being honest with myself, even if the water was cold, I'd probably still bathe in it. A set of clothes is folded over the tub. Placing the water buckets down, I pick them up. Though they consist of a white shirt, tunic, and a pair of pants, they are anything but ordinary.

The shirt feels like butter slipping through my fingers. Just as soft is the deep violet patterned tunic. It'll match my skin and hair perfectly, bringing out the green in my eyes and accentuating the various shades of my strawberry-blond hair. I'm not sure if it's on purpose or by chance, but I like it. Something I always know how to do is play to my strengths.

I'm attractive enough to get what I want. That helped me remain in the good graces of the town council and keep prying eyes away from—*stop*.

Turning my thoughts away from the home I had, I return to the bath, pouring the water into the tub. I get in and dip my head under the water, letting it clear my thoughts.

CHAPTER 21

XANDER

Ameris enters the war room with Zeke, laughing at something he whispers in her ear. Pure delight lights up her features, evident in the way her eyes crinkle and her smile widens. It is a sound that never crossed her lips throughout our entire journey to Solarium, and I'm drawn to it like a moth to flame. I want to hear more of it; be the one to bring it forth.

Jealousy flares as they walk to the table and sit next to each other over the fact that it's Zeke who gives her a moment of reprieve—not me.

From the other side of the table, Zorria's watching them as intently as I am, with a murderous gleam in her eye, like a hawk tracking its prey. She narrows in on every movement Ameris makes and every reaction Zeke has.

"Did you sleep well?" I ask, breaking the relative silence in the room and ending their private conversation, because for some reason I can no longer stand it. Plus, I don't want to know what another second of their interaction will cause Zorria to do.

Ameris snaps her head in my direction, her green eyes accentuated by the violet tunic she wears. She takes a bite from a buttered roll and sets it down before leaning back in her chair. "I don't remember how I slept. One moment I was being escorted—well, carried somewhere—and the next, I woke up in a bed. But I guess that could count as sleeping well."

Lyle chuckles under their breath. I give them a sharp look, and their hands go up in surrender. Lyle returns to eating, acting as if they're not still humored by the scene that's playing out.

"Is that where you went off to last night, Zeke? To follow her around?" Zorria nods in Ameris's direction.

"Why yes, sister, and we had a lovely conversation. Too bad you couldn't have joined us. There was a ledge you could have jumped off." Zeke lazily replies as he side-eyes Zorria, finishing with a smug smile.

"Take me there, and we'll see what happens." Zorria leans forward on her elbows, challenging her brother.

Things seem not to have changed between them. Zeke goading and riling up his sister.

Interrupting before it turns into another tiff between the two of them, I turn to Lyle. "Can you help me by working with Ameris on learning to control her magic? Zorria and I will start training again. That would also benefit you, Ameris."

I turn my gaze to Ameris, and I'm met with a stony demeanor and a cold stare. The muscles in her jaw clench, betraying her emotions.

I'm still fulfilling my bargain; I taught her how a part of our magic works in the forest. Now, I'm having someone take my place to teach her the rest. I have more important things to worry about now that I'm back than one more thing for her to be upset about.

Her eyes roll dramatically in a silent dismissal of my presence.

Ameris addresses Lyle before they can respond. "I would love your help, but wish I could have asked you myself. All around me, I can feel the magic pulsing. I can call to it, and it responds. But once I have it in my grasp, it takes over and wants release."

"I see. We shall work on this together. As equals. Soon, you will be able to control that which calls to you." Nodding, Lyle stands, inclines their head, and stops before leaving the room. "Come find me at the fourth hour of light's dismay."

"I can speak for myself, you know." Ameris spits out, narrowing her eyes at me. "I don't need you treating me like a lost puppy. Zeke can train me." Ameris looks to Zeke, and he balks in surprise as she throws him a smile.

"Of course, of course. I would love to," he responds.

"Fine." I press out in a tight-lipped smile. "Zorria, are you ready to train? I'd like to start right away."

"I'm always ready to train." Zorria's daggers spin in her hand before she stabs them into the wooden table, still blackened from the night before when Ameris lost control of her power and set the table on fire.

Ameris's power is remarkable. We have seen nothing like it since Rhiannon came into power and ruled over Elysium. All fae respected her control over the elements, naturally making her the next ruler to take the seat after Lorian passed into the stars.

By the decree of the elders, Rhiannon named me heir, but I will need Ameris by my side when I take the throne. For her magic and her reverence as our last ruler.

Though I'm still not sure if they will accept Ameris, she is a human with power she shouldn't have. But at least if she is with me, the fae can do her no harm or play tricks on her. She will always find protection under our Law of Rule, rendering the magic of deals ineffective on her.

∾

The scent of weapons and leather fills the training hall. This used to be my comfort zone, where I could release all emotions and tension. It feels good to be back in this space after so long. I remove my shirt and face Zorria, a sly smirk lifting the side of my mouth. "Do you still have it in you?"

In response, she dashes forward, slicing her blade against my chest. I jump back, expecting her attack. "Now, now. No weapons. Hand-to-hand combat."

We circle each other, each step a calculation, like predators poised at the edge of attack.

Tension coats the air as we wait on one another to make the first move. My heart pounds, the quickly beating rhythm thrumming in my ears, along with the rush of adrenaline surging through my veins.

Before I make my move, Zorria lunges, punching out with her left hand. In a fluid motion, I react instinctively, deflecting her strike. She's quick to follow up. Her right arm arcs toward my face, but I lean to the left and counter.

Swiftly moving behind her, I bring my arm around her neck and catch her in a chokehold. She slips under my grasp, twirling into a low kick that sends me to the ground.

"It doesn't seem like you were doing any training. What? Were you ogling that mortal girl the whole time? I know how you used to fawn over Rhiannon." As I rise, she beckons me with a taunting wave of her hand.

I oblige.

Offering no hesitation, I surge toward her, feigning a punch but pulling back just shy of making contact. Zorria, anticipating the hit, moves to counter, leaving herself open at the waist.

Unguarded, I take the opening and wrap my arms around her waist, lifting her before slamming her against the ground. She lands hard, the impact expelling the air from her lungs in a sharp exhale. I step back, giving her space to recover. Sweat beads on my skin, ready to slip from it with every movement.

My breaths are quick and short as I reply, "No. While she is pretty, we didn't get off to the best start. If you can't tell, she can barely stand me."

"Well, that might be the only thing we have in common." She snarls, standing with rage burning through her irises. She hates being bested.

"She is not Rhiannon, Zorria. Give her a chance."

"That may be, but looking like Rhiannon is enough for me to want to sink my dagger into her heart."

We continue training for what feels like hours, until Jesper walks in. Telling time in these caves used to be impossible. We installed a bell—one chime for every hour of the day—that makes its way through the passages.

Jesper told me last night that since there are no longer inhabitants, the bell is no longer used. Instead, he keeps an hourglass running. If he's here, that means it must be mid-day. He watches for a while as we exchange blows and end up on the ground, trying to outmaneuver each other.

His deep chuckle slices through our focus. "Nice to see you two at it again. But we need to talk about how we plan on getting our numbers back up and about confronting Oberon." Jesper waits for us, arms behind his back, standing in the doorway.

He won't leave until we go with him because he knows there always has to be a winner when we spar.

Neither one of us can pin the other down, so we both nod, ending our fight. Our labored breaths come out heavy, and our skin glistens with sweat, a testament to the intense session we had. I wipe the sweat that still clings to my body with my shirt as we head out of the room. We selected this spot for the training center because the cavern has four large alcoves, perfect as break-out rooms.

The expansive main section has a large platform in the center for group training. But it's off to the side that I notice Ameris with Zeke. He's showing her basic defensive moves and attacks. A sudden, unbidden flair of desire surges—a certainty that it should be me training with her.

Exhaling sharply, my breath is tinged with irritation at the unwelcome intrusion. What has she done to me? Brows pinching as I shake my head slightly, I try to cast off the feeling and dismiss it, returning my attention to Zorria.

Her eyes narrow slightly, missing nothing. "Why do you keep looking at her like that? You say you have no interest, yet, every time you see her, you get this longing gaze."

I think about Zorria's question before answering, "I don't know...She intrigues me...When we jumped from the bridge to enter this world, she was unresponsive. I could feel her dying. Before then, I didn't realize how much I cared. I didn't tell Jesper this. Right after we got out of the river, nightshades surrounded us. Ameris fell back, and the alpha approached her. They faced off, but the nightshade surrendered, and she ran her hand along its back. I've never seen that before—and she told me they spoke."

Zorria's eyebrows arch and her eyes widen—a mix of disbelief and shock. It mirrors my own reaction when I think back on that day. "How is that even possible?" she asks.

"The magic she carries is unlike anything we've seen since Rhiannon. I will explain when we are with the others."

"What happened to you when you were banished?" Zorria changes the subject, asking with concern.

This is not a tale I want to repeat. There were many dark days following my banishment. "Humans know we exist; at least a fraction of them do. When I woke up, I was in a forest, and I wandered around for a while, calling to the water of their world. It responded, similar to the way it does on the coasts of Elysium. I knew it was an ocean, and I let it lead me."

"When I arrived, there was a port town. I tried to fit in, but somehow they knew what I was. The humans captured me and forced me onto their ships, used me for my magic to control the seas and make their endeavors successful."

"They were not kind. So, I waited for the right storm, the right time, when they restricted food and my hands could slip from the restraints. I brought the storm that ravaged their ship as they tried to outrun it. The ship remains washed up on the shore, and that is when Ameris found me."

As we walk to the war room, I tell her the rest of what happened that led Ameris and me to the bridge and the spell that Ameris had to cast to get us here.

"Wait. What did you just say?" Zorria interrupts me, holding up a hand. "Blood magic?"

"Yes. It was the only way," I say, not wanting to linger on the fact that I had to engage in magic that we outlawed long ago.

"I don't like the sound of that. Maybe the magic is why you're drawn to her." She raises an eyebrow as we enter the room.

My response gets cut off by Lyle's greeting. "Please eat, friends. You must be famished after training."

Lyle has the table laid out with a variety of food that I didn't realize I'd missed. The sweet and tart starfruit, stuffed rolls with jelly, and a steaming pot of soup with vegetables grown outside the capital.

"Lyle, when did you become such a chef?" I tease after seeing the food they prepared.

"Many things have changed since you were last here." Lyle smiles sadly as they walk around to the other side of the table and sit. "And this is what we shall discuss."

Clearing his throat, Jesper speaks. "Oberon holds the throne, even though we followed through with the original plan laid out before you left. There were many casualties, and after our defeat, those who didn't leave our cause ran when his forces showed up. We didn't stand a chance against his shadow magic. But what we have now that we didn't then is you. Oberon may have shadow magic, but he doesn't have the power granted by the elders. The power that Rhiannon left to you as named heir."

"And if Ameris can learn to control and harness her power, she can be the key to defeating him. She inherited Rhiannon's gift over the elements. She can control them all."

Jesper and Zorria look at me as if I spoke in the language of the underwater folk. Too late, I realize I haven't yet told them about the extent of her abilities. They only saw her use of fire magic.

"I'll decide if I want to help," Ameris snaps, standing in the doorway with Zeke. She shakes her head as her hands curl into fits. A disbelieving and breathy laugh escapes before she continues. "Don't forget, I already helped you by getting you here. I don't owe you anything."

AMERIS

Who the hell does he think he is? Telling them about my magic, my abilities? Anger seethes from within, flooding my veins, my muscles, every inch of my body with acid that I want to spew onto him. To scorch him, so he knows what giving up my secret feels like when he said he wouldn't.

Now I know I'm only a pawn in his game to get back his throne. He needed me to return, and he needs my magic to win against Oberon.

Heavy silence spreads over the room, so quiet that a speck of dust falling would be the only thing to make a sound. Lyle, mid-bite, gently places their fork down and folds their hands into their lap.

They look at me, the tilt of their head and the set of their eyes speak louder than any words. It makes my skin crawl, like Lyle always knows what lies just beneath the surface of my words and actions.

Jesper speaks, breaking the tension of my entrance. "You are right that you don't owe us anything. We are forever grateful that you helped Xander return. This world is dying from Oberon's magic. If you haven't already seen it on your travels, I can take you to a place where the decay is more prevalent—where there are only black husks of trees, almost as if their very life force was stripped from them. Nothing grows in these places where there was once lush vegetation."

"And how is that my problem? I had little choice in helping Xander. He's the reason I have nothing left." I can't help the anger that seeps from my words; I'm livid. I move away from the door and into the room, taking a seat across from Jesper. Zeke sits next to me without saying a word.

"There are always choices, even when you don't see them." Lyle's soft voice carries as much weight as Jesper's stern one.

Lyle stares at us all in turn, a moment too long, looking from one to the other while taking a sip of wine. The hairs on the back of my neck rise, and a shiver courses through me. There is something that makes me wary of Lyle, like they know too much, can see what others cannot. But I don't have any reason to mistrust them, so I disregard it as having to learn people's personalities.

"We don't expect you to help. Only ask that you do when the time comes." Jesper adds.

"Remember to meet me." Lyle addresses me before turning to the rest of the group. "I am going to the city today for more food and supplies. Does anyone need anything?"

I nod my head in reply to Lyle as I grab a plate of fruit and rolls. To no one in particular, I ask, "Can I go?"

"No." Xander snaps. I pause mid-bite, but he continues before I can say anything. "I simply mean, that won't be possible. They will know you are human and that you are not bonded in servitude."

Narrowing my eyes, I glare at him. Who does he think he is? I hope he knows that telling me not to do something only makes me want to do it more, that him doing this is going to rankle my nerves. If he wants to play that game, I still have control over helping him, over the knowledge of this bond. I can still get pleasure from small acts of petty vengeance.

"Let her go," Zorria says.

Turning my head in her direction, I lift a brow and shake my head. She's worse than Xander. At least she doesn't hide her hatred for me. There must be a history between Zorria and Rhiannon because I've done nothing except look like Rhiannon—something I can't help. I scoff before taking a bite of food, and notice Lyle has slipped out of the room.

"As much as I hate to admit it, we need her help." Xander responds to Zorria with impatience. His gaze shifts to me, almost pleading. "We need you, Ameris. Need your help to heal our world."

"I'll make a deal with you, Xander. If you take me to see your world—not just the outskirts but the city—explain what I get in return for helping you a second time, show me why I should care, then I'll do whatever you need."

His jaw tenses, giving away his answer before any words leave through his clenched teeth. "It's not that simple, Ameris." His tone changes, going softer. "I cannot show you the capital without the risk of Oberon finding out and coming for you. I don't know what he would do to you, and he is not someone you want to meet. You may not realize it, Ameris, but you are important."

I sit back and stare at him. Those words...I'm not sure how to take them. Am I important because he needs me for my magic, or because I am important to him? If I were important to him, it would only be because of the bond. Not for any other reason.

I've had enough. I walk out of the room and head for the same overlook I found the previous night. I can't stop thinking about Xander.

That kiss has been a slow poison making its way through my

body. His presence is so potent when we're in the same room, especially when he's training, and his heart beats rapidly. I could sense his gaze the other day. It was so palpable, like a weight was placed on my shoulders.

The bond wanted me to acknowledge it, to seek it out, and return in kind, but I ignored it for as long as I could. When I finally turned in his direction, Xander was walking out of the training area.

My gaze lingered too long, admiring his defined and sculpted back muscles, the contours highlighted by a glistening sheen of sweat. I know what his body feels like under my touch, and part of me wants to repeat what happened in the forest.

Ugh. Why do I have to find this fae so attractive?

I'm supposed to hate him, but my body craves his touch and the way he kissed me. While I am physically attracted to him, he is still the one who has caused everything to be taken from me. I'm having a hard time letting that go.

I hold on to the anger because it's the only thing I have. It comes out in the way I speak in clipped tones, in my attitude.

I can't help it. Well...I can. But I don't care to.

The ledge opens up, and I take a breath, centering myself. Clouds gather on the horizon, slowly moving toward one another until they collide. Building the wall that will eventually block out the sun. Their white forms darken as they fill with moisture, preparing for an assault on the land.

"Hello, Ameris." Lyle's melodic voice is as light as a spring breeze. They stand near the ledge, looking out over the forest and land beyond. Lyle's dark green robes sway in the calm wind, gold stitching catching in the sun.

The wind is the kind that warns of what is to come. I've felt it many times as I stood in a similar spot, but with an ocean beyond, watching as a storm formed in the distance. I like Lyle, but there's that feeling again. That something is off about them. They're too quiet, too still, and too calm, as if nothing bothered them about the failure of the rebellion.

"I've used my magic before. It always came when I was in need or had powerful emotions—" I start, but Lyle holds up their hand to silence me.

"This is normal. Our young go through this before they master their magic. The difference here is you can call to them all."

Right. I guess at some point I would have needed to divulge this bit to Lyle. But it would have been on my terms. "I've been told as much. When one of the men that attacked us stole my horse, I was so angry and distraught, using the earth's power came easily." I almost choke on the words; the memory of Honey still raw. "And, well, you saw the fire."

"Each element has a vibration. You will know which element you call to based on how it feels." Lyle turns from the ledge and sits in front of the four basins arranged between us. Each one is filled with a different element: water, dirt, coals, and one that is empty. "Sit. I want you to close your eyes and let your mind find freedom in the quiet. Listen to the wind, feel the sun on your face, focus on your breathing. Let your mind settle."

I fold my legs under me, crossing them, coming to rest across from Lyle on the hard stone. Cold seeps through my pants. I draw in a deep, grounding breath and rest my palms facing upward on my knees.

When they nod, I close my eyes and try to get my mind to settle, which is a lot harder than I expect. It races with the unanswered questions I have—about Rhiannon, about the bond, about my new life here, and what that means for my future.

Questions turn to thoughts of Marguerite and Honey, ones that linger in the deep and dark places of my mind that I've locked away. And even though their loss still haunts me, the immediate pain has subsided. It's a pain I don't mind because it will always remind me of the good things I had.

"Your eyes are moving too much. I can see them rolling

around behind your lids. Focus. Follow my breathing and chant after me."

I actually roll my eyes beneath my lids at Lyle's words. At their verbal exhales, I will my thoughts to stop and follow Lyle's breathwork and chanting. My own breath begins to align with my focus, calming me, settling my mind. A silence falls within, and my body relaxes.

"Good. Much better." A cool hand touches mine. I jerk back from the surprise of the contact. "Keep your eyes closed," Lyle continues, as if they didn't just scare the shit out of me.

Taking my hand, Lyle extends it in front of me and guides it, sweeping over the basins. A distinct vibration resonates as my hand passes over the elements. I've felt them before, but it was distant, echoing within a large void.

"The elements wait for your call. Can you feel them?" Lyle holds my hand steady, "Here, above your hand, is water."

Lyle calls out each element as they continue guiding my hand. It's as if I can grab onto the vibrations and twirl each one between my fingers. Power waiting for me to harness it. Waiting for me to take control and bend its will to mine.

"Yes, I can feel the difference in each element." The elements swirl around, each one hitting my senses. All at once, and yet, each one distinctly courses around me, through me—the sun's fire, the earth's power, the wind's whisper, and the water's ease.

"It will be important for you to remember how each element feels, and how your body reacts to them. To search out those vibrations and pull the thread of their magic to you at will." Lyle places my hand back on my knee.

I keep my eyes closed and breathe in the humid air that threatens rain before moving my hand over the basins without Lyle's guidance. I memorize the unique power of each element, each vibrational pattern. My heart races, then slows, depending on which element I hover over. They meet me in different cadences, like the galloping of the wild horses in the meadowland back home before they slow to a trot, only to take off again.

The power wants me just as much as I want it. Like an early summer day, it slowly takes over—cool at first, until it builds into an intolerable heat that wants to scorch me. I'm brought back to the times I could feel the elements running throughout the land but could never harness the power within. It now makes sense why the tinctures and salves I made with spells were so effective— the magic wanted out. It seeped through any crack it could find.

My veins thrum, ignited with the power that lies within. It's because of him. Bonding myself to him. A tornado of memories raged after I cast the spell. Painful, horrible memories of the day my parents died. Watching in horror from the edge of the forest as they were burned at the stake. Watching my mother chant before the flames engulfed her.

She bound my magic. To protect me. But the blood bond unlocked it. Broke it free of the chains that bound it so tightly. Now, all it wants is freedom—the same freedom I've desired my whole life. An unbound spirit to make my own choices, free from fear of retribution for what I am, what I can do.

And the one I owe this new ability to access my magic to— Xander—is also the one who took everything away. The irony of that doesn't pass me. Of course, it would be this way. As Marguerite would say, it's the give and take of nature. I'm close to losing focus to the dark places that want to slip through and crack me open—the pain of loss that I've shoved away.

"Next, we have fun." Lyle's voice breaks through in my moment of weakness.

When I open my eyes, Lyle is no longer sitting in front of me, but once more at the cliff's edge. And just like that, my thoughts divert away from the home I no longer have. Lyle paces back and forth, head down and eyes closed in concentration.

"Air and water," Lyle utters, followed by, "Fire and earth."

Lyle's next words are intelligible as they speak under their breath. Walking away from the edge, Lyle comes to stand behind me. It makes me uncomfortable. Vulnerable. Before I can speak, they continue. "Do you feel them? How the wind whistles, singing its melody when it blows? How the air moves when you reach out your hand? How water blankets your skin when you sit in it, or how the rain is a comforting call when it falls? How the fire burns, its power strong and fierce? The ground a steady and solid force?"

"Yes, but this magic only came to me once I entered this world. Before..." Words stick, unable to come out.

Before my home burned down, before Marguerite died, and Honey was left behind. Before my world flipped upside down.

I stop myself. *Stop referencing 'before.'* I clear my throat and try again, because all of my befores no longer exist. It all has to stay behind the wall I've built, or all the emotions of everything I lost will consume me.

"I could only cast spells we used in the human world. I couldn't manipulate the elements. But how do you know if fae can only call to one element?" I question, taking in the way Lyle's eyes have glazed over.

"I am also unique. Multi-faceted. Unbound by the conforms of the world. I cannot do magic, but I understand it. My power lies in knowing. In foretelling and in seeing what others cannot." Lyle's gaze is skyward as they speak before flitting back to me.

I'm not sure what to say, so I choose silence, waiting as Lyle circles me, their robes swaying in the wind. The gooseflesh spreading along my skin isn't from the chill creeping closer from the storm on the horizon.

"I know Ameris. I know what you did." In a blur, Lyle is in front of me, grabbing my arm as they pull the sleeve of my shirt back. With their other hand, Lyle traces the fine white lines, scars that start at my palm and run their way down and around my arm, reminders of the blood that ran down our arms when we held them up and I performed the spell. "Blood magic."

Lyle's words send spikes ricocheting through my heart. I jerk my arm back and pull the sleeve down. The wind kicks up, moving the storm closer. Clouds block out the morning sun, darkening the sky. "I don't know what you are talking about."

"Do not lie to me, child. While you may not know the intricacies of why your magic has amplified, you know what spell you performed. You also haven't told Xander the whole truth." Lyle walks away. At the edge of the ledge, they throw their arms out and move each finger slowly, letting air flow between each one. The folds of their robes move violently in the maelstrom that stirs on the horizon.

I know why my magic has amplified, and I know what I did, but that truth doesn't have to be given to anyone else. It's mine to hold on to until I'm ready to give it up.

Lyle's hands clench, fingers curling, as if they are grasping at the very fabric of the air. In a fluid motion, they draw their arms down to their sides.

In response, the storm grows closer, moves faster, and within a matter of minutes, it's upon us, engulfing us in its fury. But Lyle said they couldn't do magic. Did they know this was the moment of approach?

I throw my arms up to shield my face from the violent, howling winds, each gust a physical blow that forces me back. I widen my stance in an attempt to anchor myself to the ground. "Lyle! What are you doing?" I yell over the wind, but it's too loud, or they don't care to hear.

Lyle turns, gaze locked onto me. A devious look and a wicked grin flash before two lightning bolts strike the ground, inches beyond the ledge. I jump on instinct, nearly losing my balance as the resounding crack deafens and the spark of electricity sets my hairs on edge.

Lyle's voice pierces through the storm in a command. "Close your eyes. Let the water fall upon you, and the wind envelop you."

I hesitantly close my eyes as rain falls. Hard, large drops hit every inch of exposed skin. This better be worth it. I'll be furious if I end up soaked for no reason.

"Focus. Remember the vibrations." Lyle's voice is now a soft whisper through the roaring winds.

The only thing I can focus on is how cold I've become. Shifting from foot to foot, uncomfortable in the open, exposed to the storm with no cover, I can barely keep myself standing in the wind.

"You can manipulate the movement of the lightning to strike where you want. From lightning, create the static electricity in the water molecules and make the electrical charge to direct it. Focus on the water." Lyle's voice is closer this time, and I realize they've moved behind me again.

"I can't do this. It's not working." The only thing that I can focus on is the rain hitting my face and the storm's rage getting stronger. The chaos of the storm makes it too hard to pick apart the vibrations to know which one is water. They all separate and merge, over and over, faster than I can process.

"Stretch your magic. You have it within you. Call to your magic; it runs through your veins." Lyle puts their hands on my shoulders to steady me.

I take a deep breath and let go—of trying—because this is pointless. The storm is too distracting. The boom of thunder, closer this time, sends a warning through the air that lightning is close behind. Within seconds, the sky cracks as light flickers in the darkness behind my lids.

A memory sparks, and I'm dragged into it unwillingly as the bodies of my parents appear. I've mastered not thinking about that day. Separated what happened from the way I used to have nightmares every time a storm came through our village.

But I can't escape the hold it has on me now—how intricately it's tied to my magic. My parents are tied to a stake, hungry flames licking their way up the pyre they stand on. Mother is chanting, and the last look she gives me crushes my heart as lightning comes crashing down.

As the bolt strikes, a clap rocks the ground, breaking the hold the memory has on me. My eyes jolt open, and I shudder, heart racing. Exhaustion rolls through my muscles, which twitch in response to the exertion of trying to force the magic to my will. And I'm emotionally spent from re-witnessing that day.

I shove Lyle off, walk away, and find shelter within the cavern.

CHAPTER 23

XANDER

Drops of sweat hit the floor in rhythm with the push-ups I work through, pushing my body hard, hoping the physical exertion will distract me from the conversation I had with Ameris yesterday, but it's futile. Since we've arrived, our weeks have been spent apart.

She trains with Zeke and Lyle while I am wrapped up in planning with Jesper. I only see her when we share meals, and that never goes well.

Keeping my return and her arrival in Solarium hidden is crucial to the success of the rebellion. We must keep the element of surprise on our side, something she doesn't seem to appreciate.

Grunting from the effort, I hold the last pushup until my muscles scream in protest, allowing the pain to linger a torturous moment longer before I release the tension. Rising, I swipe away the beads of sweat trailing from my temples.

Though the silence of this place, the empty cavern, settles me, I'm not done. I need more distraction. I can't get her out of my head. Ameris must see she's vital to our plans, to taking back the throne. There is benefit for her in helping. She will be free to walk the city, to travel this world, to discover its treasures.

But she can't do that with Oberon in charge.

I approach the weapons, scanning the array. The bow calls to me. My fingers close around the smooth, polished wood like no time has passed since I've held one. I lift the bow and nock an arrow, drawing the string back. Aligning the bow with the target, I fire shot after shot like the flow of thoughts that won't stop. Finally, the thrum of the bow snapping drowns out my thoughts.

As fate loves to play games, just as I get her out of my head, she physically shows up. Ameris's voice breaks through as I nock the last arrow and let it fly. "Impressive. Where's Zeke?"

Turning, I take in the way she has her arms crossed, how her hair is pulled back and tied up in a loose bun, the tight fit of her clothing. She came ready to train. Now is as good a time as any; it's not like my efforts to stop thinking about her were going to last. I hand over the bow. "He won't be around today. I'll be training with you instead. Here. Try."

"There is no trying. I know how to use this." Snatching it for my grip, she nocks an arrow and pulls back, letting it fly. She winces and rolls the shoulder that was injured.

Not a perfect shot, but the target's hit. I fold my arms over my chest in a show of indifference, even if I am impressed. The cavern walls pulse with energy, feeding off the tension between us. Unsaid words linger between us as she shoots a few more arrows, each one hitting the target.

"We should get a healer to look at your shoulder." I offer.

Ameris puts the bow down and turns to me. "I'll be fine. I don't want to train with you."

"If you're fine, then let's play a game. How many times can you get a hit in? I know you want to." I walk to the mat in the middle of the room and motion her toward me.

In response, she raises an eyebrow, a devious smirk playing on her features. "I suppose."

I want to elicit a reaction—any response—to get her talking, so I make the first move, slow enough for her to block my advance, which she does easily. Good. Not that I doubted Zeke's training, but I'm glad to confirm she is taking it in. Even if she doesn't have our speed, she can counter with accuracy and expectation. Ameris throws a left jab, which I block with ease, moving behind her. She whips around, her fist coming with the pivot, and a hit that lands on my jaw.

My head snaps to the left as her hand recedes. She hit harder than I'd expected. I crack my neck, ready to go again. "Huh. One."

"What? You doubted I could hit you? I know you're moving slower than you can." Ameris plants a hand firmly on her hip, her posture speaking for her as one of her brows arch upward.

"No. It was a good move. I didn't expect it," I respond, hands open in truthful surrender.

"You should remember that. I'll likely always surprise you." She advances again, faster this time.

We enter a dance of movement, twirling around each other, exchanging blows. Each strike I throw is met with a parry. I'm not fighting with her like I would Zorria, but she's doing well with what Zeke's been training her on. It's his style, and I'm familiar with it, able to anticipate her moves. But she's determined, and her attacks keep coming with more force.

I jump back just in time as Ameris lunges forward, a snarl contorting her features. Her right fist cuts through the air, its trajectory aimed at my face. It hisses past, a rush of air kissing my skin. I snatch her wrist before she pulls her arm in and twist it behind her, forcing her back against my chest. Each one of her laborious breaths rises and falls against my body. She struggles against my grasp, but I hold firm.

The loose hair from her buns tickles my face as I lean down and whisper in her ear. "One."

Ameris shoves me off as I release her, throwing a punch to the gut as she faces me. I cough and then laugh. She curtsies with a glare. "Two. Stop playing nice."

"Your wish is my command." I shift tactics and go on the offense, coming after her one swift strike after another. We move in tandem with each other, exchanging blows but never landing one on the other. Ameris's frustration is mounting. There is palpable tension in the way she holds herself and expels her breaths harshly. She throws another sharp jab, but I easily catch it and twist her arm behind her back, knowing it will aggravate her already injured shoulder. A pained cry escapes from her as she struggles against my hold. "You need to have this healed."

"No," she says through gritted teeth, and snaps her head back with such force that it slams into my face. I release my hold and grunt out as pain shoots through my face.

"Why let it pain you when we have the means to fix it?" I chide.

"This is pointless. I'm not learning anything." Ameris walks off the mat and grabs a goblet of water without answering my question.

"At least you're training and learning. Even if it's not what you want." I suck in air through my teeth, knowing that was the wrong thing to say. Of course it's not what she wants.

Ameris stops mid-drink, her jaw clenching, before she storms back over to me, yelling, "Are you serious right now?"

"I shouldn't have said that." The words are softer than I would speak to anyone else.

"Damn right you shouldn't have said that." She throws the cup at me, hitting my knee.

"Three." I try to turn the conversation around with a light joke. She exhales a long breath.

"I haven't gotten what I want since the day you came into my life. I wish I'd never noticed that ship on the horizon. I wish I would have left you there, where you probably deserved to be."

Ameris's anger is tangible, like a fine mist hanging in the air, but I also sense a tinge of regret within.

It is still a stab to the heart. I didn't want what happened either, but she doesn't see that. Her judgment of past events is shrouded by her anger and grief. Ameris walks back and forth along the edge of the arena, moving and stopping multiple times as if she wants to say more. Her facial expressions morph between thoughts, each one a marker of the emotions swirling within.

"Ameris..."

She raises a hand to stop me as I try to speak. Even though she is the one who saved me, she blames me for everything, taking none of the responsibility. I was not the sole decider of her fate, and that flares my irritation at her words.

"You... You..." Each word is accompanied by a hesitation and a finger pointing in my direction. Accusatory.

"Don't forget you made the first choice. I'm not sorry you're here, but I am for what happened." I narrow the distance between us, my own irritation fueling me. The air surrounding us seems to crackle with energy. A proper fight is brewing, ready to erupt to the surface from our pent-up emotions.

"No, you don't get to do that. You don't get to apologize for it." Angry tears fall, trailing down her reddened cheeks as she strides back and forth again.

At a loss for words, I stand there, giving her the time she needs to think, to process whatever is going on in her mind. She comes close to me before walking away again. It's like she wants to say something, but words cannot make their escape.

The next time she approaches, she looks up at me. My heart breaks at the desperation, grief, anger, and hate within her green irises. Sadness takes over the irritation that was just flooding through me.

She's lost everything, while I got back what I wanted. So caught up in my own needs, I've forgotten hers. Her fists clench at her sides before she unleashes a volley of fierce punches against my chest.

"It's all your fault." Ameris's hair shakes loose with each punch, falling into her face and around her shoulders.

Each blow is weaker than the one before it, slowing to ones that have no energy behind them. Her arms go slack, and she falls into me.

Hot tears splash against my shirt.

"Ameris." Barely louder than a whisper, I speak her name. My hand gently strokes her hair. Hesitantly, I drape an arm around her shoulder, unsure if this is what she wants, but she doesn't pull away.

"Why did she leave me?" Ameris can barely get the words out as sobs wrack her body.

"She was protecting you. Giving you the chance to escape." I shift, rubbing the back of my neck before wrapping my other arm around her shoulder.

My people rarely show our emotions like this. We are too full of pride. Emotions are for the weak, and so we internalize them. But, in this moment, I can see myself after I lost my father. Wanting to rage and cry at the same time.

"But it didn't matter because they caught up to us. And now Honey is gone." She shudders, leaning her head into my chest.

"She couldn't have known that. She loved you very much and would do anything to protect you. Even making me promise that I would protect you. My kind doesn't do that lightly." I pull her into me, holding her tighter.

There is no more space between our bodies as her arms wrap around my waist and she burrows into me. Her closeness, the touch of her hand against my skin, soothes me.

I breathe deep, at odds with the way this feels. Whether it's my promise to Marguerite or the feeling of responsibility for what's occurred, I want to take care of her. To take away all the pain.

Our hearts beating in tandem fills the space of our silence. Her breathing evens out, the rise and fall of her back becoming steady.

"Will you take me to my room? I'm exhausted. I don't think I have it in me to move."

"Of course." I easily scoop her up and cradle her body against mine. Her eyes flutter closed as she leans her head against my shoulder and rests a palm against my chest.

She almost looks at peace except for the slight pull of her brows and the redness coating the skin around her eyes. As I carry her down the corridors, I'm struck by how much I'm drawn to her, even in this short amount of time.

She saved me. Risked and lost everything. What captivates me is her ability to hold her own and doesn't back down; she speaks her mind and challenges me. It rattles me because I shouldn't want this. Want her. Even if we can offer each other mutual benefits.

The door to her room pushes open easily. Her bed is made, and it's tidy in here, something I don't expect. Shifting her weight, I bend with Ameris still in my arms and pull the covers back before gently laying her down. I lay the blanket over her and turn off the lantern by her bed. Her hand grabs mine as I turn to leave.

A whisper floats in the room's silence. "Lie with me."

The whisper might have been my own thoughts or Ameris speaking, so I stand beside her bed, uncertain. Unmoving. She tugs at my hand—an invitation. I sit on the edge of the bed. "Are you sure?"

"No." Ameris turns her back to me and pulls the covers over her shoulders.

My hand is on the latch, ready to exit, when she speaks again.

"Wait." She slides over to make room for me, patting the space next to her.

I don't question her again because I want to be near her. I feel comfortable in her presence, a soothing song to my soul. So, I lay back, putting one hand under my head. I pull in a deep breath before slowly releasing it, trying to release the tension that's burrowed its way into my body.

Ameris lays a hand on my bare chest. "Relax."

Her hand against my skin sends tiny sparks of delight that dance among my heart, but it keeps my body tense. She gets up and goes to the washroom, the sound of running water muted through the closed door.

Putting on my shirt was not a thought while we were training, but now it is my only thought as I lie here and wait for her. I should leave, but she might need me to stay.

She is in this world alone, and everything is new to her. I weigh whether leaving will cause a wider divide between us. I debate too long with myself as she returns a few minutes later with fresh clothes on.

Unpinning her hair, she gets back into bed. It doesn't take long before I run my fingers through her hair, a melodic movement that eases the tightness in my chest.

I'm attracted to Ameris, but she's human. This could never work. I shouldn't have lingered; shouldn't have lain down.

Yet, my restraint is testing me. Wanting to kiss her again, like that day in the forest. "Ameris...we're toeing the edge of a dangerous game."

"Show me how you'd win."

She sits up and is on top of me quicker than I can process. I go still as she places both of her hands on my bare chest without looking at me. I grip the sides of her thighs as she languidly starts moving her fingers around the curve of my pecs, up my sternum, and back down, circling my nipples.

She rolls her hips, and my cock hardens at her movements.

"Ameris—" I grunt out.

Her eyes flit up to my face, and she puts a finger to my lips. "You're losing right now, Xander. What is your move? I'm ordering you to distract me and win."

I flip her over and lock gazes with her. Ameris raises a brow and nods. I ease a breath out and hesitate as I look into her eyes.

She wants this.

I want this.

Yet, I know this might not be the best moment. Lust wins over logic, and I bring my lips against her neck. Ameris leans away, exposing more of her skin, which I greedily devour, planting kisses along the exposed length of it.

She inhales deeply before letting a breath go.

I kiss the corner of her mouth gently, teasing her. She lets out a grunt and pulls my head to meet her fully, and I claim her in this moment. My tongue parts her lips, and she opens for me, hands in my hair, pulling me deeper into the kiss. I explore while I untie the laces of her pants.

She arches her back as I slide the smooth fabric over her hips, discarding them on the floor. My hand roams the soft skin of her hips, trailing the line of her pelvis, to the soft skin of her inner thigh. She breathes into me through our kiss.

"Tell me to stop," I rasp, pulling away, but she shakes her head.

"Your distraction isn't good enough yet."

It's permission. And I take it.

I move my lips down the line of her stomach, and when I reach the apex of her opening, I spread her thighs wide, putting my mouth against her clit. I suck gently, and she draws in a sharp breath as her fingers grasp my hair. I sweep my tongue back and forth over her flesh, giving her what she wants. For every panting breath of hers, I take my own pleasure in the way she's crying out.

She lets out one final cry before releasing a long exhale, along with my hair. "There's one more unconquered, very wet spot."

I kiss her forehead and lay next to her. "Strategy dictates I save that for next time."

She curls into me, and neither one of us say anything. Time passes as I listen to the steady rise and fall of her breaths. I turn and look at the peaceful rest that has fallen over her. Her face is a smooth canvas.

"Ameris, she made me promise to protect you." It's the one right thing I can say. To let her know I will honor my promise to Marguerite.

"Hum?" Her sleepy response is an indication that she didn't hear what I said. I wait until she's in a deep slumber, then remove her head from my chest and gently lay it on the pillow. She stirs, turning in the other direction, but she otherwise doesn't move. I fix the covers before I walk out of her room and down the hall to my own.

I already miss the warmth of her body next to mine as I lay in my cold bed.

CHAPTER 24
AMERIS

My hand slides along the bed, coming back to me empty. Rolling to my side, I open my eyes and blink away the blurry room. I should have expected this. But there was a small hope that he had stayed.

As much as I didn't want to cave—not just because of the bond—I did, and I very much enjoyed the release he gave me. Because even though I hate him, I can't help my attraction to him.

Kicking out the thoughts before they bury too deep, I remind myself he gave me what I wanted last night—what I needed. A distraction. That's all.

Getting up, I grab my satchel from the table in front of the couch. Water and food sit on a tray next to it. So, I missed breakfast—not that I cared to join. I'm stuck in these caves. Like a caged bird that can stretch its wings, but only so far. The silence of my room eases the nerves that fire off around Xander and his friends.

I pull the grimoire out and run my hand along the aged spine and across the decorative cover, tracing the details. Plopping down on the couch, I open it and study spells while I eat my breakfast. I read through the spells, studying them.

Now that I have access to elemental magic, can I fuse it with human magic and create my own unique magic—a union of spell and element? Magic that would give me an edge.

In the human world, I struggled with even basic spells, but the ones I've tried since being here come easily. Flicking my wrist, I ignite the wood in the hearth, sparking a fire to life.

I always wondered why Marguerite was so pushy, keeping me engaged in crafting spells. She knew I had it in me—that one day I could perform magic like no one else. After hours of reading through spells and running through the incantations in my head, I put the book away. Stretching, I get up and bathe before leaving my room.

I walk along the cave's corridors, feeling for air pockets, anything that might lead me to an opening—a place where I can escape.

Even though part of me wants to be near Xander, I won't allow him or his friends to trap me in these caves like I was trapped in my village. All I find are light shafts, open to the sky above. I end up in the main cavern, where everyone sits around a table with a decadent meal spread out in the middle.

Xander's gaze latches onto mine, his icy blue depths giving nothing away. Not even a crack that would give me insight into how he feels about last night.

Maybe he doesn't want anyone to know. Definitely a dangerous game that two can play.

"We'll be going into the woods tomorrow to scout. Lyle will be around if you need anything," he says.

I nod. I've told myself I should be more talkative and responsive, but when the time comes, simple replies are all I can manage. Because even though we want each other, there's still tension between us. Whenever we try to talk to each other, it's like there's a veil I struggle to see past.

I know it's my fault, but I cannot help it—it just happens because I'm too scared to let the veil fall. Too afraid of what I would do without him as my outlet.

It is not okay, and I know that, but time will be the only healer of my heart. Or so I hope.

"Ameris, how is your training coming along?" Jesper asks.

The sound of another's voice releases the tension coiled within me. Grabbing a plate, I fill it with roasted vegetables, buttered breads, and spiced potatoes. Everyone watches my movement, waiting to see which of the two empty seats I will take. Judgment is something I expect from them. I sit across from Jesper, as far away from Xander as I can. Might as well give them something to talk about.

"Zeke's a great trainer. If every day ends with me being sore, then I think he's doing his job well." The easy laugh slips out, genuine, and I wink at Zeke. And it is true; I have been learning a lot from him. "He's teaching me defensive moves and ways to disarm anyone who tries to keep me restrained. We went through training drills to build my stamina and endurance."

Zeke smiles and nods, his curls bouncing at the movement as he takes a bite of his roll. There is a light chuckle from the group, but otherwise, the food keeps their attention. I'm unstable to them, a fuse ready to blow.

They aren't wrong. Zeke told me that since fae have abilities humans don't, we have to train harder to give me some advantage. He's made it clear that I will never be as fast or as strong as the fae, but that doesn't mean I'm helpless.

"And Lyle has been helping with your magic?" Jesper inquires, cutting through a piece of cured meat.

"Oh. Yes, that...They have." I notice Lyle isn't present. When I entered the hall, I could have sworn I saw them. "I have been learning a lot."

"Good." Jesper gently nods, satisfied with my answers.

I like Jesper; he reminds me of the village elder, the one who knows everything going on, but still inquires. The one that cares about how everyone is doing, but can put someone in their place as quick as a lightning strike. He reminds me of the father I wish I still had. The one I can barely remember, who was taken too soon.

Pouring myself a goblet of wine, I take a long drink. Its sweet and tart flavor hitting my tongue makes it easy. I have a lot of ghosts that haunt me—ones I haven't laid to rest. I hold on to them to make sure I remember what it feels like to lose something. To know what it feels like to wish you had something that was taken from you.

To remember what it's like to feel in the first place.

Taking another drink, I finish what's left in one gulp and refill it. I don't have to glance around the room to know everyone's eyes are on me, watching me. That, I can feel. Because they know my human body handles the wine differently. I've had a glass here and there, but nothing like that first day. I've worked myself into drinking the fae wine. Zeke told me to add elderberries in order to dull the effects. How he knows that, I don't want to know.

I listen as they discuss strategies to gain the numbers they need to fight against Oberon. Picking at my meal, I take in each of their faces, etched with determination, even though each word uttered is heavy with a sense of uncertainty and dread.

About whether fae will return after their past failure, and the reality that this will cause conflict, a battle even. Xander chugs his third glass of wine. He must need it as much as I do.

My third glass of wine goes down too smoothly. It's gone sooner than it should have been. But then conversation turns to me—how people will receive me. What they think is the best way I can use my magic against Oberon. Now it makes sense why he's avoided my gaze.

Of course, I'm not asked once how I feel about any of it.

"Will she be ready?" Jesper asks.

Xander's voice is somber when he finally looks at me. "She has to."

"I am sitting here, you know." My words are venomous. I've had enough of being talked about as if I'm not at the table. I stand up, but unfortunately, that has become harder after three glasses of wine. My eyes betray me as I awkwardly push the chair back and stumble to the side.

Zeke reaches his hand out to steady me, but I reject him. "I'm fine."

I grab a full bottle of wine, taking it with me, and move around Zeke. The room tilts sideways at my next step. Xander flinches as I grab the back of his chair, righting myself. I wave my hand behind me as I take my leave. By now, I know where I am going in these dark and lonely caves.

Each languid step is a chore. Every few feet, my heavy limbs catch on the cold stone, jolting me one way or the other. My eyes lose focus, and I move as if through a dream, searching for the place I know exists.

"Ameris!" My name echoes along the barren walls in a voice I prefer not to hear right now.

"Yes?" I slur out.

"Let me walk you to your room." Xander's words are distant yet so close.

"I don't need your help. I'm just buzzed, not drunk." The words come out harsher than I intend, but I guess that's the truth in the wine.

"I know you don't need it." He whispers as he puts his hand low on my back.

My body shivers at his contact—not from the cool air flowing in this corridor, but from the feeling that comes from him touching me. From the memory of our kiss. Of last night, and his lips on my body. His heartbeat pulses faster, and my stupid heart skips a beat in return, bringing with it the butterflies that ricochet around in my gut.

The stupid bond—that has to be it, because I wouldn't be able to stand being around him without it. I'm sure of it. At least, that's what I keep telling myself.

"I'm not going to my room. I'm going outside because I need some fresh air." Slipping out of his touch, I continue my graceless walk to the cliff's edge, where I first trained with Lyle.

"Ameris." Xander's voice floats from behind me, open and inviting.

I ignore it. Fight it.

The passage opens to the place I want to be. The cool air covers me like an early spring wind, and it takes everything in me to stop the tears from falling.

Then he does it again—he touches me. It's gentle, a light brushing of his fingers on my bicep, an unspoken ask that I stop moving closer to the edge.

But instead of comfort, I can't help but jerk my arm from under his touch. Coldness rushes in where his warmth was.

"Why do you do that? You act like I repulse you, but what was last night?" Xander shouts at me in frustration.

"I don't know." The only answer I can give. Because I don't know. Everything is wrong. I inch toward where the earth abruptly ends, drops off, and surrenders to the black emptiness beyond. A huff of amusement escapes at how this is where I find comfort. I sit down and dangle my legs over the edge.

Xander sits beside me and drops his head into his hands, running them through his auburn hair. The moment I put the bottle down between us, he picks it up and takes a drink. He offers me a bundled napkin in exchange—an offering. I take it and unwrap the crumpled fabric. A handful of elderberries lay within.

When I look at him, he shrugs. "I figured you could eat them, and it would help. Now you can drink more."

He lifts the bottle in a mock toast before setting it down between us. I pop a few elderberries into my mouth. They aren't over-sweet, the perfect balance between tart and earthy, with a finish. I take another drink of wine before eating the last few elderberries. It amazes me how this fruit can have a countereffect on the wine and how quickly it works.

Sighing, I hand the wine to Xander. It's a weak attempt to bridge the gap between us. Silence surrounds us. Not even the wind or the murmurings of animals reach us as we pass the wine back and forth.

Awkward tension floats in the way we refuse to acknowledge the other, both gazing to the stars and back to the dark landscape stretching out before us. The crescent moon doesn't provide much light, and I'm rather enjoying the dark, cool night. Yet, I find myself stuck between hating him and liking him.

It's worse knowing the bond complicates my feelings; never sure of what is organic or simply the magic of the bond.

A flash of light interrupts my ruminations. Xander is playing with globs of water, moving them between his hands and fingers. What light reaches us catches in the clear liquid, sending flashes of light into the night. It's mesmerizing.

"Try it," he says as he looks at me. "Call to whichever element you want. Control the flow of it and bring it to your palms."

"I don't think I can." I hesitate, taking another drink of the wine.

"You can. Talk me through what you are feeling. I will help guide you." He sends a glob in my direction. It floats in front of me for a few moments before he sends it over the edge and releases it, letting it fall.

I close my eyes and open myself to the surrounding energy—the air vibrating more rapidly than it should, wanting to be used. I pull it to me, and the magic floods, making me gasp.

"Talk to me, Ameris." His voice is soft against the rigid rush of magic.

"I can feel the magic pulsing, but it rushes in, coming all at once. I don't know how to control it—to only take a little. It's like it wants me to use it."

"The magic is responding to you. It's good that it comes to you easily. Now, find the place where the magic enters, and slowly close yourself off. The magic will resist, but you must exert your control. Hold on to a bit of the magic and tell me when you've done so." Xander instructs.

As I search within myself and slowly push against the magic, it resists, wants to rage, and I struggle to wrangle it, but it eventually caves to my control. "I have it."

"Now, make what you want from the element; form the image in your mind. If you want wind, conjure the image of a cyclone. If you want fire, conjure the image of a flame. You are clenching your fist. Open them, and open your eyes; allow the magic to live within your palm."

My eyelids and fists open in unison. Nothing happens.

"Focus. Breathe," Xander reassures me.

I let go of my inhibitions and fear of failure, and with that release, sparks of light flash. And there, sitting in my palms, are lightning bolts, flickering in and out as they spark within the air. They're smaller than I thought they would be, and my expression sours.

CHAPTER 25

XANDER

I chuckle at her disappointment. "Let in some more of your magic, but slowly. Cut it off when you're satisfied."

The lightning bolts grow, and she lets them bounce back and forth between her hands as she laughs. The sound coming from her is pure delight. And this time, I helped it come about. I watch her play for a moment. Her eyes sparkle, and a smile plasters her face from ear to ear. "I knew you could do it," I say. "You should laugh more often. I like it."

"Thank you." She laughs again before the silence returns between us.

"Anytime." I smile back in earnest, offering a gesture of friendship and hoping it shows her how much I care. She shoots a lightning bolt at me, its jagged edges sparking in the night before stinging my arm. Laughter takes over. I throw a side eye and return a jet of water. The other bolt of lightning fizzles out as the liquid douses it.

"Hey!" She shoves me to the side and shakes the water off her hand.

"Try a different element." Leaning back, I support my weight on one arm and take another drink of wine. "There is enough for one more pass." I extend the bottle, but she shakes her head, so I down the rest.

The stars and moon are the only light until an orange flicker appears in my peripheral. Fire licks back and forth between her hands. She turns to me, the excitement stripped from her face, replaced by a heavy look.

"Marguerite..." Her eyes go glassy, and water pools, tears threatening to fall as she continues. "Do you think she..."

I straighten and reach out instinctively, rubbing my hand along her back before she can finish. "She knew what she was doing."

Ameris's head drops, hanging limp, and the fire dancing in her hands goes out. She covers her face, and her words come out muffled. "How do you do that? Act like things aren't a big deal?"

Leaning back again, I shift my gaze to the forest beyond the cliffs before I respond. "I've lived a long time. Death is a part of life, and we all must face it. They teach us not to fear death. To sacrifice yourself for a loved one is the ultimate gift. And again, she made me promise to protect you."

I look at her, knowing she heard me this time, but is choosing to ignore it. Ameris doesn't want my promise to Marguerite. But though she might not want it, I gave my word to someone, and I will honor it, even after death.

"So, you didn't care when your father was murdered in front of you?" The shift in her tone is immediate. She crosses her arms, her body going rigid under the weight of the accusation.

Sighing, I take a moment to respond, not wanting to say the wrong thing. "Of course I cared."

"Your great fae strength must have kept you from feeling. You know, that explains why you don't understand what I'm going through." Her eyes go cold, and her jaw hardens.

"I hate that you have to be in a place you dislike so much—that being around me reminds you of what you lost. But we need you. I need you." The tenor in my voice shifts with the frustration that mounts again.

We can never have a normal conversation. It always turns heated, always ends poorly, and this one is heading in that direction too. I understand to an extent, but that is a battle I won't win. I'm trying to give her the time to open up and tell me what she wants. But she ignores and avoids me.

"That's just it, though. You need me. Yet, you haven't involved me, and you're deciding for me. I'm not the type of girl that lets a man make my choices." Ameris stares at me, anger rising at what I assume she thinks is my lack of understanding. "You send me off to be trained by other people and barely talk to me. Then, when I am around, you talk over me. You don't do that to Zorria. I see how you act around her. You respect her. You don't respect me."

"You are now the one misunderstanding, Ameris. I have known Zorria for decades, just as I have known Jesper and Zeke. We grew up together and have fought together. Our friendship runs deep. They are like family to me," I explain, but she gets up and walks away. I won't let her walk away again, not this time. Not without first really hearing me.

"But you involve her in the plans. I am only told what you want me to know. If I am so important to your plans, I should be involved in the planning. I'm at my breaking point in these caves. I need to be above ground!" she shouts, the words echoing in the night air.

"We can't do that. Humans are vulnerable to fae influence, and if anything happens to you, our secrets would be no more. Our plans ruined." She wants the one thing I cannot give her. True freedom.

The reality is, right now, she is a caged guest. And there is nothing to be done about it. "If anyone sees you, they will take you to Oberon. Why do you not get that?" I'm almost upon her, ready to pull her toward me, shake her by the shoulders, and force her to understand.

"I do get it!" Ameris spits out. She turns around and stops short. We're inches from each other. "I know that, but do you truly have no way of masking me? Why can't we go into the forest? You can't keep me in these caves forever."

Her shoulders sink, and she looks to be on the verge of crying. "It's too much of a risk. How many—"

"You cannot keep me here Xander!" she cuts me off. "Being restricted to one place brings me back to when I was stuck in that village. I had to hide who I was, hide my magic. Please don't do that to me."

Ameris moves past me, returning to the edge before kicking the wine bottle. It flies into the air and disappears from view. "I'm no stranger to being in dangerous situations. I'm not a damsel in distress who needs protection."

"Ameris." I grab her arm, pulling her back. When she turns to me, our faces are so close, I can feel her breath on my skin. I hold her shoulders, look down into her green eyes flecked with gold, then sweep across her features. She makes me blaze with frustration, yet when I'm around her, I feel more alive than I have in a long time. "I know you can take care of yourself."

Ameris places her hands flat against my chest. Looking up at me, her gaze is intense, and it's in that depth, I see the truth she buries.

She feels something for me too.

Snapping like frozen branches, she breaks the moment and looks to the forest beyond the cliff. I place my hand along her cheek and bring her focus back to me. I groan. "Please. Can we not fight? There are other things I would rather do with you."

Ameris's breath hitches as I lower my face and trace the outline of her mouth with my thumb. I want to kiss her again, but I wait for her response. The seconds stretch longer than possible, the anticipation eating away at me.

She leans in, torturously close, her lips a phantom touch against mine, and whispers, "I'd rather you compliment my intelligence. Include me in the decision-making and take me to see something other than these caves."

Ameris removes her hands from my chest and steps back, leaving me on the cliff's edge. Immediately, I'm struck by the coldness of the night that replaces her presence. I step forward to follow, but hesitate. There is no reason to. She leaves me in the cold, in the dark, as she's swallowed by the cave's mouth. She doesn't want my help and can hardly stand my presence. If only she would let go of her anger and see that I'm trying to protect her. I run a hand down my face and blow out a frustrated breath.

Jesper's voice fills the space that Ameris just occupied. "What did you do?"

I tell him everything. I have no reason to hide what happened with Ameris. He slaps my back and gives a low whistle. "She'll come around."

Running my fingers through my hair, I sigh. "She's impossible, and I like her for it. She challenges me in ways I've never been challenged. Before Rhiannon's banishment, she chose me as the next ruler. Everyone followed my orders without question."

"Ameris has a point. We should include her in the meetings. She needs to know how important this is and what is at stake. Have you taken her to the wastes?" Jesper responds in a knowing tone, goading me. He knows I haven't taken her anywhere and why.

"You know it is too much of a risk. Even if we use glamour, the guards could still recognize us. There are wards throughout the city to protect against glamour. I'm concerned she will fall into the hands of Oberon. That would be our end before we could begin, and right now, we have the element of surprise with my return and Ameris's power." Jesper has been around for centuries and has seen many wars. I trust his advice, but this is something I am not willing to budge on. Ameris is too important to risk.

"Take her. She needs to see it for herself. Xander, look at me. She is not the type to be kept stationary for too long and not be involved. She brought you home. You owe her." Jesper makes a demand I cannot deny.

"I know." My words come out clipped. Everything is riding on her, but I want to make sure she is ready when the time comes. Oberon has been alive and living with his magic for over four times her life span. All of this is new to her, and I am trying to protect her for as long as I can.

Sighing, I turn to Jesper. "I know I need to take her. I will when we get back from scouting."

CHAPTER 26
AMERIS

Under any other circumstance, I would want to kiss Xander with every fiber of my being. I have nothing else to say to him that won't end in an argument, ruining the nice evening we've had. It comes out of nowhere, the outbursts and mood swings.

Words leave before my brain can process that I should stop them. I'm well aware that it is mostly me causing our arguments. I need to get a grip. Accept that it's also my fault. And, of all things, he made a promise to protect me. Even if we didn't have this bond, he would fight for me.

"Ugh." I've been an asshole to him. I stop walking and lean into the wall to steady myself, releasing a long, shaky breath. Taking a few moments, I inhale and exhale deeply, recentering myself before continuing down the corridor.

But it is all too much—losing Marguerite and Honey, learning to control magic—especially bonding myself to someone forever. It was necessary to escape the human world, but now I have a piece of me that will forever be controlled by the blood bond that connects us. It will always force me to consider him and to want to be near him.

Even though life wasn't the best in my village, I had a sense of stability, and that is gone. I can't seem to find my balance anymore. What I want my role to be and who I want to be.

Again, the bond will dictate parts of those decisions, and I hate that. I've only ever wanted to have the opportunity to make my own choices.

What makes it all worse is that I know Xander won't include me in the plans because, in his eyes, being a human isn't good enough. Has he even thought of training me on the tactics of this so-called fae influence that would have me babbling like the old maidens in town who tell everyone's business the minute they find it out? Likely not.

So, my prickliness feels justified. Although his crew makes the caves feel like a home with how they've decorated, there are people and things I want to leave in the past.

Zeke approaches with his usual chipper attitude, but I can't deal with it right now. He smiles when he sees me, a joke ready to be released when we get close enough, but I beat him to it. Raising a hand to stop him. "Don't."

"But you're walking all wonky. Even if it's in silence, can I walk you back to your room?" Genuine concern seeps from him as he walks next to me.

"No. I'm fine," I say more forcefully than I need to.

His face falls, but he nods and falls back. Zeke feels like my only friend here, if I can even call him that. Accepting his help would have been the smart thing to do. Oh well.

The path to my room is now muscle memory. The wine's influence surfaces as I trip and bump into the wall. It happens more than once before I reach my destination.

Closing the door behind me, I lean against it, my head falling back against the wood. The moment I'm alone in the silence of my room, my breaths become erratic, and the more I try to control them, the worse it gets. There isn't enough air to feed my hungry lungs.

My chest tightens, and my body trembles, shifting between hot and cold.

A dryness forms in my throat, begging for water.

Thoughts swirl.

Pulsing between blaming myself for everything, hating everyone, and wanting to disappear forever.

They don't stop there.

They flit rapidly between things I wish I could unsee.

Marguerite. Honey. Home. The men in the forest. Blood. Lies.

My body fails me, my legs giving out, and I crumple to the floor in a heap, letting the hot, angry tears fall. They stream down my face, one unrelenting wave after another. Crying is something that has been happening more often than I want. I am suffocating, losing it, and I don't know how to breathe under the weight I bear.

I need to leave this place. I have to get out. I don't care what happens to me. Maybe Xander will learn to care once I'm gone.

I talk myself into breathing slowly before I pass out from hyperventilating.

One, in...

Two, out...

Three, in...

Repeating the count until my body relaxes and my breathing steadies, I crawl to my bed and climb in. The sheets envelop me like a hug. One last thought escapes before darkness takes over. I can't help it; it slips past my barriers in this fragile state—Xander's lips so close to mine.

Some time later, voices echo outside my door, coaxing me from sleep before fading. Unlike the memories of last night that come flooding back, accompanied by a pounding that settles between my eyes. My mouth morphs into the desert, dry and in desperate need of water. I sit up and immediately regret it.

Pain flares as if little pins want to push out from behind my forehead. Moving my fingers under my brows helps, kind of. Dressing is a chore; it takes forever to put on a shirt and pants. A wave of nausea floods through me as I bend over to put my boot on. Picking up the grimoire, I leave my room to find something to fill my empty stomach.

The cool air from the corridors soothes the heat under my skin. I'm delighted to see a table of food when I enter the war room. Xander tracks my movement until Zorria elbows him, and he returns to the conversation he's having with her and Lyle. Jesper is at the head of the table, filing through reports, likely coming up with more strategies.

"Is there any food that will cure the pounding in my head?" I take the seat across from Zeke, who can't keep the delight from his face at my discomfort. I plant an elbow on the table and lean my head into my hand, rubbing my temple as I push a fork around, deciding if I want to eat or go back to sleep.

Zorria snorts. I shoot her a glance, and she shrugs. "If you can't handle the wine, don't drink it."

Xander tenses, knowing I'm about to throw an insult, baiting Zorria for a fight—physical or verbal. Jesper pauses, raising his head to watch us. My hand tightens around the fork I was playing with. I contemplate throwing it at her, but I settle for words. "If you can't handle me being here, you can leave."

Before she can respond, Jesper speaks, his voice a command. "Enough."

"I'll get something for you." Zeke jumps up from his seat, chuckling as he walks away. I can barely stand the sound of the others talking when he returns. "Here, this will set you right. Don't drink so much next time."

My nose pinches, and I stick my tongue out at him, snatching the vial from his hand. I can't help but smile at him, however. "Thank you. What is it?"

"A cure. Just don't smell it." Zeke goes back to eating as he watches me twirl the vial. The dark green liquid swirls with gold and black. It looks like poison, not a cure. If Zorria had given it to me, I would suspect as much, but I trust Zeke.

I plug my nose and down the contents. My hand flies up to my mouth, barely able to hold it in. The back of my throat burns as if I've just swallowed acid, ripping through my insides before settling in my stomach.

"You could've…told…me…" Coughing, I look at Zeke. He definitely gave me poison.

"Where would be the fun in that?" He hands me a plate of food. "Eat. You should feel normal within the hour."

"Is there anything you need from the city?" Xander directs his question at Jesper. At the shake of his head, he looks at me. "Ameris?"

"To see it." In my panic, I forgot about their scouting and resupply trip.

This gives me the perfect opportunity to follow Xander and his crew to the city above. I tried finding the exit that leads to the capital myself, but there are too many tunnels in this cave system.

Part of my many training sessions with Lyle has been to recognize the flow of outside air that circulates through the caves. To learn the vibrations of air in order to control them.

Instead, I've used what they taught me to search for exits. But all I've found are small openings overhead—or dead ends.

"I will take you, but not today." Xander huffs out a breath and shakes his head. "We've talked about this. When the time is right."

Turning back to my plate, I rip a piece of bread violently in response. I shift my attention to my grimoire and say nothing for the rest of the meal, tuning out the conversation, not wanting to know what else I'll be missing out on. When they get up to leave, I follow everyone to the main cavern.

Xander turns to me. His muscular arms flex as he crosses them over his chest. "You can't come with us."

"I'm not. I can't change my scenery to continue reading?" Waving the grimoire at him, I continue. "I'm going to sit out here and practice spells."

I stalk away and plop down on a plush, green velvet couch among the lounging space. Faelights float about, giving off the perfect glow. He's still watching me, but Zorria watches both of us, her usual *I'm going to murder you* stare directed at me.

Jesper and Zeke are watching all three of us; they look at each other, shaking their heads, before taking the second corridor to the left.

"Have fun." I wave them off and open my grimoire to the page I marked, but Xander stands there, considering me. His jaw clenches, his chest rising and falling with a deep breath, as if he wants to say something more. I jut my chin out, my brows raising along with my hands. "What?"

No question or answer comes. He grabs Zorria's arm just as she opens her mouth to respond. She shakes out of his grip, and they walk away. He looks over his shoulder at me. For a fleeting moment, his expression bears a tangle of anguish mixed with concern, but he turns around too quickly for me to be sure.

Zorria shakes her head and asks Xander loud enough for me to hear, "Why do you let her get to you? She's trouble."

They round the same corridor Jesper and Zeke took. I'll never know if or what he answered. I close the grimoire and set it down on the wooden table next to me. Sticking to the shadows, I follow them. I'm unsure if I'll get away with it, but it's worth a shot.

Even though their hearing is better, picking up the faintest of sounds, I've learned enough to now control my magic, giving me an advantage. I haven't let on how much I've grown in controlling it, in being able to manipulate the elements to my desire.

And in practicing spellcasting, I've poured over the grimoire every chance I got. Murmuring the words, I weave a spell around me, masking my presence. My footsteps make no sound on the stone floor.

Voices and snippets of conversation echo back to me—The Fringe, drinking hall, glamour—all words that are foreign to me. The further down the corridor I get, the more the muscles in my legs burn.

Of course, this is an inclined path.

I'm thankful for whatever Zeke gave me, because I no longer feel the after-effects of the wine, which would have been horrendous if I'd felt like shit and had to walk uphill.

Training with him has strengthened me; my arms and legs have leaned out, but my stamina and endurance could clearly still use some work. I can only run around the passages so many times before getting bored.

Light filtering in from holes and spaces where roots have burrowed through cuts the darkness, trying to thwart my plan. If the incline wasn't an indication that I'm close to the surface, the light is. I stick to what shadows remain. When there are no more to hide within further ahead, I wait, feeling as though a century is passing.

Each time I want to move, doubt creeps in about whether it's safe to go forward. Getting caught isn't an option because I want this—want a different view, to see others, to smell what a city in Elysium is like, and to feel different ground under my boots.

Xander still hasn't shown me the dying world he claimed would change my mind about joining their fight against Oberon. It's not that I don't believe Xander about the danger, but when you reach a breaking point, you don't care. You take the risk.

Tentatively, I inch forward, toward the end of the passageway. It ends in a solid wall of dirt, as if the tunnel just ends with no exit. There were no other corridors along this part of the passage, and yet they've disappeared. I close my eyes and open myself to the elemental magic within, searching for oddities in the vibrations. The air surrounding me isn't stifled by the dead end; instead, it flows beyond it. Opening my eyes, I run my hand along the cool stone until it falls through, disappearing as if it's been cut off.

A fake wall that looks like a dead end. Clever. I still my breath and listen for any movement beyond. Nothing. I take a step forward and pass through.

CHAPTER 27

XANDER

Instead of answering Zorria, I change the subject. "Is everything ready at the tavern?" Recruiting people will be easier when they see me and know that my return is real. A tale they can spread to other rebels. I want to see the walls of the underground filled with people again. We lost many in the last battle, but that was different. It was for control. The battle to come is for the life source of our world.

The further we get into the passage, a clammy dampness coats my palms, and my heart skips a beat, mirroring the way my nerves fire through the excitement of finally getting to see my city again. A grin forms at the thought.

The heavy earthen smell lifts as we reach the exit, fresh air seeping through the cracks in the hidden entrance. I understand Ameris wanting to get out because I want that too. I'll bring her a gift from the city. We have to start over from somewhere. And when I can determine its safety, I'll take her with me.

"Of course it is," Zorria responds incredulously. "Would you doubt me?"

"No, I would never doubt you." I laugh and sigh. "Listen, about Ameris..."

She holds up her hand, interrupting me. "I think she's hiding something."

"What could there be to hide? Are you sure it's not just because she looks like Rhiannon?"

"Partly." She smiles and elbows me. "Xander, just be careful. I just got you back. I don't want to lose you again. And all I see from her is trouble."

Before I can respond, Zorria walks through the stone wall with Zeke, leaving me behind with Jesper. We wait, giving them time to vacate the area outside the exit, just in case anyone is around. As I push through the invisible barrier, it ripples and shifts around me.

The glamour keeps our image melded to the background of the wooded area until we are feet from the entrance. Unless you are looking for the entrance, you will only see a grouping of trees—nothing unusual for a city's garden.

I pull my hood down and walk out of the tree's cover and onto the pebbled path. The sights and smells of the garden are amplified by the falling rain. They fill a part of my soul I didn't know was lacking. It grounds me and settles the ache of missing my home. When we leave the gardens and step onto the street, the city greets me in a way I've never seen before—its luster is gone.

Guards swathed in black armor patrol the brick roads. Fae walking nearby cross the street or turn in a different direction when they see them. Down another street, I see two guards accosting citizens, their raised voices making it clear that they think the fae look suspicious, questioning them for information about a renewed rebellion.

As we move toward the center of the city, another pair of guards holds a blade to the throat of a boy while the other checks his pockets. I want to intervene, but Jesper holds out an arm and shakes his head.

"You can't be seen, and if we risk attention, we risk our plans."

A clear indication of the power Oberon wields. He can do whatever he desires with no regard for the citizens of this city or world. His darkness stains anything he touches.

What he expects to rule when decay takes over must be of little consequence compared to the power he craves.

I must keep Ameris from his grasp. Not only for her own protection, but for the future of our world. My thoughts drift to last night. Ameris's lips inches from mine, my thumb against her skin, and how her touch sent pulses through me.

When she is nearby and our bodies touch, sparks fly, but when we are in the same room, the events that led us to Elysium stamp out all else.

Tonight, when we return, I will sit down with her and go over what we have been planning. Seek her input. Because Jesper is right. She deserves to know. I'm not doing any good keeping her at a distance.

Before I know it, The Fringe fills my vision. When I look upon it, raindrops splash onto my face, dripping down from my hood. The blackened wooden exterior gives away its age and lack of decorum.

Nestled between the shops on the outskirts of the inner city, it's always been a gathering place for a mixed crowd. Always at odds with the neatly cared-for shops and cafes that line the rest of the street. Situated perfectly at the end of the street and between the homes of those in the upper and lower courts.

Jesper enters, and I follow close behind, pulling my hood further down to conceal my face. A haze lingers, and laughter floats around the room, mingling with the soft clink of coins and the sour stench of sweet wine mixed with sweat. Nothing about this place has changed since the last time I was here. The same fae are here, drinking their fill and playing their games as if nothing has changed, as if our world isn't dying.

"They pay the guards well to stay out of here," Jesper whispers as we make our way to the private room to the right of the main hall. "If you couldn't tell, that's why we chose it."

We sit at a round, oaken table with nicks, gouge marks, and engraved initials. I continue to watch the patrons through the cutouts in the paneled wall until a figure walks into the room. The woman who enters is human. Her eyes are kind, but suspicious.

Thin skin showing off blue veins underneath betrays her old age, despite her wrinkle-free and youthful face. The tray is steady in her hands under the weight of drinks and bread. Humans age slower in our world, and she's been here for a long time.

As she approaches the table, I grab the tray to ease the weight from her old bones and set it on the table. She looks into my hood briefly before bowing, unsure of my gesture. The hood of my robe still shadows my face. The city is not a safe place for me either. No one has returned from being banished. I wonder if anyone knows banishment sends us to the human world.

She stops mid-rise, looking at my arm that's slid too far from my robe, revealing the scars that remain from the magic Ameris performed. Another reminder of the price we paid to return to Elysium.

"Blood magic," the old woman says under her breath. It drifts up to me as if on a breeze. She steps closer.

I rise out of instinct, taking a step back, letting my arm fall beneath the robe once more.

"Let me see your arm." She stands tall, a demand to her tone.

Jesper rises and slowly approaches her. "Who sent you?"

"Your companion ordered the drinks and bread." She nods toward Zeke. Turning her gaze back to me, her stare bores through my robe, as if she can see the scars beneath. "But that scar...That is something I have only seen one other time. You are the one that has returned to this land." She looks up, peering into the hood that hides my face.

"What madness do you speak of?" Zorria seethes, still seated at the table.

"That, my dear boy, is the mark of a blood bond. A powerful bond that can never be broken." She motions for my arm again, and this time, I oblige.

"Tell me what you know," I demand, my words harsh at her revelation. Her fragile fingers take the fabric of my sleeve and roll it up. She traces the white lines from my palm, down my wrist, and around my arm, exploring and inspecting the scars that should never exist. We heal and are only ever scarred by iron.

"You are bound by blood to whoever cast this. Just as your blood flows through your veins, so too shall the blood of the one to whom you are bound. There are rules to these bonds. You were brave to agree. Few would."

"What rules?" A snarl escapes. I jerk my arm back from her grasp. I roughly sit, almost fall into my chair, and cross my legs. Folding my arms over my chest, I wait for her explanation.

She takes a step back, head cocked to the side, as she studies me before speaking. "I see. You didn't know."

"What did you say your name was?" Jesper takes another step forward, filling the void she created.

She doesn't move; only puts her hand up in a peace offering. "When the human you bound yourself to dies, so will the magic you possess, for the bond buries deep and feeds off the magic that now flows between the two of you. If you die, the human will die. If one of you kills the other, you both will die. It is the only magic strong enough to rip the seam between our worlds. But there can be no returning to the human world."

By this point, I'm seething. Words escape me. Pain forms in my jaw from clenching it so hard. I flex my hands, roll my shoulders, and take a deep breath. Ameris and I have a lot more than plans to discuss.

Zorria was right. I may have agreed to the spell, but I didn't agree to be bonded. Although I'm not sure if I would have cared, I desperately wanted to get back.

"And how did you come to know all this?" Zeke leans against the far wall, his foot resting against it.

A knowing smile crosses her lips before she turns to Zeke. "My tale is too long for this night, with the business I can only assume you came to do. But know that once a bond mate dies, there is no coming back from that loss."

Her smile fades, and it's then that I notice scars reaching through her long-sleeved dress, ending at her wrist. "I vow on the maker that the words spoken here and things seen will never leave my lips. And one more thing: once performed, nothing can undo the bond." The old lady bows her head before she leaves the room.

"Well, that was awkward." Zeke takes a sip of his drink. Pushing off the wall, he walks to the table and sits next to his sister.

"I told you she was trouble. I knew it." Zorria spits, her knife sinking into the table. "How did you not know?"

"Would you have known?" I throw a look at Zorria, silencing her.

"We will all sit down and discuss it in the morning." Jesper hands me a cup of mead and bread. "We have business to take care of tonight. We don't need this distraction right now."

As if there is anything else that I can think about after that revelation. I down the mead and slam my cup against the table, anger flaring. Ameris lied to me—she had to know the magic she was performing.

Was this her way of getting back at me? To bind our fates in the cruelest way? And that's when the realization hits. The way I'm drawn to her. Amplified... Stronger after we entered this world. Dammit. She could have done it all on her own.

Doubt creeps in—are any of my feelings for Ameris real?

"Also, we have to verify the truth in her statements." Jesper sits next to me, hand landing on my shoulder, drawing me away from my thoughts.

I shake my head. "It was the truth. The old lady has similar scars."

Sounds from outside the tavern flood through its open doors, and our attention is diverted to the ruckus that begins in the main room. Patrons scramble for the exit, wanting to see what the disruption is—likely a fight between two fae.

Whispers of a name echo around the hall, one that haunts and strikes fear: Rhiannon.

But my fear is for an entirely different reason.

CHAPTER 28
AMERIS

Brightness fills my vision, forcing me to squint as I leave the dark passage behind. I throw my forearm over my eyes to block the light. When they adjust, I'm greeted by a marvelous view of a garden.

Beautiful oak and ash trees litter the area. Bushes and flowers snake along walking paths made of small pebbles. The garden stretches as far as I can see. The palace, in all its majestic beauty, sits high upon the hill, surrounded by an expanse of water and trees that span out around it. Only the tips of distant buildings at the bottom of the hill peek over the treetops of the garden.

I search the vibrations in the air for disruptions, like Lyle taught me, but it's quiet. There is no one around. A smile pulls at my lips as I take in the perfectly laid-out plants, seeing many I'm familiar with.

Leaning in, I inhale the scent of lavender; its floral yet herbal aroma is euphoric, calming me instantly. I pull the hood of my cloak further down to hide my face and walk along the path.

Tulips and roses make a colorful appearance before the path

ends. Additional walkways fan out around a bubbling fountain like the points on a compass. The air shifts as two female fae walk hand in hand, doting on each other as they come toward me from the east. I check my hood and step off the path, back into the trees, waiting for them to pass.

I shouldn't be surprised, but their beauty is beyond anything I have ever seen. What must it be like to live in a place where everyone is beautiful, not a flaw to be seen? But the more I think about it, the more I find it incredibly frustrating.

They take turns feeding each other what looks like a purple star, wrapped in each other's arms, they are ignorant to anyone but themselves. I decide to head in the direction they came from. The air shifts around me as I walk, mixing with various scents.

Sweet and savory smells drift in my direction—notes of cinnamon and sugar, roasting nuts, and baking bread. They all make my stomach pang with hunger.

Murmurs from the city weave through the trees, the distant rattling of carts, and the hum of daily life. The pebbled road morphs into a cobblestone pathway, leading into a square buzzing with merchants and fae.

Buildings made of white stone that shine like pearls flank the marketplace. Another fountain sits at its center, where fae mingle, laughing and eating. Each vendor has a different colored cloth covering their stall, giving life to the white backdrop.

Four main roads cross through the center of the market, with smaller alleyways all around. Vendors yelling about their goods for sale mix with chatter, filling the space with noise. The hustle and bustle is so much like the market at home.

Marguerite would love this—my heart drops. I push the emotions down. Force myself to forget what home was and replace it with the wonder of this place. I wander around, browsing the goods for sale.

A stall with a multi-colored cover of spring pastels sells stunning bouquets of flowers. The one next to it has every kind of fabric, some so decadent, I could only dream of wearing them. I dare not touch anything or linger too long in one spot. Turning around, I cross the road and find a stall selling magical items: amulets, cloaks, pendants, goblets, and an assortment of other objects that hum with magic.

My gaze lands on an amulet made of gold with a jade inset surrounded by sapphires and amethysts. The elements in the amulet sing as I walk closer. My body responds quicker than my mind, as I'm pulled forward by its melody. Everything else around me is fading away. As I approach, I'm barely aware of the merchant, who watches my every move.

"Another whose gaze falls on the Amulet of the Forlorn." He raises a brow at me, studying my shaded face.

Snapping my attention away from the amulet, I look at him from under my hood. "Why is it named that?"

"Because all who try to use it fall into despair and find their endeavors in using the amulet fail most horribly." He removes the necklace from the peg and rubs his finger over the jewels.

"Then why do you have it for sale?" I can't stop the questions that come. I need to move on, not linger in one place.

"Because there are those who want to own a piece of the past. It was Rhiannon who cursed this amulet. Who is your overlord? That will determine the price."

Rhiannon may be gone from this world, but her influence and memory will never fade. I hesitate, unsure of how to answer his question.

"Um...wrong amulet." The merchant's features turn from annoyance to disgust as I retreat. I pull in a sharp breath. It took me all of ten minutes to make a rookie mistake—time for me to go.

He catches my wrist in a swift motion, halting my departure. His grip is firm, and I can't yank free from it as he pulls the sleeve of my cloak up to my elbow. "Where are your gold bands? No human is without an overlord."

I recall the move Zeke taught me, and twist out of his grip. Turning on my heel, I walk away as fast as possible without attracting attention. How did he know I was human? He couldn't see my face. Humans can't be that obvious. Can we? I run through every moment of our interaction and glance back. He's pointing at me while talking to two fae dressed in black, adorned with armor.

Shit.

This was stupid. I shouldn't have come. Xander's warning echoes through my mind. Anger washes over me at the poor decision I made, fueling my body to run as the guards approach. Knowing they're faster than I am, I turn into an ally, following it until another path opens.

A blur of white stone and bright curtains pass as I veer right down another pathway. I continue to make left and right turns where I can, hoping to throw the guards off my trail. Darkness quickly approaches. Good. That'll give me more cover.

Not stopping, I veer down another alley, but it comes to a dead end. I take a moment, keeling over to catch my breath and take in my surroundings. Stacked crates line the wall at the end of the alley. I climb up and hiss as the muscles in my shoulder pull, sending a jolt of pain through me.

Before jumping down into yet another alley, I look back to see if anyone has followed. No one. I lean against the wall and steady my pounding heart, letting air fill my aching lungs as I massage my shoulder. I should have let Xander have someone heal it.

Blackened stones lined with grime greet me on this side of the wall, and trash is littered along the alley. The homes are also starkly different from the ones I was just running through. Some have broken windows, and most of the buildings are almost beyond repair.

So, not everything is beautiful here. I furrow my brow, unsure why, if they have magic, they don't just wipe it away. Interesting.

But this is not where I need to be, getting farther away from the garden. I should have run toward the garden and hid in the foliage, or in a tree, and waited until nightfall to return. Stupidly, I've made it further into the city.

Pushing off the wall, I exit the alley that spills onto a main road. There are shops along it, but nothing like the ones I just came from. Only a few fae walk along these streets, wearing hooded clothing, just as I am.

This is a place for those who want to buy things can't found anywhere else. Glancing back a few times, I check if any of the guards followed me, but only silence is behind me. I hold my side, pinching the stitch that's formed.

Light from the setting sun fades into night, but the moon is already high above, gracing us with her radiance. Pulling my hood up, I walk on, looking for another main road that connects the two neighborhoods. I pass the only crowded place on the street; fae loiter around the entrance, drinks in hand.

If I want to avoid attention, I should get up high. I cast my gaze to the rooftops, searching for pipes or other ways to scale the buildings. That way, I can get a lay of the city, and hope the garden is visible, to reorient myself.

"Stop," a voice from behind me demands.

My pace doesn't stall, and I don't hesitate, acting as if it's not me they're talking to. But another figure emerges a few yards in front of me. He's fitted with black leather armor over a muscled body. Golden hair flows around his shoulders, half of it pulled up into a topknot. "He said, 'stop'."

I halt this time, but my mind continues to whirl, searching for a way out of this. Two guards wearing the same fitted black armor stand about six feet behind me. More fae appear, all in the same armor, surrounding me. Five against one. My odds are definitely not good, but I won't give up without a fight, and I'm foolishly too confident for my own good.

"We know you are a human. Your stench is unmistakable. And

yet you do not wear the gold bands. No human in Elysium is without them."

"Well, now you have met one without them." I curtsy. "A human that is too smart to fall prey to the riddles of fae and find herself in a lifelong bargain. I belong to no one." I hope that works. Surely there are other humans that aren't in a bargain. We can't all be that gullible. Then again, humans might not know better than to bargain with a fae.

"We shall see about that." They all advance on me, their boots striking the pavement in tandem.

Each foot fall makes my heart pound, my adrenaline spiking. I've made a fatal mistake by coming to the city. I'm about to face death or capture. Xander was right, even though I hate to admit it. He warned me, and I ignored him.

My palms sweat, and my mind blanks. The wind around me swirls, and my magic flares, showing me the way out, begging to be used. It's telling me to trust myself and my magic. I've learned enough, and now it's time to trust my instincts.

I spin in a circle, taking in all the guards. One of them twists their hands, manipulating the air. Silvery blue hair whirls, and I catch a glimpse of a scar that crosses over his brow and down his cheek.

Another imperfection. His smile makes the hair along my arm stand. He pushes out his hands, and I feel it in the way the air shutters and vibrates as he uses it to force me toward the golden-haired fae.

But I raise my hands in a welcoming gesture and let the wind he pushed out fuel me; let it embrace me, building until it's almost too painful to hold.

"You shouldn't have done that." I clap my hands together and spin on my heel, forcing out the magic I was holding onto. It slams into each one of them, knocking them to the ground. I crack a smile when their looks of shock and confusion surface.

"Shall we go again?" I taunt.

As they rise, hatred and anger seep from them. "Who are you?" A female guard cautiously approaches, her white hair gleaming in the moonlight.

"No one you need to worry about. Now let me leave." They're quick, but I'm ready. Zeke's training kicks into overdrive.

She lunges toward me, but I block her attempted chokehold. Using her own strength against her, I pivot, grabbing her arm and twisting it behind her. She cries out, but before she can retaliate, I put all my strength into a kick to her lower back. It sends her stumbling forward, the momentum taking her to the ground.

The second fae hesitates a moment too long. I take the moment to my advantage, sending a gust of wind toward him. He flies back into the wall, his head hitting the stone.

One down. Only four to go.

Arms wrap around me, pushing my arms against my sides. I jerk my head back. It slams into the face of the fae holding me. A grunt escapes my captor, so I repeat the movement and hear a crack.

My head throbs from the impact, my eyes squeezing shut from the pain. But the grip on me slackens, and I twist away as the fae drops to his knees.

Two down.

Or so I thought. The two I took down get back up. Cursing, I want to kick myself for forgetting they heal faster than humans.

"You will pay for this," snarls the golden-haired fae.

I grind my teeth and get ready to bolt, but before I can react, a branch flies in my direction. I duck and let out a small laugh at his feeble attempt, the branch hitting the ground beside me. A sinister smile dances on his lips. He flicks his wrist, and I see the next branch too late.

It hits my wrists and morphs into restraints, tying my hands together.

A hand lands on my good shoulder, *thank the stars*, forcing me to the ground. My knees take the brunt of the impact. A curse escapes me at the jolt of pain that ricochets up my thigh.

The guard leans in, a rough voice whispering, "Did you really think you would win?" I jerk away, and he stands, addressing the fae who bound my wrists. "What are your orders, Captain?"

Their captain strides toward me with a commanding presence, each step as deliberate as the last, planted with authority and confidence.

My eyes narrow, hardening into a steely glare as a surge of anger wells within. I may not be as strong and experienced as them, but magic is my weapon. Something none of them expected from a human girl. I focus and open myself up to the magic lying in wait, placing my hands on the ground, seeking the vibrations laying beneath the cobblestones.

"It's time to see who you are. I must compliment you on keeping your hood up this whole time. A worthy opponent for a human." His compliment might be genuine, but it's laced with contempt.

I look up as his feet enter my field of view. It's only then that I notice the crowd that's gathered, filling shop entrances, standing and staring, to see what all the commotion is about.

Right now, I don't care who gets hurt. I would curse them all to hell if I knew that was where they'd go.

I want to hurt them for all the humans they have tricked into a life of service. While some may have sought the fae out, a life sentence in a world where their life is no longer their own is not right. Today, they will learn about the one who won't stand for it.

Just as I lift my arms, ready to unleash my magic—to rip the cobblestones away from the earth and send them out against the night like loosed arrows—he slaps a set of cuffs on my wrists. As I slam my hands into the ground, a jolt shoots up both arms.

Realization washes over me as I stare down at the polished black stone encased in iron that now rests on my skin. My magic has become no more than a whisper in the wind. Once more, behind a barrier.

It's gone—the energy that moved beneath my hand—like I never had it. Like before. Frantically, I pull at the metal cuffs, trying to force them off, but it's no use. I let out a stifled scream in frustration. *Not again. Not again.*

"Yes," he purrs as he squats in front of me. "You can no longer use your magic. You've lost."

Well, I'll show him. I launch forward, my hood flying back as I wrap my arms around his neck and twist behind him, pulling him to the ground with me. I hook his neck with the crook of my elbow and squeeze. Bringing my lips against his ear, I whisper, "Never leave yourself open."

His breath comes in fits, his voice is barely audible as he yells for the other guards. I know this will make things worse, but I want to embarrass him once more. Especially now that there's a crowd. The other guards struggle but succeed in removing me from the lock I created around his neck. He remains on the ground, coughing, as they bring me to my feet and push me forward.

When he approaches, the look that stains his face is a memory I'll cherish forever. Hatred mingles with disbelief. It hangs in the air like early morning dew.

I can't help the smile that comes. "Hello."

"Take her directly to Oberon. And put her hood back up," he commands, ignoring me as he walks away.

The crowd outside the drinking hall is larger now, patrons flow out of its doors, flooding the streets. I can't help but smile when I see every onlooker standing in silent shock. Two guards flank me, pulling up my hood, but it's too late. The crowd has already seen me. They drag me through the street, but I don't struggle, because this time I've lost. The guards yell at the onlookers, telling them to mind their business and that the show is over.

Xander repeatedly warned me about Oberon, and now he's the

one I'm headed toward. I set my intention: Do not show fear. I imagine him as the type who expects fear and groveling. But I won't give that to him. Even if I'm the captive, I have the upper hand. No more letting men decide for me. I have the power to control my destiny. And I'll be damned if I don't start acting like it.

CHAPTER 29

XANDER

"Ameris!" Dread pools as I bolt out of the hall. The light breeze delights in my anguish, repeating her name among the whispers that float through the air. I shove someone aside, making my way to the front of the crowd, when arms wrap around me, pulling me back and putting my hood up.

Zeke's voice is harsh and commanding. "No. There's nothing we can do without meeting the same fate."

I push against him, ripping out of his hold and clawing my way to the street, but a strong hand grips my shoulder, stopping me short. "Zeke is right."

Jesper's words hit, and I freeze under his tight hold on my shoulder. My heart pounds as they approach. I want to rush toward her, disarm the guards, rip their hearts out with a feral desire to protect her. To take her back to the safety of the underground.

Ameris's gaze sweeps over the gathered crowd, taking in each person her eyes rove over, assessing them, flaunting her capture. My own gaze is locked onto her, hoping she feels it and turns my way. Moments pass in agony before her head turns to me, and the facade she put up falters for the briefest moment. Regret flickers, but she returns to the girl who confidently walks down the road, looking pleased with herself.

Almost as if she wanted this. I can't help the thoughts that bombard me—did she do it on purpose? Let herself get caught so she could escape the underground? Did she want so badly to get away from me?

"We have to go. Now." Jesper pulls me to the back of the crowd. But still, I want to follow Ameris and remove her from their grasp.

Even though she lied to me about the bond.

Even if my desire to protect her comes from our connection, it's still something I want. I brought her into this world without properly explaining the threats she faced.

"Before they come to break up the crowd and find you, Xander," Jesper says under his breath. "It is not safe for you to be out either."

I don't lose sight of her until the brick wall of the alley blocks my view. Leaning my head against the white stone, thoughts continue to flow at my failure to protect her. My fists tighten.

The scene plays over and over in my mind: her face, the guards, the crowd. All our time together since entering this world. Moments I could have said something and didn't.

Striking the wall, my knuckles crack, and the tan skin splits like the fissure forming within me as the distance between us widens. Crimson liquid paints the wall and leaves a trail, dripping from my hand as we depart the tavern. I'm barely aware of Zorria wrapping my hand as the city passes by in a blur on the long and torturous walk back to the garden.

Silence has fallen over our group; only the sounds of the night accompany us. My feet fall into their known rhythm of movement as I follow the others through the hidden entrance and into the war room.

Quiet permeates the space, each person taking a seat at the

table in a mood of their own. Zorria's expression is smug, like she knew it was only a matter of time before this would happen. Zeke looks like a child whose favorite toy was stolen, distraught, and defeated. Jesper is deep in thought, likely processing what our next plan of action should be.

Lyle enters the room, an urgency in their voice. "She is gone."

"We know," I say through gritted teeth. "The palace guards have taken her captive. We need to put a plan together to get her back. We don't know what Oberon will do to her."

Oberon hated Rhiannon, and there is no predicting his behavior. It's worse that they look so alike. He'll extract what he wants until there's nothing she can offer, and what follows is a place I do not let my mind wander to. We will get her out of there before then.

"She was following us," Zorria comments casually, like it's of no consequence.

Her statement strikes like a knife to the heart. Rising, I pound my fist against the table. "You knew? When were you going to say something?"

"I didn't know she would do something stupid enough to get caught. That is her problem, though, isn't it? She's blinded by her own needs. Just like you." Zorria folds her arms, sitting back against the chair.

"Tell me what you are inferring." I kick the arm of her chair. She rises as it skitters across the floor. Zorria's anger rises with it. She jumps at me, knives swinging as I parry her attack. We trade blows back and forth before she pins me against the wall with a snarl and a knife to my throat.

"Enough!" Jesper yells.

"What has occurred was meant to be," Lyle offers in their melodic voice. "So tell us, Zorria, what do you mean?"

She releases me, sheathing her blades, and takes a step back. She rights her chair and sits, throwing her feet onto the table before offering her explanation. "She walked around here.

demanding what she wanted, insolent, and immature. And you, brooding about like you are in love. Which we now know is only because of this bond you share. I won't have any part in rescuing her."

Zeke addresses his sister. "You have every right to choose that. But Ameris is the key to fixing our world, whether you like it or not. And she hasn't been insolent. Maybe to you, but that's because you are an ass to her. You get what you give, sis." Turning to me, he finishes with, "I'm with you, Xander. She doesn't deserve to be left to Oberon's whims."

"I've heard enough." Zorria glares at her brother before storming out of the room.

"What is..." I start, but Zeke cuts me off.

"It's because of you. She waited for you, hoping you would come back. But you came back with someone else. Someone you're bound to be with. It hasn't sat well with her," Zeke says, shrugging.

"Waited for me? She was with someone else when I was banished. And I'm not bound to be with anyone." I'm seething by this point, pacing back and forth, too agitated to sit. "Besides, no one's ever come back before. There's no excuse."

Zeke rolls his eyes. "You are bound to Ameris. You heard what the old lady said. Whether that takes a day or years, it will happen."

"Let's start," Jesper interrupts, motioning for me to sit down. "We know Oberon hosts a dinner party for the elite every quarter moon. The next one is in two weeks. I have some contacts inside the palace. I will get them to provide me with intel on her whereabouts. Once we know where she is being kept, we can work around the party's security and guests. Until then, get some rest. We'll continue in the morning."

Zeke walks with me to the corridor that houses our rooms. "Ameris will be fine. We've been training every day, and she's strong. Stronger than you give her credit for. She picked up what I taught her quickly. We also went over the trickery of our words when we choose to use them." He slaps me on the shoulder, like it will make me feel any differently about how the night has gone.

I shrug him off. "I pushed her to leave. We made a bargain when she saved me. I didn't think humans had magic, so I agreed. I was supposed to teach her magic. But I got around it by asking Lyle to do it on my behalf."

"Perhaps, but she probably would have done it anyway. Restless type. And it's not unlike us to worm our way out of bargains. Phrasing matters—you know that." Zeke never has it in him to see anything but the good in a situation.

"Hmm. Doesn't take away from my role in this mess," I respond.

"True, but being hard on yourself won't do you any good." Zeke nods, stopping outside his room. He gives me a stern look. "She'll be fine, Xander."

I take the last few steps toward my own room, but instead of going in, I keep walking, roaming around until I arrive back at the main hall.

Ameris's grimoire rests on the table where she was last sitting. I curse myself for not noticing her following us. She had to have been using magic, or I would have heard her footsteps, her breathing. I pick up the book and skim through the pages. They're filled with remnants of her ancestors. An overwhelming urge to turn to the end of the book takes over. My fingers obey, and in the margin is a message written so small it would go unnoticed by human sight: *She will need you. -M*

Marguerite. Too wise to have wasted her days in that cottage. She gave everything to give us the head start we needed. Zorria's right. My need for revenge blinded me to the deep pain Ameris carries—pain she believes I caused.

While I had a part to play in her loss, we all did. It was not a singular event that ripped Ameris's life apart.

A drawing of the nightshade falls out when I fan through the other pages. She drew their meeting with precision. I wonder if what I felt that day was because of the bond, or if I truly felt it.

The bond... The old lady in the tavern comes to mind. The scars on her wrist were like the ones I now wear. I need to speak to her again to find out what I can do about this bond. She said it was absolute, but all things can be broken. I replace the picture of the nightshade and shut the book, putting it back down.

Ameris's presence lingers; an emptiness deep within starts to bloom. I walk around with no intention, letting my body find the places it wants to be, while my mind drifts to what horrors she is undoubtedly experiencing at the palace. The training room opens up before me, and I take to the floor, running through training drills. Letting the motions wash over me, giving me something else to focus on.

"You'll have to do better than that if you plan to get her back." I turn to see Zorria leaning against the entrance to the training hall, a smirk playing against her features. We never could stay mad at each other for long.

I wave her in. "Come. Let's play."

She drops her knives on the ground as she approaches. Her walk turns into a run. She launches into the air, coming at me in a downward attack. I block, but her momentum takes me down.

Rolling out from under her weight, I jump up and wrap my arm around her neck, pulling her into submission. Her elbow slams into my stomach, forcing the breath from my lungs. At the same moment, she snaps her head back. I move my head to the side, avoiding a skull to the face.

Zorria grabs my wrist and twists, pulling her head from under my arm, while forcing my arm behind my back. She kicks the back of my knee, and I hit the ground.

"Gah!" I reach for my magic, searching for the moisture in these caves, and pull it together. Throwing the water out in tiny darts, they hit her in the face. She sputters. While she's distracted, I pivot on my knee and swipe a leg against hers, knocking her to the ground.

She spits, sitting up. "So, you want to play dirty?"

Zorria snaps her fingers, and fire springs to life in her hands. She launches a ball at me. Crossing my arms, I create a shield of water, and the fire turns to steam. I glare at her. I meant to distract where she meant to harm. She jumps to her feet at the same time I do. We both advance with fists flying, trading blow for blow.

She catches my arm as I extend it and pulls me to her. Her free hand grabs the back of my head, and she pulls me into a kiss.

The passion of our fight burns into the kiss. She pours her desire into it, and I lose myself in it. But it isn't Zorria I'm thinking of, it's Ameris—her lips that I imagine myself falling into.

I push away, chest heaving with the exertion of the fight and the breathless kiss. Zorria stares at me. "You kissed me back, but it wasn't me in your mind." She reels, landing one last blow to my jaw. I don't defend against her accusation because she's right. She stalks out of the room, grabbing her knives before disappearing.

"Zorria!" I run after her, catching up to her in the main hall. "Zorria. Stop."

She turns, throwing one of her knives at me. I duck as it whooshes past, slamming into the wall behind me with a clang. Fury, like that of the maker, emanates from her. "I waited for you. And you come back with a human you bound yourself to? One that looks like *her*." Repulsion lines her words.

"It had to be done in order to return. Plus, we didn't end on good terms," I snap back.

Zorria throws another knife at me. "Lover's quarrel."

"No, Zorria. You wanted her. You chose Amalise." I pick up her knives and hand them to her.

"I wanted you both." She snatches them from me, sheathing them.

"And I wanted you. What happened to her?"

"She died in the raid. Along with many others." Her hard exterior falters. A shadow passes before the facade returns.

"You should want Ameris back so we can get revenge against Oberon," I offer, hoping to shift her hatred from Ameris to Oberon.

"I don't trust her."

"I do."

"Your judgment isn't to be trusted. Not when it comes to Ameris."

I shake my head. For all I don't understand about the bond, I know it doesn't take away my ability to think for myself or process other emotions. I loved and lost Zorria, but time brought closure to that wound, and I moved on, my desire for revenge against Oberon taking its place.

When I don't respond, she walks away before stopping a few paces later, calling out, "She will die before you see another hundred years. Human lives are fleeting, insignificant to our immortality."

She turns the corner, planting seeds of doubt for any future I might have with Ameris.

CHAPTER 30
AMERIS

"Aren't you curious? You already know I'm not her—I'm human. You could get information before anyone else. All I ask in return is that you loosen your grip on my arms." I bat my eyelashes, swiveling my head between the two guards. "Imagine all the fame you'll gain from being the guards that escorted me to the palace. Even more so if you have inside information."

I'm met with silence. Nothing. Not even a facial movement that I can exploit. But I keep on. At least it gives me something to do during this long walk. As we make our way up the city streets, they become less crowded. The homes become larger and more pristine the closer we get to the palace.

"I hope you teach me how to do that. Not move a muscle. Do you think a human can learn that? I mean, I did kick your companions' asses. I think I have your magic mastered." The tone of my words rolls off my tongue, intentionally impertinent.

The guard to my right tenses slightly but keeps his silent vigilance. I continue my single player game, still hoping to break them before we get to our destination. "You haven't told me your names. I'm Ameris. It's a pleasure to meet you. Sorry about that little show back there. I know you didn't expect a human to ruin your night."

The guards roughly jerk me between them and push me forward. I stumble from the forward momentum and land on my knees. They've tired of my attempts to get them to talk. I huff indignantly as they jerk me up by my arms. "Rude," I mumble.

We round a corner, and the palace comes into full view. Pearlescent white stone walls shine under the starry sky, the same material as the buildings in the city square. A lake opens around the palace, and thick, dark woods surround it. The clear water reflects the palace walls, giving them an unearthly glow.

It's too perfect to be done by hand; its beauty is unbearable. They must have constructed it using magic.

Beyond a grand staircase, whose height hides the palace entrance, is where I'll find what my future holds. I stop antagonizing the guards as we ascend the stairs.

The landing spreads wide; large red doors stand tall in the distance, their color stark against the white stone walls. Menacing. Flanking each side are guards standing at attention, spears in hand, dressed all in black. Still like statues, they are unmoving as we walk by, except for their eyes, which track me.

I smile deviously at each one of them, even if they can't see my face under the shadow of the hood.

The doors groan under their weight as four guards pull them open, and we pass through. We enter a massive, welcoming hall with fifty-foot vaulted ceilings that cross and merge, supported by rows of pillars. Between each pillar, windows let the moonlight shine through.

We stop in front of grand wooden doors, the black paint imperfectly covering the intricate design etched into them, like this was an addition after Oberon took control. Two guards standing outside cross their spears as we approach, denying us entry. The male from the fight in the street—who they identified as their captain—walks up and the guards straighten further in his presence. "We need to see him now."

They look at each other before one of them responds shakily. "Sir, we cannot interrupt his majesty when the doors are closed."

"You will for this." He pulls back my hood. They gasp, shock and disbelief morphing their features when they gaze upon my face.

This is going to get old quickly. The one on the left nods and slips through the door. A few minutes pass before the guard returns and motions for us to follow him. He returns my hood before we enter the throne room.

So, they did take me straight to him, without dragging me around different routes. At least, it seems that way. Good to know.

Either they don't think I'm a threat, or Xander was right, and I've made a grave mistake.

Flickering torches mounted along the white stone walls cast the only light to fill the expansive space. Even with the moon at its zenith, light doesn't penetrate through the many windows set high in the pure white stone walls.

Everything else is cloaked in shadows, lost to obscurity. Except for the dais and throne, where torches are perched on the steps leading to and around the throne, illuminating the scene before us.

Oberon sits on the throne, leaning back to the side with his legs crossed, assessing a fae who's kneeled before him. He's half hidden in the shadows of the dim lighting; a shaft of light crosses his face, showcasing his violet eyes. They spark with delight when they flit to me before returning to the fae. He tilts the male's head so the light catches on his ears. It's not a fae, but a human.

"Let this be a lesson to those who defy me." Oberon's voice echoes through the space like a sharp blade slicing through the shadows, cutting to the bone. Precise. Deadly. Shadows come forth from Oberon and wrap around the man, surrounding him like a slow-moving tornado, swirling and pulsing.

A piercing, shrill scream fills the hall. It's unbearable the longer it goes on. I want to plug my ears, but my hands are firmly secured behind my back. Just when I can stand it no longer, silence descends.

The hairs on my arms rise, accompanied by the shiver that runs through my body. The limp form of the man, a human, thuds against the marble floor in front of Oberon. The tang of iron coats my nostrils and tongue as blood pools under the dead man. It slowly cascades down the steps of the dais.

The guards shove me forward and force me into a kneel, inches from the crimson liquid that slowly spreads. A hand palms my head, forcing me to bow before Oberon. The pressure releases, and I look from beneath my hood to see the guards put a fist over their hearts as they bow before their king. I try to rise, unwilling to kneel, but a hand lands on my bad shoulder, forcing me to my knees again, and I grit my teeth through the discomfort.

"Rise." The voice is sharper than before, and there is a promise of punishment within it.

I try to rise again, but the hand remains, keeping me down. "Your Majesty. This couldn't wait. We found a human in the streets. She looks like Rhiannon." The captain removes my hood once more.

"Don't forget to mention I kicked your asses before you finally got me," I insert before he continues, unwilling to contain myself.

"She used magic against us." His fingers, like talons, dig into the pressure point on my shoulder. My muscles tense, and I clench my jaw through the pain. It's a clear message to hold my tongue.

Oberon rises and steps into the full light of the torches. He snaps his fingers, and the shadows around the room lift, letting moonlight stream through the previously dimmed windows. I blink a few times as my vision adjusts.

His violet eyes rove over every inch of my body, pausing the longest on my face, and an intense hunger fills his gaze. I can't determine if it's a good hunger or a deadly one. I am, after all, a vicious reminder of his past. Her name slips off his lips in a snarl as he walks toward me. I still—going rigid as he approaches. His black hair, which is partially pulled back, highlights the angles of his face and the arch of his brows.

Everything he wears is black, from the leather vest, loose at the neck, coming down at an angle to show off his thin but chiseled frame, to his overcoat, lined with metal shoulder caps and a stiff collar that sits just below his jaw. Except for the rings he wears on multiple fingers. They are crafted from different metals and jewels and range from plain to ostentatious.

His gait is that of a man who knows he rules with power and fear. Within a few strides, he reaches me, circling and looking me over. When he reaches my other side, he takes a lock of my hair in his hand, twirling it with his long, black, pointed fingernails.

"Come." The word is cool and controlled, enunciated with precision as he walks back to the throne and sits, perching on the edge like a predator waiting to strike. He's a master in the art that he practices, a sculptor who molds himself into other's damnation.

To say I'm intimidated is an understatement. The stories about the type of person he is play on repeat as I rise and walk toward him, stepping through the blood that still pools on the floor. When I reach the steps leading up to the dais, I stop and look up at him.

"Oberon," I say his name in defiance, the only thing I can do right now, feigning indifference.

He grins. "I'm pleased you know my name. Now, tell me. How did you come to look so much like our beloved queen?"

"You haven't earned that answer," I reply, just as cool and controlled as he is. A risk, but what do I have to lose? I've already lost everything. There's nothing for me in this world. Besides, I'm right; he hasn't earned the right to know that answer. He may think his power and position entitle him, but they don't.

I don't expect what he does next—his eyes pull together as he doubles over in laughter. It's as if this is a different person entirely, his laughter full of glee, without a care in the world. He halts just as quickly as he started, his serious demeanor returning. "Well, that was delightful. I hope we don't have any trouble from you, like we did her. And watch your tone with me." The last words cut, sending a shiver down my spine.

I'm not sure if he expects me to grovel or answer his original question, but I do neither. Instead, lifting my cuffed hands, I ask, "What are these?"

"Those are binders." Oberon leans forward, his brow arching as another crooked smile forms.

Of course. Is this the game we're going to play? *Play nice, Ameris,* I remind myself.

"Thank you for providing the name of the item. But what are they made of? And how do they work?" While I essentially know how they work—they block the wearer's magic—I'm hoping to glean information that might be useful in helping me figure out a way to remove them.

"Enough of this. Take her to a room and post guards outside her door." He sits back on the throne and waves us off. A dismissal. Pain from my shoulder injury flares as the guards yank me back and drag me away, my heels scraping along the marble. *I should have taken Xander up on the offer to have it healed.*

We stare at each other as the distance between us grows. I try to keep my composure, but my skin crawls under his gaze. The way it makes me want him seduces me, and yet at the same time, makes me want to run as far and fast away as possible.

I call out, "I would love it if you removed these." I smile sweetly but know my request will go unanswered. The guards halt. I straighten my body, standing tall as I hold out my wrists.

Oberon regards me as he drums his fingers against the arm of the throne, a countenance of thought etched into his beautiful face. The heavy silence lets me know no one demands anything of him.

I asked nicely—well, that might be a stretch—it was more like I passive-aggressively requested. I consider speaking again, adding more to my request, but he senses it and stands.

"I will remove them." He descends the throne, coming toward me again. Snapping his fingers, a servant rushes off, returning moments later with a box. The gold casing is elaborate, with precious stones set into the corners, coming together in the middle with a large black stone.

Oberon grabs one of my wrists, his hand is soft but calloused against my skin. So, he hasn't always been served upon. He turns my wrist, pushing the sleeve of my cloak up to expose my wrists. He pauses, inspecting the thin, white scars, trailing one of his fingernails along them. "Interesting."

He drops my arm and shifts his gaze to me. His violet eyes burn with questions, but he says nothing. I watch as he caresses the box the servant hands him. Oberon runs his fingers along the edges and over the large black stone in the center. Gently lifting the lid, he nods to the guards behind me.

At his command, four of them approach and place their hands on my shoulders, securing me. Two of the guards hold my arms outstretched, gripping my forearms so I can't move. This is excessive, but I also can't blame them now that they know I possess magic. Their captain removes the cuffs, and I immediately feel my magic spring to life.

But it doesn't last long. Oberon removes two individual cuffs from the box—solid black stone, polished to a silky finish, set into a gold border—quickly replacing the ones that were removed. The magic is snuffed out once more.

"Beware of what you ask for. You are no longer among friends." The corner of his lip tugs up, his eyes sparkling with wicked delight. Oberon lifts my hand, brings it to his lips, and places a kiss on the back of it. "Goodbye."

I knew it wouldn't be so easy.

Zeke warned me of how the fae love their trickery with words. I take in any and every detail I can in the soft light of the moon as I'm escorted through the halls. We enter a long hallway and stop before a tall set of wooden doors etched with ivory vines. I'm shoved into the room, and the door slams shut behind me. I bang on it, releasing some of the pent-up anger and frustration at my capture.

Turning, I take in the bedroom, which far exceeds my expectations. This is a room for a visiting noble, not a girl who reminds you of your enemy, from the billowing silk curtains to the open armoire, which shows off all the dresses it contains.

Across from the hearth is a four-poster bed. I walk to the window, opening it as wide as it will go; moonlight spills into the room, casting everything in a pallid glow. The ground below is a four-story drop. Looking around the room, I make a mental note of all the things I might use to escape.

These cuffs will prove to be an issue. But I didn't have magic for most of my life, and I won't let that stop me now. I reel at the message he sent by placing them on my wrists—the cuffs are gold, a sign of human servitude.

A reminder that I belong to him. A mistake he will soon regret.

After inspecting the rest of the room, I return to the window, and assess the courtyard below. Leaning over the ledge, I don't see any windows below, which eases my fear of being seen when I make my descent. There are multiple entrances to the courtyard. I trail each one, gauging where they exit, seeking the best escape.

Tomorrow's nightfall will be my companion. Until then, I will rest and prepare.

CHAPTER 31
XANDER

My head rests heavy in my hands, elbows perched on the table as I wait for the others to arrive. It's been two days since they captured Ameris. Two days of waiting for an answer from Jesper's contact. Two days of my nerves being shot.

No one has seen Zorria, not even Zeke. He knows something happened between us. If Zeke's calm, then I know she's alright. Even though we parted on harsh words again, she'll come around. I hope. I need her—not in the ways I used to—but for her friendship and skill.

Smoked meat and freshly baked bread make their arrival seconds before Jesper and Zeke do. They walk in, heads together in discussion, carrying part of our morning meal. Lyle follows behind with the rest. They lay the platters of food on the table before taking their seats. Jesper looks at me, stern-faced, as he fills his plate. One thing about Jesper: He always eats breakfast before discussing business. I haven't forgotten, so I follow suit, collecting items onto a plate.

"Any news?" I stare at the food with no desire to eat any of it. Ameris is likely in a dungeon, getting fed scraps—if anything.

Jesper assesses me before issuing an order. "Eat. She is not being treated like a normal prisoner."

His words ease some of the anxiety that's bundled up within me like a knotted rope. Yet, a flood of other questions rise to the surface of my mind. There is no other thing she can be but a prisoner, so what is Oberon's game plan? Because he always has one.

The first bite of a roll brings forth the hunger I was too busy to consider the day before. I haven't eaten since we returned, and the fight with Zorria drained me more than I realized. I devour the plate before me and wash it all down with wine, letting the sweet sensation fill the void of Ameris's absence, which haunts me at every turn. Zeke considers me as he meticulously eats the fruit on his plate.

"I'm fine." I stare back at him. But I'm not fine—this is all my fault.

"Sure. Except you've never acted like this. I've never seen you this undone." One brow arches as he twirls the star fruit on his fork before taking a bite.

"Why do you eat like that?"

"One should always consider their food before it enters their body." He leans forward. "Stop deflecting Xander."

Jesper pushes his plate forward, propping his elbows on the table. He laces his fingers together and places his chin on his hands. "Ameris is a guest at the palace. She is staying in the old queen's quarters."

My face pales. A cruel trick with intentional messaging. Oberon knows he has spies in his court. It's always been this way. No ruler has a completely devoted following, especially ones who are cruel. "What is he going to do with her?"

Jesper leans back. "No one knows."

"He will use her when the time is right," Lyle offers. Their statements come few and far between, but are always piercing in their delivery.

"Are we still planning to infiltrate the party?" Zeke asks, twirling his knife against the oak table, watching it spin.

"Yes, but we must be very careful. He will know she did not come here by accident. He'll expect us," Jesper responds as he runs his hand along his chin in thought. "Lyle, what can you tell us about these parties? You've attended a few of them?"

"Yes," Lyle draws out. "They do not station extra guards because no one has wanted to face Oberon since the fall of Rhiannon and the ruin of the rebellion. Getting out will be your struggle."

"We need to go back to the tavern and gather the recruits for rebellion. We cut our last trip short. Zeke, can you arrange that for tonight?" The words leave me too hastily. I want to go back to talk to the old lady. But they don't need to know that. If I get dual use out of the trip, then so be it.

"I'm on it." Getting up, he nods, then turns to leave, but Lyle stops him, handing him our plates.

"Help me." Lyle picks up the food platters before they leave the room.

"What is going on, Xander?" Jesper gets up and moves around the table, putting a hand on my shoulder before sitting next to me.

"I've been thinking about the bond. About Ameris. I can't tell if my attraction is true or if it's because of the bond." I drop my head back into my hands. Since the old lady told us of the bond, I've been thinking of nothing else. What I entered into without knowing, and how it affects my decisions regarding Ameris.

"What did you think the first time you met?" He raises an eyebrow as if he already knows. He waits for me to speak the words aloud. Whatever Jesper is thinking is wrong.

"I thought she was Rhiannon, and I almost killed her." I scowl.

Jesper barks out a laugh, causing his whole body to shake.

Clearing his throat, he asks, "Yes, I can see you doing that. After that?"

"But then I saw the differences—her fire for life and the beauty that is her own. On our way here, she took down four men with magic she didn't understand how to use. It was majestic, bold, and terrifying.

Although she pulled me from the shipwreck, I take some responsibility for what happened. I agreed to Marguerite's wishes instead of staying back to fight. And one of the men escaped with her horse. Now she's lost the two souls that were closest to her. I wanted to be there for her, but we were at odds. She's bewitched me, but it wasn't until we entered Elysium that I wanted her this much. Now, I know that's because of the bond, and I cannot tell the difference."

"Does it matter if you cannot tell the difference? Your own words tell me you cared before the bond. I don't take that lightly coming from you." Laying his hands on the table, he stands. "Let's get ready for tonight. The maker has spoken; our fate has been dealt. Now we respond."

Walking to the tavern brings back memories of Ameris being dragged through the streets. I'm determined to get her back, but I need others on my side before I can do that. Smoke floats out from the tavern as I pull the door open.

The air is heavy with datura, the white flower of the highlands that's popular for its delirium-inducing state when wine isn't enough to cause a little mayhem. It's lethal in high doses, but it's a game those with long lives like to play. It's enough to ease the mind.

Zeke and I enter the hazy room. The same fae are at the tables, drinking and playing card games. We make our way to the room behind the paneled wall and wait for Jesper.

"The same words—" I'm cut off by two voices, loud enough to piece through the paneled wall. I look at Zeke and nod. We stand ready for a fight.

"Let me see him. That bastard."

"Calm down!"

"I'll calm down when I rip his head off."

I smile at the deep timbre of the voice. A figure with jet black hair barrels into Jesper, forcing them both through the door. Jesper gets pushed against the wall as a fae stares at me in disbelief. His hulking, muscular frame is imposing. Torches reflect the golden threads in his deep blue tunic, giving him the aura of a warrior bathed in sunlight.

"Ronan!" A laugh escapes as I step toward the fae standing before me with open arms. Instead of an embrace, a punch lands, slinging my jaw to the side as pain explodes through my skull. Righting my head, I rub my face. "Deserved."

Ronan embraces me and pats my back. Pulling away, he holds my shoulders. "How come you didn't find me? Or tell me you returned? I would have come sooner."

"They didn't know you were alive. The raid took a lot of us out, and some have been too afraid to return." I clasp arms with him before stepping back.

"Bah. I'm not that easy to kill." Taking off his black cloak, the scars on his arms show themselves, and he's missing two fingers on his left hand. Things have changed for us both; stories to be told at a later time. "Tell me about this human girl I've been hearing about. The one with magic. The one that looks like her."

Zeke gives Ronan a slap on the back before he leaves to get more drinks. The chair creaks beneath him as we sit at the table. I fix Jesper, who sits across from us, with a look. Understanding my unspoken question, he imperceptibly nods, giving me his agreement on bringing Ronan into the fold about Ameris.

We've been friends since we were younglings, spending long summers together and then fighting side by side in the battle of

Rhiannon's fall. Ronan saved my life the night I tried to go after my father, and then held me as I watched him die. He was there when we formed the rebellion and led the charge with me against Oberon. That was the night I saved his life—my life debt repaid.

"Her name is Ameris. I woke up in the world humans come from, and spent time in captivity until she found me in the ruins of a ship that I wrecked as it came to shore. There are humans born of the banished fae that have magic, but not in the way we understand and wield magic. Ameris is born from Rhiannon's line and can control all the elements."

"I don't fully understand her human magic, but she is the one who enabled my return. We're staying at the old headquarters and plan to revive the rebellion. Now that we have her, we can use her control over the elements to finally best Oberon."

Ronan shifts in his seat. "I'm all for kicking that usurper's ass. But how do you expect her to do that when Rhiannon was centuries older than this human and still failed?"

"Not to mention they captured Ameris," Zeke adds, setting the drinks down in the middle of the table.

"We're going to get her back," I press out through gritted teeth. Tension roils through my body at the thought of her in captivity.

"Well, what's the plan, then?" Ronan takes a swig of the fermented honey water, then swipes his arm over his mouth. He's a warrior and has the demeanor of one. Not like the delicate manners we hold our nobles to—like me. It's why I like him.

We talk into the night, discussing the plans for the dinner party and how to get Ameris out. Zorria never shows up, so we'll have to brief her when we get back. When Ronan leaves the room to get another round of drinks, Jesper gets up. "I'm done for the night."

I stay seated. "I'm going to stay back and talk to Ronan. Catch up." Ronan hands me water this time. I look at the cup, and he shrugs.

"It's still a drink and about time. Don't want a headache tomorrow." He laughs and downs his in one gulp.

"See you in the morning," Jesper says. Zeke follows him after first clasping arms with Ronan.

I don't actually want to stay and talk to Ronan. What I want is to find the old lady and talk to her again. Find out more. The conversation drones on as we catch up on what we've missed since the fall of the rebellion and my banishment.

It's not that I'm not interested in the topic at hand, but Ameris is my priority now. She's the key to our success. Ronan notices my responses have become automatic, dull.

He finishes his drink and sets the empty goblet on the table. "Ready to call it a night?"

"Yes, but I need to find someone before I leave. It's been a pleasure. I'll see you in a few days' time." We both rise and clasp arms, going our separate ways. I flip up the hood of my cloak before leaving the side room.

The barkeep watches me as I lean against the bar, trying to see who's beneath the hood. But he knows not to ask. Asking can get you killed. Scanning the space, the crowd is rowdy tonight, clinking mugs together and reveling in debauchery. I finally spot the old woman and follow her movements until she disappears down the hall beyond the bar.

I catch up to her with ease, as one of my footfalls equals three of hers. Her movements are slow but steady. I push open the door to the storeroom, checking to make sure no one is occupying it before I grab her arm and pull her into the room.

"Hey! Let go of me." A yelp of surprise escapes, filling the small space.

"Hush." I cover her mouth and hold her against the wall as I check that no prying eyes are upon us. My eyes flit to hers as I lower my hood with my free hand.

"Meps uuh." Her words come out muffled under my hand, but I understand them as 'it's you'.

"You need to tell me more about the bond. I saw you have similar scars." I release my hold on her and step back.

"It was far too long ago. There is nothing else to tell. You've wasted your time." Standing with her arms crossed, she continues. "They will notice my absence."

"What bargain did you make to end up here?" I demand—heat rises to the surface of my skin.

"I came here willingly. Eventually, I exchanged my service for immunity to the smoke and wine." Dropping her arms, she holds out a hand. "Let me see once more."

Pulling back the sleeve of my shirt, I let her inspect the white lines. Her hands are soft, but the skin is thin and lined with wrinkles. She moves my arm around to inspect the lines that run down it, tracing them back to the cut on my palm. Holding her finger to my palm, she closes her eyes and mumbles under her breath.

The room becomes a void; there is no longer any sound that penetrates the space, and a harrowing silence takes over. Her eyes reopen with force. Sounds come crashing back in, and my scar burns. I try to pull my hand back, but her grip is stronger than it should be for a human. Her eyes glaze over, unfocused, as they move back and forth. I pull again with success, and the connection breaks. She blinks like there is nothing more than a hair in her eye.

"What was that?" I shake my hand out, trying to get rid of the burning sensation. It hits me that, in order to have gotten to this world, this woman must also be a witch. She must've had to cast the same spell Ameris did.

"Bonds react differently between each pair. I was searching yours."

"I thought you didn't know anything else," I interrupt.

She continues, ignoring me. "You're here because she was taken from you. And you want to know how to tell your feelings apart. I no longer have magic, but I can still sense it. This bond runs as deep as the wounds it was born of. You will need each other. You must be strong, for the worst is yet to come. That's all I could discern."

The worst is yet to come. Deep. Born of the wounds she bears. Her words settle into my brain, heavy like a summer thunderstorm. The weight of the bond solidifies the truth that I must protect her. To protect myself. Shouting comes from outside the door, shattering my thoughts.

"Go now and do not return. You are not safe here. Take your rebellion elsewhere. The patrons talk, which is why I stay. I hear everything." Her hand rests on the handle of the door, cracking it open.

I try to thank her, but she shakes her head. "Take the back door. It was once said that Rhiannon would return with a vengeance." She steps out into the hallway but turns back and utters one last word. "Survive."

She disappears into the smoke from the bar, swallowing her whole in its thickness. The arguing increases, and I know it is time for me to leave. I lift the hood of my cloak and turn in the opposite direction.

"You!" The command echoes behind me, and I know it's intended for me as I reach the rear door. Peering down the hall before I exit, the same captain that took Ameris to the capital—Cortez—stalks in my direction. An urge to slam my fist into his face threatens to overcome me, but I center myself. That fight will have to wait for another day. "This way! He's taking the back exit!"

I take off at a run down the alley. Crates stacked against the wall become an escape route. I use them to propel myself onto the nearest roof and run along the adjoining rooftops, jumping from one to another until I'm a few blocks away. Slowing, I drop to a crouch, listening for the racket the guards create. Shouts echo in the distance. It's not long before they grow faint and fade into the night.

The soft hum of the crickets and the call of nighthawks fill the darkness. I lie back and stare at the stars and wait. I'll stay here until I'm comfortable and the way back is clear. The stars remind me of the nights I spent with Ameris in the human world. The nights I lay awake, thinking about Solarium and what I wanted to do when I got here. All that has changed, the bond complicating everything.

The old lady's words return, and I mouth them over and over —our bond runs as deep as the wounds it was born of.

We will need each other. My thoughts drift to when I saw her outside her cottage in the garden, slamming the hoe into the ground, the marks on her neck a fresh reminder of what I had done.

As deep as the wounds it was born of.

The wounds we inflicted upon each other.

Losing everything she knew.

Ameris's lies about the bond.

We will need each other.

We both have to survive.

I make a vow, speak it out loud to the stars that wait. I will protect Ameris, no matter the cost, until my last breath.

CHAPTER 32
AMERIS

Knuckles rasping on the door break my pensive stare at the ceiling, admiring the decorative plaster that coats it. I groan and roll out of the comfortable bed, which is nicer than anything I've ever slept on.

Not that it'd make me want to stay. But I can appreciate the luxury. Whoever is at the door either left or is patient, since I'm taking my sweet time answering the door. Pulling it open, I expect guards to bring me to Oberon, but it's a servant holding a tray of food.

"Oh, hi. I can take it." I reach out a hand to the tray, but the female wearing a golden smock, stitched with black thread, pulls it closer to her and shakes her head. I marvel at what she's wearing; it's beautiful. Half of her hair is pulled up, a braid flowing down the center to meet the rest of it. I push the door the rest of the way open, letting her inside.

"Really, I don't need you to do that." I watch as she quickly and meticulously lays out the food. She turns to leave in a hurry when realization dawns. "Wait, are you human?"

She says nothing but pauses before walking out and closing the door behind her. The click of the lock slides in place, reminding me I'm no guest, even though I'm being treated as such. I grab a roll and eat it as I pace around the room, sitting on the couch for a few minutes before moving to the bed to lie down.

Oberon has human servants. How are humans even here? My mind is restless, burning with questions about how they got here, what life is like as a human in Elysium, and the bargains that they entered unknowingly. All I can do is wait for the light of day to fall and darkness to fill my room to keep me company before I use its cloak to my advantage.

I wake with a start, my heart ricocheting against my chest cavity. Dammit, I fell asleep. Jumping out of bed in a fervor, I throw open the window to see the moon, a quarter of the way up. Phew. It's a few hours past dusk. The pounding in my heart slows and my breaths normalize, knowing I didn't sleep for too long.

Gathering the sheets off the bed, I tie them together. Pulling the curtains down, I add those to my makeshift rope. I only need it to be long enough to get me a safe enough distance to drop to the ground below. I check the window again and estimate I'll be able to get about four feet from the ground. Securing the sheets to the bedpost, I pull the knot as tight as I can, the thickness of the material not in my favor.

Before throwing the material out the window, I squat a few times, getting my blood flowing and muscles pumped to prepare for landing. I lower the fabric out the window, slow and steady, to avoid any noise or sudden movements.

Using the wall as my anchor, I slowly descend, taking each move with caution, for this drop will end my life should I fall to the hard ground below. The silk curtains make my descent particularly difficult.

The material is slick beneath my fingers. I wrap my hand around each piece, locking it into the fabric as I lower myself. This takes more time than is ideal, but none of this will do me any good if I'm dead. At least I tied the silk between the cotton sheets and used a more complicated knot to secure the fabric together.

I wrap my hands in the cotton material at the end of the rope and let my legs relax from the wall. Letting go, I drop to the ground and scan the courtyard. There's no one in sight, and the only sound is coming from the gurgling fountain in the middle. I keep to the shadows as best as I can and make my way across the courtyard to the exit I mapped out earlier.

A shiver crawls its way down my spine. It's quiet—too quiet—the kind that warns you and pushes blood through your veins faster, betraying your sense of safety. I keep moving even as I continue to feel the unease creep through my body, bringing my fine hairs to attention on my now pebbled skin. I know something's wrong, but I'm going to get out of here all the same. Better to try than sit around doing nothing. I will control my fate.

Hedges line the walkway, white flowers blooming along its height, so tall I can't see beyond them. Sticking to the edge, I keep my footfalls light and quick, just short of running. I look around every so often, but no one follows.

The hedges open up into another courtyard—no, a garden, a well-manicured one, flanked by stone walls. Raised garden beds litter the grounds, filled with different plants—lavender, yarrow, lemongrass, valerian, echinacea, roses, citrus trees, and so many more that I've never seen before.

A sharp pang hits as it reminds me of the garden I had back home.

Again, that word.

Home.

What it means to me now, and what that tells me about where I belong. But it's neither here nor there. I move on before I think too much about the subject. Before panic rises again and I find myself in a heap in the grass. That won't get me anywhere, so I shove the emotions down.

I can't help but walk to the edge of the terrace, looking over the expansive gardens that extend beyond and the one road that leads out to the city. The city lights twinkle below me like a thousand fireflies dancing at my feet. As much as I hated being trapped within those cavern walls, I wish I was there, where my hands weren't bound, and my magic could flow freely.

I feel his presence before the words drift down to my ear. Silent as a wraith, he approaches. "Hello, my stygian." The last word rolls off his tongue in an endearment.

Oberon comes to stand beside me. Placing his hands on the terrace wall, he drums his fingers against the stone beneath, the same motion he made earlier in the throne room. As he moves his fingers, his rings catch in the moonlight and glimmer in the darkness. Among the intricately crafted rings inlaid with gems is a simple golden band.

"I am not your stygian. Whatever that means." Scowling, I assess him.

He's a head taller than me. His light skin and violet eyes clash with the black clothing he wears. It's not a pallid complexion, but one that reminds me of the stars that shine bright against the night sky. His lean but muscular stature is accentuated by the way the moonlight reflects off his fitted leather coat. The way he can meld into the shadows and darkness is admittedly alluring and beautiful. His eyes hold so much depth; he's attractive in a dark and menacing way.

"Maybe, but you will eventually. It means you will become my darkness, the hellish thing that will haunt me always. For love or hate, it will be you." His voice is as silky as the curtains I used to escape.

"What do you want?" I ask, annoyed that my plan has failed.

"I want your power. Your face. And the love the people have for their lost queen." The intensity in his gaze causes me to step back. "You still haven't told me your name."

"Ameris."

"Ahh." His fingers drum against the stone once more. He studies me, a tilt to his lips, as if ready to smile.

"Ameris, I may have tricked you before." His eyes flit to the gold and black cuffs on my wrists before he continues. "But I want you to know that I do not intend to harm you. You intrigue me."

Scoffing, I reply, "Most men say that. But it never tells the tale of their hearts' intent." I stare at him then, and he stares back. Why do these fae men have to be so beautiful? It's unfair. I can easily understand a failed bargain with one of them. They used their beauty as a tool to get what they want. The human heart is so fickle about the outward beauty of a being.

He pushes off the terrace railing. "Let me show you the shadow magic that only I possess. Why I rule."

"Why would I want to learn that? Isn't it destroying your world?" I fold my arm across my chest.

"By whose definition is it being destroyed? For darkness and death appeal to me. One may call me villain while another calls me savior."

I don't have an answer to this, so instead I ask, "What about your food supply? The other creatures that live in the forest, and the dwellers of spring and summer? What happens to them when the world becomes too cold? When you can no longer feed even yourself? Everything has a price."

He regards me. "Do you know all stories have a beginning? Even the evil ones?"

"One I don't care to hear about." I keep my arms crossed and lean against the terrace facing the palace. Taking in all its beauty in the moon's lowlight. The turrets spiral high, with intricate stonework like the massive cathedrals I've seen in the human world. Not that I have seen many, but I can imagine what they all look like from the descriptions I've heard from other travelers in town.

These memories keep creeping up when I least expect or want them. How long is this going to last? How long until I no longer see the things from my past weave into my experiences of the present? I wonder if they will ever leave me.

"I am going to tell it to you anyway. For it may change your mind. It is a long story, as our lives are infinite, and I have forgotten some details to time. But what remains are memories of pain and fear. My father was the king before Rhiannon. And the throne was mine, or so I thought, until she came into the picture. Oh, my father never loved me, or thought me worth his time. I couldn't find an affinity for any of the elements. But, you see, she could call to them all."

He looks at me, asking without words if I have the same ability. When I don't give him a response, he continues. "And so the king took her under his wing and raised her as his own daughter. She didn't have an ounce of royal blood, yet she was more valuable than me."

"Time is a funny thing. It can morph you into something that was lurking just under the surface. Propelled by that which could have flourished if nurtured, yet, when left out, that same thing rots and decays. I tried everything to gain my father's favor as I saw my throne slowly slip from my grasp."

"In the end, my father named her next heir and ruler, and I was all but forgotten. Fate has a way of making its rounds. Being forgotten allowed me to manifest my desires and seek the hidden things in this world. Things that live in the shadows and hide from us. It didn't take me long to figure out that shadows are my calling. And the darkness is my comfort."

"So, you didn't get what you wanted, and you turned evil because of it?" I look at him, but he's staring out over the grounds and at the city beyond.

"No, Ameris, I found what I had been missing, and it saved me. And all of this," he motions to the grounds and the city below, "was mine to rule before she came along."

"So, why do you need me if you have everything you ever wanted? Everyone fears you, you won the battle, and you rule the land." What is he getting at? I don't know what he thinks I have to offer. Sure, I have my witch abilities and now elemental magic, but I can't do anything with these binders on.

"The shadow magic needs you. It sings of you in my sleep. Songs about the one that would come. A girl that will save us all or destroy us all."

"Right. A chosen-one prophecy? I don't believe in things like that. There are tales told like that in the human world, and people live their lives depending on them. They waste away hoping for something that will never come."

"No. These are melodies sung only to me in the dead of night. A curse Rhiannon left behind when I banished her. She promised to return."

"Well, I'm not her. And she is dead."

"You know pain and loss. You want control. I can give you everything you desire."

His offer startles me. I didn't take him for the kind to give things away so freely. I search within those words for a trick. For a mistake. One that would have unforeseen circumstances in the future. Being human, I can lie, but I wonder if my fae lineage also gives me the power to bind someone with their words. I choose my next words carefully. "What kind of control can you give me?"

"I will teach you the power of the shadows. Give you freedom from the bond, so long as you remain in the palace. Be mine."

Well, that's not freedom, but better than the guards constantly watching me. I lift my chin in defiance, not wanting anything to do with him. "And if I don't accept?"

"I thought you might say that." He snaps his fingers, and a guard appears from behind the hedges. His eyes narrow, and his lips pull back into a wicked grin.

A whimper escapes, and my knees buckle as I see who the guard is escorting. Honey. Cool stone bites as my fingers curl into it, steadying myself. I must sound so pathetic and weak to Oberon, but that's exactly what seeing my horse has done to me.

Without thinking, I move forward, ready to hold her, unsure if this is even real. But the smooth black leather of his coat wraps around my shoulders, firmly pulling me against him. I push against his hold, but he remains steadfast, a stone barrier that halts my advance.

A soft tsk fills my ears. One that echoes his dominance in the game we've entered. His hold tightens, a silent declaration of control, and his words are laced with a threat. Gone is the gentle and charming demeanor, replaced by violence. "I may not be willing to harm you, but I have no qualms about harming that which you love to get what I want."

"Bring it."

The guard walks toward us, and Honey whinnies as they approach. My hands tremble as I lean weakly against Oberon's arm. He lowers it, allowing me to greet her. As I approach, my heart thrums with a mix of relief and fear. She's safe, but still in danger. The moment my fingers graze her sleek and warm hide, she responds, pressing her body gently against mine. A sign of her recognition and trust, of our familial bond reaffirming itself.

"How?" A tear slides down, its heat breaking some of the ice that formed around my heart.

"You haven't earned that answer." Oberon throws my words back at me. He grabs my arm and pulls me away from Honey. "Take the horse away. And bring the other."

The other? I don't care for anything else. Yet, my breath hitches when they drag out a fae, the male's feet trailing behind on the ground, head bobbing along as the guards draw near.

"Ameris. Nice to see you." Zeke coughs out and flashes me a crooked smile, his normally cheery voice rough as if he hasn't had anything to drink for days. Dried blood cakes his face from his temples to his chin. His left eye is swollen shut. My lungs constrict at the sight of him.

"Your only friend will die if you do not. It's not just his loss that you will suffer; it's the repercussions of his death, what it will mean to the others in his group, who are surely to come after you. What will they do, knowing his death was a result of your actions? Think on it, Ameris. Comply, and everyone will survive."

I'll do anything to keep harm from coming to Honey, and now he's not only threatened her, but he also has Zeke.

I turn, and want to slap the menacing smile off his face. Collecting myself, I word my agreement carefully. "I will stay at the palace if you give me what I need. No harm is to come to Honey or Zeke by anyone's hand or magic. They are to be cared for and protected." I hold out my hand.

Oberon takes it, but instead of shaking it, he lifts it to his lips. He places a featherlight kiss on the back of my hand. "A deal is a deal."

His violet eyes sparkle as he chuckles and slides my hand into the crook of his elbow. "Now, let me escort you back into the palace. You can come here tomorrow to see the splendor of the garden in daylight."

He doesn't let go as he walks us back to the palace. I expect his skin to be cold against mine, but his touch is warm.

I should fear him, but I'm angry.

I want to see how far I can go—how much I can get him to give me. Sink my own talons so far into his flesh that he won't be able to escape my grasp. To become the predator he doesn't see coming.

CHAPTER 33
AMERIS

A folded piece of paper floats from under my door before it lands gently on the floor. My feet slap against the cold floor as I slide off my perch from the window. I pick up the yellowed paper. It has a lingering scent of leather and sulfur.

This isn't the first, and I don't expect it to be the last. Since Oberon found me on the terrace, I've seen him once, during breakfast, with a long table between us. I tried to speak, but he held up his hand in a command of silence. When he finished eating, he left without a word, never even glancing my way.

And now, another letter. Be ready at the sun's zenith.

Ripping the paper to shreds, I forcefully throw it into the fire. I scoff at Oberon's beckoning, annoyed. Opening the wardrobe, I shuffle through the old clothes.

Finding a plum chiffon dress, I step into it, shimmying the slightly too-tight fabric that hugs my wide hips. The queen was a bit slenderer than I am, but the tightness accentuates my hourglass waist and shows off my cleavage. Mid-length lace sleeves connect to a solid bodice that flows out past my hips, with more lace overlaying the deep purple fabric.

It's beautiful. I can't deny it, but I still prefer pants and a top. Hoping to grab his attention, I forgo comfort. I'm tired of being ignored. It doesn't help my brewing plans.

Looking in the mirror, I braid my hair, moving from one temple to the other, making a crown. The rest of my hair flows down my back. I let the baby hairs that frame my face—those that never want to cooperate—retain their wildness.

A knock comes. I let my lungs expand, take in another breath, and slowly release it while I count to three. I open the door to find Cortez. He looks me over before smirking. "Well, well. What do we have here? I thought I'd be finding the feral creature I captured in the street."

I scoff. "She's still here. Don't get too close. I might bite."

He laughs before he pulls my arm and shuts the door behind me. I want to take him down again, in this dress, just to show him I can. But my better judgment wins after reminding myself it's only a matter of time. Nothing is as it seems here, and I'll be the same. I will be whatever I need to be to get what I want.

He escorts me past the dining hall and through the main hall, but the rooms are empty. No other fae are present except for the guards.

"Why are there guards if no one is ever here?" I mutter, but it's loud enough in the empty spaces for Cortez to hear.

He looks down at me. "Why are there thorns on a rose?"

"Ugh." Rolling my eyes, I remain silent as we continue through the entrance doors and into the blinding light of day. He escorts me to the garden terrace, where Oberon found me the night I tried to escape. A rainbow of colors comes alive in the daylight. The light wind teases the plants below, their leaves swaying in the breeze. It's utterly beautiful and mesmerizing how the colors move amongst each other.

I reach out a hand to feel the vibration within the air—the way the energy moves through the plants in the garden. But nothing comes, and I remember, a second too late, that I don't have access to magic. He took it from me. Gold and black cuffs, harsh against the colorful background, serve as my reminder. Dropping my hand, I dig my fingers into my palms, frustration rising.

I need to find out what these are made of and figure out a way to get them off. The black looks like stone but reflects light as if it's glass. It reminds me of obsidian, but it can't be that simple. Regardless, I need magic again.

"Hello." The silky and low timbre of Oberon's voice comes from behind.

I'm losing the ability to know my surroundings and to sense when someone approaches because I'm distracted, and it's showing. Twice is two times too many. I turn around to find him standing a few feet from me, dressed in a deep purple tunic, far deeper than the plum I chose. A black vest rests over the tunic, matching his black pants. The color choice we both made intrigues me, a message to the other to signify our nobility, power, and ambition.

"The color suits you, Ameris." His eyes never leave my face. He raises a brow as a slow smile builds. A wicked and hungry gleam sits in his eyes, like I'm a feast that was just laid before him. One that he cannot wait to devour.

"As does yours." The color of his tunic amplifies his eyes. They burn with an intensity I haven't seen before. My heart flutters, a reaction I can't control, along with the heat that builds. He's dangerously beautiful. I turn back to the garden and release a breath. "What are we doing here?"

"It is not here. Come." Oberon holds out his hand, offering to guide me down the stairs he's standing before.

I clinch my fingers and shake my head, declining his offer. He's too handsome. I don't need to be any closer than required. He nods and places his hands behind his back. Without waiting for me, he walks down the stairs leading into the garden.

We walk through the garden and see more herbs I recognize

from my time in the human world. Herbs used for the tinctures and salves I made, infused with our magic. Almost everything I need to make the things I used to is here.

"Are these plants natural in this world?" I ask.

"Most are, but some came from the humans," he responds, continuing forward.

Stopping in front of some lavender, I run my fingers through the soft green spikes and over the purple flowered tips. Closing my eyes, I take a deep breath, fill my lungs with the calming scent, and let it wash over me. I let it bring me back to a place where there was joy and love.

When I open my eyes, Oberon has stopped and is watching me with an interested expression that's short-lived. With a wave of his hand, he beckons me forward. I rip a few of the stems away from the plant and follow.

Grand oak trees that loom beyond the garden rise up upon our approach. The entrance to the forest, the one I was trying to reach the other night, is before us, and we enter, sunlight fading the deeper we go. My eyes adjust, but it's not just the blocked light that's causing the darkness. The tree trunks are as dark as night the farther we walk into the forest.

"What is this?" Everywhere I look there are varying shades of blackened trunks. Above us, strings of light weave through the leaves, but their glow never reaches where I stand.

"The Black Forest. My Forest." Oberon walks to a tree and puts his hand on it, rubbing it along the trunk. "Come. Feel."

I approach and hesitantly reach out my hand.

He leans down, his lips inches from my ear. His voice is a soft caress as he instructs me. "Close your eyes and let it find you."

The hairs on my neck rise, sending a shiver down my spine. Placing my hand next to his on the trunk, I follow his instructions and close my eyes. At first, nothing happens, but then, just under the surface, I feel the decay, the shallow and slow pulse, like a heart that is a beat or two from death. A cold sensation reaches my fingers, and I pull my hand back.

"How?" I'm surprised I can sense it with the cuffs on.

"Ah. So, you felt it. I thought it might be so," he says, more to himself than me. Turning away from the tree, he holds out his hand for me. This time, I take it. Oberon leads me away from the tree and back the way we came. "That Ameris is the magic of the shadows. It feeds on life within the world and turns it toward death—at least, that's my favorite part."

"How do you expect to survive in a world where there is only death? Where will your food come from?" I ask, continuing to let the weight of his words sink in as I look at the dead trees around us. There are only a few shrubs alive. This forest floor is as barren as the one Xander and I traveled through on our way to the capital.

"I only need enough alive to control the world." He walks alongside me with his gaze on the horizon.

"But you're already in control." Confusion crosses my features as I wait for his reply. When he doesn't immediately respond, I think he doesn't have an answer, but it comes after several beats of silence.

"No, Ameris, I rule as king. I am not in complete control. I want the world to need me, to beg me for what they need, to feel what desperation is. To know what it is to have everything you thought was your right taken away."

"The garden." The realization hits me, the words coming out as a whisper.

But he heard me. "Yes." His answer comes as we leave the shadows of the forest and walk into daylight. The garden looks different now. More important.

"Why are you showing me this? Telling me this?"

Oberon stops and pulls up our linked hands to inspect my arm. He removes his hand from mine and wraps it around my wrist, holding it still. His black nails delicately trace the thin raised lines that marred my skin after I cast the bond, following them to the source on my palm, reaching the scar left by the blade that sliced it.

He lingers there for a moment before the intensity in his gaze shifts. A fire burns within his violet irises when he looks upon my face. It could be his delicate touch when he traces the marks along my wrist and arm.

Or the way he speaks to me.

Or the surety of himself and the purpose with which he walks.

There is power in his presence, and I want to bathe in it, to let it seep into my skin and settle like the missing nutrients I need.

My reverie is broken the moment he speaks. "I know what these are. Why are you really here, Ameris?"

I want to jerk my hand back in surprise at his knowledge. I thought we were the first to return to this world. How would he know what my scars mean? "I'm here because I had no other choice. I don't want to be here. I couldn't care less if this world burned to the ground."

The words come out hard and laced with hatred. I surprise myself, but don't regret it. All the freedoms I thought I would enjoy were only a delusion. I am just as caged here as I was in the human world.

I hate it here, and that I am linked to someone. My bond with Xander causes me to have lingering thoughts of him. To fill my dreams with him. Making me want to be near him. I fight it with every fiber of my being because I don't want anyone or anything to have control over me.

"There it is." Oberon brings my hand to his lips, kissing the scar that runs along my palm. I release a shuttering breath. His touch is intoxicating, giving me permission to hate the world, to be angry.

With my silence, he continues. "I want to set you free from this bond. I want you to show me how to use your human magic." Oberon kisses my scarred palm once more.

The scar that burned my soul.

The scar that gave me power.

But took away my choice.

I want more power because I want control. To be free from the things that bind me—including Oberon. But it's also what he's offering, for a price. Fae don't operate on their own goodwill; there is a bargain to be made, one that I can manipulate for my own goals. "What do you want in return?"

He already asked me to stay at the palace. This must be how they trap humans into the bargains they make. One bargain topped by another, securing the life of a human.

"Your help to ruin the rebellion. For you to teach me how to use your human magic." Oberon steps back as he gently releases my arm.

It falls to my side, the warmth of his touch gone in an instant, at odds with the disbelief coursing through me that I know shows on my face. My hands stiffen. Unsure of what to do, I hesitate.

If I take too long to answer, he might take my hesitation as a sign of dishonesty. Even though everything I said is as true as the sun rising in the east, I grapple with it because a part of me still wants to protect Xander and his rebellion. Yet, the only option is to comply; that's the only thing that will save Honey and Zeke from certain death.

"Yes." My answer comes before I can continue to think too long upon friends who won't be in my life forever. Someone who can be my friend can just as easily turn into my enemy. "But," I stop to add my part of the bargain and to add my need from the night we agreed I would stay. "First, you never asked what I needed the other night. I need my grimoire. Second, I want you to teach me how to control the shadow magic, not just show me."

"I shall make it so."

Words are tricky, as are bargains. I didn't say how I would help end the rebellion, just that I would. He gets what he wants, and I get what I want. I'll figure out how to deal with these cuffs another time.

CHAPTER 34

XANDER

"We're headed out for supplies," I call over my shoulder. Ronan and I gather our satchels and head out to the market.

"Be careful, Xander. They'll know you're back now that they have captured her." Jesper's stern voice carries, even as we walk farther into the tunnel that leads out of the underground. He's staying behind with Lyle to go over plans.

The new moon offers its protection as we leave the garden and enter the city. The market is a different beast at night. Fae are out in their midnight finery, drinking and dancing with each other. Their bodies move in rhythm with the music playing from the band. The revelry is palpable. Even under the threats brought on by Oberon's rule, we still take time to enjoy what we can. There are still guards roaming about, but even they are more relaxed; a few even partake in drinking.

I remember the nights I thought all was in my favor for the future. The parties I planned to throw, and the semi-sweet wine I wanted to get from the winterberries of the north. It was all I wanted then. I didn't have a care in the world.

Envy licks at my insides as I watch these fae, living freely. I think of Ameris and wish I brought her here. Let her have a night of enjoyment. Maybe then our lives wouldn't have come crashing down for a second time.

Weaving through the bodies, I grab a drink and down it in one gulp, tossing a coin to the merchant. Music floats through the air, seeping into my skin, urging me to lose myself in its melody. To forget everything that has happened over the past few days. Fae dance in time with the music, scattered in groups and as couples around the fountain in the middle of the square.

The melody is as entrancing as it was in my youth; the beats moving up, down, and all around. As I move through the crowd, beautiful fae approach me; their hands slide along my arms, enticing me to a dance. They reach for my hood, but I swipe their hands away and push them aside. I lean against a makeshift bar, waiting for another drink.

Ronan dances with a golden-haired fae whose pale skin is decorated in blue swirls and crushed pearls that make his skin shimmer. The male's muscles show through his skin-tight tunic as their bodies undulate together, matching the rhythm of the song.

"I've been scouting for you." Zorria's black braid falls over her shoulder as she saunters toward me. "Would you like to know what I saw?"

There's a delightful venom to her words, and the target is my heart. She knows I want to know, and she's enjoying the upper hand. I shouldn't give in to her whims, but I do. "And what would that be?"

She places her hands on the bar, boxing me in, and leans close. Her whisper is only meant for me. "Your human was in the black woods with Oberon. They were talking. Laughing, even. She wears gold bands." I don't miss the glint in her eye as she pulls back. "I'm thirsty. Care for a drink?"

I stare at her as she shrugs and walks away. I follow her form through the thick crowd to a different merchant. She orders a drink, taking it down in one gulp, then turns and leans against the bar. Her gaze roams over the crowd, finding her victim for the night. Once she's found them, she winks at me and pushes off the bar and through the patrons.

A whistle comes from Ronan as he joins me. "Geez, now you have to tell me what you did. She's angry." He watches as Zorria joins a group of fae in the square.

"Thank you for pointing out the obvious. She kissed me. I returned it. But it wasn't her I was thinking about." I also tell him what she just told me about Ameris and Oberon in the Black Forest.

"Ouch." Wincing, he buys me a drink. "Is she worth it?"

"I don't know. I think so. This bond is messing me up. I cannot tell what is real and what's forced. Did Zorria tell you anything else about what she saw?"

"She hasn't said anything to me." Ronan shrugs down his drink. "Maybe she went to find Zeke? Where is he?"

"He went out to meet with some rebellion members the other night. You know how he likes to stay out." We watch the crowd in silence for a few more moments before he pushes off and joins them in their revelry.

This time, dancing and kissing a female fae with tan skin and snowy white hair. Downing another drink, I make my way through the merchant's stalls. Jewels sparkle in the light of magical lanterns. I locate the source of the multiple colors that spread over the square. Compelled, I approach the merchant and see the necklace Rhiannon wore during her last battle; labradorite surrounded by blood red rubies.

"Another one drawn to the Amulet of the Forlorn." The merchant stands behind the counter, leaning against the stall.

"It has another name. You can't sell it because of its reputation." My focus goes to the dark-haired fae. "I'll give you a hundred crons for it."

"It hasn't been called its true name since Rhiannon fell, and it went with her. The amulet was lost for decades. Now I have it. And it'll cost you five hundred," he responds.

"Two hundred fifty." I would pay anything to get this, but the merchant doesn't need to know that. Ameris was here; the trace of her lingers. I feel it through the bond; she wanted this amulet.

"Fine." He sticks out his hand, and I place the money into it.

He grabs my wrist and studies the white scars along it. Lifting his head, he tries to peer into the shadows of my hood. Jerking my arm back along with the necklace, I turn and take a few steps before pausing at his words.

"I'll buy it back when you're down on your luck. That necklace is nothing but trouble—starting now." He chuckles, then yells, "Guards!"

Dammit.

I tuck the amulet into the inside pocket of my tunic and take off through the crowd. My heart beats in tune with the acceleration of the music. Risking a glance back provides the incentive to pick up my pace; the guards are not far behind.

Whipping my head around, I don't have time to stop as a fae suddenly steps into my path. I slam into them, and we fall to the ground, but I waste no time getting up and sprinting forward, offering no help to the bastard who got in my way. Getting out of here is my priority. Ronan and Zorria can handle themselves, wherever they are.

Shouts from the guards are closer than they were before, but I'm almost to the garden where I can lose them. At my last turn onto the gravel path, vines begin to curl around my waist, snaking their way down my legs. My heart races as panic sets in. Something isn't right. I rip at the vines, but for every vine I destroy, two more spring forth, multiplying faster than I can remove them.

Distracted by the vines, I don't see the fae that blocks my path. When I look up, it's too late. He throws a branch that comes to life as it nears me, binding my hands. I fall forward as the vines wrap around my legs, securing me from escape.

"Hello Xander." The arrogant voice is one I know all too well.

"Cortez," I grit out. It was intentional. He's the fae who stepped into my path, planting his vines on me, letting me get up because he knows better than to fight me. "Cheap trick." A guard puts obsidian binders on in place of the branches, cutting off my magic.

"But a trick that works." Cortez's sly smile is barely visible in the darkness of the gardens. "So, the girl is yours?"

I want to snap out that Ameris is nobody's, but I hold back. Better that I don't openly admit anything. "I don't know what you are talking about. How about you untie me and we fight like old times?"

"I think not. You have a much more entertaining future that I cannot wait to witness." He stands over me, looking down, before he crouches. "How pathetic. The false prince, lying here, unable to do anything."

"I never called myself a prince, but she chose me to rule next." Frustration flares as I throw an elbow at his face. Cortez hops back before it can make contact and gets up.

"Well, chosen one, you have a lot to look forward to now that you have returned." He turns to his guards. "Take him."

I jerk as they lift me from the ground, but their grip is too tight, and my efforts to shove them off are futile. Cortez snaps his fingers, and the vines unravel from my legs, moving up to pin my arms against my body. "What makes you so loyal to Oberon? What has he done other than ruin this world?"

"Better to serve the new ruler than to live in hiding," Cortez says without looking back as he leads the company of guards back into the city.

"Sir, do you want us to put his hood back up?" one of the guards asks Cortez.

Cortez turns and studies me before answering the guard. "No. Let the people see their fallen prince has returned, only to be captured again."

I can't help the growl that escapes. Cortez and I have unfinished business, and he's gloating that he has me captive.

"Won't that make them want to rally?" the guards probe.

"Do you think Oberon isn't already aware of Xander's little reorganization talks? There are plans for Xander, none in his favor. No more questions. Let's move," Cortez commands.

He's baiting me, hoping for a reaction, but I won't give him one. I steel my features as the guards shove me forward. How does Oberon know we are meeting again? It must be a trick to get me to reveal our secrets. The only thing he would know by now is that a human girl has entered this world, one who looks like Rhiannon. Unless she told him.

No, she wouldn't do that. She has no reason to—I hope.

Just as we leave the garden, a movement in the shadows catches my attention. The glint of blades, ready to find purchase in the guards that hold me. Zorria sits under the cover of tree branches, but I shake my head. It isn't worth fighting them off. There are too many of them, and I don't want to put anyone else at risk.

Zorria shakes her head as she sinks deeper into the shadows. She will return to the underground and let the group know what's happened. Ameris is no longer the only one they'll have to free during the delegates dinner.

In the fashion of Cortez, he walks us through the city square. I'm escorted through the crowd, but it takes a while for the dancing to slow and for the fae to take notice of who is being escorted through the middle of the revelry. The guards' silence is intentional, and I do nothing to break it, holding my head high, gazing straight ahead.

But I hear the whispers.

This parade goes on all the way to the palace. They take me straight to the dungeon. Torches line the walls, illuminating the grime that covers everything. It's a place I have been many times, but as the one escorting others to their cells. Two guards shove me into the dirtiest one, with only straw on the ground as a bed.

"Enjoy your stay," Cortez says as he motions with his hand. The vines that pin my arms to my body crumble as they dry out and die.

I lean against the wall and slump down onto the straw that is piled in the corner. I pull the amulet out, turning it over and over, wondering why Rhiannon wore it when it would block her magic. Thinking of Rhiannon brings me back to Ameris. The closer we got to the palace, the stronger my connection to her became.

CHAPTER 35
AMERIS

The midday sun is out in full force, beating down on me and the guards that escort me to a different part of the forest. The coolness of the forest cover is an instant relief. The browns and greens are luminous in the light that filters through the branches.

There is no decay here, only life. We make it through and into the heat once more. Oberon stands in a circular glade, waiting for our approach. It's been two days since I last spoke to him, and there has been no sign of my grimoire.

I've asked the guards assigned to watch over me every day to find out about it. They don't respond or give me any information. It's quite annoying to have guards all the time—for my protection, I'm told. Not everyone is a fan of my presence; too many reminders of the past.

He may not want me, but he wants the magic I have. A type of power he doesn't have—cannot have. Simply put, I am a threat. But a threat that the king desires. He thinks I've bargained my freedom away. That he is in control.

I'll let him think that for as long as it takes.

Sweat beads on my neck, the heat searing my light skin like I'm baking in an iron stove. Thank goodness I chose white clothing. A loose linen shirt paired with matching pants that tighten around my ankles gives me the mobility and comfort I prefer to dresses. It's a simple outfit. I'll keep the fancy dresses for special occasions. Oberon nods to the guards, and they retreat to the shade of the forest.

"Aren't you hot?" I ask as I take in his all-black attire—simple pants paired with a leather vest that covers a bare chest. His exposed, pale arms are more muscular than I thought they would be. The curves of his biceps are prominent as he stands with his arms crossed.

He smirks. "If I get hot, I'll undo my vest."

"Well, then." I choke back my surprise at his response. So he has a sense of humor. "How will I be able to do this with these cuffs on?"

He walks up and inspects me. Moving my loose hair behind my ear, he leans in and whispers, the phantom touch of his lips against my ear, "Close your eyes and trust me."

I oblige. His presence is palpable, cool, and heavy as he slowly moves around me. Hands settle on my shoulders, gentle but firm. I relax under his touch, the coldness of it seeping through the linen, sending chills along my spine. The scent of him reaches me, like he is made of leather and fire in winter.

"Think about all that you hide. All the anger. The frustration. The hatred." His words are demanding, strong, and harsh.

It isn't hard. Those emotions sit right under the surface. They hover, waiting for a chance to be released. His voice comes again, this time silky and encouraging. I let his words put me in a trance. "Feel the fury closing in. Let it bury deep within. Then pull at the havoc it creates."

I remember the way I felt when my hand was against the tree in the Black Forest—the way the magic left a pulse so subtle yet cold and willing. Wanting to be found, waiting for the right person to seek it out.

All these months of holding in my anger, my frustration, and my despair burst forth. I let it fuel a fury within myself I have never known. Let it burn within my soul. Let the chaos within take over. The way the storm must have felt that day—the one that brought my life into disarray.

"Yes, keep feeding it." Oberon's voice is a beacon amid the momentum of my emotions, guiding me to the edge.

The chaos builds and builds until it reaches a breaking point. My arms open wide as I lose control and let out a scream, releasing the tide of darkness within. I fall to my knees, and the angry heat of the sun falls away. Dropping my head back, I open my eyes to see the sky has become a tangle of shadows. Oberon's form blurs above me as my vision goes in and out.

I release a sigh as the weight of the emotions and magic hits me. Pulling my head forward, I draw my gaze to the border of trees that are now black. Charred from the release of magic.

Black pants fill my vision before he leans down.

"Very good, my stygian," Oberon says, accompanying a look of admiration.

There is no coming back from this. He's broken me open in a different way. In a way that feels good to be pulled under. To feel what it's like to lose control. To let dark things take over. I'm sinking into the deep end, and my breath is catching. The current is about to take me out into the darkness. A command against my soul is being made.

Dropping my arms, I close my eyes again. It felt so good to feel magic pulsing through my body once more. He's letting me have his magic, even though these cuffs block out all my other magic.

But I want it all.

My body shakes as I attempt to stand and fail, my legs giving out. Before I hit the ground, his sturdy arms catch me. As he rights me, I lean into him, his muscular body hard beneath my palms. His heart beats slowly under my touch. It steadies my breathing as exhaustion washes over me. He runs a hand over my hair in soothing motions as his other arm holds me. "The magic wants you...I want you. Need you."

Leaning my head against his chest, I push my body back and take a few more breaths. I grab his arms to steady myself. The grass that was once under our feet has turned to dirt.

This magic comes at a price. Destruction.

As the exhaustion fades, a feeling of excitement takes over. I did it—tapped into a magic only one other has mastered. That will be my next goal—to learn to control it and know when to wield it. A memory floats to the surface. The nightshade, Lor, sensed great power within me. It flows through my veins, pounds in my heart, fills my lungs, along with every crevice of my body, just waiting to be unleashed.

My hands glide up the length of his arms, tracing the contours until they rest on his shoulders. I press my palms gently against the firmness of his chest, feeling the rhythm of his heart beneath. Lifting my gaze to meet his, I begin to unbutton his vest, each motion deliberate, unraveling the barrier between us with a mix of anticipation and hesitation.

Oberon doesn't move. Doesn't stop me. We search each other's gaze. His is questioning, searching my face for understanding in my actions. But he won't find that because there is nothing to understand. I am just reacting to the surge of magic and what feels good right now.

With the final button released, my hands find the warmth of his skin, our eye contact breaking as my fingers, guided by a silent curiosity, wander across his torso, mapping the landscape of his body. They stumble upon two scars.

One sits beneath his heart, a jagged line that trails down his ribs. The other is a mark of survival near his navel. Gently, reverently, I trace the contours of his scars, mirroring the way he once explored mine. The healed wound along his rib was meant to be a fatal blow. I've seen them before—treated them.

But most don't survive. I wonder what caused them, since fae are supposed to heal so fast that scars are rare.

When I look up again, I bring my lips to his.

Surprising him. Surprising myself. Even though the high is still buzzing through me, I know what I'm doing. My need to know what he can do for me heightens with the intimate contact between us. The cool touch of his lips mingles with the heat flowing through my body. My bond fights the sensation, but I revel in it. I feel a little wicked, and I want more of it.

As his lips press against mine, the world narrows to the space between us. The rich scent of leather and fire envelops me, a heady mix that is unmistakably him. In an effortless motion, he lifts me, as if I weigh no more than a feather. Instinctively, my legs wrap around his waist, drawing us even closer as the kiss grows more intense.

This is purely a mutual exchange of physical touch. After he held me, it made me realize how much I wanted to feel another's touch. Yes, I'm physically attracted to him, but there is no genuine desire here, or want, other than what he can give me in this moment.

Pulling back, I catch my breath and gently smooth his hair back into place, fixing the dishevelment my hands caused. I smile. "Thank you."

Oberon places me back down but doesn't say anything; he just watches, waiting for my next move.

I button up his vest before stepping back. "You looked hot."

His laughter echoes through the dead glade, and it makes me smile. It's the second time I've seen him laugh, and it looks good on him.

"I'm famished. I would like to eat." My stomach growls in agreement.

"Of course, my stygian." Oberon grabs my hand. We walk out of the glade and into the forest.

I forgot about the guards until we pass them. They fall in line behind us. I catch the glances that pass between them. I look back and give them a devious smile.

When we approach the palace, Oberon snaps his fingers. "Have the kitchen prepare us a meal and serve it in the dining hall. You can leave us now."

The guards run off into the setting sun at a pace that far exceeds what a human is capable of. When we enter the dining hall, food sits on the table, ready for us. Plates of cheese, fruit, and bread are laid out in front of the seat at the head and the one to its immediate right. We take our seats, and servants rush over to pour us wine. I down the sweet liquid, raising my cup for a refill. Tearing the bread, I savor the warm, fluffy inside, encased in a crispy shell that replenishes the energy I spent this afternoon. We finish our plates in silence.

When the servants clear the table, Oberon leans in, excitement plastered over his face. "I have something for you."

"Oh, is that so?" I raise an eyebrow in return, folding my arms over my chest.

"Fetch him!" he calls out.

A servant scurries away. Using the word 'him' causes an uneasiness to pool within my stomach. For all that I told myself in the glade, I still have to battle this bond that can't bear to have harm done to Xander. And then there is Zeke. Whom I haven't seen in days.

The servant re-enters the dining hall within minutes, a hooded figure following behind them. As the figure approaches the table, my nerves fire on high. This could be anyone. I need to respond in a way that pleases Oberon. I still have a game to play.

When the figure removes their hood, I cannot control the shock. My jaw drops, and my eyes widen. The last fae I expected to see stands before me. So much for playing the game. I lost this round.

Lyle.

"Hello Ameris." Lyle's voice removes me from the shock that had me frozen.

He approaches, handing me a parcel, and I know immediately what it is. My grimoire. I am grateful to have it, but it's at the expense of learning who the spy in the rebellion is. Oberon already knew I was in Solarium. It was only a matter of time before I fell into his hands. I know I'm a pawn, but irritation flares at thinking I had an advantage when I never did.

Lyle already passed information to Oberon—about me and our training. That's how he knew about the bond, how to draw me in, and what I wanted. Which means he knows I'm bonded to Xander. The one he banished is the one I returned with.

It takes this moment to know he will never remove these cuffs, so long as I remain under his control. I have been under someone else's control my entire life.

"Lyle," I force out as I gather myself and return my features to neutral. "What an unexpected surprise."

I turn to Oberon and give him a sweet smile. "You're so thoughtful."

I make a promise to myself.

Take them all down.

CHAPTER 36

XANDER

Four days have passed since I found myself confined to this dreary dungeon. Each day stretches longer than the last, filled with a monotonous blend of silence punctuated only by the incessant drip of water from the damp stone walls, and the scurrying of rodents that claim these shadowed depths as their domain.

Isolation wraps around me like a suffocating cloak, leaving my thoughts to chase themselves in endless loops, seeking escape in a place where none seems possible.

Warm light pierces the darkness. Pulling me from the familiar tug of thoughts that threaten to spiral once more.

At first, it's no more than a faint glimmer. It quickly intensifies, swelling into a brilliance that overwhelms my eyes, long accustomed to the shadows. The sudden flood of light is jarring, searing against my retinas, forcing me to shield my eyes against its merciless glow.

"Xander." A voice dripping with malice that reignites every ember of hatred I hold for the person it belongs to pierces the silence.

"Oberon," I return through gritted teeth.

"What a shame you returned." He perches against the wall in front of the cell, melding into the shadows, barely visible in the torchlight.

"Someone has to stop you." I spit at his feet. Anger roils through my veins at his presence.

"That is unlikely." He chuckles. "I should actually thank you. For the human. What a find. But Ameris is mine, and she doesn't even know it. You see, we've struck a bargain."

My insides churn at the implication that he's made a claim on her. Ameris is smart and wouldn't let herself get tricked. "If you think you can control her, you are sorely mistaken."

"Oh, Xander, you should have learned from your mistakes. I see your arrogance is still your weakness. You bound yourself to her. But she doesn't know the consequences, does she?" A haughty smile spreads, filling what light there is with evil.

"I can't kill you, Xander, or she dies." He steps forward, casting his gaze to the ground with a tilt to his head, as if lost in thought. There's a deliberate pause before he continues, landing a predator's gaze on me. Like he's won. Knows I'm the prey he's about to devour. "But that doesn't mean I can't make her want to kill you. And turn against you and your rebellion."

"I'll kill you if I ever get the chance." I snarl and launch forward, but he slides back. My hand grips air, just missing his tunic.

He clicks his tongue against his teeth. "You're going to tell her what I want, or your friends die. In fact, Zeke rests only a few cells away from you. And I know you've holed up again in that cave."

Zeke. I've failed my friends and the rebellion again. Failed to keep our secrets—our safety. My next breath comes out ragged as my heart pounds behind my ribcage. I thought we were so careful. Was it the night in the tavern when someone spotted us? I slam my hand against the bar, letting out a wave of frustration. "What do you want?"

"You will tell her you never intended to let her help you and that you were using her for the magic she possesses," Oberon commands.

"She won't believe it. And you know we cannot lie." I glare at him.

"Doubt is the seed that, once sown, grows wild." Oberon's words are a vicious poison. "But is it a lie? You didn't want her to help, and you did want to use her for the magic she is capable of."

My heart aches at his words because of the truth in them. I seek solace in knowing there is no way she will fall for the web of deceit Oberon is spinning. But I cannot risk the death of my friends. Moments pass before I nod, defeated.

"Ever the diligent heir." Oberon motions for the guards to open the cell. They cuff me once more and shove me out of the cell. Defeat hits at each step I take. I have no energy to fight them. "Take him to the atrium."

A vast stained glass ceiling vaults overhead, casting the room in an array of soft colors against walls made from white pearlescent stone meant to emulate serenity. Lush green foliage offsets the white to bring calm into the space. I used to love coming here to clear my head. To breathe in the earthen scents and ground myself.

Heaviness settles over me as I'm escorted forward, flanked by two guards, with another pair leading the way. Each step closer to the heart of the atrium amplifies a sense of Ameris's presence, an invisible thread pulling taut with anticipation and dread. It's a paradoxical comfort and curse, feeling her so near in a place twisted by Oberon's will.

The emptiness that wanes and waxes within me since her

capture fills the closer we are to each other. I can sense when she's close to the dungeon or away from the palace.

Her voice echoes around the atrium, before they reach us. It's different, more determined, yet lined with suspicion and an undertone of ease. She isn't suffering in this place, like she was with me. I hang my head—another layer of defeat that will weigh on me.

"How come you've never brought me here before? It's lovely," Ameris says.

"Today is special. I have something to show you." Oberon's voice is gentle, almost caring. As if he's a male who wants to impress his lover. Maybe he does. He was obsessed with Rhiannon, according to the stories my father told.

The two guards in front of me move aside, and when our eyes meet, her surprise can't be mistaken, but she corrects herself before Oberon notices.

"I don't want to see him." Ameris turns away abruptly, as if making to leave.

"He has something he wants to tell you." Oberon grips her arm firmly, stopping her, and forces her back around to face me.

Anger flares, and I want to rip his head off. I don't want to do this. My shoulders tense, and I strain my neck back and forth, as if a snake is wrapping itself around my throat and I'm trying to fight it. It goes against my instincts, my promise, and everything I stand for. I hate that this will cause her more suffering at my hands.

Oberon's eyebrow raises, and his piercing gaze bores into me, each word laced with a veiled threat—a warning not to cross him. 'Well, Xander, what do you have to say?"

My eyes flit between Oberon's glare and Ameris's watchful stare. She's like an oracle, her eyes intent upon mine, reading me as if she can uncover the layers of my thoughts with her gaze alone.

Inhaling deeply, my eyelids fall shut for a brief moment while I gather my resolve. With all the focus I can muster, I channel my true intention into the silent, unseen tether that connects us. It's a silent plea, a wordless message sent through the bond we share, hoping she understands the complexity of my position.

The words I'm about to speak will hold truth, but not entirely. My reluctance to draw her into this was real, but my need for her magic is undeniable. Yet, buried deeper than any scheme or necessity, lies my willingness to offer her everything, anything, if it meant it would protect her.

When I open my eyes, I lock onto her. "I used you. I only needed your magic to help with my plans to get to Elysium." The words leave me with no emotion.

Ameris stiffens and stares at me. My composure threatens to break as her eyes fill with clear liquid. Before her tears fall, she turns and walks away.

"Not being able to lie can often be the source of our greatest weakness," Oberon says as he waves us off.

"You bastard." I shove off the guards, ready to tackle Oberon. Even though my hands are bound, I can still knock him down. It would feel good if nothing else.

The atrium darkens, and inky blackness swirls in the air, giving pause to my advance. The guards grab a hold of me again, jerking me back. He brings the shadows close—a phantom touch—but it's enough to sting and send a message.

"Just because I can't kill you doesn't mean I can't hurt you." Oberon saunters away, shadows trailing him until he snaps his fingers, and they disappear. He can turn anything vile. Even sanctuaries like this are not spared from corruption.

Sunlight returns, but rather than being warm and inviting, it pours in with an intensity that feels almost aggressive, casting harsh shadows that slice through the space. The plants are no longer green. Brown leaves fall from trees, and blackened flower petals fall from their stems.

Groaning in frustration, I take it out on the guards. I elbow the closest one in the face and kick the feet out from under another. It doesn't take long for them to tackle me to the ground, but I don't stop fighting. I keep lashing out, causing any damage I can, before Cortez walks in and sets his vines upon me once more. Deep, ragged breaths come out as I'm lifted by different guards to face Cortez.

"How does it feel to be helpless, Xander?" My head whips to the side from the punch he lands on my jaw.

The tang of iron fills my mouth. I pull my blood in and spit it at his feet. "You'll regret that."

"I doubt it." Cortez snorts, "And there's more of that coming. Maybe the arrogance will finally be beaten out of you."

I don't make the walk back to the dungeon easy for the guards. We know each other, but they act indifferent. They are the same palace guards that served Rhiannon. So much for loyalty.

When the guards leave, I'm left in the darkness of my cell once more, with thoughts that threaten to break me. My knuckles connect with the wall more times than I care to count. When they are bloody and raw, I turn my back against the dirty stone and slide down until I reach the floor. I grab my cloak and rip off strips to wipe the blood and wrap my hands.

I lie on the straw and stare into the darkness.

Silence presses its weight against my skin. Thoughts race, keeping me from sleep. If I get out of here, I will come back and take the throne. The only benefit of being left alone is the time it gives me to come up with the plans I'll need to put in place to secure my takeover. Not a takeover, but a righting of the wrongs that Oberon has consistently done to my world. He is a plague that needs to be eradicated. Along with Cortez.

I will sit on that throne.

CHAPTER 37
AMERIS

Every night brings discomfort. If it's not my thoughts on how Xander's here in the dungeons, it's how the thick black and gold bands that encircle my wrists bite into my flesh no matter which position I lie in. I thought I could finally bury the way the bond was drawing me to him. But no, he is within a few hundred feet of me at all times, making it harder to fight the pull of the bond.

I toss my grimoire aside and lift my arms into the sliver of silver moonlight that spills through the window. The light reflects off the black stone and golden metal. Putting Xander out of my mind, I turn to contemplating whether it's really as simple as obsidian, a stone I'm familiar with from the human world. I close my eyes, focusing intently on the coolness of the bands, seeking the secret.

The attempt is futile. Resigned, my arms fall back to my sides, a heavy sigh escaping me as I sit upright. These bindings must be removed if I am to reclaim my power. The resolve hardens within me to break free from these chains and access the magic that lies dormant, waiting.

Thankfully, guards are no longer posted outside my room. Their prompting questions about where I'm going or what I'm doing is not something I want to deal with in the middle of the night. Maybe it was the kiss that let Oberon think I've fallen for him, or that he knows I won't be able to do any magic outside my budding ability to call forth the shadows, which does me no good in an empty palace.

What I want is my magic back. I didn't realize I would miss the way it thrummed just beneath the surface, waiting to be fed and called upon, until it wasn't there anymore. It feels like a part of me is missing, as if I'm ever so slightly off balance.

I head to the library—at least, I assume there is a library in this place. What would a palace be without one? I have no idea where I'm going. Too late, I realize this was a bad idea. But I've committed, and so I'll see my mission through. Find a library and search for any clue as to what these blasted bands are made from. Records of creation or crafting. Anything I can do is better than sitting around and accepting my situation.

Committing to memory the layout of the palace, exits, and paths while I was escorted is one thing, but navigating on my own in the dim light of night is another. I venture down the corridor that I know leads to the main hall.

My breaths and the beat of my heart feel too loud in the silence. Rounding the corner, I peer down the hall. Guards are stationed along the corridor, in front of entrances to other parts of the palace. Figures this wouldn't be easy. I was so wrapped up in not having guards for myself that I didn't think about the ones stationed everywhere else.

A sweet voice carries down the corridor. "My Lady, do you need something?"

I jolt and clutch my chest. A servant appears to my left, a questioning look on his face. "Oh, my goodness, you scared me!"

"I'm sorry, My Lady... please... I didn't mean to." The servant shuffles his feet while looking at the ground. He's dressed plainly

—a simple grey shirt tucked into black pants. His shoes look worn as he stands with an air of defeat.

Another human in this place, serving the fae for a bargain gone wrong. I wonder what wish landed him here, how humans end up within the palace walls, and if there is anything I can do to change it.

"Will you please take me to the library?" The servant hesitates and looks at me quickly before nodding his head. I don't know what I said to make his body relax at my request. Oberon is doing a good job of keeping me from interacting with—or even seeing—the human servants.

"Of course. Please follow me." He walks in the direction I came from.

My bare feet make no sound against the marble floor—an intentional choice. I didn't want shoes clacking around, giving me away. I'm not sneaking around per se, but I also don't want to alert everyone to my schemes. Questions burn through my mind—ones I want to ask this young man to find out more about his life within here.

We approach the corridor that leads to my room, but take the one across from it instead. I commit the path to memory for the next time I want to go out on my own. Twin oak doors come into view; nightshade flowers intertwining with vines are etched into the wood, life and death circling each other.

The servant grabs the golden handle of one side, pushing it open with apparent ease. I would have thought the weight of the door too much for him. When I step inside, I greedily take in the view. A domed glass ceiling spills moonlight into the chamber, and the high ceilings are adorned with filigree made of stars and whorls. Rows of tall, rich mahogany shelves line the long walls, filled to the brim with books. This is exactly what I need—to have access to all of this knowledge and find the answers I seek.

"Thank you." I shut the door behind me, barring him from leaving. "I have a few questions for you. Follow me."

His hesitation is unmistakable. He's never been asked to sit in front of what he assumes is a fae. He looks around for a moment. "I assume you must listen to anyone that commands you within the palace walls?"

He nods. I turn my back to him, confident he'll follow. A short distance from us are two plush, green, velvet couches facing each other. Two black leather chairs flank each end of the couches, completing the rectangular sitting area. "Sit."

I wait as he shifts uncomfortably in one of the black chairs. When he settles into a position, his eyes stay downcast.

"Look." I lift my hair. His eyes go wide, looking at my ears, then my face, and then my wrists. Pulling up my sleeves, the bands are on full display. Instead of a question sitting beneath his gaze, I'm greeted with fear, which is not what I was expecting.

"What is it?" I want to hear it from his lips, even if I already know and don't want to admit it.

"It's you. The human with magic. I shouldn't be talking to you. Can I leave, please?" He pleads and looks around as if someone will barge in and discover us at any moment.

So, word has gotten around. I should have realized servants gossip just as much as the old women in my town. It is all they have to do to fill the time outside of their duties. I consider making him stay to answer all my questions, but I don't want him to get in trouble. "Yes, after you tell me where the books on metals are and how long your service contract is."

"I don't know. But those," he nods toward my wrists, "are not metal. That is glass. It's obsidian and only comes from—"

A sudden sense of alarm overtakes his features, causing his eyes to widen and his eyebrows to shoot up. Fear flickers across his face as he claws at his throat. The blood vessels in his eyes burst; red slowly seeps inward to his pupils. His chest shudders from his inability to breathe.

My own breath hitches as my body freezes, unsure of what to do as this man chokes in front of me. Shadows wrap around his body and he stills. Only the thin wisp of darkness around his throat is visible, cutting into the pale skin of his neck. But the anguish is clear. He's suffering in the darkness that is consuming him.

Oberon's voice cuts through the moonlit room like a blade slicing through bone. "Hello, my stygian."

"Stop! You're killing him!" I plead, looking to Oberon, who has materialized from the shadows. He's standing behind the couch at the man's back, calm and composed, unaffected by the man he's killing. Not even a flicker of emotion is present on his disgustingly beautiful face. I hate myself for even thinking that.

"What will you do for such a request? His life is in your hands, seeing as he has broken his oath to me."

"I'll do anything. Just stop." The words are ash in my mouth, leaving me before I can register their weight.

"Very well." With a flick of his wrist, the shadows disappear.

The servant collapses to the ground, sucking in breath, the redness in his face fading back to pale. I drop beside him and reach out a hand, but he jerks away from my touch and shakes his head.

"Let us leave this place. You are free to return tomorrow if you so choose." Oberon holds out a hand, an offering of help that I refuse.

We leave the library in silence as he guides us outside the palace. Stars shine brightly among the barren night sky; there are no clouds or moon tonight. Like my soul, a dark and empty vastness with only pockets of light that keep me sane in this new life. Yet, they provide enough to navigate through the treacherous darkness.

A wooden structure comes into view, a dark shadow against the white stone wall beyond. Large trees loom over the wall, like giants standing watch. A soft glow from lanterns fills the stables. He's brought me to see her.

Undoubtedly to showcase he's not a total ass and has a heart, black as it may be. I find Honey's stall and click at her, making her aware of my presence before entering. When I do, I hug her, burying my face in her neck.

Hot, angry tears fall before I can stop them. I'm losing this game, and I better figure out a way to turn things around, or I'll never win.

I don't want him to see my distress. But maybe I should; the perception of weakness might suit me in pursuing my goals. "How did you find me?"

"I will always find you where shadows are present." Oberon leans against the doorframe of the stables, one leg casually crossing over the other, mirroring the nonchalance of his arms folded across his chest.

His effortless grace, every line of his lean body showcased through his fitted violet coat screams to proceed with caution. Paired with a white shirt that's unbuttoned at the top and his signature black leather pants, it's a manicured but slightly unhinged look. An intentional display that he is powerful.

A ruler who knows he has nothing to worry about. It makes me envious. I want people to regard me in such a way. To think twice about coming after me.

"Is that supposed to turn me on?" He can't know that if it wasn't for the gilded cage he's put me in, I might be drawn to him. Drawn to his darkness.

"Does it?" Oberon doesn't react, but there is a watchful alert-ness that pulses beneath the surface of his calm gaze.

"No."

He scoffs, but his violet eyes glitter in the torchlight. "Take it how you want. A warning, or a turn on I would gladly fulfill." He pushes off the frame and stalks toward me. "But for tonight, I have other plans. We made a bargain, and it's time for you to show me your human magic."

"It's the middle of the night."

"You are awake. And my responsibilities do not occur at this hour." Oberon removes my grimoire from inside his coat, handing it to me. The one that was in my room. The one I was just looking through before I left to find the library.

He came to my room in the middle of the night? Was it a coincidence, or did he sense I'd left my room? *I will always find you where shadows are present.* Shadows are everywhere, unless I never leave the light of the sun. He can't possibly know everything that happens—I hope.

Begrudgingly, I follow as he walks out of the stable and into the coolness of the night. I rack my brain for a spell I can teach him that isn't dangerous. Something useful.

He takes a seat on an oak stump around a roaring fire, spilling its light beyond it. I take the seat next to him and watch as the flames dance in the slight breeze. Our knees touch when he leans over and gives me an expectant look.

It would be so easy to fall for him—for his beauty alone. But under the surface lies a deadly force. One that tempts me, as if it knows my soul and calls to the parts of myself I haven't explored —parts that yearn to be used and that urge me to become just as deadly as him.

Enough. Focus on teaching him human magic.

"There are two parts to a spell. First, you must concentrate on the object or direction intended. Then you channel your magic needed, letting it grow, until the spell is completed." Opening the grimoire, I select a page for the growth of crops. Fitting, I think.

He raises an eyebrow. "Interesting choice."

"You might need it when you go too far." I shoot him a glance. "I need a seed of something."

Oberon walks to a guard nearby. Speaking in low tones, he sends him off. He returns to his position next to me and leans back, arms holding him as his face stretches to the stars that shine brightly above us.

I consider Oberon, what he stands for, and what he just did in the library. Is that enough for me to hate him too? After what he went through to get his power and the throne, the thing he was born to inherit, which was taken from him for the simple reason of not having magic.

"Your thoughts are loud. It's almost as if I can hear you thinking about me."

I'm about to retort when the guard returns and hands me a seed. I place the seed in Oberon's hands. Shaking my wrist, the gold bands swirl, catching in the firelight, the black reflecting off them. "Can't do magic."

His low chuckle sets me on edge, but not in a threatening way —the kind where he has the ability to push me in a direction I don't want to go.

"Right. Walk me through it."

Rising, I distance myself from the fire, and kneel on the cold earth. "Here. Away from the fire pit."

Across from me, his knees gently touch the ground. For all his hard edges, he has a softness about him when no one is around and it's just the two of us.

Reaching out, I curl his slender hands around the seed. "I don't know what impact being fae will have on this. When channeling magic into the object, repeat the words I speak. You need to believe what you're saying will come to pass."

We speak in unison, repeating three times: "What is to grow, may it find speed from seed to sow. I give my power to make it so."

I turn his hands over and guide them down to the soil. "Open your palm and press the seed into the earth."

My touch lingers on top of his smooth skin longer than necessary. A silent tension brews as we look at each other, probing each other's souls, seeking truths that remain elusive.

Not only does he want to learn my magic, but he taught me his. And now, if this works, we're creating new magic together. He leans into me, and my traitorous body gives in.

Our lips meet, and it's as intoxicating as ever. He explores my mouth, his tongue tangling with mine. He pulls my lip between his teeth so gently, a caress that begs for more. It's enough to right my senses.

A grunt of dissatisfaction rumbles from him when I break away. But I need to pull myself together, because he's a danger I can't let myself fall willingly into.

Refocusing on the spell, I tell him, "Direct your magic into the seedling. Not your shadow magic, but the magic of your being. A witch's magic doesn't come from the elements, but the magic our fae ancestors inherently had was a part of themselves."

There is a faint pulsing from beneath his hands, the binders blocking anything else. I sit back, distancing myself from him. The cool air nips at the skin of my palms in the absence of his warmth. When he pulls his hands away, green leaves sprout from the ground. A black-stemmed sapling follows.

Gasping, I watch as the tree continues to grow. I scramble away from its widening trunk. The bark of the tree is as dark as night, as if made from Oberon's shadow magic itself. Yet it held onto life, the green leaves multiplying along the growing branches. I can't believe it worked, let alone that he created something both alive and born from decay.

A manic laugh breaks my trance. "An elder tree of my making." Oberon runs his hands along the black trunk, looking up at the tree that is now grown, like it's been there for a hundred years. "It's singing to me stygian. Can you hear it? A mixture of shadows and light." His voice is low and seductive.

His greedy gaze lands on me, and I quickly stand, moving away from him. I take in a startled breath, clutching my heart, when I bump into a guard. He pushes me forward, and Oberon grabs my wrist. He leads me to the tree, forcing my palm against it. I look up and see a small cluster of white flowers has bloomed. The tree is beautiful, but unnatural, commanding attention even in the middle of the night.

Yanking my hand back, I break from his grasp. "I can't."

It's a lie. I felt it. A chaotic melody from two opposing sides fuel each other, giving life to something that shouldn't exist. What have I done? I've given him the ability to create life after he takes it all away. He will remake this world in his image. I cannot allow that.

I couldn't live with myself, let alone be stuck as his consort, knowing I enabled it.

CHAPTER 38
AMERIS

Sunlight streams in through the narrow gap in the curtains. Rolling over, I try to block it out, but it's no use. I flip back the other way and open my eyes. A haze hangs over the room. Blinking, I stare at the rays of light and watch the dust in the air.

Watching how the particles float around in an unknown place, trying to find solid ground, resonates with how I see myself in this world. After last night, I wonder where I'll land.

But I'm not a speck of dust; I have more power than that. I will choose my path. Besides, this life would become so mundane and boring if the only thing that happened was waking up and having people knock on my door.

"Yes?" The word is lazy and loud. I roll my eyes because I know it's just someone else wanting something from me.

"You are due to attend the garden party. I'm here to help you dress; may I come in?" The voice is young and soft.

"If you must." Another servant who won't talk to me for fear of punishment. Lovely. I'm not looking forward to it.

Two bodies enter my dark room, save for the light that

harassed me awake from my slumber. The same voice speaks. "Put that down and open the curtains."

I raise my hand to shield my eyes from the onslaught of sunlight that now pours in from the window. Peering through narrowed lids, I wait as my vision adjusts to the brightness.

A female fae stands in the middle of the room. Her soft, curly black hair is cropped closely against her scalp, and her golden-brown skin shimmers in the sunlight, as if dusted with starlight. The blue silk dress she wears flows about her, rippling with every movement she makes. Her brown eyes narrow and scan the room before landing on me. She is breathtaking to behold, and I feel her scrutiny wash over me. An uncontrollable shiver passes as I stare back.

Well, I wasn't expecting that.

"Hmm. You look alike, but you—you do not glow in the way she did. Everyone felt her presence before she walked into the room. You look like a crumpled piece of paper." She scoffs, turning toward the trunk. "I'll have you looking the part by the time I leave."

Closing my jaw after the insult takes longer than it should. But it stings. I might look a mess, but I just woke up. It must be nice to be so beautiful upon waking. "Who are you?"

"Oberon asked me to make you a dress for the dinner party. I am the best fashioner in Solarium—actually, in all of Elysium." Facing me, she pulls out a measuring tool. "Undress."

She commands it like I'm expected to follow without question. "The clothes I have are just fine."

Tapping her foot, she folds her arms and looks at me like a child she doesn't have the patience for. "You are going to the party within the hour. I don't have time for your opinions."

"Fine." I look from her to the man still standing beside the window. Another human servant. "But he needs to go."

"Humans. So modest." At the snap of her fingers, he exits the room.

When her poking and prodding are done, she hands me a small mirror. I marvel at my own reflection. I look stunning, radiant, even. My hair is curled in soft waves that rest gently on my shoulders and down my back. Red tint paints my lips, and both eyes are lined with brown, which emphasizes my green eyes. A black mixture coats my lashes, completing the look.

She lays a dress gently on my bed and walks to the door. "You have twenty minutes before your escorts arrive."

The dress is white, its tight bodice flowing into an airy skirt that sweeps out at the bottom. Pearls and crystals are scattered throughout the skirt, meant to catch light and be the center of attention. It's beautiful. Slipping it on feels like a well-worn glove; the fabric is tight but soft and movable. My shoulders and arms are exposed, but the front comes up to my neck, covering my chest.

Guards bring me to the terrace entrance that overlooks the garden. Even with the high afternoon sun, the air is cool. The garden is full of fae today, and I notice no one else is wearing white.

I easily spot Oberon in black among the sea of color. He's standing with a group of immaculately dressed fae near the tree from last night. These must be the nobles and court members—the ones that flit from one ruler to the next. Their only interest is selfish survival.

They marvel at the tree as he engages in conversation with them. The guards go no further, leaving me to enter this snake pit alone.

Conversation becomes hushed as I'm noticed, followed by the gazes of everyone present. Whispers float to me on the westward wind, too delicate to be understood but heard nonetheless. I know what they say and what they see—that which should have never graced their sight again. Rhiannon.

But I am not Rhiannon, and I will make that clear.

"Hello, Ameris." Oberon moves through the crowd, his voice

triumphant over the whispers. He holds out a hand when he reaches me. I don't decline this time.

"Oberon."

His hand curls around mine as we move into the crowd.

I try to take in everyone that we pass, but there are so many. A fae to my left with tawny skin in a green floral dress lifts her brow as she says something to the fae next to her. The male couple standing together, outfits complementing each other, give me murderous glances.

Individual. Couple. Group.

It all comes in faster than we are walking. I thought I could handle their distain, real or fake. My stomach coils, the dress feels too tight, and my throat goes dry. I keep a placid smile for everyone who looks my way, but if they look closer, my eyes tell a different story, questions fire, and apprehension prickles my skin. "What am I doing here?"

He leans in, close enough that only I can hear him. "If you're to be my consort, the court needs to see you. They have only heard rumors." The bastard. He dressed me in white. Not just the tree, but a message to them. I curl my free hand into a fist, clenching my fingers before releasing them as he continues. "Whispers reach me. They say I'm a madman on the throne with a ghost for a lover. But they will fear us, Ameris, and we will own them. Fear is the great ruler."

He kisses my jaw before turning back to the crowd. A shiver I cannot control runs through me, the feelings he elicits clawing their way into my heart. Dammit. No. I don't understand my lack of resolve around him. I harden my heart with the promise I made to myself. I will take them all down.

We're at the end of the garden, where two thrones sit on a decorative wooden dais—a large, black throne sits next to a smaller, white, marble one. I am to be his queen in all but name, but not his equal.

We'll see about that.

Each step up to the dais gives me three reasons to win this game: vengeance, control, and destiny. I am grateful Oberon took back his throne that day; otherwise, I wouldn't be here in this place. Be alive. Except that's not enough.

Pivoting to face the crowd, he waits for them to bow before sitting down. I don't sit on the white throne.

"Ameris, take your seat next to me." Oberon grabs my hand, gently pulling on it, a command to sit.

"No." Looking down at him and our hands, I remove mine from his grasp. I walk around the black throne, inspecting it. Running my hand along the intricately carved edge and over the tipped point as I come to his other side. I hear a few gasps from the crowd. I look out at them, standing there, waiting to see what Oberon's response is. No one defies him, and their desire for blood shows in the way they lean forward, eyes focused, and minds alert.

But I am *not* no one.

I smile wickedly at the crowd before sitting on Oberon's lap. My crossed legs are bared to the crowd thanks to the slit in my dress. I run my finger along his jaw, returning the gesture, hoping to pull him into the web I've begun weaving. Closing the gap between us, I lean in and whisper against his lips, "My place is equal to yours."

Pulling back, I look across the garden, soaking it all in—the energy, the tension, the anticipation—before returning to Oberon.

I kiss him, opening myself to the claws that want to sink in—to the darkness that encircles me, waiting to take over. His body responds of its own accord, his cock hardening against my ass that rests in his lap. I rest my hand on his chest, the spiked beat of his heart thumping beneath my touch.

Oberon's hand grips my other thigh and squeezes. He quietly moans, deepening our kiss. Claiming me.

It would be easy to fall into him. To not care what happens to the humans here, about the world that is dying. And not care about what happens to me, to live under another's direction. But I won't let that happen. I want to control what happens to me—to control my destiny. Not be at the whims of a male. To live freely with my magic, not used for what it can do.

"My throne will be as big as yours, or we will share the same one," I say against his mouth, ending our show.

He exhales a breath, his whisper devious, meant only for me. "The things I want to do to you, stygian."

"We can do more once you agree." Forcing a smile has never been easier. I run my hands through his long hair and twirl a strand among my fingers. He rubs his hand up and down my exposed leg, his thumb reaching for the sensitive skin of my inner thigh. Butterflies bound around in my core. I can't control how my body responds to his caress. I try to ignore it.

Turning to the fae gathered before us, unmoving as they watch the show unfold, he says, "Meet Ameris, human descendant of Rhiannon."

Oberon mentions nothing about my power, but they all see the black bands around my wrists. He puts pressure on my lower back and raises my hand, a message for me to stand. I oblige, and he follows.

Walking us to the edge of the dais, he pulls me close, sweet venom lacing his words. "They all see it, but they won't ask, and you won't tell."

Oberon makes it clear I'm not about to talk about my magic before leading me off the terrace and into the garden. I nod. The fae gathered don't need to know; they will eventually see it for themselves. Mingling in the garden gives me the opportunity to gather more herbs and find out what other unknown treasures live here.

I'm busy picking valerian when Lyle's voice cuts like a blade to the throat. "They will come for you."

"I have nothing to say to you." I fill my voice with hatred at his betrayal.

"I suspect not. Know that if you do not take the action Oberon wants, your own plans will fail." Lyle's last words trail off.

"Excuse me?" I whip my head up to where Lyle stood, but another fae fills the space, one I wish I never had to see again if I could help it.

"Do you have anything you wish to tell me?" Zorria stands there, one hand on her hip. She inspects the fingernails on her other hand, acting so casually, like it isn't a problem that she is here.

I look around, but there is no one around us. Oberon is deep in conversation with a regally dressed fae and the captain. I watch their interaction. Oberon clasps the captain on the shoulder and smiles after he speaks, his delight unable to be masked by his usually controlled manner. I can't help but find him attractive. There's something about the way he dresses and holds himself—his powerful presence—that I'm drawn to.

I realize now that's what I want for myself.

My attention shifts back to Zorria. The triumph in her gaze is an obvious message that she saw my display with Oberon. "Not to you."

"I hate that he wants us to save you. Have you not felt him? Do you even care? And where is my brother?" Zorria questions, twirling a dagger in her palm.

"What do you want, Zorria?" I don't give in to her prodding. She's trying to get a reaction out of me. Of course I've felt Xander through the bond, even though I shove it down, but she doesn't need to know that. "Your brother is unharmed, but that is all I know."

"I came to see what state you were in. But I have the answers I need. It doesn't seem like you need our help."

"You're right. I don't." I leave her standing there and make my way back into the crowd toward Oberon.

CHAPTER 39
XANDER

My vision moves in waves.

Blackness waxes and wanes as light from the torch flickers along the wall. Each day is marked by its replacement. The guards light one in the morning, and one in the evening when they bring food. It burns for hours before darkness swallows me again.

But today is different. Light floats down the long hall until it illuminates my cell. I sit up as a figure approaches, standing beyond my cell, staring down at me. With a movement of the torch, the face clears. I can't tell if I'm imagining what I see—it's been too many days since I've been down here, the binders and iron bars jilting my magic and mind.

"Hello Xander." The figure steps forward, bringing the torch closer, inspecting me under the glow of the light. Their presence and voice are too real to be my imagination. I jump up and slam my hands against the bars.

"Lyle." My response is hoarse, but the words are still full of anger. "There is only one way you can be here." I reach through the metal bars, grab their cloak, and press them against the cell's barrier.

"You are the one with obsidian cuffs on. Be careful." Flames from the torch expand, and I release my hold, backing away from the sudden heat.

"What are you doing here?" I spit out.

"Ameris is becoming dangerous." Lyle takes a step back. Light fills the space between us, expanding onto the dark stone walls behind them.

"Your words hold no meaning. We trusted you. You helped fight against Oberon in the days of Rhiannon." I return to the cell bars, gripping the iron even as it burns my skin.

"I am here to serve this world and nothing else." Lyle nods in a subservient way.

"What do you want?" I growl, more from the pain under my hands, but I let it fuel me.

"What you feel for Ameris will be key." Lyle recedes further into the darkness of the dungeon, leaving the torch in the bracket on the wall. "Be the light." With those last words, they disappear.

"Lyle!" I scream out, tearing what remains of my vocal cords. My voice echoing back at me is the only response I receive, and when it fades, the only sounds that remain are the flickering of fire and the scuttling of rats.

I retreat into the corner of my cell and sit on the cold stone floor. I process Lyle's words: Ameris is becoming dangerous. My feelings for her. Be the light. I stare at the torch, the undulating flame whipping back and forth, repeatedly gaining strength and then failing.

Dangerous.

What is she doing while I sit uselessly in this cell? How many days has it been, or has it been weeks? Even though I try to count them, they blur and warp as my mind and body falter.

I raise my hands to the light. Where it would normally heal

quickly, the singed skin takes its time knitting itself back together. This dungeon is nothing but death to any who linger in its depths.

The food they provide is sufficient to sustain me. But the quiet loneliness and desperation causes my thoughts to betray me; I have to fight them to survive.

I stand and pace. I must break out of here. Frustration mounts as every thought ends in failure. Because there is nothing I can do. A roar of anger tears from my throat, and I slam my fist into the wall. I have no way of doing anything in here. No escape. The only way out is to place my faith in others rescuing me.

So I sit and wait in the darkness for Jesper or Ronan to come.

Until then, I take the time to plan. Find Ameris, get her out of the palace, and away from Oberon's clutches.

CHAPTER 40
AMERIS

Golden rays from the setting sun pour through the high-set windows. The contrast of the flickering candles and light streaming in against the darkness of the ballroom is intoxicating. It matches the way I feel inside—light fighting for space in the darkness that closes in on it.

Oberon is waiting for me when I step into the ballroom. He's wearing an all-black velvet jacket with matching pants. The lapels of the jacket are blood red, and the shoulders are studded with metallic spikes. It's expertly tailored to enhance his features and frame.

A crown made from black metal, shaped into spikes and inlaid with luminous gemstones, rests atop his head. It's the first time I've seen him wearing one, and it enhances his already striking features. He embodies power tonight, his presence commanding, and I can't help but find that very attractive.

Oberon holds out his arm, and I link mine into his. We walk along the rows of tables, making our way to the head table. A glimmer catches my attention, and I glance down to see the diamond chains adorning the bodice of my black gown sparkling in the light.

Each step I take makes them glitter like stars in the night sky. I'm dressed up again in finery, like the accessory he sees me as.

I hear the always-persistent whispers. The gathered courtesans stand as Oberon parades me around. There are more fae present tonight than during the garden party. He stops every so often to greet others as we proceed to the front.

He's showing me off.

I hold my emotions back. Another forced smile paints my face for the fae who, at present, has taken Oberon's hand and is kissing his ring. When the male's head rises, his gaze goes to me. Searching. Waiting. Wondering.

When we finally get to the table, he motions for everyone to sit but still grips my arm. We are to remain standing. "Guests, welcome. This is a special evening, and I am delighted you could join me." His tone is anything but innocent.

I know only a handful of them are here willingly. From what I learned in the caves, there isn't much love for Oberon, but he's too powerful to stop, and no one challenges him. Not yet, that is.

I suppress the cough that would give me away when his words reach me, as I was lost in my thoughts. He speaks of special plans for me, just like Xander. *Xander*. I've been avoiding thinking about him. But as Oberon's poisonous words echo around the room, I let down the walls I've built. It hits me full force. I almost stumble back, but grip Oberon's arm to steady myself. Oberon returns the gesture, thinking it was for him.

But no, it is Xander's essence that I react to through the bond. It hits me full force, filling the emptiness in my soul, one I didn't know was so vast. Wrapping me in an embrace so permeating it feels solid. I shut it off again, but it fights me, wanting me to remain open to it. I can't, though; I have things I desire that leave no room for this connection. The hollowness returns heavier this time, now knowing what I could have—what's missing.

Oberon raises a chalice high. "Now, we dine."

I pick up mine and follow suit, with a pleasant and warm smile on my face for everyone to see. The crowd is glued to the scene in front of them. Watching us. After taking a long drink, I set my goblet down and place my other hand on his arm as we sit, ever the doting consort. Not.

For all the things Oberon's taught me, he is also using me. The role he thinks I'm going to play will be of his deciding. That I am his, belong to him, and my magic is too chaotic for a human to control.

Throughout dinner, I watch the fae at the tables below and how they steal glances at us. Oberon is too busy drinking, dining, and reveling in his supposed continued victory over the rebels to notice. Or maybe he thinks himself too powerful to care how his guests behave.

Musicians begin playing their strings and drums. The melody that floats up to the dais we sit upon calls me to the floor. Excusing myself, I walk down the stone steps, weaving through the fae who are dancing. Bodies move away from me as I head to the middle. They give me a wide berth, unsure if they should approach. I spin around, regretting my decision, as I'm surrounded by all the unfamiliar and unfriendly faces that stare at me. The music slows to a song meant for pairs. No one approaches me, and I turn back, defeated, when a voice calls from behind me.

"May I have this dance?"

I know that voice. Turning, I stare at the male fae standing before me with his hand out. Jesper. He bows and steps forward, palm open. He shouldn't be here. I look around, but Oberon is still distracted. I take Jesper's offered hand so as not to draw attention to my hesitation. He gently places a hand on my waist and guides me across the dance floor.

"What are you doing here?" I whisper. While his presence is a relief, I'm concerned for his safety. "Oberon knows who you all are. Or at least about the rebellion and your plans." I look around at all the other fae that twirl and move about us, hoping we stay well hidden.

"Ameris, you are more important than the thousand years I have lived." His smile is gentle, like a father doting on their child. "We are here to rescue you, Xander, and Zeke."

"Who is we?" I cast my gaze to the crowd, looking for Zorria since she would be the only one left of the group I met. I don't see her, only Lyle who is standing near Oberon. My eyes meet Oberon's, who is now watching me intently. I offer him a smile before he leaves my view. "Lyle is your traitor."

"Who is not important." Jesper expertly weaves me in between the other couples dancing. If it weren't for our given situation, I would have enjoyed dancing with him very much. "Lyle is a steward to our world; they see things that others cannot. I trust their intentions."

"I can't say I share the same sentiment," I respond.

"I understand. You've just met them. But you did get your grimoire?"

"I—" I'm not sure what to say. So, I say what truth runs through my heart. The words come out harsher than I intend. "I don't need to be saved. I have my own plans."

Even though Jesper was always kind to me, I'm sure he knew of Xander's plans and didn't have an issue with using my magic. He spins me away, and when I come back into his arms, I feel the need to speak these words aloud. "I'm done taking orders from others."

"I'm not ordering you to do anything. Just know that Xander was beside himself when they captured you. I've never seen him like that. He went looking for answers about the bond you two share and got himself captured."

"He knows." It's more of a statement than a question. Jesper twirls me away, and when he pulls me back in, he continues speaking.

"Yes. He told us to get you out, no matter what happened to him. Let's go while we have the opportunity." Jesper leads us toward the edge of the room. Closer to the exit. I push out of his embrace just as the song ends, masking my sudden movement as other couples disengage.

"I cannot leave the palace. I made a bargain." Saying it forces me to admit what I did. That I might have made a mistake. The disappointment is plain when understanding dawns. "I'm not being harmed here." I quickly add.

His look hardens, focusing across the hall before turning back to me. "Ameris, we'll find another way."

"Don't bother." Twirling around, I land in Oberon's arms. I look back, but Jesper is nowhere to be seen. I'm unsure if he heard me.

"Dance with me." Oberon hooks his arm around my waist and pulls me close, his mouth a gentle caress against my ear. "You're a smart girl. I watched your every move. I know who that was."

"Yet you didn't kill him?" I question.

"There is a time and place for violence." His hand is firm on my lower back as he leans me back and sweeps me around before pulling me tight again. We move around the dance floor.

I pull away and take in his features. He offers me a crooked smile. Desire and need fill his gaze when he looks upon my face. I softly kiss his lips. Luckily, I can lie. Unlike the fae. I only need to tell him what he wants to hear. Make it believable. I swirl my finger on his shoulder and look up at him with a devilish smile of my own. "I told him I am yours."

He has no idea what is coming. Who he has at his side.

We return to the dais and finish course after course of food. He keeps stroking my back and whispering in my ear, speaking of all the things he has planned for us. If I were a genuine lover, I would revel in this moment. Fall deeper into him.

But I'm most certainly not falling. For every plan he recounts,

I mentally recall my own. *Find out how to get these bands off. Claim the throne for myself.*

I may not have been raised to rule, but I am a direct descendent of the late queen, the bloodline that gives me a right.

Instead of being ruled, I will be the ruler.

Oberon finally rises and proclaims, "I have a gift for Ameris."

I sigh. Why does he keep giving me gifts? I was hoping for a dismissal. Not whatever this next show is. Twelve guards appear at the entrance to the ballroom, in a squared formation, three on each side. They're so close the space between them allows for no prying eyes.

The room's energy visibly shifts, every human and fae straighten, and silence falls as the guards march toward Oberon and me. When they reach the dais, my heart lurches. Holding my composure takes great effort as they drop Xander before us. The crowd gasps, matching my internal reaction. I take in each face, looking for Jesper among the captivated fae. He stands in the entryway to the ballroom, part of his face shadowed, before he slips away into the hall beyond.

I steal my features before they crack, giving away how I really feel. Xander looks awful, his clothes filthy and torn, his head hanging in defeat. It brings me back to the first time I saw him on the ship. My thoughts run wild while Oberon speaks.

The day I saved Xander feels like yesterday, yet it also feels like a lifetime has passed since then. So much has happened. I'm no longer the same woman who was bound by other's choices. Now I'm willing to take what I want. To fight for myself and not let other's rules dictate my destiny.

Oberon calls my name, and I snap out of my reverie. I look up at him, my eyes landing on what he holds out to me—a dagger. Red rubies are set in gold against the black casing. The blade glints off the light from the torches. It's a beautiful item, but I know this isn't a gift to use for my protection. It's not really a gift at all. It's a tool to rid himself of what ails him most, to be wielded by his consort.

He leans in. "Take it. Use it."

His words drip poison into my ear. He offered to sever my bond with Xander. To free me from the chains that bind us together. But death is the only way out of the bond. Death at the hand of the caster. I have to be the one to deal the blow. Is this something I can really do? Is it something that he deserves? But my anger at his abandonment strikes again as I think about how he was absent when I needed him most.

My body moves of its own accord, walking around the table and down the steps, time slowing to a crawl. Thoughts race as I consider what Oberon requires of me and what I really want. My dress becomes too tight, the fabric scratching against my skin. Even if I keep my movements fluid, my breath comes in panicked expansions and contractions. I focus on my breathing as I reach Xander. Standing in front of him, my heart lurches. His head hangs deeply; lashings scar his back.

I'm not ready for this. I didn't sign up for this. Not only have they kept him captive, but they've also tortured him. We're both in chains. My dress is laced with them. The meaning is clear. And here before me is Xander with his own set of chains around his hands and feet.

Oberon's eye for detail hits. He knew this moment would come. I don't have to turn around to know Oberon watches me, waiting to see what I will do. He's judging me, assessing whether I am loyal to him and his desires. Lyle's warning floods back in. If you do not take the action he wants, your own plans will fail.

The dagger's weight burns in my palm. I lift the dagger and place it under Xander's chin, lifting his head. He doesn't resist the movement. His long black lashes slowly lift as he opens his eyes.

"Ameris." My name is a whisper on his lips. His stare never leaves mine. Seconds creep by as every unsaid thing passes between us. His eyes tell a story of regret and longing, of lost moments, and of words never spoken.

Venom slips from Oberon's tongue as he says my name. "Ameris." It's a warning.

The moment breaks and my resolve returns. Xander searches my face for understanding as the words come out. Words that I didn't know I would say. "You deserve all the pain you are suffering."

I slide the blade against his neck, cutting only deep enough for the wound to bleed, a wound that will heal in a matter of hours, if not days, given his state.

Blood slowly runs down his neck. I drop my hand, and rivulets of blood drip onto the white marble from the dagger that is now by my side.

Play the role, Ameris.

Be what Oberon wants you to be. It's only for a little while longer. Stepping back, I lift the dagger once more and run the blade along my lips, his blood painting them red. I don't know what makes me do it.

Maybe it's his blood calling to mine, or knowing that it would send a clear signal to both of them. Avoiding any further thoughts that might break me, I walk back to my place at the table. When I turn to face the room, Xander's eyes are unfocused, yet they rest solely on me.

What I really want is to say how much I missed his face, and even though I felt trapped underground, I had more freedom— more choices. To apologize for leaving and admit my feelings are more than the bond. But it's too late for all that.

Eyes to the crowd, I proclaim, "Let that wound sting and fester while he rots in the dungeon. I will repeat this cut three times; each slide of the blade will go deeper. That first one was, for the wounds you inflicted upon others. The second will be, for the harm your rebellion has caused the people of Solarium. And the last one is for me." I turn to Oberon. "This is what I want."

Oberon lights up with satisfaction. He runs his fingers along the exposed skin of my back in a loving gesture that sends a chill through me. Yet, it also proves I'm ensnaring him in my own trap. His hand moves into my hair and pulls me close, our faces inches apart. He gently kisses me, then trails his lips along my jaw before whispering in my ear. "Oh, my stygian, you delight me."

At the nod of his head, the guards remove Xander.

Oberon stands and addresses the crowd. "And that, my friends, concludes our exciting evening!" He claps and bows in merriment. When he turns his back to the crowd, his face transforms into a mask of anger, and he barks an order at Lyle, who diligently sat by Oberon's side throughout the entire evening. "Take her to her room."

Before I have a chance to respond, Oberon rushes off in a flurry of shadows through the exit in the rear. Lyle stands at my side, waiting for me to rise. I bristle at the dismissal and stand. "I can find my own way."

"I know you can." Lyle smiles and bows. They offer me their hand, and I take it. I don't know what Lyle has up their sleeve, but Jesper trusts them. We walk into the crowd that still lingers, dancing and drinking. Lyle leads me to the side of the ballroom, where staff have been coming and going all night. "I must go. Follow the kitchen staff, but return to your room before anyone questions your whereabouts."

Lyle leaves me without further explanation, their red cloak disappearing through the crowd and beyond the doors of the ballroom. When the next set of servers open a hidden door along the wall, I catch the door with my fingers as it closes. I prop it open for a breath, making sure no one is watching before I slip through it.

Keeping my distance from the servers, I take each twist and turn they do. I make my footfalls as silent as possible, but the two humans are lost in conversation and remain oblivious to my presence. It seems luck is on my side. No one has made their way from the kitchen to the ballroom. I would have nowhere to hide, and I am still in my overly extravagant dress.

The smell of vanilla, cinnamon, and caramelized sugar from the deserts that were served still circulates through the corridor. Sounds from the kitchen get louder the closer we get. Voices mingle with the clattering of pots and the slosh of water. My luck ends when a server heads in our direction. She nods to the two I've been following but stops, her mouth hanging open when she sees me.

"I wanted a snack for bed, so I followed the two servers." I nod in the direction of the two servers who disappeared around a corner.

She collects herself, but stutters when she responds. "Uh..miss..you could have rang for us."

"It's really no problem." I keep walking, leaving her behind. I round the corner and enter the kitchen, but all the staff are looking out the windows; jobs left unfinished. This can't be good. I push through them, and when they notice me, they all step aside. No one says anything. All eyes are focused on what's going on outside.

I move along the wall of windows to the open door, and I'm just as glued to the scene as everyone else. Oberon stalks across the large cobblestoned courtyard from the left side toward Jesper, Lyle, Zorria, and another fae I've never seen. They race towards the trees that make up the back edge across from the kitchen entrance.

Zorria and another fae I've never seen are with them. Night has fallen, but the ball of fire floating in fae's hand illuminates his tanned skin and the hair he has pulled into a bun. He towers over Zorria and his tight clothing shows off all the solid muscle he's built from. My gaze is pulled away from his presence by the fae they're holding between them. Zeke has his arms around their shoulders, supporting his weight. Other than looking drained of energy, he appears unharmed, as promised.

"Go!" Jesper yells at them as he turns to face Oberon. A deafening silence falls over the space. Even the birds cease their chirping, a sign that danger is present.

"I think one life is a fair trade for the three guards that were killed." Oberon proclaims.

My heart lurches as his ribbons of black and grey lash out and wrap around Jesper, pulling him off his feet and into the air. The shadows also enter his body through his nose and ears, leaving only his eyes unaffected. Eyes that widen as he gags and scratches at his throat. I cover my mouth, silencing my gasp.

The rest of the group stops running and turns. The horror written on their faces mirrors everyone in the kitchen. I slink back a step and stand behind one of the kitchen staff, trying to hide my presence in case anyone looks my way.

"Let him go!" Zorria screams at Oberon. The wind kicks up and viciously swirls around Jesper, trying to remove the shadows, but it does nothing against Oberon's magic.

"Dammit." The other male fae exclaims while fire pulses in his hand. "Your call Zorria. I don't want to burn Jesper, but I will put him out of his misery."

"No." Lyle says and steps to the side of Ronan, taking Zeke from him. Lyle leans into the other fae male, but his words don't travel. Once the tall fae nods, Lyle sharply flicks their wrist. A glint in the moonlight flashes before a palm-sized dagger embeds itself in Oberon's outstretched hand.

"Grah!" Oberon's outcry is deep and abrupt. His shadows instantly recoil and release Jesper, who falls to the ground. Jesper lies unmoving on the cobblestone ground; his once unmarred skin now shows his veins, which have turned black. "Lyle, that was not nice. Using an iron blade."

"Grab him, Ronan, and let's go," Lyle calls out as they retreat into the forest with Zorria and Zeke. Ronan rushes to grab Jesper and throws him over his shoulder, following the others.

"His death will be slow and painful." Oberon laughs as he

yanks the blade from his hand and throws it to the side. "You'll never have her, and you'll never win."

A male I don't recognize makes eye contact with me as he throws Jesper over his shoulder before turning to follow the others. I don't linger, having seen enough, and move further into the gathered servants. I'm aware they are all human, something I'll need to process later. Right now, I need to hurry back to my room.

Oberon may have already been informed that I never arrived since Lyle was with the others. I've certainly stayed too long, but Lyle wanted me to witness this. I'm not sure for what purpose.

With Zeke's rescue, a weight has been lifted off my shoulders, and I no longer have to worry about him being used against me. But was it to show me that Oberon is every bit of a threat that Xander warned me about, or to show me that I am flirting a dangerous line in thinking I can take on Oberon by myself?

When I round the corner of the corridor that leads to my room, I stop short. Oberon is leaning against the doorframe to my room, the door wide open. He's wrapping his hand in a cloth when his eyes flick up to me and he raises a brow.

"Where were you?" He tucks the white bandage into itself and straightens.

"I was getting a snack for later from the kitchen." I meet his intense gaze and walk up to him, flashing the bread I grabbed on the way out. "So, was that the violence for another time?" I don't try to hide that I saw what happened.

"Did you think you could go with them?" He roughly pulls me against him, our chests pressed against one another as he holds my wrists.

"He knows I made a bargain and cannot leave the palace. They won't be coming back for me. If I must, I'll repeat what I told you earlier tonight. I told Jesper I was yours. While I feel bad for Jesper, they shouldn't have moved against you." I smile up at him and slowly move my arms out of his grip.

Oberon releases my wrists but doesn't step back. I don't break his gaze as he assesses me, trying to find the lie within my words.

I remove myself from his closeness and enter my room. "Goodnight."

When the lock clicks into place, I release a breath. Tonight was too much. I draw a hot bath and strip off my dress. Getting in, I relish the way the hot water stings, doing what it can to wash away everything that happened tonight as I breathe in the steam.

This might be the last moment I get to relax and process everything before things either go my way or very poorly.

CHAPTER 41
AMERIS

Oberon has kept his promise to me. Xander must have healed from the cut I made if the next dinner is to happen soon. I was stalling when I spoke of the punishment I wanted to deliver. I still have things I need to figure out.

It's been two days since I ran a blade against Xander's throat. Seeing him in such a manner has done something to me. Set a fire against my icy insides. And then there is Oberon, who, as harsh as he may be, evokes a part of me that wants out.

Yet I was always drawn to Xander. And it's not just the blood bond; this started before that. The bond strengthened my feelings and completed them. I noticed the little things he did during our travels.

The gentle touches and the care he took in dressing my wounds. The times he let me pummel him with punches before pulling me in and holding me while all the tears I'd shoved down were finally released. I hate it because I know things can never work between us.

Deep down, I know my anger and irritation aren't because of

him. I bear responsibility for my home being destroyed. But in those moments, I wanted someone to blame, to be angry at, to hate.

Stars, I am at war with myself.

And I hate it.

My thoughts and actions are the one thing I have—those and my plan to take the throne for myself. It's the only way to truly be free from the control others have always had over me. Like the way I had to hide being a witch in the human world, then Xander using me, keeping me in the caves without letting me in on his plans when I was the key all along. And now Oberon, blocking my magic and wanting me only as a consort because he knows the threat I am.

I tell the first guard I find to escort me to the dungeons. They give me an odd look, but do as I say. If I've done my job well enough, then Oberon will believe any lie I give about why I wanted to visit the dungeon. He keeps tabs on my whereabouts and actions. I'm always watched in this place—not exactly a prisoner, but I might as well be.

So, I soak in every detail—the twists and turns we take, the way certain hallways look, and which ones connect to each other, because this trip serves a dual purpose. I need to learn more about the palace's layout, like which doors the servants enter and exit from. One day, it'll be mine.

When we make it to the dungeon entrance, I nod my thanks and instruct the guard to wait for me there. "I'll be fine by myself. No one down here can harm me."

I take the torch from the wall and head down the stone steps, large enough for three people to walk side-by-side. The air turns sour and the light fades the deeper I descend. Outside the torch I hold, it's dark, giving the prisoners no sense of time, and the cold chills me to the bone. Wrapping an arm around myself, I hesitantly open myself to our bond, and let it guide me to his cell.

Mounting the torch on the wall, I stand there, staring into the dark. A figure sits hunched in the shadows. No words come to me. I huff out a breath. I'm not even sure what I'm doing down here.

"Ameris," Xander says, as if it pains him to speak the words. He stands, grabbing something from the dark corner, before he approaches the bars of his cell. "Is that really you?"

Again, no words come. I just stare at him, taking in how broken he looks.

"I'm sorry, Ameris. This is all my fault." His voice cracks. He appears in the light, standing just behind the bars.

"No! You don't get to apologize. You left me... left me when I needed you the most." Frustration ripples through me.

"I didn't think you wanted anything to do with me," he replies.

"You're a fool!" I spit. The iron bars stop me as I rush forward, my face inches from his. "It could've been easy. If you would've just let me help."

Before I can say or do anything else, he grabs the back of my head and pulls me to him. In the next moment, his lips are on mine. They linger for a moment, his kiss forgiving and loving.

I pull away, but one hand is still in my hair, not letting me back up, but I don't try to either. He finally releases me and holds up an amulet. "I got this for you. Somehow, the bond led me to it. I knew you had to have it. It was Rhiannon's."

It's the same one I saw in the market. The one I wanted. He puts it around my neck, clasping it in place. My anger wanes as the cool stones sit against my chest. He was thinking about me.

"It suits you." He's looking at me as if I am the single source of his joy.

I lean forward and bring my mouth to his. This kiss is nothing like the first one. His lips are hard against mine; his tongue reaches into my mouth, and I part for it, both of us exploring and devouring. The kiss is full of passion and fire. Loss and longing. Our bond, ravenous, needing to be fed. This is everything I want in a kiss. I want it to last a lifetime—to get lost in the feeling of his hands holding my face. I shiver and break for breath.

Faltering, I fall into the brick wall behind me.

I can't. I have other plans and kissing him will take me far from them.

"Let me taste your lips once more," he begs, the yearning in his voice and expression ready to break me.

"I have to go." I turn quickly and walk away. My heart races. The tingle of his lips lingers as I near the entrance to the dungeon. Leaning against the wall, I gulp down air, my lungs and breath constricting. I know all my frustrations were wrongly directed at him. That I was angry at the village for the wrongs they committed against me and full of grief when I lost Marguerite, and then Honey. It was easier to stay angry than to feel everything else. I grapple with my emotions, bouncing between longing for him and not wanting anything to do with him. I know it's not just the bond. The bond is only amplifying what I already know.

He's good, and I'm teetering on the edge of becoming his villain. Xander could save me, but I'm not sure if I want to be saved.

I take a moment to center myself, taking a deep breath and letting my heartbeat even out and regain my composure. I vow not to return. I can't. Everything I've been working for will fall apart if I let him in.

But that kiss. That feeling.

No. Forget it.

Move forward with the plans you've made. I remind myself of what I stand to lose if I continue to let others control how I live. It will be the same as living a half-life like I did in the village. Everyone in Elysium will want to use me for the power or the lineage I have. Including Xander. My life will be my own. I'll look out for myself because no one else will. It's me against the world.

When I get back to my room, I pull out my grimoire and sit in the middle of the floor. I flip through the pages until I find the spell I've passed over every time I read this book.

The spell for release. I can't believe I didn't think of this before. Normally, we use this spell for negative energy or emotions. Rising, I gather the ingredients—things I've collected during dinners and garden walks.

I grab a bundle of sage, rosemary, salt, and a bowl of water before returning to the floor. Taking a few pieces of the sage and rosemary, I mix them together in the water with the salt, making a paste. I spread it over the binders. Taking a breath to center myself, I light a candle and the rest of the sage smudge. I release a breath and move my wrists over the flame while swirling the smoke around me.

"Unbind the chains that hold me fast, Release the weight of burdens past," I begin the incantation. The amulet sparks to life, sending a jolt through me. The rest of the words come out in a tenor I've never spoken, hurried and frantic. Whatever magic lives within this amulet is aiding me, pushing me to finish. "Be free, as once before, Ensure I am bound no more."

The binders clatter to the floor.

I'm flattened against the ground by the force of the magic that wells within me. It needs to be expelled, or I fear I'll burst into flames from the inside. Raw magic claws at me, burning within my veins. I crawl to the window and struggle to pull myself up. Forcing the window open, I release the magic, channeling a windstorm.

I ease into the release of magic so it doesn't give me away, expelling just enough to ease the pressure. I slump against the wall below the window, clutching my chest from the breaths that can't seem to fill my lungs.

With shaky legs, I reach the center of the room and grab the binders. I bend the latch just enough so they won't click into place, but I can still wear them. I put the binders on again, this time knowing I control their removal.

Everything settles as the binders don't block my magic entirely anymore. But they help with the overwhelming power that wanted out. I'll have to slowly release my magic, balancing myself out again.

I clean up the evidence of what I did and fall into my bed. Sleep takes me the moment my head hits the pillow.

CHAPTER 42
XANDER

She came. How long has it been since her lips were on mine? Days? Weeks?

My vision blurs. The walls come and go with the flickering torchlight.

In and out.

When the light comes, it dances against the stone, casting images that haunt me.

Uncontrollable shaking seizes me; the cool stone is the only comfort against the heat that crawls over my skin. Infection spreads from the open wounds that mingle with the sweat and blood dripping down my back.

Iron. They have iron, and it burns like fire.

The wounds don't heal as they should, slowed by the cruel metal.

Unrelenting itching.

She is there again. Standing there, watching me. I reach out to her, but she doesn't move.

"Why have you come?" My voice is harsh from words not spoken.

There is no reply—only the tilt of her head and a gleam behind those green eyes.

"Leave me." I swipe my arm out, and she vanishes.

Darkness falls once again.

Time has left me.

Light comes, and she returns.

Again, she stands and watches me, but this time, she reaches out with an open palm.

I no longer feel the itching or the heat.

My body stops shaking.

But she says nothing.

She stares.

I reach out again.

Darkness falls, and she leaves once more.

CHAPTER 43

AMERIS

Ever since that kiss, I haven't been able to get Xander out of my head. Gah. I don't have time for complicated emotions. Tomorrow is the next dinner party. In order to save myself and take the throne, I must rescue Xander. I need his rebellion to make a stand against Oberon. I will use him, just as he wanted to use me. Xander will get me closer to what I want, even if it also benefits him.

The amulet he gave me rests against my chest. I wrap a finger around the delicate chain and hold the centerpiece up to the light. The jewels sparkle and fill the room with their reflective colors. I haven't taken it off since Xander placed it around my neck, hiding it under my clothing when Oberon is around. It thrums with power, a comfort when I can't feel my own.

Removing the binders, my magic surges. I place them on the side table next to the herbs I've gathered and enter the bathing chamber. I will enjoy this bath, soaking in the hot water, before I go to the dungeons. Before I do something that might get me killed.

One last luxury in my gilded cage.

When I've finished, I collect what I need from the table and pocket the binders before leaving my room. Following the path I committed to memory, I'll be at my destination with the next turn. Along the way, I nodded at servants and guards, demurely smiling as I do every time I go to the stables to ride Honey. I gave them nothing to consider out of the ordinary.

I round the corner to find two guards who are talking to each other. They're relaxed because they expect nothing to happen under Oberon's rule. I take the sachets I made of mandrake, valerian root, and lavender out of my pocket. As I walk down the corridor, I seek out the vibrations in the air, gathering and swirling them through the cloth. Pulling the properties of sleep from each herb before pushing them toward the guards.

When the infusion reaches them, it doesn't take long for their bodies to drop. I drag each guard down a few steps so they are out of sight. They'll be out for a while, and nothing will wake them until the herbs wear off. I take the keys from a guard and lift the torch from the wall.

I descend, leaving the grandeur of the palace behind for the filth of the dungeon. Smells I'd rather not know the source of offer little comfort in the face of the condition I expect to find Xander in. It's been close to a week since my kiss with Xander—longer than I expected. I told Oberon to keep him well fed, that I wanted him aware of what was going on, not in a delirious state of deprivation.

Before visiting Xander the other night, I hadn't wanted to come down here, knowing he was here. Approaching the cells, the torch offers enough light to see Xander. He's hunched in the corner, his head resting against the wall. His white shirt now hangs in shreds off his shoulders. The rise and fall of his scarred back tells the story of his time down here.

Oberon kept his word about keeping him fed but said nothing about not hurting Xander. I curse him to whatever fae hell there is. How could I have ever thought being with Oberon was a possibility? He may not be outwardly cruel, but he shows it in other ways.

"Xander." My voice sounds too loud, even though I whisper his name. I move toward the bars, filling his cell with light. He pulls back, then raises his arm, looking at me with shadowed eyes, his expression blank.

"Leave me. Your presence has haunted me enough." His eyes droop, barely able to stay open.

Has he been seeing visions of me? I take a shuddering breath and falter, my feet moving backwards until I hit the wall. I'm unsure how to process the fact that I've been a source of his torture in this place. I set the torch in the bracket on the wall. The keys sit heavy in my hand, their weight a reminder of how my decision to free him took so long when it was so easy. The path that led here plays over in my mind. All the mistakes and decisions we made. No—decisions I made.

The key that slides into the lock is my salvation, or my damnation. Once I open this door, there is no going back. I am committed to the destiny I intend to create.

Rotating hinges break the silence as I step into the space Xander has occupied for weeks. He looks over again as I approach. Xander's skin is streaked with dirt, and a red-stained cloth is wrapped around his knuckles. But it's his eyes that pain me, the icy blue now dull and faded.

When my hand touches his skin, he startles and jerks back. Gently, I say, "I'm really here."

He looks at me with such intensity, and when his hand touches mine, he squeezes it hard—too hard.

"Xander, stop." I try to pull back, but his grip is too strong. Panic threatens to take over as the pain increases. My magic flares in defense, but I push it down and focus only on him, willing the pain to recede to the back of my mind. Placing my other hand on his face, I caress his skin, hoping to soothe him, to let him know that my presence is real. "I'm not a vision. I'm here."

Xander leans into my touch and closes his eyes. Letting go of my hand, he says, "I wish this was real."

I run my hands through his hair, pushing it out of his face. I lean in and whisper against his cheek, so that my breath caresses his skin before pulling back. "Open your eyes."

The shift in his expression gives me the answer I need. He sees me, feels me, and I take it—I lean back in with a gentle press of my lips on his. And then he truly knows. Xander's hands move to my face, his fingers in my hair, pulling me deeper into the kiss.

"You came for me." The words are a whisper against my lips.

"Yes, but we need to go. The guards are unconscious, but someone else could walk by and realize something is wrong." I loop his arm around my shoulder and help him up, but he can hardly stand. I look down to see his ankle is swollen. "What did they do to you? I thought you healed fast."

"Iron. It keeps us from healing." Xander says.

I know he won't tell me what they did to him down here. My imagination is more than capable of coming up with answers. All I can think of is the pain he has been experiencing—pain that I've caused—and that sends cracks through the walls I built, ones that were already falling. Stars. I have a feeling I'm going to regret this. Because when I'm this close to him, I want nothing but him, and as hesitant as I am to admit it, it's not just the bond.

I take the torch with us as we move through the dungeon. Prisoners call out for our help as we pass, some reaching through the bars, begging to be saved. I pay them no mind. Instead, I focus on the vibrations of the earth's signature, and once I've tapped into its power, I search for the best way out. "This way."

We reach a dead end, a solid wall of stone. I focus on the element, on the way the earth's subtle vibrations thrum. The amulet amplifies my magic, aiding me by giving me more power as I push my hand against the wall in front of us.

Stones begin to move, crumbling into dust or falling into new places. An arched exit with a ledge extending beyond the drop-off is now in the space where the wall was. Wind funnels through the opening, whipping my hair around. The opening drops off twenty feet into the lake that sits beside the palace.

"We need to jump together. It's going to be cold and wet."

Xander's head hangs, barely conscious, but he manages a nod. As we take the step off the ledge, I twist my hand, closing the opening behind us. Before we hit the lake's crystalline surface, I direct my magic to the water. I force it to rise and meet us, padding our plunge into the water below.

I pull Xander up, our heads breaking through the surface of the water. I do my best to swim with him toward the edge, but it's difficult. The cold water brings back memories of our entrance to this land. We've come full circle, to another moment when a choice must be made—what path I will take.

Will I let my heart lose to his male or stay the course and win for myself? It might be selfish, but what's so wrong with that? Why shouldn't I want things for myself, without the strings attached that the other choices offer?

All I've ever experienced is others making decisions for me. Xander jerks, pulling me from the thoughts that begged to spiral.

Xander groans as he comes to. "I can swim."

I let go and swim the short distance to the shore. Water laps against my waist as I wait for him to reach me. I hold out my hand when he gets closer, helping him out of the water.

"Are you okay? You're limping," I say as he struggles in the light waves.

"Yes. Now that I'm no longer in the dungeon, I'll heal quickly." Xander nods, putting his arm around my shoulder as we leave the water and head into the forest.

We've barely made it a few hundred feet when a force stops me mid-stride, like I've hit an invisible wall. Xander turns to watch me, his brows pulling together as he leans against the nearest tree.

He reaches his hand out for me. "What are you doing?"

I try to force my body forward, his hand just out of reach, but it's to no avail. "I can't go any further. I made a bargain." I leave it at that because I don't want to explain.

"I see." He limps toward me.

"Xander, you shouldn't." When he passes the barrier, I surge forward to stop him from putting weight on his ankle. I find myself inches from his face, my hands on his chest, with his arms around me.

"It's not broken, Ameris." He chuckles. Looking down at his foot, he moves it in circles and smiles. "See? Already better."

I push away from Xander, walking back toward the palace. "You need to leave."

"Ameris, come here!" Xander calls after me.

I stop, knowing that I should keep walking, that I shouldn't linger here. The longer I stay, the more I'll want to. Leaves crunch and twigs snap as Xander comes up behind me. Before I can decide, his hands are on my shoulders, his wet hair falling into my face as he leans in and kisses my cheek.

"Thank you," he breathes against my skin. His breath is warm against the cool air.

CHAPTER 44
AMERIS

The tug-a-war that I've been playing has met its match—the bond holding us together as I pulled away. In this moment, the rope that was pulled taut slackens, thrusting us together and into each other's arms. I turn around and bury myself in his chest.

All the tension that's been wound tight within my body releases as Xander's arms wrap around me. I finally open myself to it in this moment of weakness. In need of this reprieve from my own machinations. I knew I would fall into him the moment our bodies touched. That kiss undid me. It broke my walls and melted the icy anger I'd built around me.

I never thought about how good it would feel to be held against another's body. I can feel every curve of his body through his wet clothing. He is still solid, even after the time he spent locked away.

Xander's hold is an anchor, as if he wants to keep me from drifting off and being taken from him again. If only it was strong enough.

But it's not.

Oberon's bargain is stronger. The separation after this moment will shatter our souls once more, as we continue in the roles we have to play in the larger game, a game that can win the war against Oberon.

My thoughts are eradicated the moment Xander moves his hand up my back, trailing over each vertebra until he reaches my neck. He's pulling the water from my clothing, the same way I challenged him that first time in the frozen north.

It sends a dizzying feeling through my body, igniting want deep in my core. I exhale, letting everything go. All the frustration, the pain, and the anger.

Xander's warm touch is gentle as he lifts my chin, bringing my eyes to meet his. Small droplets of water drip from his hair onto my skin. My heartbeat quickens as he studies my face. The depth of his emotions is reflected in the sky blue of his irises, and there is a fire once more behind his eyes. "You came for me."

"I am bound to you and will always come for you." The words leave me without a second thought. It's always been true. I've been fighting against it. His lips crash against mine with a force that matches the way he looks at me.

Xander's tongue roams, moving with mine. It's a dance of ecstasy as his hands move to my cheeks, cupping my face. I'm lost in his touch. My hands roam his body, anywhere they can touch, along his biceps, up and down his back. I want this—want him— and I know he wants me.

In a frenzy of moans and stolen breaths, I rip off his tattered shirt, pulling the wet fabric away from his skin, and throw it aside. When my fingers trail down his chest, I pull away from the kiss. My gaze drifts from his face to scars that litter across his tan skin, wounds that healed like a human's, remnants of his time in the dungeon.

"I—I'm sorry. These are here because of me." I did this; I left him there in my anger over past events.

"The only thing you have to be sorry for is this." He moves my finger to the thin line along his neck—the scar I created from the dagger I slid across that very spot.

"I..." Words stick in the back of my throat, choking me. How can I explain? How can I apologize for something I'd wanted to do?

"I'll take your apology in the form of a kiss." He smiles softly at me and rubs a finger along my cheek. "I'm the one who should be sorry. I should have been there for you."

I press my lips to the scar on his neck—my scar, the one I made. But I don't stop there; ever so slowly, I carve a path up his strong jaw. His muscles flex and he tenses, my name vibrating at the back of his throat, barely audible. At that, my own desire peaks, wetness builds between my legs, and my nipples peak.

I need his hands to touch me, skin to skin. I resume our kiss, this time controlling the movements, tasting him, and devouring him at the same time I work the button on my dress. Fumbling with the urgency of want. In this moment, I wouldn't even care if we got caught.

Soft and calloused hands touch mine, stopping me. "Are you sure?"

"Yes." I nod, then bring his hand to the buttons, reassuring him and letting him continue what I started. His movements are as deliberate as they are slow. Each button he undoes releases the now-dry fabric from its hold on my shoulders. He savors every button that comes undone, exposing more of me.

As my dress slips from my shoulders and falls to my ankles, I let him take his fill, seeing me for all I am. Seconds pass before my hands work at the buckle of his pants, trying to slide the fabric over his hips, but they're still wet from the lake.

Xander grabs my wrists and places my hands on his chest as he works them off. My fingers roam over his skin, following the contour of his muscles.

He manages to remove his clothing faster than I could have and swiftly grabs my thighs, lifting me up and spreading my legs around his waist. I lace my fingers behind his neck and press my body against his, grinding my hips against him.

A low rumble escapes him as I bring my lips to his again. He squeezes my thighs as his tongue sweeps over mine. It's lust, or passion, or feelings I don't want to admit, and desperation that's fueling me. Before I know it, my back touches fabric as he breaks our kiss, hovering over me while I lie on the ground.

I want him in me, to close the gap between our bodies. I want him to give me the release I so desperately need.

He looks at me, a devious smile playing on his lips. "I've thought of nothing more than wanting to be the source of your pleasure again."

I let out a whimper when he takes my breast into his mouth, tongue flicking at my peaked nipple, while the other hand cups my free breast, rubbing his thumb over the pebbled skin.

"I haven't forgotten the way you sound when you come for me."

"Stop teasing me," I gasp out. Returning the favor, I wrap my hand around his hard length, and move up and down in slow strokes. "Because two can play that game."

He sucks in a breath, releasing the hold he had on my breast and chuckles. He moves down my body, forcing me to let go of him. He plants kisses along my stomach, to my left thigh, then my right. My chest is heaving, my breath ragged at this point. "Xander."

He looks up from between my legs, hands gripping my thighs. "Say my name again."

I'm so wet, so aroused by this point that I can barely think. "Xander."

When his name leaves my lips, his tongue strokes between my folds, finding the most sensitive bundle of nerves. I'm panting, already about to come, when he drives his tongue into me, sending a wave of pleasure through my body. My hips buck, but he holds me tight, giving me more. My hand goes to his hair, gripping it, while the other rubs at my nipple, pushing me closer to the edge.

He slows, and I cry out. "Don't stop!" I should stop him, knowing this will complicate everything. But I can't. Won't.

"I wouldn't dare."

Two fingers slide into me as he returns his mouth to my clit and I am undone. Consumed by the rapid firing of pleasure coursing through me. When I can stand it no longer, I force his head away and rise, pushing him under me. Not wanting to wait, I rub my still-sensitive parts against his, and now it's his turn to moan. I silence him with a kiss and, inch by inch, lower myself onto him.

Rocking my hips, I slowly rise until only his tip remains within me before thrusting back down. He cups my ass, guiding me in and out, increasing my speed. He growls out, head back, and my lust for pleasure increases with the way I feel every pulsing throb of his blood. Not just in his length, but in the way the bond is flaring, filling me with his essence and giving mine to him. Whatever he needs, it takes; what I need, it gives. It's healing him and shattering me. My plans. My vengeance.

I don't hold back, and neither does he. I arch back at the mounting wave threatening to drown me. And when he rises, deepening inside me, taking my breast into his mouth, I cry out.

He wraps his arms around me, moving his mouth to my exposed neck. His own grunted cry is forced out as he comes. "Ameris."

He flips me over, tenderly kissing my forehead, before lying beside me. Both of us are panting, and when my senses return and the last of the pleasure leaves, I curse myself.

Fuck.

That was so good and so, so bad. I immediately shut off the value that burst open. If I give myself over to him, then I'll just be a pawn in the game again.

And I will not cave to the whims of these men. Getting up, I gather my clothes and quickly start dressing.

CHAPTER 45
XANDER

"Leaving so soon?" I sit up and reach out a hand to pull her back to me, but she evades my touch.

"I have to go. Oberon might already know by now." Ameris shakes out her cloak and puts it around her shoulders.

"There is nothing he can do to you. He cannot harm you. We are bound—"

She cuts me off before I can continue. I try to interrupt her, but she talks over me. Resigned, I fall silent to let her finish.

"But he can harm you through me. Oberon doesn't know I can do magic, and I'm not hiding in the woods. I'll figure something out." She stalks away from me.

"Ameris!" I jump up and rush after her. She turns around and shakes her head while flicking her hand. Roots spring from the ground, their rough exterior bringing me to my knees and holding me in place. "Dammit, Ameris! Let me go!"

The tail end of her strawberry blonde hair disappears into the trees. I don't understand how we just did *that,* and now she's running away, discarding me like I'm nothing more than a speck of dust on her shoe. I am going to kill Oberon for whatever threats he's made and whatever bargains he's coerced her into.

Dirt and sweat coat my hands as I struggle, twisting and turning my body, trying to free myself from the roots. I've been at this for so long that the late afternoon sun has started its descent.

Needing a break, I sit back on my heels and observe the surrounding forest. It has browned too early in the season. The more I look, the more I see Oberon's decay seeping into the world.

I'm making headway on freeing myself when I hear the snap of a twig and the crunch of dry leaves. My pulse spikes at being so exposed and vulnerable, unable to protect myself. Ronan and Zeke appear through the foliage, and I sigh in relief.

They look at each other, then me, and Zeke lets out a laugh. "Naked and bound?" The corner of his mouth turns down in jest.

"It's not like that." My brows pull together as I huff out. "She left in a hurry, concerned about how long she'd been gone." Saying it aloud flares my irritation at being left here in such a state.

Their chuckles sound in tandem as they work to rip the roots away from my body. Ronan pats my shoulder and hands me clean clothes from his satchel. "Been where you are, my brother. Are you sure you didn't get your release before hers?"

I growl, and he steps back, laughing with his hands raised. "I assure you that was not the issue. She made a bargain with Oberon and cannot leave the palace."

I can't be sure she knows about the effects of the bond and that Oberon cannot harm me without harming her. "Wait, how are you even here?"

"A note appeared on top of a document I was reading to Jesper. It was from Ameris." Ronan shrugs, and hands me the paper.

Meet me in the forest next to the lake.
The fourth bell after sunset.

The magic she carries can do far more than the elemental magic we possess. She impresses me once more, and I regret not including her before. This could have all been avoided if I hadn't been so protective. I can't be sure she knows about the effects of the bond and that Oberon cannot harm me without harming her.

Ronan speaks up again, but his voice is heavy. "About Jesper, Oberon got to him when we went to rescue all of you. He's on death's door."

"What? What is wrong with him?"

"Oberon's shadows are spreading through his veins, slowly draining his lifeforce." Zeke answers.

"Let's not linger. I need to see him." We mount the horses they've brought and start our ride back home. Before I think too long about how quickly she left, I divert the subject and ask, "What of the rebellion?"

"We have more than enough to launch our attack. Yet they fear Ameris. Word has spread through the Solarium, probably through all of Elysium, after the garden party and the ball. Rumors are spreading of the girl who sits at his side. Who appears to be his—under his control."

"But they also saw the binders?" I ask.

"Aye. Either she gave a good show or she's playing us on his behalf. Enticing us, you, to face him." Ronan gives me a questioning look.

"I don't think she would have risked saving me." I can't blame him for wondering; that was everyone's reaction. I saw it myself during the dinner party. When she sliced my neck. Though the iron had weakened me, I was alert enough to see the slight hesitations; the way her eyes didn't hold the same conviction she spoke. There was a performance to her that night.

We make it to the entrance of the underground, and I dismount, ready to breathe in the deep earthen scent of the cavern. It welcomes me, enveloping me in its comfort as I enter the passage leading home.

I'm not prepared for the immediate darkness that takes over when the opening closes behind us, bringing me back to a place I don't want to be. It feels as if eons have passed before the lights flick to life. I release the breath caught in my lungs and suck in a deep breath, willing my taut muscles to relax.

Before we get to the end of the passage, music, laughter, and the scent of food greets me. I am not disappointed when the view opens before us. Holding onto the railing, looking over the main hall, this is not the place I left. It's alive. Fae fill the cavern below. They have erected stalls with food and wares for sale, and they are dancing. I cannot help but smile.

"It is a beautiful sight." Jesper takes the last step onto the landing and holds my shoulder. He's wearing a long sleeve and high-neck tunic, but the dark lines along his skin still show just under his jaw. "It's good to see you." He nods to Ronan and Zeke, who leave us.

"Yes," I say, making a silent vow to keep it this way. I failed once before, but I will not fail again. "But you shouldn't have walked up all these steps."

I support Jesper as we make our way down the stairs until someone spots us. The one playing music points, halting the tune that had so many mesmerized. Confusion passes over the crowd at the sudden silence until he yells, "Xander! He's back!"

They look toward his outstretched hand, their gazes landing on us. Disbelief and excitement pass through the crowd. It doesn't take long for the cheers to erupt, and arms are thrown around each other in celebratory hugs. I shake hands and nod at people as we pass them and make our way into the privacy of the war room.

Just before we enter, Jesper is suddenly overcome by a fit of coughing, and he clutches my forearm for support. I place my hand on his back, worry coursing through me as I steady him. "Jesper, we need to get you help."

When he's finished, his voice is low and serious. "It's too late for that. We already tried. You need to convince Zorria that this is worth it. That it is not just about Ameris. She has only expressed her concern about Ameris to our inner group, but I'm worried about her speaking to others"

Jesper is rarely bothered, but it's clear that whatever he is referring to needs to be addressed. I nod in understanding, follow him into the room, and help him in the chair closest to the door. Zorria and Zeke are deep in conversation, and Ronan leans over documents scattered across the long table.

"Xander," Zorria greets me coolly. "I'm glad you're back, apparently unharmed."

"It's good to see you too." I pull her into a hug, and she tenses for a moment before returning my embrace. Her loyalty is unwavering, and I cannot blame her for her concerns about Ameris.

She steps back and leans against the wall, arms folded over her chest. "We haven't seen Lyle around since they helped us save Zeke."

"Lyle is likely back at the palace with Oberon. I don't always understand their wisdom, but if Jesper trusts them, then so do I."

"Well, at least we know who gave us up." Zeke sits at the table, scratching his head with a pensive look on his face. "Even though they also helped save us."

"I still don't trust her." Zorria tilts her head, assessing me.

The air is heavy; unspoken words hang like sharp daggers waiting to drop. I know Zorria has something to say. She always does when I come to Ameris. "Say it, Zorria."

"Ameris is no longer with us either. She kissed Oberon very passionately, mind you, in front of everyone. They looked like lovers on a spring day. Disgusting." Zorria throws a set of knives at the wood target that hangs on the wall, each one hitting the center, and I know she wishes Ameris was standing there.

"She's probably just playing his game." I say, but her words are a poison slowly working their way to my heart. But what we just did in the forest—it felt too real to be a lie.

Zorria's sigh of disbelief is so loud it could be heard across a courtyard. She looks at me and throws her last dagger without aiming. It hits perfectly in the center. "She will be the death of you."

Jesper's cough cuts the conversation short, and he directs us back to the task at hand. "Enough, Zorria. We need to make a move, and soon. Ronan, can you go to the other courts and ask for their allegiance in this fight? We're going to need as many fighters as we can get."

"Right away." Ronan gathers the papers from the table and leaves.

"You really think the other courts are going to come?" Zorria scoffs and sits next to her brother.

"Zorria, cut it out. Are you with us or not?" I place my hands on the table and lean in, getting as close to her as the table will allow. "You can sit here and sulk or be part of the solution. Ameris is a part of me, and you need to get over whatever hatred you have for her."

I fold my arms across my chest. I've given myself away, calling her *a part of me*. A common phrase used when we become intimate with someone, but I can't hold back anymore. Bond or not. Ameris is my priority, second only to taking Oberon down. I would do anything for her. I would give up my throne for her. And I still have a promise to uphold to Marguerite.

Zorria's eyes widen, immediately recognizing the meaning behind my words. "You laid with her? I shouldn't be surprised. I take back what I said. You will be the death of us all." Fury laces her words as she stands and turns toward the room's exit.

"You will not leave. Sit and let us make the final plans," Jesper cuts in again before she can leave the room.

A flick of his fingers brings her grudgingly back into the chair. She doesn't sit gently, and now she's the one with crossed arms. I sigh, and Zeke shakes his head at us but says nothing. I'm at a loss for what to do. It's going to be an uphill battle to get Zorria and Ameris on good enough terms to be civil.

"Let's begin. We meet on the battlefield at dawn. Hand me that map," Jesper says to me.

CHAPTER 46
AMERIS

Oberon is waiting for me when I return. Standing next to the hearth, he holds my grimoire. His slender fingers, decorated with gold jewels, thumb through its pages. The fire behind him cracks and pops, begging to be fed by the paper that lingers above its reach. This can't be good.

"Tell me, Ameris. What have you done?" He rips a page from its binding, looks at me, and throws it into the fire. I flinch. The flames devour the page. They must have discovered Xander's empty cell. Knowing I'd be the only one to help them escape, there is no point in denying it.

"I did what this bond requires of me." It is the truth. I may have wanted to do it, but I couldn't have left him there. Xander's pain and suffering became mine the closer I physically got to him. It didn't have to come through the bond; I could feel it, could see it when I saw the state of him in that cell. I turn toward the bed, throw my cloak down, and act as indifferent as I can. I need time to refocus.

Oberon moves with such speed that I'm caught off guard. Before I have time to react, he spins me around and presses my back into the bedpost, a sharp blade at my throat. My breath catches for a moment before my chest starts rising and falling in sharp, quick gasps at his quick advance and the danger in his gaze. The ornately carved wood presses into my palms as I grip the post for support.

I take a deep breath, lower my chin in defiance and push forward onto the cool metal. I bite my tongue as the sting of sharp metal cuts into my skin, and I give Oberon a look of defiance. "Do it."

I push further against the blade. He falters for the briefest moments before the pressure of the blade returns. So, he doesn't want to kill me.

"Xander will come for you. He will die because of you. As will his pathetic rebellion." He sheathes the blade and takes a step back.

I shove him, but he doesn't move. He takes another step back, taunting that he is still in control. I try again, harder this time.

Oberon falls back against the couch. Fury runs rampant through my veins. Yet, he is just smugly sitting there, like he allowed my shove to land him on the couch. He cocks an eyebrow at me, and I grab the closest thing to throw at him. The hairbrush misses, crashing against the wall before clattering to the floor.

"You don't know you'll win!" I scream at him, bursting with fiery anger that these fae think no one is better than them. Especially me—that all I am is a pawn. Oberon stands and walks up to me. I attempt to shove him again, but he grabs my wrists and pulls me to him.

He presses his body against mine, holding me, bringing his face into my neck. Oberon takes a large inhale. His mouth hovers above the sensitive skin along my collarbone. I don't react, don't lean into him the way my body wants me to. He leans his head back, searching my face.

He is searching for something he won't find—love for him.

I might be drawn to him, but I don't love him. There isn't any reason for me to. Speaking of love, I'm still not sure if I want the love that Xander has given me. Love makes things complicated.

Maybe in another time or place I would, but not here, not now.

"You've been with him."

And there it is.

"Are you jealous?" I can't help myself.

His eyes sharpen. "I will have you, Ameris. You may have a bond with Xander, but I've noticed the way you look at me. The darkness within you wants out. I intend to release it and make it mine."

Oberon relaxes his grip and pulls me into a kiss. It's fierce and full of fire—a claim on me. Stars, I love kissing him, so I let myself enjoy it. I need to bring him back into my grasp. But he pulls away and rubs his finger against my jaw, the sharp point of his fingernail trailing across my neck, a message that he isn't done—he hasn't fallen for my antics again.

He inspects my wrists and turns them over, looking at the binders. "So, you didn't act alone."

I try to shove him off, but it's no use against his strength. The light from the open window blots out as he envelops us in shadows. "We could have been great together. Do you feel the shadows? They will devour anything I allow."

At his words, the shadows push in, and when they reach my skin, it burns. I knew they left decay and destruction in their wake, but I hadn't expected this. It terrifies me.

"I don't want to be great as someone's consort," I hiss.

Tears make their slow descent down my face. I scream, the pain becoming unbearable. My body goes slack against him. My head falls forward, and salty drops hit the wooden floor. They soak in, then disappear into nothing.

A representation of my life, the pain and suffering I bury within the outer walls keeping me safe—or so I thought. Until someone else breaks them down.

"You have no power here." Oberon rests his chin on my head. The shadows pull away. Instant relief comes to the fire that was my skin. When I look at my arms, there are no wounds. My skin is as pristine as it was moments ago.

"Shadow magic is all about pulling out the worst fear, or memory, someone has. The one that haunts them. Killing them from the inside. When the heart can no longer handle the pain, it stops," Oberon says.

My parents' and Marguerite's deaths return in a flood of emotion. The one thing they all perished from—fire. Tears continue to fall, and I don't have the energy to stop them as he continues.

"Xander will come with his friends. You will fight for me, and their destruction will be on your hands."

Oberon walks me to the couch, releases my arms, and sits me down. He takes the couch opposite me, leaning back with outstretched arms and legs crossed in front of him, sitting as though he didn't just put me in what he thinks is my place. I collect myself from the emotions and the pain that is real, even if the burning wasn't.

"What if I refuse?" I'm not sure if the tough act is going to work anymore. Maybe I should play vulnerable and scared. Then, when he least expects it, I'll strike. I will not let him control me. He taught me how to use the shadows. And I will use them.

Oberon pulls a golden ring off his finger, moving it to another. I've noticed the way he plays with the ring mindlessly while in thought, and I know it must hold significance because I never see him without it. "What's with the ring?"

"Loyalty." He laughs softly before finishing, returning the ring to his index finger. "I like to say *loyalty* instead of *control*. But it gives me security that the people who serve me won't betray me."

"Someone will always betray you." It's my turn for a warning. He's too arrogant to expect the warning to be from me.

He leans forward, resting his arm on one leg. "Your friends will die. And, for Xander, there are worse things than death."

A plan forms while he speaks. I said I would take them all down. And now I have a way to do it. I need this battle to happen so everyone will be in one place. "They aren't my friends."

"Regardless, you will listen to all my commands. You will do what I tell you."

"For how long?"

"Until the battle is over. Now agree."

"I agree to listen to you until I no longer have to." I smirk, a look of contempt accompanying it.

CHAPTER 47
AMERIS

Heavy grey clouds fill the sky, a threat of temperament weather on this chosen day for war. Oberon's forces blot the landscape like a dark stain. Their black armor with spiked shoulder plates and arm guards poses a menacing threat. Lined up in perfect formation, foot soldiers stand at the forefront, forming a wall of impenetrable mass. Behind them, archers take their positions, bows ready, poised to make the first move.

"The day has come, stygian." Oberon looks out over the gathered armies below the hill we perch on.

Across the field, Xander's forces are amassed in armor in the varying shades of the seasons. Red and Orange intertwined like autumn leaves, pure white of winter snow and like the nightshade's fur, deep emerald of the spring forest, and the muted golds of wheat fields in summer. Xander's forces have shown up, gathering once more to fight against Oberon, to end his reign.

Even so, Xander's forces are outnumbered by a few hundred.

Xander promised he would come back for me. This time, he's kept his promise, but he's not only here for me. He wants the throne he was promised. Wrapped in another bargain with Oberon will force my hand at fighting against Xander's rebellion, likely making it appear I've joined Oberon's side.

Except they both know nothing of my access to magic. Or that I chose my response to Oberon's demand carefully. Oberon's shadows pulse around him as he takes in the army that has gathered. Not wanting to get caught in the darkness's terror, I take a few steps away from him.

"More than you expected?" I give a small laugh.

"Ameris, you know what the shadows do. Their efforts are futile." He turns in my direction, and the corner of his mouth turns up.

Arrogant asshole. They all tried to cage me, but no one took the time to get to know me, or what I wanted. I was a pawn in their game.

They will find out soon enough that I also play to win.

I will break my cage and take the throne.

"You will shoot at them," Oberon commands me.

I nod, but seethe under the hard expression I wear. I want to take an arrow and shove it through his back. Xander's forces are just close enough that I can make out their features. I haven't been here long enough to know any of the faces I stare at. But one catches my attention, and it cuts at my soul.

I don't have to see the details on his face to know the hurt it holds. Zeke is staring straight at me. Xander stands next to Zeke, his hand on his shoulder. I have to fight the urge to go to him, especially after what happened in the forest.

Xander is a pillar of morality to bring me back from the pain I endure. *He is good.*

Part of me still wants that.

Part of it is real, but there are remnants of this damn bond that I want to rid myself of.

He has power over me. He has control.

I dig deep within myself, rebuilding the walls against the bond. I have to do this. I have to fulfill the promise I made to myself.

I don't have a side. The only fight I have is my own.

Oberon pulls the shadows in and pushes me forward, down the hill, between the rows of the royal guard, and to the front of the line. He wants to make sure there is no mistaking my presence or my forced allegiance; he will manipulate anything to his advantage. To convince them I am on his side.

"Let Ameris go! This fight is between us." Xander walks a few paces forward, calling out across the field.

Oberon waits a few moments before answering, twirling a dagger in his palm. His calculated tone cuts the silence. "You're a fool, Xander. You can't think it would be that easy."

Oberon deftly pulls an arrow from my quiver and extends it toward me. The invisible chains of our bargain tug against my flicker of hesitation. I'm compelled to accept the arrow, and I do, with resentment. I want to spit fiery words at him, but I tighten my jaw, sealing them within. It wouldn't do anything but make me feel better. There is nothing I can do as his command comes.

"Do it."

With a steady hand, I rest the shaft on the bow and nock the arrow between my fingers. As I pull back on the bowstring, it resists at first, mirroring the reluctance in my own heart. But just as the string finally gives way, so too do I yield to the inescapable bargain.

The bowstring brushes against my cheek as I inhale deeply, aligning my shot. He only commanded me to shoot at them, not to kill. While the arrow is destined to fly, I will direct its path. On my exhale, I release the arrow, marking the first move on the battlefield.

Zorria steps back, the arrow lodging in the ground at her feet. Probably not my best choice, but I feel strongly about her and how she's treated me, and it's the best way I can repay her. Plus, I knew she wouldn't fall so easily.

Her head rises, shifting from the arrow to me. I cannot see her expression from here, but I don't need to imagine what it is. I know by the way she grabs a bow from the fae nearest her and sends a return shot. She's pissed.

The arrow never reaches us. Shadows envelop it, the shaft disintegrating into black ash midair while the metal tip crumbles, falling to the ground at our feet.

Oberon gives the signal to Cortez. "Xander is not to be killed. Let him get through to us; kill everyone else." Cortez nods, and the guards engage.

The sound of a thousand feet pounding the ground drowns out the way my body thrums with tension. Waiting for my moment. Oberon's hand wraps around my wrist in a vice grip, dragging me back to the hill. "Don't miss again."

"My aim was true." I yank my arm away, but his hold is firm. "Are you really going to just stand on this hill and watch the battle?"

"No, you are going to stand here and watch the battle. You will release your arrows on the same command as the other archers." He releases me as his attention diverts to the men rushing toward us. He watches them with the precision of a predator about to devour their prey. "Understood?"

"Yes," I grit out.

He doesn't look back as he slides his sword from its sheath and makes his way into the thick of the battle. Just as with everything else, his movements are precise and deadly, cutting down his enemies with steel instead of magic. At each command to release an arrow, I hit my target, but never with a killing blow.

Xander rushes his way through the fighting, delivering debilitating blows but never killing a fae. He's heading straight for me. His path isn't easy, but he doesn't care; it's clear all he wants is to reach me. His heartbeats break through the walls I put up against the bond, rapid with his exertion. The desire to reach me threatens to knock the breath from my lungs.

CHAPTER 48

XANDER

Atop the hill, Ameris stands shoulder-to-shoulder with Oberon. She is clad in black armor, its sleek, menacing form in stark contrast to the white gambeson she wears underneath. Light and dark intertwined, the very image of clashing sides embodied.

Focusing, I close my eyes and tune into her heartbeat. It beats slower than mine, calm amid the chaos that's sure to erupt. She is ready for whatever will come. My eyes flit open at the whistling arrow flying through the air. It lands where Zorria stood mere moments before.

"That bitch," Zorria fumes.

"Zorria, no!" I yell from down the line and run to where she's positioned, but she has already let an arrow fly. It soars through the air, glinting in the sunlight before Oberon's shadows engulf it, turning the arrow into black ash before it gets close to Ameris.

Dammit. Not a moment passes before a sea of black descends the hill.

But my focus is on the one whose heart is bound to mine. I

need to get to her, and the only way I will is to fight my way through the oncoming swarm. There are things I need to tell her: regrets I have and apologies I never gave.

I raise my sword in the air, giving the signal, and we charge forward. Our most experienced magic wielders remain behind, using their magic to support our front line. As for the rest of us, there is nothing quite like the thrill of engaging in physical combat, and we relish the clash of metal on metal as our magic pulsates through our veins.

Magic isn't meant to destroy, but to create. But, like anything else, magic can be used for destruction, depending on who wields it.

My hand tightens around the hilt of my sword as I swiftly slash downward, leaving a deep gash in the thigh of a soldier. Blood spurts out as she screams and falls to the ground, painting the grass beneath her red.

I push away any thoughts of the person under the helmet, focusing instead on getting to Ameris. Another soldier charges towards me, and I swiftly twist my blade in the opposite direction, plunging it into the weak spot in their armor with precision.

The clashing of metal echoes around us as I keep pushing up the hill. I would prefer not to fight the people I once served with, but they have no choice but to answer Oberon's call as the current ruler. There is no point in killing these fae who will serve me after this battle, so I keep my blows non-fatal whenever I can.

I divert my attention to Ameris as often as I can. She's still standing on the hilltop, nocking another arrow. I track its trajectory as she shoots into the warring forces.

Her aim is true, yet she avoids lethal shots. As she repeats this several times, it dawns on me that she's not participating in this conflict of her own volition. Oberon must be controlling her, compelling her through another bargain. My resolve strengthens as I push myself harder to get to her.

More soldiers surge toward me, a relentless wave of steel and menace. Breaking the rules of engagement, I summon water with a flick of my wrist, conjuring a swirling cyclone that hurls them aside, clearing my path. My legs pump furiously as I sprint up the hill, slashing through more fae who dare to block my way.

"Ameris!" I shout with desperate urgency as I crest the hill.

CHAPTER 49
AMERIS

My eyes lock on Xander as he comes into view. I draw another arrow from my quiver and set it against the bowstring, pulling back until the fletching brushes my cheek. My next shot is aimed at him. His forward momentum halts abruptly, as if he's hit an invisible wall.

Confusion flickers across his face; his eyes dart between my drawn bow and my blank stare, trying to decipher my intentions. Slowly, hesitantly, he steps forward. Just as he's within arm's reach, a voice calls out from behind me.

Oberon issues another command that I must heed. "Put your bow down."

Xander raises his sword, swinging it in an arc across his body, an invitation for Oberon to advance.

Oberon doesn't. He comes to stand beside me, burying the tip of his bloody sword into the ground before leaning into it. "Well, we meet again."

"Fight me without magic. Metal to metal," Xander challenges.

"But banishing you was so much fun. I would love to do it

again, but you've gone and bonded yourself to Ameris." Oberon lifts my arm and rubs his thumb over the scars on my wrist.

"Don't touch her," Xander growls, taking a step closer.

Oberon's lips brush the top of my hand, his eyes lifting to meet Xander's in a taunt. "We've already done much more than that. Isn't that right, Ameris?"

I don't react, even though Oberon's touch still makes my body act of its own accord. Wanting him. "Yes."

Xander doesn't let the heartbreak show that hits like a punch to the gut, but it's so strong I feel it through our bond. "It doesn't matter. She doesn't belong to you."

Xander is so close now that he could reach out his sword, and the tip would touch Oberon's chest. The tension between them is palpable; a clash of wills and steel brewing between these two males. Over me. Xander wants to save me. Oberon wants to keep me. But they both want to cage me in their own way.

Perhaps Xander's love for me is real. Perhaps he wants to save me from the perceived threat of Oberon. But I'm too far gone to be saved. I've already chosen my path, and I will fight the bond even if it kills me.

"Oh, but she does." Oberon swiftly shifts his body, blocking me from Xander.

Oberon's hand tightens around the hilt of his blade, ready to pull it from the earth.

This is my moment.

With their attention on each other, I hastily remove the obsidian binders, slip them into my hands, and readjust the latch with my finger. They're open and ready to be put on a new pair of wrists. Rounding on Oberon before he can advance on Xander, I slap the cuffs onto his wrists and pull the golden ring off his finger, one swift move after the other.

He looks down at the binder, then to the ring I'm twirling between my fingers.

"How does it feel?" I can't stop the insolence that caresses my voice. Slipping the golden ring onto my finger, I hold my hand out and admire how it morphs into the perfect size. A devious smile settles as I look back to Oberon, then to Xander. "I think it looks great on me."

Before either of them can react, I reach for the earth, pulling the roots that lie beneath the surface and wrapping them around both of their legs, forcing them both to kneel.

Tears fall freely from the satisfaction of victory. I release a laugh, full of mania and pride. I did it. It shouldn't have been that easy. But when no one takes you seriously, this is the consequence.

Oh stars, take me.

While my magic lay dormant, it was building. The pain was no longer present, but the pressure beneath my skin threatened to explode. I don't know what's about to happen or if I can control the magic wanting release. Lyle's training wasn't enough for the overload of vibrational signatures from each element swarming around, finding me atop this hill as the battle rages below.

Yet, it's a delicious nectar to my need for power. I greedily take it in, letting it fill all the empty places within my shattered soul.

Tears continue to flow down my face as I drop to my knees, chest lifted to the sky, arms falling behind me.

I'm about to lose control.

Magic consumes me, and I surrender to its will. The shadows come first, pulling out all the emotions I've been battling—pain, loss, hate—and the magic explodes. Darkness washes over the battlefield; screams echo around as I envelop everyone in their worst nightmare. Lightning strikes the ground. Within seconds, heavy rain falls in sheets, blurring everything in sight.

Wind roars to life, sending the rain sideways, ripping trees from the ground, and picking up fae in its wrath. The debris swirls, whipping around before being released and falling to the ground.

I hear Xander's voice through the magic that thrums in my

ears, but I ignore him. I don't want this to stop. The release feels right. The suppressed magic is finally able to be used. This is the moment I have been waiting for.

To take what I want and be what I want.

CHAPTER 50

XANDER

A gut-wrenching scream comes from Ameris. Not from agony, but release. She's basking in her freed magic. Every element pulses out at once, wild and free. The battlefield has become chaos, a maelstrom of magic threatening to destroy everything in its wake.

The ground violently shakes, and anyone still standing is forced to their knees. The fighting has stopped, and all eyes are on Ameris. They watch her in awe. In their gazes, I see the reverence Rhiannon once held and how, only now, do they realize she has the same abilities. This is the danger Lyle spoke of.

What you feel for Ameris will be key. Be the light. Damn Lyle and their cryptic messages. I continue yelling her name.

There is no response. It's like I don't exist. Frantically, I search the bond for her to bring her back. But I can no longer feel her. She has blocked me out. I struggle against the roots that bind me, trying to loosen them.

My magic is rendered useless while she pulls all the energy from the area. Right now, it responds to her, and only to her.

An eerie silence falls as her magic wanes, as if time has stopped and placed us in a void. Ameris falls forward, palms in the mud, pulling in deep, ragged breaths. Light slowly returns when the clouds begin to dissipate and the air around us calms. She should have blacked out from using that much magic. I am once again shown that there is more to her than I expected.

"Ameris!" I call once more, and this time, her head drifts in my direction. She flashes me a wicked smile and stands, heading toward me. "Unbind me, and let's end this."

"No." Her cold fingertips brush my cheek as she passes. All the warmth has left her touch and voice. "I am going to end this."

Oberon studies her and smiles, his lips pulling back into a full-toothed grin that radiates amusement. "Hello, my stygian. That was fun to watch. If I knew you had that necklace, I never would have let you wear it."

"And that is why you are there, and I am here." Ameris picks up his sword and lets it drag along the ground behind her as she circles him. Coming back around, she brings the sword to his heart, holding it there.

Oberon watches her, full of glee. "I'll give you anything you want. I won't bind you anymore if you agree to marry me and rule by my side."

"I will never let that happen." I jerk against the roots. "Will you unbind me now?"

Ameris drops the sword and ignores what we say.

She lifts her hand, the gold ring on her finger glinting in the sunlight. "I understand what you meant about control."

"Stop this, Ameris. What has Oberon done to you?"

"He's done nothing but help me." She motions to the field below the hill. "This was always the path I was bound for, but you were both in my way. You never truly saw me."

"No, it's not. You let his shadow magic get to you," I plead with her.

"You wouldn't know." She turns away and leaves us bound on the hilltop.

Oberon laughs. "We underestimated her."

CHAPTER 51
AMERIS

Power and control. They are finally mine, and no one can stop me. This is what it means to become a villain; to want something you know you shouldn't and make decisions that get you there anyway.

When I turn to the battlefield, I am met with every fae's gaze upon me. All of their attention is drawn to my presence, their expressions mixed between fear and awe, mingled with relief that the battle is over.

Amidst the fae who are still kneeling, I spot Lorcan sprinting through them in my direction. The fae scramble back in terror as he passes, but he pays them no mind. His white fur shines in the sun of the now-clear skies. As he crests the hill, he slows to a smooth and confident gait. He's a magnificent beast, with all the grace and power of a predator.

Ameris. I will accompany you from now until I am no longer needed.

I bow to Lorcan and run my hand down his spiked back. He sits next to me, patiently flicking his tail. Standing at the edge of the hill, I pull the necklace from beneath my armor so all can see that I have Oberon's ring and Rhiannon's necklace.

They never knew the power of the necklace—not even Xander, when he gave it to me. But it spoke to me when the cool stone touched my skin and whispered its secrets. Her secrets. The necklace in the hands of the one it serves blocks all other magic in the vicinity and gives foresight to know when harm is coming.

"Leave them bound and take them to the courtyard. Set up the throne on a platform. I'll be there shortly," I command the guards, who stand in shock nearby. They look at each other before they comply, knowing they cannot refuse me. I chuckle at the way it feels to be not only in control of myself but others too. Oh, how the coin has flipped since I found Xander.

I walk fearlessly down the hill and through the crowd. The royal guards bow as I pass them with Lorcan at my side. Even with hate in their eyes, they also hold fear and reverence. I'm forcing them to serve and protect me, but they know I have the same power as Rhiannon. More power than her. I have shadow magic and a mythical beast that accompanies me.

One of them tries to rush at me. I don't flinch; I just keep walking as his sword, which was raised against me, never falls. The magic of the ring protects me from his intentions.

Instead, he's forced to drop it to the ground. He then stabs himself through the heart with a dagger he pulls from his baldric. His knees hit the wet and muddy ground, slick from rain and blood, before he drops and never rises again.

I stop and address the guards standing around. "Find Cortez and tell him I want everyone gathered in the courtyard. You're all dismissed, and make sure you tell the citizens of Solarium as well."

A smirk involuntarily plays at the corner of my mouth. The knowledge that the guards cannot harm me and that the other courts know they can't let anything happen to me fills me with satisfaction. So, I keep walking toward my target.

It doesn't take me long to reach the one who is too shocked to do anything but stare at me. "Hello, Zorria. You can drop that sword."

Her blade is against the neck of a royal guard. She tightens her grip on the guard's collar and starts shaking with anger. Zorria's gaze bores into me like daggers, but it doesn't penetrate; it's merely an annoyance I can never get rid of.

I shake my head, sensing her movement before she takes action. "I wouldn't do that."

As the blade nicks the neck of the guard, intending to slice it open, I flick my wrist, and her hand snaps in the other direction, forced to swing the blade the other way. Her eyes widen before she lunges in my direction. Guards move to stop her, but I signal for them to let it happen. This is a moment I've wanted.

We fly back into the mud and roll a few times, each struggling to pin the other. When she pins me, I buck my hips, sending her over my head. I turn onto my stomach and grab her leg, pulling her under me. She tries to rise, but I punch her in the back, and she slams once again into the ground. Pinning her arms under my shins, I pull her head back. Her strength is no longer an advantage to the raw power I now wield, coupled with the necklace and ring. I've become the ultimate ruler.

"If you didn't hate me so much, we could've been good friends. I think we're more alike than we know," I whisper in her ear as she bucks under my hold.

"You'll pay for this, Ameris," she spits out.

"Maybe, but it feels good right now," I return.

I motion for the guards, and they approach. "Secure her and take her to the dungeon." They grab her arms, and I get up, releasing her. They pull her away from the gathered crowd as she thrashes under their hold, yelling curses at me.

I swipe mud from my face. When I look up, Zeke is staring at me, wide eyed, mouth open. Seconds span into minutes as we stare at each other. He hesitates as he takes a step forward. I nod, giving him permission to approach. When he reaches me, he pulls me into a hug.

I don't know what to do. It's not something I expected, especially having never visited him while he was rotting in the dungeons. He easily forgave me when I rescued them. If anyone could save me, it would be him.

"Don't hate me." The words are sheepish as I look up at him.

"Never." He shakes his head. He looks at me like he knows there is something hiding beneath the surface but is too afraid to say anything.

"I'm not so sure about that." I shrug and step out of his embrace. I look in the same direction he is, toward the guards that are cresting the hill with Zorria in tow. "She's your sister."

"Well, she kind of had that coming. She's been nothing but unkind toward you." He gives me a small smile and squeezes my shoulder.

Jesper comes up to us, Ronan on his heels, and briefly embraces me before I can stop him. "Ameris."

I feel so conflicted. These fae have helped me, and I have nothing against them, but I know their allegiance won't lie with me. I must assert myself like Rhiannon would and demand it.

"Where are you taking him?" Jesper's voice is too soft as it cuts through my thoughts. He looks terrible. I'm surprised he's still alive, and that he's here. His cheeks are sunken, and a sheen of sweat coats his brow.

"To the courtyard," I answer. "Everyone is to head there."

Ronan supports Jesper as he walks off to spread the instructions I've given. I return to the hill and look out over the battlefield at the wasted lives of all these magical beings. Zeke follows and stands next to me, taking it all in. Judgment seeps from him like sap oozing from a tree. I try to ignore it, but he grabs my arm and makes me face him.

"Ameris, look at me." I hesitate for a moment before raising my gaze to meet his. "Are you okay?" he asks me with a raised brow.

My breath hitches as his question hits. I think this is the first time someone has asked me how I am doing. If only someone had asked me before now. If anyone had cared to ask...

"Ameris?" he probes when I don't respond.

I shake it off. "Yes, yes, I'm fine."

But really, I'm not fine. I'm exhausted. The magic took a toll, and adrenaline fuels my body at this point. I can tell my answer doesn't satisfy him, but he doesn't press. We leave the field and head toward the palace. Lorcan follows me, always by my side.

"Where did you get that?" He changes the subject, asking about my necklace.

"Xander gave it to me." I lift it away from my skin, play with the chain, and admire the jewels.

"I see. Do you know whose necklace that was?" he asks.

"Yes. And now it's mine," I answer, not wanting to talk about it. I know why he's asking, and don't have the patience for it right now. Even if it means losing the one person who might care about me, I have to stick to my plan. I don't need anyone to care, so long as I am in control. At least then, I will always remember to think twice about the information I'm given.

Never trust; always question.

I remind myself that I'm not doing the same thing as Oberon, because he didn't have everything I possess. And I don't intend to ruin this world. When we get to the town's entrance, I stop before passing under the gates. "Zeke, I have to do this next part alone. You won't like it, but I can't risk another uprising like this."

His face falls farther than I thought it could. "What are you talking about?"

Instead of responding, I call out to some guards passing us. When the four of them approach, they bow and stand at attention. I turn away from Zeke. The guards respond without direction, and flank me as I head toward the palace. With every step, my heart breaks a little. I use the hurt I'm causing Zeke—and myself—and flit the small, inky blackness of shadows between my hands. The guards follow a little further behind.

As a hostage, guards flanked my first entrance to the palace. Now, I return with them at my command.

CHAPTER 52
AMERIS

The last piece of armor Oberon made me wear drops to the ground with a dull thud as I lean my back against the stone wall. Coolness seeps through the thick material of the gambeson, giving me much-needed relief.

Murmurs from the gathered crowd drift through the open doorway to the courtyard. The hushed conversations carry an air of anticipation and curiosity about this morning's battle and the human girl who possesses the magic of their lost queen and the usurper.

These few solitary breaths are needed, as I refocus on what I've set out to do—the first ones I've been able to take without being under someone else's control. Not the village's. Not Xander's. And not Oberon's.

Under my own control.

My fingertips dig into the wall as I take a final breath before pushing off and stepping into the evening sunlight. Three rows of guards line the front of the platform, serving as a barrier against the gathered fae. Oberon and Xander are kneeling before the black throne that sits on a secondary raised dais, facing the crowd.

Just as I asked, good.

My fingers slide along the side of the intricately carved throne, over the top, and down to the armrest before I sit on it. Observing the crowd silently, I wait until someone looks up and notices me. The fae turns and taps the shoulder of the one standing next to them.

Silence ripples through the crowd, and when there are only the sounds of nature, I rise.

My footfalls break the silence as I step between Xander and Oberon. "A human may only be a tool to you all, but that ends today. You may pay us for our work, but I shall henceforth ban all bargains that aim to use humans knowingly. Those I appoint must approve of all contracts or bargains. Any human currently in a bargain must be released or kept on for hire."

Xander's head tilts in my direction, and he softly says my name, but I ignore him. I know this will not make me popular, but I don't care.

"I may look like her, but I am not Rhiannon. When Oberon banished her to the human world, he didn't realize the consequences of giving humans the chance to have magic. As Rhiannon's descendant, I am claiming my right to rule." I put my hand on Oberon's shoulder. He tries to shove it off, but I hold steady.

I motion to the guards, and they bring Oberon forward, front and center, so there will be no mistaking what I do or what my brand of punishment looks like. I take the iron and obsidian from my pocket and hold them in the palm of my hand.

He arches an eyebrow and laughs. "What do you think you can do with such small pieces?"

A few of the fae in the crowd chuckle. I let it wash over me. They won't be laughing when I'm finished. "Even the smallest splinter can cause the most pain. Remember that."

It is my turn to laugh, and he goes still.

Rolling the two pieces between my hand, I search for each material's vibration, its essence. When I find them, I weave the two together, while keeping their integrity. I open my palm to show Oberon the splinter I formed, then hold it up for the crowd. The setting sun glints off the black glass.

"A punishment worse than death, worse than exile, is a life without magic and the ability to heal yourself; to know what it is like to be human." The crowd tracks my every move. "Such will be the punishment for the one who stole the throne, who tried to use me, and who is responsible for the decay in this world."

Oberon's eyes widen as I approach. He fights the guards, manages to break free, and lunges at me. With a snap of my fingers, roots from the surrounding trees spring to life. They pull him back before he has time to grab me. Standing with his arms pulled back, I rip his shirt open, exposing his chest.

My hands trail over the curves of his muscles. "We could have been great, you know. But I will not bow to a man. And I want this world to flourish, so I can rule over it." My voice was low enough that only he could hear me.

He tries to move, but it's no use. "You don't know what you're doing. Don't do this." His harsh words turn soft. "Please."

"Too late for that," I say as I push the sharp end into his chest. He tilts his head back and screams as the iron rips into his flesh. The crowd gasps, and the murmurs start again. When the obsidian hits, he calms, but his head falls forward and hangs in defeat. But I don't stop pushing, using my magic to propel the splinter into his body. I let it sink in just above his heart. When I'm satisfied, I remove the binders.

"It's just...gone." It's barely a whisper, but I hear it and I understand it. Understand what that feels like, because he did it to me.

"It doesn't feel good, does it?" I've never seen him look like he does now. But every ruler meets their end, whether by time or by force.

"We need to talk." The last words are barely audible before his eyes close and he collapses.

"Take him to a room. Guard him. I am the only one to approve his requests, and no one enters his room unless I am present." I release the roots that hold him. The guards nod as they remove him from the platform.

I stand at the edge of the platform facing the crowd and announce, "The reign of the tyrant is over. Oberon is no longer a threat to your world."

"What about Xander?" a voice calls from the crowd.

No one else speaks, but they rustle and shift as words pass between them. I know they are waiting for Xander to say something, but he's been silent since he whispered my name, so I continue, answering their question.

"There can only be one who is destined for the throne. And that person is me," I say.

Movement catches my eye in the otherwise still crowd. The air shifts in tandem with the movement, the vibration accelerating, my magic warning me that a threat is near. My instincts kick in, and I quickly step to the side, narrowly avoiding an arrow aimed at me from the back of the gathered fae. I hold up my hand and bend the air to my will, stopping the arrow just before it would have impaled Xander in the chest. The sharp metal tip glints in the sunlight as it quivers against my hold. Gasps and murmurs of surprise spread through the crowd at my display of power, their eyes wide with fear and fascination.

"Whoever fired that sealed his fate." I close my eyes and pull at everything within, like Oberon taught me. A shadow barrier forms between the fae who have gathered and the platform. It will destroy anyone or anything that tries to cross it. I know how destructive the shadows are, that somewhere I have destroyed a part of this land, but this is the only time I will use them—a sacrifice that must be made to protect myself and finish what I started.

I kneel in front of Xander, my heart beats faster at the choice that presses against my mind. I hesitate, placing my hand on his heart, and sigh. *I have to do this. I have to do this.* I repeat the words over and over to make sure I go through with it. The dagger slides out of its sheath with ease, and I hold the tip against his chest, above his heart.

"I'm sorry." Wet heat hits my cheeks, and I cannot stop the tremble in my words. "I have to do this. I can't have someone telling me what to do anymore. And I don't want to be bound to anyone."

"You can't. You'll die. We are bound forever. If I die at your hand, we both die." There is no anger when I search his face. I want him to be angry. I want him to hate me because that would make it easier.

I drop my head and stare at the oak floor of the platform, at the patterns that swirl in the wood. The many rings that were cut off before they could grow.

He has to be lying.

I don't know what's real anymore. It figures that this bond would curse me and be my undoing, but this might all be a dream. Thoughts flit across my mind as fast as a shooting star. One moment, a thought is there, only to be replaced by another.

"I will gladly give up my place for you. I would give you the stars and the moon."

My head snaps back up at the words. "Take that back. You don't even know me."

"I know enough." The words are gentle, his breathing steady.

"You had your chance." I push on the blade, drawing blood. He sucks in a breath and winces.

"Why didn't you tell me you were suffering?" His voice strains under the pressure of the dagger.

"Why didn't you notice?" Before he can answer, I do. "Because you were too busy trying to win that throne. I was your second thought. Now that we are here in this situation, I am your first."

He doesn't respond. He can't. Any response would contain a lie.

Am I willing to risk my own death if what he says is the truth?

My hands shake so violently that the dagger I hold clatters against the wood. Leaning my forehead against his, I close my eyes.

"Fully open yourself to the bond, and you'd know. You'd know if I was lying. Being this close to you, I can tell that you try to shut it out. There is a difference between the other day in the forest and now."

"I need to do this." But I don't know if I can. "And if what you say is true..." I'm cut off before I can finish my sentence.

"Then don't." The voice that answers isn't his, and it's one I thought I would never hear again.

A hand gently lands on my shoulder, and a form kneels by my side.

It can't be real.

My exhaustion has gotten to me.

But the weight of the hand is there, and no illusion would feel this way. I turn my head to see a hand lined with wrinkles before moving to the face that shatters my soul and fractures the walls I have built around myself.

I lean into the old woman. Even if she isn't real, I want her to be in this moment. I need her.

Marguerite's voice, soft and stern, echoes around me. "Ameris, what have you done?"

ACKNOWLEDGMENTS

I'm not sure what to say now that I've reached this point. I finally did it? Finally finished the monumental task of not only writing a book but also taking it to publication. It's been a wild ride, and I wouldn't be here if it wasn't for the endless support of the people who have helped me on this journey.

If you've made it this far, thank you for choosing to read Ameris's story. Thank you for supporting an indie author. Self-publishing is challenging, but it is also rewarding to know that people will finally be able to read Ameris's story. She is special to me, and I hope you loved her character arc.

To my family: A big thank you to my husband for endlessly supporting my antics of traveling to writing retreats and taking craft courses over the last four years. Also, I'm sorry for all the time I spent in my office, ignoring you for the fantasy world I was building. Mom, you are the root of my love for reading, which led to writing. Mom and Dad, I don't think I can express how much your support has meant to me. I want to thank my sister for reminding me of how I used to force you to write stories with me when we were young. I wish my grandmother were still alive to witness this. I used to create plays and act them out in the living room for her. She would have been proud. It's been a long time since you've left us, but I love you dearly and miss you.

To my writing community: Adrienne Young, you have been a pivotal force in my writing journey. From that first feedback session you did with Kristin Dwyer (hi, I love you) to Writing

With The Soul (WWTS), and all the events and retreats you've hosted. I wouldn't have all these people to thank without you. Kristin, you are also so important to my journey as a writer, and I can't thank you enough for every conversation, laugh, and hug.

To those who were there from the very beginning. *Okay, cue the endless tears now flowing.* Toni, we brainstormed and talked through the plot in those very early days, and you've been with me ever since. As Ameris grew, our friendship grew, and I have been blessed by it. You are a wonderful friend and an amazing storyteller. Also, thank you for helping me with the endless horse questions.

Siena, as our lives shifted and changed over the past four years, we evolved from CPs to soul sisters. I love you dearly and thank you for everything you've done for me and Ameris.

Jazzi, you are my bright star in the shroud of darkness that writing and publishing can bring. You pushed me to stay true to my intention for Ameris and not change her because other people may not like her.

Emily freaking Varga, that's it, right? All I have to say? Kidding! You read that early draft and I still laugh at what you said. It was true. Yet here we are four years later, and I am so glad we are friends and have been on so many adventures together.

Morgan, thank you for all the craft conversations, travel, and writing sprints. You are simply the best. I love you.

Mary Alyce, I cannot thank you enough for your willingness to let me run things by you and for sharing your knowledge of the industry.

Chinelo, I love you so much and am so grateful you slid into my DMs all those years ago. I cherish our friendship. Thank you for all the sprints, for keeping me on track, and organizing a writing retreat where I got to meet more wonderful people.

Deanna, thank you for all the laughs and good conversation during our FaceTime quiet working sessions. They helped me so much, and I am thankful for your friendship.

Bri and Maggie, I am so glad to have you both as friends and am thankful for all the fun times we've had together talking story and craft.

Hazel St. Lewis, I love that I get to go on this indie joinery with you. Despite all the ups and downs, I've had so much fun. I can't wait for where our futures take us. Brittany, Amanda, Dianna, and Carrie, I want to thank you all for letting me join the Chat, Chat. It was the perfect timing for me, and I am so grateful for our friendship.

Thank you to Lacie, Liv, and Libby, for reading the very early draft and loving my story enough to encourage me to keep working at it. The Scotland Green group, you have my heart. You all encouraged me when I shared my opening chapter for the first time to a large group. To everyone who was at the Spring Retreat, the second Scotland Storyteller's Retreat, and the Research Expedition—thank you for all the laughs, feedback, and support.

I know I'm probably going to leave out naming people, but as a collective group, my Writing With The Soul community and the writing community at large, you all are the best people. Every single one of you that I've had an interaction with has impacted me in some way. I'm serious. If you even have an inkling that it might be you I'm thinking of, IT IS. You all are such lovely people. I have never been part of a community that rallies behind other writers so willingly and passionately. It is a beautiful thing to be a part of.

I have said this before, but I truly believe that without all the various sprints, events, chats, and trips I've been on, I would not be writing this right now. You all mean the world to me. THANK YOU.

There is another community I want to thank, and that is the indie author community on Clubhouse, specifically the morning chat rooms. Those morning chats have given me the courage to pursue the indie path, and you all have provided me with so much guidance. Everyone who is a part of that group so freely shares their knowledge and I love starting my mornings off with you all.

And finally, Farrah, you were there from the very first time I said I wanted to write a book. You excitedly listened as I told you my original story idea that went nowhere to this idea and all the others I've mentioned. You've read countless drafts of this book and have been there for each change and shift in Ameris's story throughout the years. You kept asking for more chapters and new drafts, and you stuck with me through the delayed revisions. It has been so fun to have such an amazing advocate and friend that kept pushing me to get to this point. You are cherished.

ABOUT THE AUTHOR

Jamye Smith is a Las Vegas-raised author who was diagnosed with ADHD as an adult. She has a penchant for daydreaming about fantastical worlds, loves traveling around our world—having traversed thirteen countries thus far—and has lived in multiple states. Jamye currently works as an Agile Team Lead for a tech consulting firm and recently co-founded a tech startup.

instagram.com/thejamyesmith

tiktok.com/jamyesmith

goodreads.com/jamyee